Praise for the Ever After series

"This fast-paced combination of middle-school realism and fairy-tale fantasy will appeal particularly to imaginative readers."
—*Kirkus Reviews*

"A fresh take on the whole fairy-tales-made-real theme. Full of action, humor, [and] realistic school dynamics."
—*Booklist*

"There's plenty of magic and enough twists and turns to entice even reluctant readers. . . . [A] light, fun look at fairy tales after the 'happily ever after.'"
—*School Library Journal*

THE EVER AFTERS

OF SORCERY AND SNOW

SHELBY BACH

Simon & Schuster Books for Young Readers
NEW YORK   LONDON   TORONTO   SYDNEY   NEW DELHI

SIMON & SCHUSTER BOOKS FOR YOUNG READERS
An imprint of Simon & Schuster Children's Publishing Division
1230 Avenue of the Americas, New York, New York 10020
This book is a work of fiction. Any references to historical events,
real people, or real places are used fictitiously. Other names, characters, places, and
incidents are products of the author's imagination, and any resemblance to actual
events or places or persons, living or dead, is entirely coincidental.
Text copyright © 2014 by Shelby Randol Trenkelbach
Cover illustration copyright © 2014 by Cory Loftis
For information about special discounts for bulk purchases, please contact Simon &
Schuster Special Sales at 1-866-506-1949 or business@simonandschuster.com.
The Simon & Schuster Speakers Bureau can bring authors to your live event. For
more information or to book an event, contact the Simon & Schuster Speakers
Bureau at 1-866-248-3049 or visit our website at www.simonspeakers.com.
Also available in a Simon & Schuster Books for Young Readers hardcover edition
Book design by Chloë Foglia
The text for this book is set in Usherwood.
Manufactured in the United States of America
0515 OFF
First Simon & Schuster Books for Young Readers paperback edition June 2015
2 4 6 8 10 9 7 5 3 1
The Library of Congress has cataloged the hardcover edition as follows:
Bach, Shelby.
Of sorcery and snow / Shelby Bach.
pages cm— (The Ever Afters ; 3)
Summary: Rory Landon sets off on another tale from The Ever After School in order
to end the reign of the Snow Queen.
ISBN 978-1-4424-9784-9 (hc)
[1. Characters in literature—Fiction. 2. Magic—Fiction. 3. Fairy tales—Fiction.
4. Adventure and adventurers—Fiction.] I. Title.
PZ7.B1319Oh 2014
[Fic]—dc23
2013029637
ISBN 978-1-4424-9785-6 (pbk)
ISBN 978-1-4424-9786-3 (eBook)

To Colby and Clint,
I would cross frozen
wastelands and fight evil
sorceresses to save you,
too, just so you know

The wolves might not have attacked if we had left right after school. If we'd headed for Golden Gate Park on time, they might never have sniffed us out.

Of course, I wanted to hurry for a completely different reason. I squinted up the hill. Half of our classmates had clustered behind my best friend, trying to convince him to borrow their skateboards.

"We don't have time for this, Chase! We need to get to EAS!" I told him.

Even thirty feet away, with a giant homemade ramp on the sidewalk between us, I could see Chase rolling his eyes. "Trust me, we won't miss the tournament," he said. He knew how much I wanted to wipe the smug look off a certain sword master's face. "This'll just take two minutes."

"What's the deal with that Ever After School?" asked the freckled kid who sat behind us in pre-algebra. "You, Rory, and Lena go every day."

You could tell by the way he said it: He thought eighth graders going to day care was the lamest thing since kids started bringing their teachers apples.

Ever After School wasn't day care. It was a program for fairy-tale Characters-in-training. I'd been going for about two years, my other best friend Lena for a little longer. Chase *lived* there with his dad.

But we obviously couldn't tell that to a kid who didn't know magic was real. I hadn't even broken that news to my parents yet.

"It's awesome. That's all you need to know," Chase said coldly. "Hey, Rory! Move, or I might land on you."

Sighing, I trotted halfway up the steps to our school, Lawton Academy for the Gifted. It wasn't that foggy today, but the sky was gray, the clouds close.

The door opened behind me. Lena came out wearing yellow rain boots, a yellow raincoat, and a waterproof backpack over her shoulder. "Ready! I—" Then she stopped. "Oh, hold on. I forgot my umbrella."

She rushed back in, and I sighed again.

All I wanted to do was get to EAS, sign up for a duel with Hansel, and kick the sword master's butt. I'd been fantasizing about it for months—no, *years*. During my first sword lesson, Hansel had told us, *You have no idea what you might be up against. You would all be dead in two moves if the war hadn't ended. Especially you girls.* When I'd told him that we might grow up to be even better than him someday, he'd just sneered at me.

Well, today was the day I'd prove it.

But I couldn't do that if we missed the whole tournament. EAS only held it every three years, and it would end in an hour and a half. Plus, we had a pretty long walk ahead of us—four city blocks and the whole Golden Gate Park before we even reached the Door Trek door. If I lost my chance just because my friends were too slow . . .

No. Never mind. I still remembered how much school sucked before Chase and Lena started coming with me.

Because my mom's job made us move every three or four months, I'd been the new kid more times than I could count. I'd gotten used to it. Most of the time, it was just lonely.

Then, one morning last spring, Chase had shown up in my homeroom, and Lena had arrived the week after that. I hadn't asked them to come. My family had moved twice since then, and both times Mom had dragged me to a new school. Chase and Lena had been there too—even if they had to enchant every teacher, secretary, and computer to get themselves into the school's system.

Skateboarding and excessive rain gear were no big deal. I definitely had the best friends in the whole world, magical or otherwise.

"Rory! You're not looking!" Chase called.

I turned back to the top of the hill. "If I watch, can we do a warm-up match when we get to EAS?"

"Only if I hear a big round of applause." Chase hopped on the skateboard and rolled down the slope. He didn't brake or even take a few turns like the other boys had. He just barreled full tilt for the ramp.

The door squeaked open again, and a second later, Lena clutched my arm. "He's not even wearing a helmet!"

The skateboard's wheels clattered when they hit the ramp. Then Chase sailed off the end, way too high, and he grabbed the front end of the board. Gravity dragged him back down, and he hit the sidewalk smoothly. The boys rushed down the hill after him, cheering.

"I thought you were going to fly straight into traffic!" Lena told Chase. He just swerved to a stop right in front of us and grinned expectantly.

But I didn't have good news. "That jump wasn't human," I said, and his face fell.

Chase was half Fey. He had wings, which were invisible most of the time, and he couldn't resist using them to show off. It hadn't taken him long to figure out that he was a natural on a skateboard and that regular kids were a *lot* easier to impress than Characters and fairies. He always asked me to watch, so I could tell him if he overshot.

"About eight feet too high, I think," I added gently, and Chase nodded.

Lena looked at me funny, not getting it. She didn't know that Chase's mom was Fey. I'd tried to convince him to tell Lena a hundred times. She was the smartest person I knew. She was eventually going to figure it out, and then she would probably be furious with us for keeping such a big secret from her. But Chase refused.

So, except for all the grown-ups, I was the only Character at EAS who knew.

The boys reached us, and every single kid was begging Chase to teach them how to get that much air. His grin immediately reappeared.

Lena and I exchanged a look.

"We'll meet you at the crosswalk," she told him, and we skirted around the crowd, down the sidewalk, to the street corner. We knew from experience that Chase liked to bask in our classmates' admiration for a while, but when he noticed we were leaving without him, Chase broke away and caught up.

I stared at the crosswalk signal and willed it to change. Underneath it, a college student in a red sweatshirt was chatting on her phone. Her enormous black dog stood higher than her waist, and it didn't have a leash. It turned toward us, its eyes glinting yellow.

Chase looked at the bank sign clock over Lena's shoulder. "Wait.

Is it really three twenty-two? Registration for the tournament ended at six fifteen, Eastern Standard Time. I totally forgot."

Seven minutes ago. I froze. He'd spent weeks helping me train. He *knew* how important this was. I couldn't believe he'd—

"Rory, he's messing with you," Lena said.

Chase laughed. "April Fool's!"

He loved April Fool's jokes. He'd also tied my shoelaces to my desk in English, stolen Lena's textbook in math, unplugged all the computers in the computer lab, and cast a glamour over our chemistry experiment, turning the sulfur bright blue. Our teacher had a hard time trying to explain that one.

I rolled my eyes to hide my relief. "I can't believe I fell for that."

The light changed, and we hurried across the street. The giant black dog sniffed at us as we passed, its ears pricked forward. We turned down the hill, the park very green ahead of us.

"*I* can. You're taking this tournament way too seriously," Chase said, obviously trying to sneak in one last lesson before we reached EAS. "You're never going to beat Hansel if you don't loosen up. Getting all nervous is going to make you stiff. It'll slow you down a fraction."

"No, Rory—you're going to do great," Lena said firmly, but she was just saying that to be a good friend. She was more of a magician than a fighter. "You'll beat him easy."

"I hope so," I said.

I'd been watching Hansel for two years. I knew his habits. He always fought with a broadsword, and he always finished duels in one of two ways: If he wanted to lull his students into overconfidence, he struck high with a one-handed strike, then low, faked a blow to the left—and *always* left; I think he had an old injury that made him a little slower coming from the right—stepped inside the kid's guard, and disarmed them. If he just wanted to get the duel over with quickly, Hansel switched to a two-handed grip, locked swords with the student, and kind of leaned on the crossed blades until the kid either buckled or freaked. *Then* he did the disarm. I'd never seen him end a fight any other way—not even with his advanced classes.

Chase and I had run through both scenarios until I was sure I could outmaneuver Hansel. All I had to worry about now was if the tricks I planned would work on an opponent bigger, stronger, and heavier than Chase. And more experienced. And not nearly as likely to go easy on me.

Right. I wasn't worried at all.

The street was full of traffic. Some smoke wafted toward us, and Lena waved it away, shooting a glare at the driver who'd rolled down his car window for a cigarette. He didn't notice. He was too busy turning up the radio.

". . . a frightening case of misreporting," said the announcer. "The incident in Portland was not an April Fool's joke. Those children *are* missing. The mass kidnapping is still under investigation, and the authorities have yet to name any suspects."

Mass kidnapping sounded serious. So serious that my worry-wart mom would probably want to see me as soon as she heard about it. *That's fine,* I thought, walking even faster, *as long as I have my match with Hansel first.*

We stepped into the park, and the trees closed over our heads. Pine smells replaced exhaust. Tourists passed us on their way to the exit, see-through ponchos over their I LEFT MY HEART IN SAN FRANCISCO T-shirts. No other humans were in sight, but two huge dogs sat beside the trail ahead. The dark gray one with white paws tilted its head at us and whined, but the brown one nipped its ear. Golden Gate Park had some weird strays.

Suddenly Chase flinched. "Did I just feel a raindrop?" He hated the rain, especially getting his wings wet. He told me once that they itched while they dried.

As I pulled up my hood, Lena shook her umbrella open, happy to be prepared. "I can share!"

"We'll just hurry," Chase said, practically running down a sidewalk lined with benches. "It's not bad yet."

My eyes landed on a puddle forming on the concrete ahead, the perfect revenge for earlier. I grinned. "Lena, are you thinking what I'm thinking?"

She spotted it a second later. "Yep!"

Lena and I ran up to it, bending our knees dramatically. Catching on, Chase sprinted out of the splash zone.

We didn't jump.

"April Fool's!" I said, and Lena and I cracked up.

"Hilarious, you guys." Chase turned onto the next trail.

"Ooooo, I see," I teased as we veered toward the bridge. We always crossed Stow Lake and followed the path around the island. Lena was sure gnomes had built and hidden a colony between the waterfall and the gazebo. She was hoping to find one of their hats for an experiment. "You can dish out the April Fool's jokes, but you can't take—"

Three enormous dogs stood on the bridge, blocking our path. I stopped in my tracks, wondering how they'd caught up to us so fast.

"I've seen those dogs before." I was sure they were the same ones—the black one from the crosswalk, the older brown one, and the little gray with the big, white paws. All three triangular faces turned toward me in unison, pink tongues hanging past long teeth, and the hairs stood up on the back of my neck.

Lena squeaked and ducked behind a tree so she could unzip her backpack.

"Crap." Chase thrust his arm in the front pocket of his carryall—the one Lena had designed specifically for easy access to weapons—and drew out his sword.

If these two started freaking out, then we had a battle coming. So I started searching my backpack too. Somewhere in there was my sword, but since my carryall was the older model, it didn't have the convenient sword pocket—my sword could be anywhere.

"Rory, those aren't dogs!" Lena whispered. "They're wolves."

I could tell from the way she said it that these weren't the regular, endangered variety. The Snow Queen sometimes made wolves for her army, transforming criminals to create a soldier with the intelligence of a human and the teeth and claws of an animal.

Magical creatures sometimes snuck into human areas, like the bridge troll we'd once caught in Boston, but I had the awful feeling that these wolves had been waiting for us.

"At least there are only three of them—" I started, trying to make myself feel better.

Behind us, something howled, and a half dozen other wolves joined it, including the ones on the bridge. Forget the hairs on the back of my neck. Every hair on my body stood up.

"Looks like you're going to get that warm-up fight after all, Rory," Chase said.

But they weren't attacking. The three furry guys on the bridge hadn't even moved, except for the younger one, who tilted his head a little. Maybe they were here for some other reason. "So, what do we think? Did one of us just become the new Little Red Riding Hood?" I asked.

Lena shook her head, kind of apologetically, like she knew how much I hoped that was true. "I think one of us would have to be wearing red for that."

"The Snow Queen just sent something new to kill us," Chase said. "You know, since dragons, ice griffins, and trolls didn't work."

I'd been afraid of that. The Snow Queen liked to send her minions to kill Characters.

She especially liked trying to kill *us*. This was the second time her forces had ambushed us out of the blue. In February she'd sent a squadron of trolls after Lena at home. Luckily, Chase and I had been visiting. We'd managed to fight them off and transport Lena's whole house to EAS's courtyard.

"We've never been attacked in public before." I stuck my head half in the carryall, determined to find my sword.

"First time for everything," Chase said. "We have company. Four more wolves at two o'clo—*Watch out!*"

I looked up. The big black wolf had run forward, snarling seven feet away. Chase raised his sword to defend us, but he didn't notice the little gray one running at us.

Neither did Lena, who was busy tucking a baby food jar labeled 3 into her raincoat. When the gray wolf leaped, teeth bared, I shoved Lena down with my right hand and swung out with my left.

The punch connected with the wolf's muzzle. It sailed back thirty feet and hit the lake with a splash so big that lake water doused the top of the bridge. Whoops. Definitely overkill.

I was still getting used to the silver ring that gave me the West Wind's strength. I hadn't learned how to totally control all that power yet, but at least I had gotten better at not smashing stuff accidentally.

The little wolf didn't surface. His brown pack mate on the bridge howled, probably calling for backup.

"Thanks." Lena peeked inside my bag, pulled out my sword, and pressed the ridged hilt into my palm. "Remind me to put a hook in here for your sword belt."

"We need to get out of here, before the rest of them catch up," Chase said, as Lena and I slung our carryalls back on. He sprinted down the path along the lake, not even looking twice at the pile of black fur he'd left behind.

My stomach squirmed. Chase killed bad guys so easily, and I knew he wanted me to do the same. But I couldn't imagine killing one the way I slayed dragons and ice griffins. These wolves had been human before the Snow Queen enchanted them. I didn't want to go home knowing I'd taken a life, without being able to tell my mom why I was upset.

Something snarled at my elbow. I spun and crashed my hilt between the eyes of a small red-brown wolf. It fell, legs sprawled out in all directions, its breath whistling through its black nostrils. It didn't get up.

Knocking a wolf out with one blow felt pretty satisfying though.

"We need a doorway," Lena said, huffing just ahead. "We're not going to make it to the Door Trek door."

She was right. The director of EAS frowned on temporary-transport spells, but for emergencies, Lena had premixed some paint with just enough powdered dragon scale to magic the three of us back to EAS. This definitely counted as an emergency.

"What about the museum?" Chase said.

"In this rain?" Lena asked, incredulous.

"It'll probably be filled with tourists right now," I agreed. "We need to look for a shed or a public bathroom or something."

Lena read the sign we sprinted past, her hands on her glasses to keep them steady. "Or the Shakespeare Garden!"

Chase snorted. "You want to go *there*? What'll keep the wolves away? The flowers or the poetry?"

"No, the fence has a *gate*," I said. "Where is it?"

Lena double-checked the sign. "Oh," she said in a small voice. Then she pointed at the far side of the lake.

"You mean, back *toward* the wolves?" Chase said, obviously not a fan of the idea.

But Lena was right on this. "We need a door frame. It's better than losing time searching for one."

"Time's not the issue." Chase said. "Wait, are you still afraid we'll miss the tournament? I was *joking*."

A wolf howled in the distance, and we all turned to stare in that direction. All we saw were trees.

"There's probably more than one," I said.

"Lena, can you check?" Chase asked.

We ran up the path. *His* way, unfortunately. Since he had the most fighting experience, he was used to taking the lead during attacks.

Lena fumbled inside her jacket and pulled out a fabric-covered square—her mini magic mirror. This was an improved one. Since the first walkie-talkie M3, she'd added a video recorder, a flashlight, texting capabilities, and most recently, a radar for bad guys.

"Lena?" Chase said, sounding impatient.

"It's a lot harder to read when I'm running! Wait, just a—" Before we rounded the corner, Lena gasped and threw out both arms. Chase and I skidded to a stop. Four wolves stood shoulder to shoulder across the trail, growling. White teeth gleamed in their black gums, gray fur bristling around their necks. The second pack had outrun us.

"Rory!" Chase grabbed a fallen branch from beside the trail, hacked some vines to free it, and tossed it to me. I passed my sword to Lena, so I could catch the branch with both hands. The wolves plowed forward. I swung. A gust of wind built up over my left hand, and then the branch connected. Three wolves whooshed backward. With a crunch of broken glass, two hit a car parked thirty yards away; the other smashed into a tree as big as the one in EAS's courtyard. It slid to the ground, leaving a canine-shaped scar on the tree bark.

It whimpered, its forelegs bent in an impossible direction.

Lena handed my sword back. Chase had taken care of the fourth wolf. Red spilled into the fur above its heart. With his sword, he pointed at the injured wolf beside the tree. His blade was covered in fresh blood. "Are you going to finish that one off?"

I scowled at him but didn't answer.

I tried to explain it to him once. As much as I loved EAS, being a Character wasn't easy. It forced me to do things I would have really liked to leave to the grown-ups. Because I had to, I would face off with the Snow Queen and her minions. I would keep Chase's secrets from Lena, and even lie to my family, but I drew the line at killing. Not forever, of course—I knew I'd need to kill enemies *eventually*, but it could wait until high school.

Maybe I hadn't explained myself all that well, because Chase had only replied, "Waiting won't change anything, Rory."

He still bugged me about it too. And *only* me, even though I knew for a fact no one else in eighth grade had slain anyone besides beasts, like dragons and ice griffins. Even Lena, who had been in almost as many battles as me and Chase. It drove me *crazy*.

Chase rolled his eyes. "Come on, Rory—"

Lena sprinted back the way we'd come, cradling the M3 to her chest. "Tell her off later, Chase. More are coming, and one of them is *really* big."

Chase wheeled around too. "Better to take on two than five."

We dashed around the lake again. It was pouring now. The ground was soggy, and mud splattered up the back of my clothes.

Lena led us down a sidewalk between the road and some trees. Three cars passed, and I really hoped it was raining too hard for the people inside to notice that Chase and I both had swords. The path opened up, and I saw buildings—one was big and boxy, another had a lawn and glass bubbles on its roof. Between them was a sunken courtyard.

Chase wiped the rain out of his eyes. "Last call for the museum."

"I don't think so." A very big group of tourists, all with cameras, stood under the awning. *They* saw the swords. A few even took pictures.

I turned away, shielding my face, and dashed down the stairway to the courtyard. The last thing I needed was someone recognizing me and selling the photo to some tabloids. I could see the caption now: DAUGHTER OF HOLLYWOOD ROYALTY CARRIES WEAPON INTO GOLDEN GATE PARK, WOUNDS ENDANGERED WOLVES.

The courtyard was full of bald-looking, knobby trees. Their leaves had barely started growing in, so it was easy to see the wolves stream down the steps after us.

Lena glanced down at her M3. "*Eleven.* Oh my gumdrops. Oh my gum—"

"Don't panic," Chase said. "We've faced worse odds than this."

"*When?*" Lena asked. "Because this is looking pretty bad."

Near the museum, someone screamed. We looked back.

An enormous wolf trotted down the steps, easily four times as big as the others. The rain had soaked its black fur, but you could see red-brown streaks running down its sides—exactly the same color as dried blood. When it saw us looking, it howled so loud that it rattled the concrete under my sneakers.

Sometimes villains are so bad that you recognize them instantly, even if you've never seen them before.

Ripper. As in Jack the Ripper, the serial killer who was famous in Victorian London even before the Snow Queen made him a wolf. He had held the Big Bad Wolf title for one hundred and fifty years.

He'd never been captured. He'd never been defeated. He hadn't even been *seen* since his mistress, the Snow Queen, had lost the last war.

"Scratch what I said about panicking," Chase said in a tiny voice.

"Is that who I think it is?" Lena squeaked, starting to slow down. "Oh my—"

It didn't matter. We still needed to get of there.

"Lena, quick—before they catch up." I shook her shoulder, and she looked at me, her eyes enormous behind her glasses. "Where's the Shakespeare Garden?"

"It's behind the Tea Garden." She leaped up the stairs and sprinted past a line of benches. Chase and I followed.

I glanced back one more time before we reentered the trees. The smaller wolves were only a hundred yards behind us, but Ripper hadn't sped up at all. He just prowled behind the others, his jaws open in a smug doggy grin. Like he had all the time in the world. Like he knew he was going to get us.

I *hated* it when bad guys underestimated us.

"Here!" Lena dashed along an iron fence and through the

opening. She pulled the baby food jar of green-gold paint from her pocket. "Oh no—where's my brush?"

Chase reached the gate next. He grabbed the iron bars and waited under the sign that read SHAKESPEARE GARDEN, its letters decorated with metal leaves. "Rory!" He pointed over my shoulder. "Wolf!"

Without looking, I spun and punched. My fist caught a white wolf right between the eyes. It flew back with a whine, and its pack mates slowed to dart around him.

I swung myself inside, and Chase slammed the door. Breathing hard, hands over my knees, I scanned our defensive position—a smallish garden, about the size of eight parking spaces, encircled by a tall black fence. The garden didn't have that much in it, just a brick walkway that led to a couple benches and a low brick monument.

"Lena, can you set up a temporary portal with a *closed* door?" Chase shouted, holding the gate shut. "Please say yes."

"No, but just lock it." Lena inspected some small doors set straight into the brick and opened them. A metal bust of Shakespeare sat inside, protected by a sheet of clear plastic. "I've got another idea. Just give me a second to get the Plexiglas off."

"Awesome. Rory, help me look for something to tie this closed with," Chase said, kicking through some leaves. "The park must use a chain to lock up. Check the bushes."

A wolf yipped, just up the trail. We didn't have time to search the whole garden.

I pulled my carryall in front of me and groped around until I found my sword belt. I tugged my sheath off and wrapped the sturdy leather strap once, twice, four times around the gate before buckling it closed.

Through the fence, I spotted three wolves—smallish with dark brown backs—tearing up the trail.

Chase stepped back, studying my handiwork. "They might try to chew through that."

"You can stab them when they try," I pointed out.

One of the wolves threw itself against the door, trying to open the gate. Not a great idea. The belt latch held, and Chase slid his sword through the metal bars, straight into the wolf's throat.

It collapsed in front of us, and I felt kind of guilty for suggesting it.

"Lena, they're catching up!" Chase said.

"Two more minutes!" Lena shouted back.

Another little wolf trotted up the trail, water dripping from its gray fur. I recognized its big white paws—it must have swum out of Stow Lake, and it looked absolutely thrilled when it spotted the belt. Definitely too smart for a regular wolf. It jumped up, rested its front paws on the gate, and angled its teeth toward the leather, but before Chase could even lift his sword, a brown wolf shouldered its pack mate aside.

"Mark, you heard the boss's orders," it said.

I stumbled backward, my mouth open. I'd run into a bunch of fairy-tale wolves in the Glass Mountain, but I'd never heard a wolf *talk*.

"I know, I know," said Mark, the gray wolf who tried to gnaw through my belt. "We wait till he gets here."

He even *sounded* younger than the others, maybe the same age as Lena's brother George. He skulked back to the other wolves, his tail between his legs, and it was easy to imagine the teenager he'd been before the Snow Queen enchanted him—probably as gangly and clumsy as George had been when he'd had a growth spurt last fall.

Great. I could *never* kill them now.

Chase's eyes bulged. "Rory, this is bad."

"No kidding," I replied, as six more furry blurs ran along the fence.

"No, I mean, these are *fresh* wolves," Chase said.

I glanced at him. I didn't think he meant fresh as in cheeky.

"What's the holdup here?" said one of the new arrivals—a black wolf with an X-shaped scar on his snout.

"Waiting for Ripper, Lieutenant Cross," said Mark. "Just like he ordered."

"The boss's exact orders were to keep them busy," said Cross. "The magician is working a transport spell. Besides, we know how to deal with fences, don't we?"

Immediately, one of the big white wolves stood beside the iron bars. A brown wolf shuffled off into the trees, so deep in the shadows that I couldn't see it anymore. Then it sprinted out. It jumped on the back of its white-furred pack mate and leaped again, clear over the fence. Chase slashed once—the wolf's body hit the ground first, and its head dropped next, a few feet away.

"The same will happen to anybody else who comes in here," my friend told the wolves, his face dark.

Every once in a while, Chase *really* freaks me out.

"Okay! The portal's up," Lena called.

But all the biggest wolves were standing by the fence now. Their smaller partners were disappearing into the woods for a running start.

"We kind of have a situation here, Lena." Swallowing hard, I raised my sword. I couldn't let Chase do all the work. He would never let me forget it.

"A *big* situation," Chase added, looking up the trail.

Ripper padded into sight. My throat clenched. He was bigger than a buffalo.

"It's okay!" Lena said. I could hear her rummaging through her carryall. "I have an invention for that."

I thought she meant her new retractable spear, the weapon she only got out when we were so outnumbered Chase and I weren't sure we could cover her. This was definitely one of those times, but I honestly didn't see how Lena's fighting skills could save us.

Three wolves sprinted out of the woods. Their pack mates beside the fence braced themselves, standing very still.

"Found it!" said Lena. "Up, bat! Beat!"

A wooden baseball bat sailed into view. At first I thought she'd thrown it, but as soon as the first wolf cleared the fence, the bat swerved. It walloped the wolf's ribs and sped down the fence to smash another wolf across the nose.

I'd never seen *this* invention before.

"Oh, good—it works," Lena said. "Come on."

Ripper must have realized that his pack was losing. He began to run.

We were faster. "Ladies first," Chase said, gesturing at Shakespeare's head.

The frame around the bust shone green-gold. I sprinted for it, sliding my sword in its beltless sheath and hoping that Lena had finished her paint job. Otherwise, I would head-butt a metal Shakespeare.

Growling, the ginormous wolf lifted a paw over the fence.

I squeezed my eyes shut, dove . . .

. . . and I promptly collided with someone. She fell over when I hit her. "Oww," she said when Chase and Lena flew into me.

I looked up. The Tree of Hope's leaves shaded us. Branches stretched out and around, dipping to the grass and arcing back up to the sky, and we were surrounded by familiar Characters.

Ever After School. My favorite place.

"Made it!" I cried, still out of breath.

"Geez, Rory," said the kid I'd knocked over. Miriam—an eleventh grader and George's girlfriend—flipped her long black hair out of her eyes and shot me an irritated glare. "You don't need to tackle anybody. The tournament's not over yet."

The weirdest thing about the wolf attack was that nobody seemed to notice. The tournament had taken center stage.

The courtyard's usual mismatched furniture had disappeared, but the Table of Never Ending Instant Refills had to be somewhere in the crowd. Some kids snacked on popcorn as they watched the events—the longbow range, crossbows' moving targets, the dueling court, that stupid jousting lane where you were supposed to gallop straight at a post and grab as many rings hanging from ribbons as possible. So many Characters were squeezed onto the remaining patches of grass that you couldn't see any of the doors set into the walls.

"You can apologize anytime, Rory." Miriam dusted herself off. Something had made her crabbier than usual.

"Sorry. It was an emergency." I rolled to my feet and helped Lena up.

"What makes you think you're the only one with an emergency?" Miriam said, and before I could apologize again, she stomped off through the crowd.

"Lena, what's with the baseball bat?" Chase obviously wanted one.

"Classic spell from the Tale 'The Donkey, the Table, and the

Stick.'" Lena sounded extremely proud of herself. When she wasn't inventing, she liked to unravel and recreate old spells. "The stick portion, obviously. I was going to test it in the workshop today, but I guess it works fine."

Chase and I exchanged a look—the last time Lena took a new invention out for a test run during a fight, it had malfunctioned and almost cost us the battle.

"Well, I'm glad we made it out of there with all our teeth." Then Chase did what he usually did in these situations—he changed the subject. "Here's what I don't get. Where are all the freaked-out grown-ups when you need them? The last few times we set up an unapproved portal in the courtyard, the EAS army was on us like poison on Snow White's apple."

He had a point. "Do you see anyone in the Canon?" I asked.

Lena stood on tiptoes, peering over the crowd. "Ellie and Rumpelstiltskin," she said, pointing. "Right on the other side of the jousting lanes."

We squirmed our way through a clump of tenth graders holding crossbows, waiting for their turns. One of them, Lena's big sister, Jenny, called after us. "Be careful!"

Just ahead, I spotted Ellie's broad back, her apron strings hanging in a limp bow at her waist, her brown hair even frizzier than normal. "Ellie!"

She didn't bother to stop when she heard my voice. She just kept ushering Rumpelstiltskin, our dwarf librarian, through the crowd, her hands clamped on his shoulders. "Rory, I'm a little busy right now. It will have to wait until after the tournament."

"No, this is important." I grabbed her elbow.

Lena pulled up next to me. Her gaze fell on the three-foot-tall book Rumpel was hugging to his chest. It was bound in purple leather, and its pages had gilded edges. Books like that only came from one place. "Is that the current volume? Why did you take it out of the library? Is there a new Tale? Did the Director ask to see it?"

Ellie and Rumpel exchanged a glance. It was the look grown-ups give each other when they're trying to decide how much to tell the kids. My stomach sank down to my toes—something else had happened, something bad.

Chase obviously didn't pick up on that. He shoved his way to Ellie's other shoulder and told her about the attack. She didn't seem surprised, not even when he told her about Ripper showing up. Then he added, "Ellie, they were talking. They were *fresh*."

Ellie shuddered, which honestly freaked me out more than the ominous way Chase said "fresh."

"We'll tell the Director," said Rumpel in a dull voice. Then they shuffled off through the crowd, leaving us behind.

We stared after them.

"They should have made a bigger deal out of that," Chase said.

"Well, it's not exactly the first time it's happened. We do get attacked a lot." But Lena sounded a little uncertain.

"What do you mean when you say they're 'fresh'?" I asked.

"You know that the Snow Queen *makes* the wolves in her army, right?" Chase said, and I nodded. "Well, after a few years, they forget how to speak. The wolf takes over. So none of the Snow Queen's old army should be able to talk."

"Except for Ripper. He's the only one who never stopped talking," Lena added.

"So they've been turned into wolves recently," I said. "What's the big deal?"

"It's a *huge* spell, Rory," Lena said. "Only two sorceresses have been known to perform it successfully: Solange and General Searcaster."

Solange was the Snow Queen's real name, and Genevieve Searcaster was her four-story-tall general. "But the Snow Queen's in prison, and Searcaster's under house arrest."

"*Supposed* to be, but we know she still gets out," Chase reminded me. We had seen her and her eye patch in person when we went up the beanstalk during Lena's Tale.

"It had to be Searcaster. The Snow Queen couldn't have done it in prison," said Lena slowly. "The Glass Mountain limits her magic too much."

"So she's starting to move. Again," I said.

The Big Bad Wolf leading an army of freshly turned wolves. Maybe Ellie and Rumpelstiltskin already knew. Maybe a new Red Riding Hood had already Failed her Tale, killed by Ripper at her grandmother's house. Maybe that was why they looked so upset already.

"Rory!" I heard someone call behind me—Kyle Zipes, one of the triplets in our grade, was pushing his way toward us. He pointed at the dueling event. Hansel had just disarmed a tenth grader, who was chasing his sword across the arena's smooth flat stones.

I had almost forgotten about my duel. *Almost.*

"You're on deck," Kyle said. "Come on."

I scowled. It had to be *another* April Fool's joke. "I'm not even registered yet."

Kyle shot me a weird look. "Yeah, you are. You're at the top of the list. Chase put your name down before he left this morning."

I glanced at Chase, eyebrows raised. "He forgot to mention that."

He shrugged. "Don't thank me. I registered myself right after you. Wear Hansel out for me."

But I wasn't fooled. He just didn't like to get caught doing anything nice. I smiled. "Thanks, Chase," I said, starting to hurry.

Lena helped me push through the crowd. "Focus, Rory. Don't think about what happened this afternoon."

The rest of the eighth graders clumped around the dueling arena. When they spotted us, our spear squadron—Connor and Kevin Zipes, Paul Stockton, and Alvin Collins, who had only come to EAS at Christmas—started whooping and pumping their fists in the air. The stepsisters, Tina and Vicky, shouted, "Rory! Rory!" Even Melodie, the golden harp who was also Lena's assistant, had come out, along with the moving fairy statue she used as her legs. Both she and her dummy chauffeur were clapping their metal hands.

A herd of fifth, sixth, and seventh graders had also squeezed in. They didn't have too many kids actually *entering* the event, so it took me a second to realize why they were there.

Then I spotted a couple posters that said CHASE IS #1! and GO, RORY!

When the trio of sixth graders with the signs saw me looking, they waved—superenthusiastic—until I waved back, smiling.

Some of the younger kids had started following me and Chase around last spring, after we recaptured the Water of Life and saved a few hundred people at EAS. Chase loved the attention, but since it made me feel a little weird, I just treated them like my mom treated her fans. Maybe the movie-star wave was too much.

Adelaide, Daisy, and Candice lurked around off to the side, trying not to look too interested. Adelaide was the prettiest girl in eighth grade, and she knew it. Candice had come two weeks ago and replaced Daisy as her second-in-command. They obviously came to cheer Chase on, because I'm definitely *not* Adelaide's favorite person.

"We should just skip all this and do the ball," Adelaide sniffed. I kept forgetting about the dance. That was the *other* part of the anniversary celebration that took place every three years. "I mean, tournaments are so medieval."

She looked my way, so I definitely knew this comment was for me.

"Not really," said Kyle. "The king of the Living Stone dwarves announced a *real* tournament up at his new colony this morning. Winner gets his eldest daughter's hand in marriage."

"Dude, have you ever *seen* his eldest daughter?" Chase asked. "Not exactly a prize."

With a deep breath, I stepped up to the edge of the dueling arena to wait. Kenneth, a ninth grader, already stood on the stones, his sword unsheathed, his arm muscles bulging out from his sleeveless shirt. He glared at the sword master. "You're going down, old man."

The proctor rang the gong. Kenneth charged forward, yelling, and then he collided with Hansel, their blades clanging so loud some fifth graders winced. But Hansel just stuck to his old habits—he stepped back and did his low strike. The ninth grader stumbled and barely parried it in time. Then Hansel's fake out to the left came, and when Kenneth tried to block it, Hansel changed positions, stepped inside Kenneth's guard, and knocked the boy's sword from his hand.

Cursing, Kenneth snatched up his weapon and tore off.

The high school proctor rang the gong.

Yeah, Kenneth acted stupid, but he was actually one of the best fighters in his grade. If Hansel beat *him* so easily, I probably didn't have a chance.

I was wasting my time. I should have backed out of the tournament and focused on whatever the grown-ups were up to. I should have—

Then Hansel said, with the smug smile I hated, "I told Gretel this morning that I was getting too old for this, but you kids get weaker every year. This is easy. Who's next?"

I wanted to make it harder for him. I could at least do that. I stepped forward.

"Rory Landon." Hansel's smile grew wider. "Take that ring off before you smash up the arena, and let's see what Turnleaf taught you."

I passed my ring to Lena, and she gave me an encouraging smile. "You'll do *great*," she said again.

"Hey, Rory." Chase held up three fingers. "Iron Hans."

That was all he had to say. Last year, in Atlantis, Chase and I had run into Iron Hans, a thousand-year-old metal guy once known as the Snow Queen's deadliest warrior. I'd beaten him in three moves.

"I had the ring," I reminded him in a whisper, "and the sword's magic."

"You also had two injuries," Chase said. "And now, you have another year of training that you didn't have then. You're better than you think you are. He'll be flat on his back in a few seconds," he added, grinning, and I believed him.

I turned. The proctor rang the gong. Hansel stared at me, and I stared back, not at his face, at his arms. After a few beats, he grabbed the hilt of his broadsword with both hands. If I was reading him right, he was planning to go straight for the disarm—he wanted to finish this quickly.

"Scared, Rory?" Hansel said when I didn't attack, and I just smiled.

Chase said that the strongest position with Hansel was the defensive one.

Hansel reached forward with his sword, as he'd done with plenty of other students. Our blades clicked against each other, and I moved. With my right hand, I flipped my sword around and wielded it underhand, like a dagger—catching his hilt guard and wrenching my arm back. His broadsword clattered to the stones. His eyes widened. He raised a foot to go after it; he was off balance. I hooked my foot around the leg he stood on, pressed my left arm into his chest, and shoved. He fell back.

I had him! I pressed forward, pinning him to the ground, and I spun my sword around to its regular grip, pointing it at his throat, triumphant—

The proctor rang the gong before I managed to get my blade in the kill position. I looked down. Hansel held a small knife, its point a half inch from my belly button.

I lost. After all that training, all that work, all the favors I owed Chase, I *still* lost.

"He had a concealed weapon!" Chase shouted at the proctor as I stood up, scowling. "Doesn't that disqualify him?"

"They're allowed," the proctor replied. "It's in the rule book."

"Hansel *wrote* the rules. He's the one who *told* us the rules, and he conveniently left this one out," Chase replied. I clearly wasn't the only one who thought Hansel had cheated.

"Your enemies won't tell you when they hide weapons either." The old sword master got to his feet. He was moving a lot more slowly than he had before. Slamming into the stones had hurt him. Good. Served him right for bullying his students for so long.

"In a real tournament, he'd have to forfeit to Rory," Chase grumbled.

"In a *real* tournament, Hansel wouldn't be fighting every single dueler himself," the proctor pointed out. "You're up, Chase."

My friend leaped up, sword unsheathed, looking pretty intent on avenging my honor. I turned away, but Hansel clapped me on the shoulder.

I raised my chin. If he mocked me now, I didn't think I could control my temper.

"You did really well, Rory," Hansel said, smiling. "You would have had me if you hadn't taken the time to change your grip. Next time, assume your opponent has something else up their sleeve. Don't let your guard down when it looks like it's all over."

Hansel was being *nice*? I was so stunned that I forgot to move. Chase had to nudge me off the arena so he could have his turn. "Thanks for bruising him up. I can use that," he whispered to me as I hopped down to the grass.

I sheathed my sword and sighed.

It was a lot easier to lose when I thought Hansel would make fun of me. Now, it was like he was *teaching* me. I didn't need anyone to tell me that I still had a lot to learn.

Lena hugged me. "That was *amazing*."

"Yes, I've never seen you move that fast unless the sword's magic was helping you," Melodie added, but her mind was obviously someplace else. "I'll see you later. I have to go back to Lena's workshop. Touchy spell in progress. Portable wish. Thirty-second attempt, and it's looking very promising. Good thing too, because the Director won't give us any more Water of Life to use for experiments." She signaled to her dummy chauffeur, and they started weaving their way through the crowd.

The Zipes triplets hurried over.

"That was just *you*?" said Kevin, clearly shocked. "Not the sword?"

I scowled. He made it sound like *I* was cheating, not Hansel. The sword's magic only kicked in when I was protecting someone.

"Nobody's ever knocked Hansel down like that," Connor said.

"I still lost," I reminded them.

The proctor's gong rang again, and Chase flipped over his opponent's head and aimed a slash at the sword master's shoulder. Hansel was almost too slow to dodge.

"Why are you so upset, Rory?" Lena asked. "*Nobody* beats Hansel. Give Chase another minute, and he'll lose too."

"I heard that, Lena!" Chase blocked a high strike from Hansel's broadsword. "You suck at the cheerleader thing."

Lena looked guilty. "Sorry! Go, Chase!"

I didn't want to say what I was thinking—if I couldn't beat a stupid sword master, how could I defeat a real villain? The Director was keeping a secret from us, and Chase, Lena, and I were pretty sure this was it: that I was destined to take down the Snow Queen. So I just turned toward the fight.

Chase was on the defensive, leaping back as Hansel swung his broadsword. I guess Hansel *did* have a few more tricks after all.

"Don't forget the boundary line!" Kyle called. "You'll be disqualified if you cross it."

Chase glanced down to see how far away he was, and Hansel locked his hilt guard with Chase's and yanked. Chase's sword sailed from his hand, flipping hilt over blade in a high arc.

I wasn't worried. Handling a disarm was the first move I'd seen Chase do.

Chase leaped up to catch it, kicking at Hansel's chest on the way to buy himself time.

But Hansel knew this trick too. When Chase kicked, the sword master caught Chase's foot in his left hand and swung his broadsword to my friend's throat with his right.

The proctor rang the gong again. It was over.

"Crap," said Chase, stomping off and scooping up his sword. He stopped beside me. "*Crap*. Have I mentioned today how much I hate Hansel?"

"You stayed in the ring longer than anyone else," I said, trying to cheer him up, but Chase's scowl didn't soften.

As the gong sounded and the next match started, Lena tried to help us think about something more pleasant, too. "What are you going to wear to the ball tomorrow?"

Chase stared at her, mystified that he had to suffer a defeat *and* a conversation about clothes at the same time. "No idea."

"Contacts," Lena said. "That's what I'm wearing."

"If you're trying to make sure someone asks you to dance, I *can* be bribed," Chase said. "Lena, from you, I'll take a Bat of Destruction. Rory . . . maybe delivery service from the Table of Never Ending Instant Refills on a day of my choosing."

I rolled my eyes—he knew I wouldn't mind grabbing him a snack most days anyway—but Adelaide, who was obviously eavesdropping, looked excited about this information.

Then a bell started ringing. My whole body stiffened.

A Tale must have started. Someone was going to find out what kind of Character they were always meant to become.

Or maybe, I thought, remembering Ellie and Rumpelstiltskin's faces—*the Director is going to announce a Failed Tale*.

Every Character in the courtyard turned toward the Director's office. With all the people in the way, I didn't see the door open, but I saw the crowd ripple as kids cleared a path, stepping onto the dueling arena and jousting lanes, the tournament forgotten. The

Director walked to the podium set up just beside the Tree of Hope, like I'd seen her do dozens of times before, and everyone was falling silent, same as always. Miriam was so excited that she walked right behind the Director, so close she nearly stepped on the older Character's long purple skirts.

Even though I kind of suspected it was a Failed Tale, I couldn't help hoping too. My heart thumped hard, like it was trying to climb out of my throat.

I looked at Chase and found him looking back at me. We'd been worrying over our Tales more than usual. Most of the kids in our grade had gotten theirs in the past year. Plus, Tales were supposed to be contagious—if someone near you had one, the magic around them threw out invisible sparks that could easily ignite your own Tale.

But Chase's Tale hadn't come, and neither had mine.

"There's still a chance someone could be Red Riding Hood," I whispered.

Chase just shrugged with a tiny grin, his way of saying, *Good luck*.

The Director took the podium, and on tiptoe, I could see her face past everybody's heads. She looked kind of pale and just as stressed as Ellie had been.

"A new Tale has begun," she said. You could practically hear hundreds of Characters suck in a breath and hold it. "It belongs to Philip Chen-Moore, Evan Garrison, Mary Garrison, and Jamal Kidd."

Chase's shoulders slumped a little in disappointment. Murmurs started up around us.

People didn't usually share a Tale. If they did, they were usually siblings like Hansel and Gretel. Plus, as soon as they were named, the Tale bearers usually grinned or freaked out, and then they made their way to the podium. But no one was moving to the front.

Lena noticed too. "Why isn't anyone coming forward?"

"Must be a sucky Tale," Chase said, looking slightly less upset.

"I regret to inform you . . ." The Director's voice wavered. The whole crowd tensed. The Director hadn't lost her cool since she got poisoned last spring. Something had to be seriously wrong, something *much* worse than just a few new wolves or a Failed Tale.

"I regret to inform you that their Tale is 'The Pied Piper of Hamelin,'" said the Director.

"Does she just expect us to know all the Tales just like that?" said Candice. "I haven't had time to spend *hours* in the reference room like you people."

I did know the Tale, but not from my time at EAS. When I was little, my parents used to read me a book of fairy tales, and that was the story they always skipped. It had given me nightmares. I still remembered Dad perched on my bed, the book in his hands, the shiny princess on the cover facing me. "The Pied Piper," he'd said, and I'd shivered. "No, you're right. Too scary."

First a piper comes to a village called Hamelin, and he promises to get all the rats out of town. The villagers agree, and the next thing you know, the piper plays his flute. The rats stream out of the houses and follow the Pied Piper. Just that first part is creepy enough for bad dreams, but then the mayor refuses to pay the piper. The piper gets ticked, and the next night, his flute sounds one more time. Kids sleepwalk out of their beds and out of the town. No one ever sees them—the piper or the kids—again.

"Last night, the Pied Piper strolled through the streets of Portland with his flute," the Director continued.

"Maine?" asked a high schooler near the archery lanes.

"Oregon," Miriam called back, right beside the podium. I wondered how she knew.

The Director didn't even glare at anyone for interrupting. "In the Hawthorne neighborhood, his song called the children into the rainy streets. One thousand and one in all. Philip, Evan, Mary, and Jamal were with them. They followed the piper through a nearby portal. They emerged in the Arctic Circle, where the piper led them to the Snow Queen's palace."

Gasps ripped through the crowd. My stomach squeezed like a huge hand had closed over it.

People said that I was like Solange, and every time she did something like this, it freaked me out a little more. But it had been decades since the Snow Queen had done anything this big. When she kidnapped one thousand and one kids, most of them not even Characters, she had crossed a line, and Rapunzel would probably say that Solange was pleased with herself.

I wished Rapunzel were here. She was the Snow Queen's younger sister *and* she saw the future. If *anyone* could tell us what needed to happen next, it was her.

"Are they hurt?" Miriam demanded to know, and I remembered that Philip was her brother. Oh, wow, her emergency *was* bigger than ours.

"Yeah, the Arctic . . ." Kyle said. "Well, it's *cold*. A bunch of kids in their pajamas aren't going to last long. . . ." Then he saw Miriam's face, white and stricken, and muttered, "Sorry."

Across the courtyard, a dark wooden door with black ribbons led to the Wall of Failed Tales, the memorial for the Characters who never finished their Tales and those who died trying. The long columns of names flashed through my mind, and I wondered if we would be adding more soon.

"They are unharmed," the Director told Miriam gently. "Perhaps the spell helped them keep warm on their journey."

"But it doesn't make any sense," said a high-schooler. "Portland's a city. Why didn't anyone see a thousand kids in the middle of the street? You would think someone would try to stop them."

"What does she *want* with them?" asked Tina.

Miriam shot them a disgusted look that clearly said, *Who cares?* "Who are you going to send to rescue them? And how fast can they leave?"

Chase went still. His father, Jack, was the champion of the Canon. He was the obvious choice for this mission, and we all knew it would be extra dangerous if the Snow Queen was involved.

"Traditionally, in the Tale of the Pied Piper," said the Director, "the children are led away and never seen again."

After that little announcement, the stunned silence lasted about a second. Then everybody started protesting.

"She has to be kidding," Chase said. "It's her April Fool's joke, right?"

"She's not wrong," Lena said. "About the Tale. But the last Pied Piper was seen during World War II—the Germans blamed a bomb. A Pied Piper nowadays . . . people are going to notice. Logic can only take us so far."

I didn't say anything.

I just felt like . . . I had to go rescue them.

A plan exploded in my head, as sudden as a sneeze. It was so simple. I needed to sneak through the portal in Hawthorne, get to the Arctic Circle, find the kids' footprints, and track them to the Snow Queen's palace.

The Director raised both gloved hands, and across the courtyard,

EASers elbowed their friends and told them to shut up. "But luck- ily, another Tale has begun in answer to 'The Pied Piper,' one that provides a solution to the kidnapped children . . ."

She glanced in our direction.

My heart thudded to a stop. I was right—I was getting my Tale.

". . . and allows a sister to rescue her brother," the Director fin- ished. "Miriam Chen-Moore, congratulations. Your Tale has begun: 'The Snow Queen.'"

Or not.

Chase glanced at me. I clapped with everyone else, but I *was* disappointed.

The Snow Queen was a good Tale. In the first one, Solange kidnapped a boy named Kai, and his next-door neighbor, a little girl named Greta, goes on a quest to the Snow Queen's palace and rescues him. No Character had gotten it in *decades*, and I'd kind of thought *I* would get it.

Miriam stepped up beside the Director's podium.

"You are allowed to pick two Companions to journey with you," the Director told her.

Everybody knew that Chase, Lena, and I had the most experi- ence dealing with this villain. Miriam would probably pick one of us, to help her out. Maybe two. I might still go. . . .

"Shakayla Carey and Natalie Kasprak," Miriam said quickly.

The crowd drew aside as two eleventh-grade girls started for- ward—a short one with pretty skin and muscles like she lifted weights, and a tall pale one trailing along behind, a bow and quiver over her shoulder.

Of course she would pick friends from her grade. Of course she wouldn't take me or anyone else in middle school.

Miriam didn't wait for the Companions to swear to advise and protect her. She just marched down from the podium, grabbed Shakayla and Natalie's wrists, and towed them toward the library. "We see Rumpelstiltskin next, right?"

The Director pretended that Miriam wasn't rushing the usual ceremony. "Yes. He has research to share with you and a map that will help guide your journey."

"We need to get this show on the road." Miriam stalked across the jousting lanes and the dueling court so fast that Shakayla and Natalie had to scamper to keep up. "Like *someone* pointed out, my brother could be freezing right now."

"Sorry! I didn't mean—" Kyle started, obviously feeling bad, but the questers just disappeared into the library.

Like everyone else, I watched them go, but I still couldn't help feeling that Miriam had made the wrong choice.

he grocery store down the street from our house was one of those tiny upscale ones, everything bright and shiny and expensive. Its door was propped open with an enormous planter full of fresh herbs. Amy sailed right in, past the display of wine bottles and olive oil jars, to the refrigerated ready-made section. She flipped over plastic packs of ravioli to check their expiration dates.

Mom hung back, waiting for me. "What do you think? Ice cream?"

This store had the best frozen treat section in Pacific Heights, but I wasn't in the mood to pick one out. I was still a little upset Mom and Amy hadn't let me stay in the car—Lena had promised to keep me updated on the quest by M3, but we couldn't talk if Mom was watching me like this. Actually, I was still upset I couldn't stay at EAS long enough to see the questers off.

Mom was pretty strict these days.

Last year I had sort of run away from my dad, right after he told me he was going to marry my stepmother, Brie. I'd had a good excuse—Lena's life was at stake, *plus* the lives of almost every Character I knew—but Mom didn't know that. She just thought EAS was a "bad influence."

It had taken me two months, one week, and three days to

convince her to let me go back. I'd had to get straight A's on my report card and promise that I wouldn't spend more than ten hours a week at EAS. She enforced it too—we had a calendar and everything. When I told about the ball, she said I could go, but I could only stay at EAS an hour and twenty-four minutes during the week.

It *was* a crazy system, but not really any weirder than getting attacked by the Big Bad Wolf. You can get used to anything.

But over by the chocolate display, which was almost as epic as the ice cream section, Mom's expression hadn't changed since she'd picked me up: her smile still looked distracted, her eyes pinched with worry. She'd definitely heard the news from Portland. She kept finding excuses to touch me—tugging my ponytail, brushing mud off my shoulder—like she was checking to make sure I was in one piece.

I couldn't take this much longer. "I'm okay, Mom," I said as gently as I could. And despite the wolves and Hansel, I *was* okay. I just really wanted to find out what was going on back at EAS.

"I know." Mom sighed. "I shouldn't hover. You're a teenager now—you *hate* that. Besides, Portland's pretty far away."

Of course she was still worried. She didn't have an explanation for the kidnappings like I did. Sometimes, like today, I *wanted* to tell her. It would be nice to talk about what had happened—to let her know what I was really thinking.

Someday, but not now. I couldn't put her in danger just to make myself feel better.

"I'm sure they'll get the kids back," I told her, thinking of Miriam. I seriously hoped her Companions were up to it.

Mom squeezed my shoulders, giving me her *Oh, Rory, I'm the mother* smile. "I would never be the same if something happened to you. You know that, right?"

I nodded, guilt twisting my stomach. If she freaked out this much over something a whole state away, she definitely didn't need to know about the skirmish in Golden Gate Park.

"Maggie, what kind?" Amy waved two packets of ravioli at Mom. "Pumpkin or arugula?"

"Pumpkin!" Mom said. Her favorite. Then she turned to me. "I think it feels like a movie night."

"Definitely." As long as I could sneak to my room and get an update from Lena beforehand.

Glass shattered near the front, and we all glanced back. I expected someone to apologize profusely for knocking over some wine bottle, but the woman in front of the purplish puddle just backed away from the entrance.

A white wolf stood in the doorway.

For a second I just stared, too shocked to move.

It couldn't attack me *here*, not when I was surrounded by people who knew nothing about magic, not when I was with my *family*.

But when its yellow eyes met mine, the wolf began to growl.

I'd left my sword in my carryall, sitting in the backseat of Amy's car. Useless.

Someone near the back of the store screamed, but it sounded far away.

Mom shifted forward slightly. "Stay behind me, Rory."

Amy's hand crept into her purse, where I knew she kept a can of pepper spray. She was too slow. The wolf crouched, and if Mom was standing between us, it would just attack her before it got to me.

The wolf leaped.

I yanked Mom back so fast that her rain-booted feet flew out from under her with a rubbery squeak. Then I struck out with the only weapon I had on me: my left fist, armed with the ring of the West Wind. A gust rippled over my arm as the punch connected with the wolf's snout. The furry body crashed into the canned vegetables section. Then it slid to the floor, out cold before it could even whimper.

It also left a big dent in the metal shelves.

I glanced at Mom, checking to make sure she wasn't hurt, but she was just staring at me. Amy too. Actually, every eye in the store stared at me. My face started to burn. Cans rolled on the floor past my ankles.

"Rory, what did you *do*?" Amy whispered.

But it was the look on Mom's face that scared me the most—like she didn't recognize me at all.

With a nod from Mom, Amy went straight into damage control mode. She walked up to the cashier and offered to pay for all damages.

Mom just got us out of there before the police, animal control, or the press showed up. With a hand clamped on my shoulder, she steered me out the door, around the corner, and to the car.

She wasn't saying anything. She wasn't even looking at me as she climbed into the driver's seat, and it was freaking me out.

"Mom . . . ," I started, buckling my seatbelt.

"Hold on, Rory," she said, turning the car toward home. She sounded as strained as she did when she had to drive in a blizzard back when we lived in upstate New York—she had the same distant look, the same tense focus making her entire body rigid. "Let me get us home."

My hands shook as I unzipped my carryall. I fished around until my fingers closed around my sword hilt. I didn't pull it out, but I felt the tiniest bit better with it in my hand.

Mom had come so close to getting hurt. And it was my fault.

But why *now*? I'd been on high alert for *weeks* after trolls invaded Lena's home in Milwaukee. I'd been *sure* that my family was next, but the Snow Queen hadn't sent anyone. Chase said it must have been because my family didn't know anything about EAS. Even Solange wouldn't cross that boundary. Not knowing kept them out of danger.

But the wolf had come after me. The Snow Queen would follow me wherever I was, whoever I was with.

The normal world wasn't safe anymore.

Mom turned the corner onto our street, and I jumped. But the big furry shape on the sidewalk was just the poodle that lived two doors down. His owner trotted behind him, poop bag in hand.

We reached the cheery yellow house Mom had rented, with its pale green trim, its giant upstairs window with crisscrossed panes, and its small front garden, full of tulips in bloom. Mom parked the car and turned off the engine.

Then she looked me straight in the eye, dead serious. "Is Ever After School giving you drugs?"

This was so far from what I thought she was going to say that I didn't respond. My mouth just gaped open.

"Amy suggested that once. She thinks EAS is a cult—did you know that?" Mom asked, but she didn't give me time to answer. "And last spring, when you ran off to Lena, I almost believed her. Then I thought, No. It makes Rory so happy. But a grown man couldn't bend those shelves the way you just did. So I have to think . . . steroids."

The human mind is a tricky thing: someone can be faced with

magic, and instead of believing what they see, they'll think of some "logical" explanation that fits what they know about the world.

I could tell Mom that my strength came from the plain silver band on my finger, but she would probably still go with her drugs idea.

"Rory, you need to tell me the truth," she said.

The truth. In the two years I'd been attending EAS, I'd never once tried telling my family the truth, even if it meant getting grounded. "I'm not taking drugs, I promise."

"So if I check your room, I won't find anything?" Mom said.

"You can if you want . . . ," I replied, kind of hurt. I didn't mind her checking my stuff—all the inventions Lena has given me were disguised as regular things—but she usually just trusted my word.

"I know. I'm sorry. I do trust you. I shouldn't just accuse you with crazy things, but . . ." She pressed a hand against her mouth. Her hands were shaking too.

"It'll be okay," I said, but my voice cracked.

And, like a mask fell over her face, she donned a smile. "Okay. Let's pause this conversation and reconvene in the kitchen. Today calls for tea."

Mom only calls for tea breaks in stressful situations. She brewed it the same way she'd driven us home, distant and focused: filling the kettle and putting it on the stove, lining up all of her favorite mugs on the counter, and pulling out three different kinds of tea—mint for me, lemon for Amy, and chamomile for herself.

Moving around the kitchen, she shot me the same looks as she had in the weeks after I came back from Atlantis, like she didn't know what to do with me, but she was afraid I would vanish again if she let me out of her sight.

I definitely didn't break the silence. I didn't know what I was going to say.

Finally the door squeaked open, and Amy let herself in, looking a little harassed. She took in the sight of Mom's tea freak-out. "No trouble from the storekeepers," she said.

Mom nodded, then turned to me. I braced myself for the third degree. "Listen, Rory," she said. "What if we stayed in San Francisco? Got a house and everything?"

Well, *that* came out of nowhere.

"I'll get the folder," Amy said and left the room, which kind of upped my confusion.

"Two more productions have approached me recently, asking me to commit to other plays here," Mom explained. "I think this stage acting could be the next phase of my career. I would still do movies, but only in the summer, when school was out and you could come with me."

I guess it made sense, Mom wanting to moving here: She had college friends in the Bay Area. The dean of students at my school had been her freshman-year roommate, and the theater director who had first convinced her to try out the San Fran stage had been in most of Mom's drama classes.

"This way, you could spend all four years at the same high school and make some friends." Mom looked at me expectantly. She thought I would jump at the chance to stop moving around, to have a real life instead of just being the new girl all the time.

Two years ago, I *would* have.

Now, when I daydreamed about living in one place, I always pictured moving to EAS, like Lena and Chase. We wouldn't even have to move from city to city for Mom's movies anymore. She could just use the Door Trek system to travel the country. But my mom would never go for that. If I told her the truth about EAS, she would only see that world as a place where the Pied Piper kidnapped children, wolves invaded Golden Gate Park, and the Snow Queen tried to kill me for having some sort of freaky destiny—not the place with easy magic transport.

When Amy came back carrying a red folder decorated with a silver door, I knew what Mom was going to say next: "You wouldn't need to go to EAS anymore." That was putting it in a nice way. Staying in San Francisco meant she never wanted me to go back to EAS again.

"You could join the soccer team," Amy added.

I *had* been into soccer—before sword training took over my free time. They still thought I was the same as I'd been at eleven, but so much had changed since then. They didn't know me at all anymore.

"And I've been looking at houses!" Mom reached across the table and opened the folder. Inside was a stack of glossy flyers. She pushed one in front of me. "This condo isn't even that far from here. Four bedrooms! I thought we could go to the open house on Sunday."

Then I understood. The grocery store incident hadn't caused this conversation. It had just given Mom the excuse to bring it up. "You've been thinking about this for a while."

"Yes." Mom hesitated. "Since February—when your dad told you about, um, his news."

Dad's news had been big. I'd known that it was going to be something major as soon as he called. He never called me unless we set up a phone date ahead of time. He also didn't normally waste long seconds taking deep breaths that whistled over the mouthpiece.

Then he'd said, "Guess what? Brie's going to have a baby!"

I had been so surprised at first. I think I'd only said, *"Huh?"*

Dad hadn't noticed. "This summer. This *June*. That's what the doctor said. You're the first person we called. We haven't even told Brie's parents yet."

"Cool." I tried to remember what I was supposed to say. "I mean, congratulations."

"Thanks. Thank you. I'm just—I'm overwhelmed, you know?" Dad's voice had gone all crackly, which meant he'd either had a bad connection or he'd gotten choked up. "Hold on. I'm going to pass the phone to your stepmother. She wants to talk to you."

Brie hadn't been able to contain herself either. "We don't know if the baby's a boy or a girl yet, but we are so excited. And scared, to be totally honest. Rory, I need to ask you something."

"Okay," I'd said, still reeling.

"I want you to think about what kind of big sister you want to be," Brie had said. "Because I think it would be fantastic—and your dad thinks this too—if you were really involved. I just know that your little brother or sister is going to *love* you. I want you guys to meet right away. Maybe you could come down for the birth? What do you think?"

I'd thought, *I really need to get off the phone*, but I hadn't *said* that. I don't remember what I'd said. I just remember what happened after I'd hung up.

I had burst into tears, run upstairs into my bedroom, and slammed the door.

That had led to a few late-night phone conferences between my parents on the *how is Rory handling the baby news?* question. They didn't know I'd overheard them, but it was hard to ignore my parents working together without shouting.

What Mom and Dad didn't know was that after I'd locked myself in my room, I'd called Lena on my M3 and told her. She'd understood why I'd freaked. This was yet another way my life paralleled the Snow Queen's. Solange's father and stepmother had had a little girl when she was thirteen too—Solange had stolen the baby away, named her Rapunzel, and put her in a tower until she started her little sister's Tale. Manipulating the conditions like that is forbidden, but Solange wanted to make sure that Rapunzel joined the Canon and became immortal like her big sis.

And as much as I loved Rapunzel, she was pretty messed up, and it was all Solange's fault.

I didn't want to be involved. I didn't want to get anywhere *near* Brie's baby. It was safer—for *them*.

Remembering that made me sad.

Of course my family didn't know me. There was so much I hadn't told them.

"Rory," Mom said, and I looked up. Worry had pinched her face again. I guess I'd spaced out for too long. She reached for my hand. "I really think it would be good for us."

This was the perfect time to come clean, to explain what was really going on in my life. I was running out of excuses.

But I wasn't sure that now was the right moment to tell Mom magic was real. She was still shaky from the wolf attack. She didn't need to know that I fought like that on a regular basis.

I couldn't break it to her this way. Not yet, not when the adrenaline was still making her hands shake.

So I did what I usually did. I stalled. I *lied*.

"Can I have a little time to think about it?" I said, ignoring the guilt creeping in. "I've really been looking forward to the dance at EAS."

I didn't really care that much, but this excuse seemed normal enough to satisfy my mother. She even looked kind of relieved, like she thought this explained all of my hesitation.

Amy didn't. I knew that fierce thin-lipped look. "Maggie, you're going to let her go back to that weird place? After Rory just tossed a giant dog across the *room*?"

Here we go. I steeled myself.

"It's only one evening," Mom said. "Besides, we don't have any proof what happened today has anything to do with EAS."

"Well, we can ask her." Amy turned to me. "Does Ever After School have anything to do with that punch?"

I froze, resisting the urge to touch the ring. "I mean, all the sword lessons have made my arms a lot stronger." Wow, that sounded weak.

Amy and Mom knew it wasn't the truth. They stiffened, and I could see the indecision on Mom's face: call me on it and punish me for lying, or keep her word and let me go to the dance.

"I'm going to trust you, Rory," Mom said slowly. "But when you get back, I want you to trust me too. I want you to tell me the truth."

I nodded. It would be easier to tell her when we were calmer, when I had time to prepare. Maybe Lena would let me borrow one of her inventions—something awesomely magical instead of just dangerous and scary.

"Maggie—" Amy started, but Mom shot her a look that clearly said, *I'm the mother and the maker of all decisions.*

"She can go tomorrow night," Mom said, and I knew what she really meant.

I could go tomorrow night, but never again.

When Amy started dinner and Mom started researching high schools in our neighborhood, I snuck upstairs to my room. I made sure the door was locked before flipping open my M3. "Hello?"

Lena didn't let me down. Her face filled the mirror. "Rory. It took you forever to get home—we have so much to tell you."

"So do I—" I started, but I don't think she heard me. Noise overflowed through the M3, like a hundred Characters were shouting.

"Is that Rory?" I heard Chase ask, over Lena's shoulder. "Let me talk to her." His big hand covered the mirror for a second, and then there was Chase, scowling, his face red. "The Director, she cancelled it."

"Cancelled what?" Oh no—hopefully not the *dance*. Without a ball tomorrow night, Mom would never let me go back to EAS.

"The *quest*," Chase said. "She cancelled Miriam's quest. She said it's too dangerous."

For a second, shock made me stupid. "But you can't just cancel a quest. It's Miriam's *Tale*."

Lena's head popped up over Chase's shoulder. "That's basically what Miriam's saying."

"She's pitching a fit," Chase told me.

"Well, to be fair, everyone is," Lena said loyally. She knew Miriam better than Chase and I did. "A quest has never been cancelled before."

Obviously, *this* news blew mine completely out of the water.

"What did the Director say *exactly*?" I asked. "I mean, most quests are dangerous, right? Why couldn't she just give Miriam and her Companions rings of return like everybody else?"

Lena's voice sounded tinny, like it always does when she recited something from memory. "'The quest cannot take place. This Tale would mean certain death for its bearer, and I can't in good conscience allow her to go.'" Then she added, in her regular voice, "That's all. Miriam said that Rumpel was reading her Tale in the current volume, and he *flipped out*. Then the Director made that announcement."

"Who is she sending in Miriam's place? The twelfth graders? Your dad?" I asked Chase.

"That's just it," Lena said, sounding kind of helpless. "She's not sending *anyone*."

"The Director's just going to leave those kids up there," Chase said.

Then the feeling came back, even stronger. I saw it so clearly: the portal to the Arctic Circle, the trail of footprints in the ice . . .

But that was insane. You couldn't just hijack someone else's Tale—that was worse than cancelling it.

On the other hand, this was the Snow Queen. And if we were right about my destiny, then I was *meant* to stop her. "We should go. We should find her and go on the quest anyway."

Chase nodded. "It would be a big mission. Who knows what kind of security Searcaster set up around the Snow Queen's old fortress? If the Canon sent all the high-schoolers, that should be enough—"

"No." I lowered my voice. "I meant *we* should go. The three of us."

And for some reason, my two best friends looked at me like I'd said I should stop by the Glass Mountain and invite the Snow Queen to the ball.

"That's an interesting thought," Melodie said. I couldn't see her, but I could hear her. She must have been in the bag on Lena's shoulder.

"I don't think that's a good idea," Lena said.

"Can you think of anyone better for the job?" I hoped Chase

would side with me, but his face was blank—not a good sign.

"No," Lena said, "but Rory, rescue missions don't usually go out without the Canon's support. Missions like that, they need supplies, maps, Rumpel's research. They need *help*, and if Characters don't have it . . ."

I could see where this was going. "They die?"

Lena nodded, biting her lip.

"The grown-ups have told us that maybe a million times," I reminded her. "I'm beginning to think that they say that just to stop us from what we want to do."

"Their names were Greg, Simon, Cassie, and Shira," Chase said. "They were in the year above George. Shira's sister was stolen by Vasilica the Deathless, and they went after her before the Canon could meet and decide what to do. All five of them died. Their names are engraved on the Wall of Failed Tales. I can show you, if you don't believe me."

"Technically, it was just Shira's sister's Tale, but the Director made an exception. They're all on there," Lena whispered. "It happened two months before you came."

Now I felt like a huge jerk for wanting to roll my eyes.

But Philip Chen-Moore's name could end up there, and Evan and Mary Garrison's, and Jamal Kidd's, and maybe the names of all the Portland children who followed the Pied Piper. A thousand and one *more* names. We would need a bigger room.

"You think we don't have a chance," I said to Chase. "You think we won't be prepared."

"No, supplies and stuff aren't the problem. I know how to get into all of EAS's storerooms, and Lena can make everything we don't have," Chase said, and for a second, I relaxed, sure that he would vote for rescue. "But I don't think we should go either. I don't want to go to the Snow Queen's palace. People go in, and they don't come out."

I stared at him.

Chase didn't scare easy. He never backed down from a challenge just because it was too dangerous.

"Even powerful Fey, like Dyani, crown princess of the Unseelie Court, and her betrothed," Chase added, and I understood what he was trying to say. Dyani's betrothed had been Chase's half brother Cal. The Snow Queen had killed them both when Chase was only five. She'd probably killed them in her palace dungeon.

I couldn't say anything. I was right, I knew it, but I didn't want to force Chase to visit the place his brother had died.

"Well, that is true, but they say the same thing about the Glass Mountain, and Chase and Rory have gotten in and out of there," said Melodie, and all my hopes rushed back. "Twice, I might add. And you're all forgetting that most times, a person's Tale will bring them the help they need. You three are the newest Triumvirate. You're known for making things happen. You might *be* the help that Miriam needs."

I didn't know what I did to get on the harp's good side, but I really appreciated it.

Chase still looked unimpressed, but Lena was wavering. I could tell by the way she frowned and stared off into space, the same look she got when one of her inventions wasn't behaving and she was trying to figure out how to fix it.

Melodie sensed it too. "Madame Benne would do it. Madame Benne and Maerwynne and Rikard would never leave anyone to die alone in the cold."

That was the right thing to say. We all enjoyed getting compared to those three—they were the first triumvirate and they'd founded the Canon—but Lena could never resist being like her ancestress, Madame Benne.

"Okay, let's ask Miriam. We'll give her the choice: We'll either go with her, or we'll help her and the *Companions she picked*"— Lena glanced down at the M3 to send me a reproachful look—"get to the right place without the Canon's help. Deal?"

Oops. Somehow Shakayla and Natalie had totally fallen off my radar. "That sounds fair," I said, glancing hopefully at Chase.

He shrugged, which was as close to yes as we were going to get.

"Where is Miriam?" I asked.

Chase and Lena turned away from the mirror, searching the crowd.

"There." The harp's golden hand crossed the screen, pointing somewhere I couldn't see. "Beating against the door to the Director's office."

"Oh! Poor Miriam." Lena's image started bobbing around as she ran across the courtyard.

"Don't tell her the plan so close to the Director!" I cried. "If the Canon finds out, the kidnapped kids have *no* chance."

"Give us a little credit," Chase muttered off-screen. "We're not complete idiots."

"Here. Take Rory and go to my place," Lena said, passing the mirror over. "Gran's gone with George to a prefreshman college orientation, and Jenny's still out. I'll grab Miriam and meet you there. The Director will be more suspicious if she sees all of us together."

"But we're always together," I pointed out.

"And the Director is always suspicious," Lena replied. "Didn't you see her looking at us right before she announced Miriam's Tale?"

Chase held the M3 up as he walked. "For someone who hates breaking the rules, Lena shows a lot of talent for it."

Waiting for Chase to find the LaMarelle's spare key and let himself in was *torture*. Waiting for Lena and Miriam to come in was even worse. Especially when Amy knocked on my bedroom door and brought me back to San Francisco with a jolt. "Ten minutes before dinner."

"Okay!" I called back.

Mom and Amy. I couldn't leave them unprotected, not when those wolves were roaming around. I should have thought of that before.

"Chase. I have to tell you something." In fifty words or less, I explained what had happened in the grocery store.

"And you didn't mention this *earlier*?" Chase said in that special annoyed way he got when he was worried about me.

"Your news was more important," I reminded him. "But do you think they'll try again?"

"Of course they'll try again," Chase said. "She went after Lena a few months ago, and now she's after you."

"You think she'll attack if I'm not here?" Then I'd have to stay. I imagined the weekend ahead, wondering if I could have rescued those kids, and the weeks after that, explaining and re-explaining everything to Mom.

"You mean, if we go with Miriam?" Chase said. He thought about it for a second. "No, I doubt it. The Snow Queen goes after your family to use them against you. If we all go on the quest, she'll have two other potential targets close by: me and Lena. She wouldn't waste energy going after people in the human world instead."

Wow. I was *definitely* excited to go on the quest now.

"Besides," Chase added, "we might not go." He flipped the mirror around so I could watch Miriam and Lena crashing through the door.

"Are you *sure* you don't want to take someone from your grade?" Lena asked anxiously.

Maybe it had been wishful thinking on my part, until I heard her trying to change the Tale bearer's mind, but I didn't realize Lena had expected Miriam to say no.

"Yep," said Miriam, stalking into the room. "Do you know what Natalie said when the Director cancelled the quest? 'So, I get to use my glass slippers after all.' I don't need any Companions who are more excited about some stupid dance than saving my brother."

So we *were* going.

I wished there were three of me—one to stand guard all weekend to keep my family safe, one to tell Mom the truth without freaking her out, and one to rescue the Pied Piper's victims. But Chase said Mom and Amy would be safer without me. That meant the Portland kids were in the most danger. I had to focus on that.

"We should leave tomorrow. During the ball." It was the only time Mom would let me go to EAS, but I hated that I was planning to disappear on her *again*.

"Good idea," Chase said, resigned. "Dances are always chaos. The Director won't be watching us so closely."

"Okay." Lena grabbed a notebook from the coffee table and pulled a pen out of her pocket. "Let's write a list of everything we need."

"We have to sneak into the library," Miriam said eagerly. "I want to find out why Rumpel and the Director freaked."

Lena grimaced, obviously wishing we didn't have to, but she wrote it down anyway. "We'll do that during the ball too. I think I can find a good illusion spell that'll keep the Director from realizing we've even left the dance floor."

Chase turned the mirror back to his face, so I could see his grin. "What did I tell you? An extraordinary talent for breaking rules."

That night I dreamed of a door. The door hadn't changed from the other dreams it had haunted—it was still carved from black wood, cracked with age. A scrolling *S* marked the doorknob, and frost traced silver into the wood grain. My breath fogged the air, like it had before, but this was the first time I *felt* the cold: my ears and fingertips ached with it.

On the other side of the door, the Snow Queen had hidden something, and the fate of the world depended on me finding it.

When I woke up, my heart beat so hard I could hear it thudding in my ears. If you were a Character, dreams were never just dreams, especially if you had the same one three times. Those dreams gave you a glimpse of your Tale.

This one I'd dreamed five times. But that wasn't why adrenaline poured into my veins.

We were going to the Snow Queen's palace. If that black door existed, it would be there. I might *find* it.

My Tale might actually start on this quest.

Mom wasn't too crazy about me going back to EAS, but she was determined not to show it. Instead, she made me as pretty as possible for the ball. It was like a Hollywood glitzy version of reverse psychology.

After spending hours picking out the perfect accessories, Amy attacked my hair with a blow-dryer, while Mom sat me down on her bed, pulled up her desk chair, and opened a makeup box with an alarming spread of bottles, brushes, and powders.

You would think, with such an important quest coming up, I would be immune to getting excited about a dance, but when Mom said I could pick out one of her old dresses, I knew exactly which one I wanted: an emerald green one she'd worn to a premiere six years ago, back when Mom and Dad were still married and hardly having any problems at all. When I put it on, silver embroidery shaped like leafy vines swirled around my torso, and the gauzy skirt swished against my legs, light and cool and totally swirl-worthy.

I stared at my reflection as Mom zipped up the back. I'd thought that I would look like Mom in the dress—pretty and elegant. But my arms were a lot stronger than my mother's, and without sleeves, they looked it. Plus, with all the makeup, my eyes looked bigger, which meant that my chin didn't look so huge, and if you added Amy's handiwork on my hair, I looked as glamorous and dangerous as the superhero Mom had played in her last film.

Except superheroes didn't usually have such goofy grins on their faces.

Amy came close, tugging my hair free of my dress straps and frowning as she finger-combed it back into place. Then she snapped a pic on her phone. "Wow, Rory. You went through an awkward phase last year, but you're a knockout now."

"What are you talking about? I don't remember an awkward phase," Mom said. "But I admit you look particularly lovely right now."

"If all these eighth-grade boys don't swoon at your feet, then they're blind." Amy checked her watch. "Okay, you've got just enough time to drive over there and be fashionably late. I don't care if the hottest guy in the universe asks you to dance right at the end—I want to see you outside at a quarter to ten. If you're not there, I'll send your mom in after you. With her camera. And her most embarrassing hair." She grinned to show me she was joking. Kind of.

"Pigtails," Mom said, playing along. "Lopsided ones. Now just give me three minutes to run to the bathroom. Then we can go."

"I'll meet you beside the car," I said, swinging on my lime-green carryall. Late the night before, hours after Mom and Amy had gone into their rooms, I'd dug through my moving boxes and packed all my cold-weather gear. Plus my sword, my toothbrush, a couple changes of clothes, and *lots* of warm socks.

"Someone *is* excited," Amy teased as I reached the front door. I grinned a little sheepishly, so she wouldn't suspect anything, but that wasn't it.

I'd thought of one more thing I wanted to do before I left, and since Mom and Amy had been keeping closer tabs on me than usual, I hadn't gotten a chance to sneak away yet.

Outside, I climbed halfway down the front steps and found the tile I'd given Mom for her birthday, sitting in the bare dirt between some trees. The carving looked like a really ornate Celtic knot, and it gleamed green and gold with all the pieces of ground dragon scales Lena had baked into it. She'd given it to me as a precaution after trolls attacked her family.

When I pulled out my gumdrop translator and stuck it in my ear, I could easily read the Fey writing: *I protect this house.* Over the tile, I whispered in Fey, *"From this earth, I ask you to rise, to stand tall and hear what I advise."*

Like gnome-size zombies, figures rose up on dirt-caked feet. They didn't have heads—just a torso, legs, and arms ending in a fist. One had a petunia growing out of its shoulder. Each dirt servant left a cat-size hole in the potting soil. Whoops. I hoped the person who owned this house wouldn't charge Mom for damages done to his garden.

"Um," I said, trying to remember the next part of the spell. They all turned to me, which was actually kind of creepy. *"Still and quiet you must stay, guardians enspelled by clay. If an enemy comes in dark or light, we need you to stand and fight."*

I was pretty sure it worked, but somebody was bound to notice if they stood out front. *"And hide,"* I added in Fey, pointing at a conveniently leafy Japanese maple. It took them a second—Lena said they weren't sure you were talking to them if you didn't rhyme— but they shuffled behind the tree.

Done. If anything as magical as a mugger with troll blood tried to hurt Mom and Amy while I was away, the dirt servants would attack.

I trotted down the driveway to the car, shoved my gumdrop translator back in my bag, and leaned against the passenger side just as Mom opened the front door.

"Ready?" she asked. I nodded, afraid to glance one more time at the maple, in case someone noticed the moving shapes behind the leaves.

Amy waved from the porch. "Remember! A quarter to ten!"

Mom made me nervous when we drove away. She kept glancing at me until I was sure she had figured out my real plans. Maybe she'd spotted my sweaty palms. Maybe she'd gone to my room— I'd left her a note on my pillow, but if she'd found it three hours too early, I would have a serious problem.

"I can't believe that you're almost finished with eighth grade and this is your first real dance," Mom said finally. "If we'd stayed in L.A., you would have had maybe twenty by now. I'm so sorry."

Oh. This *was* my first dance. Working so hard on my makeup hadn't been reverse psychology. She'd just wanted to make it special for me. "It's okay."

Mom smiled, a little sadly. "It's really not okay, Rory. But I appreciate what a fine, brave, uncomplaining little girl you are."

Hello, guilt.

It squeezed my lungs flat. If I spoke, I would probably confess that she should add "lying" and "soon-to-be runaway" to that list. She didn't deserve this. She didn't deserve *me*.

I *could* tell her. I could explain everything right now—magic and the Tales, the Door Trek system and the Tree of Hope, the Pied Piper and the kidnapped children and the Snow Queen. Even if she turned the car around, dragged me back to the house, and locked me in my room, it still wouldn't stop me from going. I had a temporary-transport spell in a jar. I could paint it around my closet to get back.

Maybe that wasn't what worried me. Maybe I didn't want to see her face when she realized how much I'd kept from her.

"In your new high school, you can go to all the dances. Maybe I'll even let you and your friends take a cab there, so you won't have to get dropped off by your mother. Seriously uncool," Mom said. She was clinging so hard to the dream of staying here. Sadness rushed in and smothered the guilt.

With me gone, she was going to worry anyway. It was better that she worry just about the dangers she already understood, rather than the magical kind that would scare her more. I couldn't tell her yet.

After two whole years, one more week wouldn't make a huge difference.

Mom parked in front of the blue-and-gray house with the bright red door, the Door Trek one that would take me to EAS. You couldn't hear any music, but that didn't tip her off. Seeing that no other cars were lining up to drop their kids off didn't bother her either. When I'd told Ellie that my parents were supersuspicious of my after-school activities, she amped up the *don't question anything* enchantment so much that even Melodie was affected. Last time we'd carried her through this way, she had gone as still as a statue for almost a minute, and when she woke up, she'd said she had forgotten for a moment that she was a magic, talking, *moving* harp.

When I got out of the car, Mom did too, and she hugged me hard. "Who's my favorite daughter?"

She hadn't said that in a while. Maybe she thought I'd outgrown it, but I still liked hearing it.

I relaxed into her, dropping my chin on her shoulder, trying not to wonder if she would hug me so hard after I came back. "But I'm your *only* daughter."

"Then it's a good thing you're my favorite." She smiled, tucking some hair behind my ear. "I know it's hard to imagine a different life. We've gotten into a good routine. If we make a change, it's new and different and scary. But just remember: It was new and different and scary when we started moving around, and we handled it just fine. We're brave enough. We'll survive."

I hoped she was right. I hoped it was true for coming clean about EAS, not just staying in San Francisco.

"Nothing lasts forever," she said, hugging me again. I wasn't sure she was going to let me go. I wasn't even sure I wanted her to.

Remember the dream, I told myself. *Remember the kids.*

"I'll tell you all about it when I get back," I said.

Mom's face brightened, hopeful, and I hated myself instantly. The right thing to say had come to me so easily. I was getting as bad as Chase.

This was the last lie. It had to be. I couldn't stand being such a terrible daughter anymore.

She patted my bare shoulder. "Have fun, sweetie."

I trotted up the front steps to the red door. Mom's camera flashed three times, like my own personal paparazzi, the parental version. I turned back to wave, and I wondered if she would show those pictures to the cops—evidence of the outfit I was wearing when I went missing. I wondered if later she would notice the guilt on my face.

Nothing lasts forever. Not even Mom's trust in me.

I stepped inside and tripped—right over Chase.

He sat on the floor, staring into his M3. He obviously didn't care if he got his suit all dusty. It was dark in this corridor so often that I memorized the carvings on the walls by feel alone, but he'd managed to flip the lights on.

"You're late," he said without looking up. It looked like someone had attacked his shaggy blond hair with a wet comb. "Miriam went to the ball ages ago, and Lena just left to set up the illusion in the workshop."

It took me a few seconds to switch gears—to start worrying about the quest instead of Mom. "She couldn't set it up here?" I asked.

"According to Melodie, the spell can't be moved that far after it's cast," he said. "Pack up your carryall so we can meet her. She can't actually start the spell without us."

Supplies were spread across the floor beside him. I unzipped my pack and started shoving stuff inside: my enchanted sleeping bag; a new sword belt to attach to my sheath; an ancient SAVE THE PLANET sack, heavy with green-gold dragon scales; a clay tile that looked a lot like the one I'd just set up; a scuffed Lunch Box of Plenty, the same pony-stickered one Chase and I had taken to Atlantis.

"Did anyone grab some rings of return?" I asked.

"We couldn't find them. The Director keeps them in her office, and we didn't want to risk breaking into there," Chase said.

I stopped packing to stare at him. He shouldn't sound so calm. "So how are we going to get back?"

"Lena packed fifty extra dragon scales so we can make a portal straight back to Hawthorne," Chase said, eyes still glued to his M3. "So we can get the kids back too."

"Oh." This was the problem with not being able to chat on your M3 all day: your friends made a bunch of plans without you, and you had to play catch-up.

I peered around his shoulder to see the M3. He was staring at the ballroom.

If the well-dressed EASers didn't give it away, its pretty sky-blue walls did. Even the members of the Canon had gotten fancy— Hansel wore a suit without a tie, and the Director was in a violet ball gown with a skirt so huge it almost hid her seat, a high-backed chair engraved with thorns. Both of them looked kind of worried, which wasn't great news, but not particularly attentive, which was way more helpful.

"Did Lena ask you to spy on the Director?" I asked.

"Nope. I volunteered. Adelaide keeps trying to bribe me into dancing with her." He looked up to kind of grin at me. I say "kind of" because the grin lasted about half a second. Then he just goggled at me as if I had walked in wearing towering icicles, like the Snow Queen's favorite crown.

"What?" I said, touching my hair to check that I hadn't gotten anything in it.

"You're wearing makeup," Chase said. He never looked at me that closely unless I was doing a move wrong during one of our lessons. Even then, his eyes didn't travel up and down like that.

Suddenly the dress I was wearing felt stupid. I wished I could have spent the day researching spells to keep warm in the Arctic, like Lena, or sneaking around EAS's storerooms to gather supplies, like Chase. A blush was coming on. I wondered if he could see it under all the dumb makeup. "It's not my fault. Mom put it on me."

Chase snorted. "And you let her?"

"It was the only way she would let me out of the house," I said. "I told her I was excited about the dance."

He rolled his eyes. "Well, that explains why you haven't finished packing yet. You're worried about breaking a nail."

I shoved the lunch box into my carryall, feeling even more defensive. "I haven't finished because nobody's *helping*."

"Lena entrusted me with a very important task." Chase waved his M3.

"Then you should be staring at *that* instead of at *me*," I said.

Chase jerked his head back to the mirror. Point to Rory, but I didn't really feel any less awkward. We were silent for the minute it took me to finish packing.

"Done. Where do we leave this, then?" I asked him, pointing at my carryall.

"I'll show you." Chase hopped up from the floor and slid to a spot across from the carving of the Snow Queen. Then he whispered something in Fey. Without my gumdrop translator in, I couldn't catch the words, but I'd heard it so many times that I recognized the spell: *Break what was whole, crack what was smooth, open what was shut.*

A secret passageway. It didn't surprise me. Chase knew about most of them.

We ducked through three hidden doors, turned a corner, and came to a bright corridor with mason-jar chandeliers, a honey-colored wood floor, and three packs leaning against a wall of exposed brick. The other side had a carving too—of Evan Garrison, I think, talking to a fleet of foxes.

"This is the door to Portland. Lena and I already tweaked the spell to let the four of us through," Chase said.

"For a quick getaway?" I said, slinging my pack off.

"If necessary." Chase turned toward a door so intensely green that it was just one shade away from neon. "But you know Lena—she's definitely hoping it won't be necessary." He twisted the old brass handle and pushed open the door. The Tree of Hope stood dead ahead, one of its twisting branches touching down right in front of us, blocking us from view. That would be helpful when we made our escape.

Dozens of people had surrounded the Table of Never Ending Instant Refills. Today it was covered with a punch fountain, cucumber sandwiches, and tiny little cakes. But the courtyard wasn't nearly as crowded as it normally was. The only people in my grade I saw were the stepsisters. Tina was scrubbing at a punch stain on Vicky's sleeve with a wet napkin, and they stared at me blankly when I waved at them.

We started across the grass toward the ballroom, and before we'd gone two steps, a quiet musical voice called, "Rory."

Chase jumped about a mile.

Rapunzel stood behind us. She wore the dove-gray dress she saved for special occasions. Even her long silver braid was fancier than usual: she'd woven red ribbons and ruby-encrusted jewelry into it.

I smiled. If she was here, it was to help us. This *was* the right thing to do.

"It's creepy, the way you always know where we are." Chase folded his arms. His suit sleeves were a little too short. "I hope the Director didn't see you waiting out here. She's more suspicious of you than us three."

That was true, but it wasn't Rapunzel's fault. She couldn't help being the Snow Queen's sister.

"The Director is at the ball," I reminded Chase. "We're safe for a few minutes."

Stepping closer to me, Rapunzel pulled something from her pocket: the top part looked like a silver tree, with tiny emeralds set into it like leaves, and the bottom had a bunch of short metal sticks. It was a comb. She slid it into place right behind my ear.

Chase gave a little golf clap. "Very pretty. Can we please go now? Lena's waiting on us."

Rapunzel ignored Chase and bent toward me. I waited for her to tell me everything I needed to know to survive the quest, but all she whispered was, "Do not get caught."

Then she stepped aside. We were obviously dismissed. Chase wasted no time scooting me forward.

I glanced back, half expecting Rapunzel to rush up and tell us a few impossible-to-understand prophecies, but she had disappeared. "Doesn't she usually tell us more than that?"

He made a face. "Oh, she cornered me and Lena earlier. You know what she told me? 'Be patient with her. She'll need more time than you.'" He glanced at me sidelong, already exasperated. "That means either you or Lena or Miriam's going to be slow. My money's on you. I've seen Lena and Miriam run."

"Thanks." I rolled my eyes, but I was trying hard not to be jealous. *I* was the one Rapunzel usually singled out, not my friends. "What'd she tell Lena?"

"Something about inventing. She'll probably need a translation later," Chase said as we skirted around the Table. The doors to the ballroom were straight ahead. The sounds of violins and harps leaked through the carved wood. "'This quest won't be like the others.' That's another thing she told us in Lena's workshop this afternoon."

I might have grilled him some more, but someone was waiting for us: Lena.

She looked so different and amazing that I wondered if she might get a second Tale tonight: "The Ugly Duckling." Not that she was ugly, but with her glasses off and her hair up, her neck looked about a million miles long. That definitely screamed *swan*. Her dress was gold, and her dark skin glowed against it. It wasn't just her outfit, though—she stood up as straight and elegant as a princess. Of course, she was biting her lip and wringing her gloved hands, which kind of spoiled the effect.

"Melodie's almost ready," Lena told Chase, too nervous to even say hi to me, "but we can't cast the illusion with so many people in the courtyard."

Chase nodded. "I'll run inside and tell him we need that decoy he offered."

"Ben went in about ten minutes ago," Lena said, relieved. "He's wearing seersucker."

Ben Taylor was the only Character in the entire Ever After School who would ever wear a seersucker suit. He was full of dorktastic style, and weirdly enough, he'd become one of Chase's closest friends since his Tale last spring.

"Got it." To me, Chase added, "Stay here. It's insanity in there."

He opened the doors. The ballroom's sky-blue walls were the same as usual, and so was the gilded woodwork that made the walls sparkle. The rest had been transformed.

They'd hung seven chandeliers—golden phoenixes as big as dragons, with flames dancing across their metal feathers. The orchestra was filled with the huge metal fairy, troll, and witch dummies we usually practiced on in training. I'm pretty sure that they took requests, because the lame waltzy music had given way to an instrumental version of "Brown-Eyed Girl." On the dance floor, there were so many Characters—and so many huge frilly dresses— that I lost Chase before the doors even closed behind him.

"Ben said Lancer brought his speakers, so they're all set," Lena told me, like I knew what that meant. "Ben can do this, right? He can create a decoy that distracts the Director and gets everyone out of the courtyard."

"Um . . . sure." I wanted that to be true, but Ben didn't have as much experience as Chase with this sort of thing.

Lena didn't notice my hesitation. "I mean, he has Chatty on the M3, helping him."

"Definitely then," I said. Chatty was Ben's girlfriend—a mermaid who happened to love practical jokes. They have a long-distance relationship. "Is there anything *I* can do?"

"Cross your fingers?" Lena said helplessly.

I did, and I held them up to show her, with the most reassuring smile I could manage. But it felt weird not being part of the action. Yesterday, this had been my idea. Now it was completely out of my hands.

Then Chase slipped out again, leaving the door open a crack so we could peek through. "Let's see if the Director takes the bait," he said.

Up on the raised dais, opposite the orchestra, a row of throne-like chairs were all empty except for the Director's. Her fingers drummed on the armrest, her eyes sweeping across the floor. We drew back a little when her gaze traveled toward us.

"Not yet," I said. "Where's Ben?"

"Beside the line of potential Cinderellas." Chase pointed to the back, where a swooping marble staircase rose above the dance floor. Girls had lined up behind it. On a small platform at the top, an elf in a weird shirt and waistcoat announced the name of the girl who had reached the front of the line, but I couldn't hear him from this far away. I knew without looking that they were all wearing glass slippers with a flexibility spell embedded in them. The Director had announced a sign-up sheet for anyone who wanted to borrow a pair a while back, but I'd been too focused on the tournament to care.

The ninth graders shifted into position below them. I glimpsed Ben's seersucker jacket, and then a loud beat exploded from them.

A kid wearing a blazer covered in patches passed some speakers to Ben. Then he pulled a beanie out of another pocket, stuck it over his hair, flipped upside down, and started to spin, his legs at crooked angles.

The break-dance-at-the-ball-distraction. Perfect.

Looking like a *Draconus melodius* about to breathe fire, the Director deployed the troops. Hansel and Stu, the Shoemaker, both pushed through the crowd toward the commotion.

"It's not working!" Lena's whisper hissed with panic. "There are still way too many people in the courtyard for Melodie to bring the spell out here."

Chase stepped back and opened the doors wide. Then he cupped his hands over his mouth and called to everyone outside. "Dude, Lancer Davis is b-boying! The Director's going to freak!"

Kids rushed from the Table to the ballroom. We scooted out of the way as Character after Character passed by, craning their necks to get a peek at the action. Lena sprinted four doors down toward the workshop, way faster than she should have in those heels.

"Well done," I told Chase, and he grinned.

Soon just one couple sat in an overstuffed chair under the Tree of Hope, but they were too busy kissing to notice us. The only other people I saw in the courtyard were three figures in front of the library door. Miriam, Natalie, and Shakayla. Hard to tell in the dark, but it looked like Miriam was tapping her foot.

The metal doors to the workshop slid open, and out came Lena and Melodie, along with her dummy chauffeur. They came slowly, step by painful step, carrying a scrying bowl. It was filled with a really gross concoction: green and gold dragon scales ground down to the size of sprinkles, reeking of sulfur; random sticks and twigs; a photograph of me, Chase, and Lena; and a spoon made out of coral.

Chase inspected it too. "Please tell me the spoon isn't for eating."

Melodie hunched over the bowl protectively and sent us her golden-eyed glare of doom. "This is a very delicate spell. Almost as touchy as brewing a portable wish. If you breathe on it funny, you mess it up."

"Well, can you hurry?" Chase asked. "It's not going to take the Director very long to kick that kid out."

"Is anybody looking?" Lena said. "It won't work if people are watching us."

I glanced through the door. A circle had formed around Lancer, and now people were cheering and clapping in rhythm. Hansel and Stu couldn't get close enough to stop him. The Director looked like she was about ready to charge in herself and escort Lancer off into the dungeon. "I think we're okay," I said.

"Then, on the count of three," said the harp. Lena nodded and took a deep breath. "One, two . . . three." Then the harp and her mistress unleashed a long torrent of Fey words, in a weird sort of sing-song. I definitely shouldn't have taken my gumdrop translator out.

The scrying bowl boiled with color until it bubbled over the sides and all the way down to the grass. It streamed off in one direction and spilled upward, recreating a Lena, Chase, and Rory. Watching my green flats appear and then my ankles creeped me out so much that I had to look away.

Lena noticed. She smiled sympathetically. "I know. It's weird, but it's fast. Look—they're already done."

Three new figures stood in the courtyard, identical to us, right down to Lena's long golden gloves and Chase's too-short sleeves and the tree-shaped comb Rapunzel put in my hair. It was weird to watch my double grin and line up in the ballroom door-way with the illusion Chase and the illusion Lena. On their tiptoes, they tried to see Lancer dancing. Lena must have enchanted them to do what everyone else was doing.

With Lena's help, the harp poured the contents of the scrying bowl—now less lumpy and glowing hot pink—into a glass jar, and she put it in the satchel hanging over the fairy dummy's metal wings. Then Melodie looked at us, her golden face determined. "Better hurry."

Lena hugged the harp so hard that some of Melodie's strings twanged.

"Be careful, mistress," the harp said.

Oh. I guess Melodie wasn't coming.

"Don't tell," Lena said.

The harp nodded. "Cross my heart and hope to melt."

Then Melodie's dummy chauffeur stepped forward, and so did the illusion Lena, Chase, and Rory. They shifted down along the ball-room wall, and Melodie waved as Lena shut the doors behind them.

"Now for the library." Lena spun on her heel and rushed across the courtyard.

I glanced back once. "We're not going in?"

Considering everything, it was stupid to feel disappointed about it, but it *had* taken three grown-ups to get me ready that night. It was hard to believe I wasn't even going to step into the ballroom.

"Sucks that we won't even have time for one dance," Chase said as we fell in behind Lena.

I looked at him, trying to decided if he was teasing me or not.

He smiled, just a tiny bit. "I dance even better than I skate-board. You would have been really impressed."

Still not sure. I would have asked and possibly told him off, but the door squeaked open behind us.

Oh no. We'd been discovered. We all looked back to see the person who had come to drag us in front of the Director.

Kyle Zipes.

"Hey, Lena," he said. "Two quick questions: One, do you want to dance? And two, why did you leave a copy of yourself against that wall?"

Lena stared at him, horrified. "Oh my gumdrops."

"I'm sensing—and go ahead and tell me if I'm wrong—that you guys are up to something you shouldn't be," Kyle said, following us toward the library.

"Your detective skills amaze me," Chase said.

"Born talented. What can I say?" But Kyle glanced between the three of us with a small frown, clearly waiting for someone to explain.

"We're breaking into the library," Chase said in his most bragging voice.

Lena obviously couldn't stand not telling Kyle either. "Remember the illusion spell Gretel did for the skit last year? Well, I adapted it. It would have been easier if I was a sorceress and not a magician, but that's what Melodie carried into the ballroom."

"Okay . . . ," Kyle said. "So, I guess . . . no dance, then?"

"I really *want* to," Lena said desperately. "It's just—"

"It would look weird if people noticed there were two Lenas," Kyle finished.

"I'm really sorry!"

"It's fine, Lena. You have top secret stuff. I get it. But—" Now he looked a little nervous. "Maybe later? After you dissolve the illusion spell and—"

Poor guy. He was about to get turned down a second time, and Lena looked so unwilling to tell him that I thought the Pounce Pot forced her to swallow her tongue.

Kyle guessed. If possible, he deflated even more. Then he noticed who was waiting for us in front of the library. He stopped short, and his eyes grew so huge, I double-checked to make sure he hadn't spotted a rogue ice griffin or something.

Nope. Just Miriam arguing with her friends, so loud we could hear them.

"It doesn't have anything to do with the dance," Natalie said. "You know you could die, right?"

"Tell that to Philip," Miriam snapped.

Shakayla noticed us first. "Look, Miriam. More little kids to add to your collection. At this rate, you better just take the whole middle school to the Arctic Circle."

That was annoying, especially coming from a sissy almost-Companion.

"You're not going after the Pied Piper's kids, are you?" Kyle said.

It occurred to me *why* Lena had such a humungous crush on him. He had to be one of the smartest kids in our grade.

"Of course." Miriam pointed at Kyle. She'd painted her nails silver since I'd seen her last. "Are you coming too?"

"No, I'm not." Kyle headed back to the ballroom, walking backward so he could keep talking. "Lena, your illusion's a noncorporeal spell, right? I'll try to make sure nobody walks through your decoys."

And he offered to help without being asked? Lena had *really* good taste in crushes.

"We trust him, right?" When no one replied, Miriam clapped once, to get our attention. "*Children*. Answer."

"Crap," said Chase, looking at our Tale bearer. "You're as bossy as Jenny, aren't you?"

"We trust him," I said, but I had the sinking feeling that Chase was right. This was going to be a *long* quest.

The library door wasn't even locked, which worried me. No kids were allowed in unless the librarian invited them. I couldn't believe Rumpel would just leave it open, unless maybe the library had other defenses.

We didn't even have to search the bronze shelves, or look through the three-foot-tall books stacked on them. The current volume lay unguarded on the table. The leather cover was a deep violet, which grew even darker along the edges. The pages were gilded, and inside, all the ongoing Tales were writing and rewriting themselves, just waiting for us to read them. Maybe the Canon had booby-trapped it. Maybe an enchantment would turn us to stone as soon as we lifted the cover.

Because the Water of Life would break most spells, that wouldn't be the end of the world, but we'd definitely be caught.

I expected Lena to be even more nervous than I was, but she was a Character on a mission. She was the only kid at EAS who'd ever been invited to the library just because Rumpelstiltskin liked her. So she knew exactly where she was going, straight to the back. She knelt beside the map cabinet and tugged a long skinny drawer open. Then she began lifting maps out and laying them down one by one. When Chase got close, examining a map, she said, "I don't need help. You don't exactly have much attention for detail, and everything has to go back exactly how it was. Rumpelstiltskin can never know I betrayed his trust."

He knew better than to argue with Lena when she was like this. He stepped away. "I'll go stand guard."

That left me with Miriam and the current volume. She eyed the book on the table the same way I'd eyed Jack's wyrm when I'd met him for the first time, like it might spew fire any second.

"When Shakayla, Natalie, and I came in here yesterday, Rumpel just turned a page and his whole face went white," she whispered. "He slammed the book shut and kicked us out of the library so he could talk to the Director alone."

I took a deep breath and lifted the violet cover. Not stone yet. Maybe it was fine. Maybe the Director never expected kids to break such a big rule.

Maybe if I got so freaked out opening a *book*, I had no business going on this quest. Geez.

I flipped to the middle, where someone had slid in a ribbon bookmark. "The Pied Piper" blazed across the top of the page.

"Do you remember orientation?" Miriam said, and I nodded. I'd had mine with her and Philip. "Do you remember what he saw in the mirror?"

The mirror test sometimes gave you a glimpse of your Tale, and Philip had seen a man in red, carrying a wooden flute. He'd seen the Pied Piper.

"Philip knew who had come." Then, in a hesitant voice, Miriam started to read.

> It didn't sound like a flute. More like a cross between a kazoo and a trumpet, and its vibrations made his bones buzz. He'd

been drifting off. It took him by surprise, how quickly he shoved away his covers and swung his legs off the bed.

He was halfway down the stairs before he realized he wasn't in control of his body.

He wasn't afraid yet. This could all be a dream. He'd dreamed this before: stepping off the bottom stair and reaching for the door, unlocking it and walking through, leaving the door open behind him as he strode across the porch and down the front steps.

Philip remembered this part too—passing his sister's car, parked at the very top of the driveway, because she was out of town for a two-day tennis tournament. Like in the dreams, he told his hand to reach for the side mirror, to latch onto it and hold out against the current pulling him into the street. His fingers twitched—

I wish I never had a brother, his sister had said before she left. *I wish I was still an only child.*

That seemed kind of harsh to me, but I wouldn't really know. Philip wasn't *my* brother.

"I didn't *mean* it," Miriam told me softly, stepping away from the table. She crossed her arms over her chest. "I was talking to my parents. I didn't think he was even listening . . ."

That probably was my cue to take over reading. I leaned toward the page.

—but his hand rose no higher than his waist. He sailed past

his sister's car and his mother's station wagon, down the rest of the driveway and into the street.

Under the tune of the not-flute, other children streamed out of their homes: Jeff, his next-door neighbor, who hadn't been allowed to come over since fifth grade, when he'd convinced Philip to practice golf in the backyard. That red-haired girl who was obsessed with jumping rope. The three younger Brooks boys, who had moved here two months ago from Toronto, and who were trying to win Philip over to street hockey.

Now Philip was afraid.

These kids weren't Characters. They shouldn't have showed up in his dream about his Tale.

Their eyes were open, but their gaze shot straight past Philip, like they were sleepwalking. They wandered down to the end of the street, and around the corner to Hawthorne.

"I can get us to Hawthorne," Miriam said unexpectedly.

Philip's eyes sought out the familiar places, drinking in the sight of them, worrying he would never see them again: the grocery store his mother shopped at, and the restaurant where they ate brunch on special occasions, like the day he graduated from middle school. The bookstore where he and Miriam had bought their summer reading for as long as he could remember. The bargain movie theater his family had visited every Thursday until Miriam joined the tennis team and had to go to practice instead. The alley with a bright green door, the one that could take him to EAS.

His eyes were his own, but he could only turn his head an inch.

As his legs marched on, he strained to catch a glimpse of the door, and he noticed someone else straining to look, someone else awake among the herd of sleepwalking children: Evan Garrison, another Character who lived about a quarter mile away.

He wondered how many other Characters had been captured. He wondered when the Canon would send someone to save them.

The Pied Piper turned off the main road, onto a street threaded between a gift shop and a coffee place—

"That describes half the neighborhood!" Miriam said, annoyed.

A staircase led down from street level. A sign with a border hung on the door.

As soon as it opened, the piper's tune leaped forward, and so did Philip's feet. The children sprinted down the steps and streamed across the basement, empty except for one tall hooded figure. Dark wings rose from his back.

"You're late," the fairy told the Pied Piper. "Take them through quickly, so I can finish my task."

"A Fey is working with the Snow Queen?" Chase said, clearly ready to wring that particular fairy's neck.

"We'll talk about it *later*, when we have time," Miriam snapped. "Lena, how's it going over there?"

"I have the one of the Arctic Circle. Still working on the portal one. When I find it," Lena said, painstakingly returning map after map to the drawer, "you'll be the first to know."

I started reading again before a fight could break out.

Beyond the fairy, another door had been thrown open. The Pied Piper went through first, leading the children into a cold tunnel. Instantly, Philip's bare feet ached, and it only grew colder as the piper marched them to the cave mouth.

Outside was whiteness in every direction, blank and empty under the night sky except for a strange tower padded with fur, surrounded by a puddle of melted ice. Then the tower bent, and Philip realized it was a giant. She glared at the piper, face twisting under her eye patch. "You're late. I've wasted too much magic keeping the air warm while I waited," she snarled. "You'll have to make them run."

And so the children ran. Their breath rose in foggy bursts, but the giant's magic wrapped them in a bubble of warm air. The ice melted to slush under their bare and socked feet. Outside the path of running children, wolves prowled, and if they didn't catch an escapee, the frozen white world around them would.

Philip's fear turned to terror.

I bet those were the same wolves we'd seen in Golden Gate Park.

"Wait, do we know who that giant is?" Miriam said.

Lena nodded. "There's only one sorceress-giant."

"Genevieve Searcaster," I said glumly.

The list of villains we would be facing was getting longer and longer. No wonder the Director was worried.

Only once did Philip see a kid break away from the pack—Evan crouched over a hole in the ice, where white fox pups watched the children stampede past, but the sorceress-giant plucked the boy from the ground, carrying him in her fist.

Through the night and the morning, the children ran. They ran until Philip's feet were numb and his breaths ripped through his throat.

When the palace rose out of the bleak landscape, Philip welcomed the sight almost as much as the piper, who had begun to bleed from two fingers, and the giant, whose face had turned gray under her hood. The children were slipping now in the slush. Mary, Evan's sister, would stop and help them up, so Philip started to do the same. His neighbor, the jump-roper, tripped just as they reached the threshold—frozen doors thrown open, tall enough to admit the giant.

Philip had already grabbed his neighbor's hands before he noticed that her eyes had widened. She was awake.

"Philip?" she said. "Where are we?"

They were in an enormous room made of ice—frozen floors, white walls, and a dome ceiling glittering with icicles. It was colder here than it had been during the run, especially with the sweat cooling around his pajama collar.

Around them, other kids were waking. Some screamed. Others cried.

Philip glanced at the villains.

The Pied Piper's tune had stopped. His lips were almost as red as his suit, bruised with the effort of enchanting them for so long.

"I can't control them as well at a run," the Pied Piper panted.

The giant's face was still ashen, but her voice was steady. "It doesn't matter. Her Majesty has a plan." Then she lifted her gaze.

Following it, Philip spotted a balcony high above them. He stood, riveted, when a slight figure stepped out upon it—her silver dress edged with lacelike frost, her ivory skin shimmering with ice crystals, her fair hair bound up under a crown.

Her lips—the color of snow mixed with a single drop of blood—curled slowly into a triumphant smile.

My eyes reached the next line before my voice did, and my heart stopped.

"Welcome, children," said the Snow Queen. "You are mine now."

And then Philip's terror evaporated. Only despair was left. If this villain had stolen them, there would be no rescue.

The rest of the page was blank. "That's all. That's the last line," I said.

Now we knew why the Director had cancelled the quest. It didn't seem like such a stupid decision anymore.

Chase stared at me, like he was waiting for me to say, *Late April Fool's*. I clasped my hands behind my back, so that no one could see them shaking. Lena let a map dangle from her fingers, not noticing the crease she was making in the parchment.

"Well . . ." Miriam's voice was rough. She cleared her throat. "At least we know he's still alive."

I wondered how long she'd been worrying about that.

"Why didn't she *tell* us?" Lena said. "If the Director knew since yesterday, why didn't she announce it?"

"Panic," Chase said. "It would ruin the ball."

The Director and her stupid ball. She should have told us. We had a right to know.

I had a right to know. I was the one who was supposed to stop the Snow Queen, wasn't I?

"Lena, have you found the map of Portland yet?" Miriam asked.

Lena's eyes were huge. "Are we still *going*?"

But we needed to go. The slush the book had described should still be there, frozen over. The tracks would be easy to follow.

I made myself bite my tongue. It *was* Miriam's Tale.

Our Tale bearer just flipped forward in the book, blank page after blank page. "All this empty space. It means his Tale is still being written. We still have time to rescue him."

"But from the Snow Queen's palace?" Lena said. "What does she plan to do with her prisoners? Maybe we can rescue Philip after he gets a little farther away from the Snow Queen. . . ."

"You guys are asking all the wrong questions," Chase said, striding over to the table. "How did she get *out*? And is it really her? That could have been a doll."

"Like that Mia kid last year?" Miriam said, sounding way less stressed.

That would be nice. At least with a doll, we wouldn't have to worry about the Snow Queen's magical arsenal on top of Genevieve Searcaster's.

Chase took the book from Miriam and turned pages until he found one that wasn't blank. At the very top, it said, "The Snow Queen." Underneath, an illustration showed the villain exactly how she looked when I last saw her, her skin kind of yellow. She lounged in a throne room hung with white silk. On one side, the drapes had been ripped away to reveal the wall of her prison, the Glass Mountain. Beyond it were the forests of Atlantis.

He began to read.

FIRST STORY, which tells of a Queen and her Prison

The Snow Queen sat in her prison and smiled. True, the children had gotten away. That troublesome Rory Landon had retrieved the Water of Life and rescued the two boys.

Chase looked up. "I resent that. I did a lot in there. It was my idea to—"

"Not now!" I said, and he returned to the book.

> Doubtless, they would now be distributing the Water to all those
> poisoned. Doubtless, they thought that they'd won.

> She allowed herself a moment of frustration—yes, wiping out
> the entire Canon under Mildred's very nose would have been
> delicious. Killing the Rory girl would have been particularly
> sweet. But no matter.

> Her hard work hadn't been for naught. She had completed
> her primary objective.

> The Snow Queen reached under her throne, and from a spot
> hidden behind her skirt, she grabbed two bottles, filled to
> the brim with the Water of Life. The stupid children hadn't
> realized that she had removed them from the carryall before
> they had arrived. They hadn't bothered to count the number
> of bottles.

That was true. Chase and I hadn't checked. We'd been in too much of a hurry. Teams of wolves and trolls had attacked us almost as soon as we'd arrived.

"Wait, what did she want the Water *for*?" Miriam asked.

"*With this, she could escape,*'" Chase continued.

Black squiggles crowded my vision. I reminded myself to breathe.

Chase's gaze zipped back and forth over the page, reading but not aloud, and I didn't like the way his face was beginning to say, *doom*. Miriam leaned closer and took over.

She would do it now—perhaps this wall was weakened, still recovering from the child's blow. She edged closer to the glass, fighting as it tried to push her back. She unscrewed the cap of the bottle.

She didn't call her attendants to her, in case the attempt failed.

Then she jerked her arm forward. The water flew in an arc over the few feet she couldn't cross and splattered against the glass. For a second, nothing happened—the water only dripped pathetically down the wall, long enough for Solange to swell with rage.

"It didn't work," I said, but I didn't feel as sure as I sounded. "The spell in the bottles was the same as the spell embedded in the Glass Mountain. If the water didn't explode the bottles, it couldn't explode the wall either. Right?"

Lena shook her head slowly. "I cast the bottle's spell specifically to hold the Water of Life's magic. That's what kept it from exploding. Throwing a bunch of water on the wall would overload the Glass Mountain's enchantment."

Of course I felt like I needed to rescue the kids of Portland. Chase and I had handed the Snow Queen a way out. It was our fault they were in that mess.

Miriam started again.

But the Water was true.

The wall shattered, exploding outward. It left a hole seven feet tall and five feet wide. The force shoving her back disappeared.

The Snow Queen ran, wishing now that someone was here to see her escape from the inescapable prison, to see her step onto the grass she had stared at for decades.

She relocated to a small clearing nearby and began work on another doll—one identical to herself, one that could stand in her place when the Canon sent someone to check on her. It wasn't time to spread the word that she was free. She had so much to do before Mildred tried to stop her—a palace to rebuild, an army to reassemble, a reputation to reestablish, and wishes to make.

And—as much as she hated to admit it—her powers were not what they once were, not after years baking under that hated glass dome.

Chase brightened. "Having weakened powers is good."

"No, it *was* good," I said, mourning our lost chance. "The ball was in *her* court. If she has started to move again, that means she thinks she's ready."

Miriam turned another page. The illustration at the top had a portrait of her own worried face glaring down at the book. "There's more."

SECOND STORY. A Plan and a Piper

One day the Snow Queen needed a demonstration of power. She needed to prove two things: She had returned, and so had her might.

She decided to do what she did best: steal children.

She would send the Pied Piper—she had daydreamed about it during her long imprisonment. She'd even chosen the location a year previous, when her spy doll had carefully leafed through EAS's records—Hawthorne neighborhood, in the city of Portland, had the most young Characters of any other area on the continent. Even better, an ancient portal to her domain already existed there. She would send the Pied Piper and strike Mildred where it would hurt her the most, at her beloved EASers, at the human world the Canon believed safe.

And so she did.

And when her piper and her general delivered the stolen children to her palace, she watched the terrified young wake from the piper's song and smiled at her good work.

Miriam flapped the page uselessly. The rest was blank. "That's it? Stupid book. It's *my* Tale, isn't it? Why doesn't it mention me?"

She sniffed hard. I hovered near her shoulder, trying to decide if I should give her a hug or not.

Chase went in for distraction, his number-one tactic for dealing with someone about to cry. "Okay, admit it: Who's a little freaked out after that fun trip into the mind of the Snow Queen?" He raised a hand and peered at Lena, who was still kneeling beside the cabinet, swaying slightly. "Lena, 'fess up—I can see you wobbling from here."

Lena didn't even look at us. "I found the map of Portland."

She didn't ask the question again, but we all thought it: *Are we still going?*

Paper crinkled as Lena carefully returned the maps to their drawers. Chase and I watched Miriam blink hard at the current volume.

While we waited, the book added a few more lines. No one read them out loud.

This, Miriam Chen-Moore knew.

Safe in the library, surrounded by books and allies, she asked
herself what her brother would do, if she had been stolen in
his place.

Then the door burst open.

We froze. Well, except for Lena, who covered her eyes, probably trying to shield herself from the librarian's look of betrayal.

But it was just Kyle again. Gulping down mouthfuls of air, he slammed the door behind him.

"They saw through the illusion?" Lena whispered.

He shook his head. "You tripped an alarm. I overheard Rumpelstiltskin tell the Director. They're coming."

"We need to get out of here," I said, because I was a master of the obvious.

"Not that way," Kyle said, pointing to the door. "They were literally a few steps behind me. Connor bumped into Rumpelstiltskin and knocked him over to buy us time—"

"Is he okay?" Lena said, and Chase shot her an exasperated look.

"—but they'll see us if we go to the courtyard," Kyle finished.

"The back way, then." Beside the map cabinet, Chase pushed aside a curtain and pulled a case of tools from his jacket pocket, pretending to pick the lock while he muttered the Fey spell. I closed the current volume, trying to position it exactly the way we found it.

Lena kept returning maps to their drawers. She was the only person I knew who could be frantic and slow at the same time.

"Bingo." Chase pushed. The door tried to swing closed and lock automatically, so he had to brace it open. Beyond was a corridor with a beanstalk mosaic inlaid on the floor and cast-iron fixtures on the wall. Torchlight flickered across his face. "Let's go."

Nobody had to tell Kyle twice. He darted through so quickly that I wondered if he shared Lena's feelings about breaking rules. Lena and Miriam weren't far behind.

I walked backward, scanning the room for anything out of place as I went. There. Miriam's handbag thing—she'd left it right beside the book, where any suspicious librarian or Director could find it.

"Rory," Chase grunted when I changed directions and snagged the purse. He was losing the battle with the door. It pushed him back, making his shoes squeak against the floor. He had to use his foot as a doorstop and his arm as a crowbar, just to keep it open.

"Sorry!" I whispered, waving the purse as an excuse.

Then the front entrance flew open.

"Stop!" the Director called. "We have seen you! Students are not permitted in the library."

I squeezed under Chase's arm. Something fell out of my hair.

"Rapunzel's comb!" I turned back to pick it up, but Chase grabbed my wrist.

"Leave it," he said, yanking me forward into the hall. The door thumped shut behind us. As he dragged me down the corridor, I looked back, hoping I could spot the little comb.

I saw all right. I saw it hit the floor and bounce once, and then I saw metal bars sprout from its teeth, like iron vines snaking across the doorway, weaving together on the way up, like a chain-link fence.

Yeah. My jaw definitely dropped.

On the other side of the door, I could hear the Director saying, "The key! Rumpelstiltskin, I need the key to this door immediately!"

"Did you see what the comb did?" I asked Chase.

He obviously didn't have any idea what I was talking about. "Forget the comb. We have to hide. They're going to search this hall."

"No, we should run to the Portland door," I protested. "Hiding won't help us if they already know it's us."

"Well, she didn't actually see *us*," Chase told me. "Last-minute glamour. We looked like twelfth-grade boys. Hopefully she'll think it's a senior prank."

That was unexpectedly brilliant of him.

"She'll figure *out* who it is if you two don't stop bickering," said Lena, hands on her hips. "No one in EAS fights as much as you do."

She had found one of the storerooms, and as soon as Chase picked the lock, Miriam ran in and concealed herself behind a row of puffy ball gowns on hangers. Kyle ducked behind an urn as big as a troll's torso.

Then we heard the Director's voice, no longer muffled. She must have gotten the door open.

"Who dropped this comb?" the Director cried. Good. The bars were still blocking the way. "Get me Rapunzel." My relief drained away. We had just gotten her into serious trouble. "And tell Gretel, Hansel, Stu, and Ellie to search this service corridor. These pranksters must be found. Seniors or not, they can still be punished."

Chase grinned. "I'll take thanks and pats on the back now."

iriam made us all hide until we saw an opportunity to sneak to the Portland door. Lena ducked in with Kyle. She clearly didn't want to pass up an opportunity to hang out with her crush. I found a nice spot under the shelves of dried goods, creepy stuff like petrified newt eyes, shredded basilisk skin, and cockatrice teeth. Sadly, my cozy hiding spot became significantly less roomy when Chase decided to hide with me, too lazy to find his own. I got smushed between him and a nice large bag labeled DRIED LEAVES—TREE OF HOPE.

I hated waiting. Hiding wouldn't matter if any of the grown-ups checked this storeroom.

Apparently Lena thought so too. I couldn't see her, but I could hear her murmur, all in a rush, "I wish that they wouldn't find us, that they forget this storeroom is here, that they walk right by without seeing us, so we can get to Portland safely."

We had all been thinking this, but saying it out loud seemed pretty weird. Then Kyle asked, "Is that new?"

"Portable wish," Lena said. "They like very specific requests."

"You got it to work?" Kyle said, impressed.

"*Maybe*. This is its test run," Lena said, sounding pretty nervous.

We would find out, I guess.

Pitching her voice even lower, she started to say something else. I tilted my head to the side, trying to make out the words. Maybe you could call this eavesdropping, but really, I was being a good best friend, taking notes for the boy talk that would happen later.

"What would you have done if someone asked you to dance?" Chase whispered.

He obviously didn't realize I was listening in. "Same thing as Lena," I said swiftly, hoping he would take a hint and be quiet so I could go back to eavesdropping. "Say we were busy."

"But did you *want* someone to ask you?" Chase asked. "Is that why you wore so much makeup?"

Those questions were so weird I turned to look at him, but I couldn't really see much in the dark, just the glint of his eyes watching me. "I *told* you. Mom wouldn't let me come unless she thought I was excited about the dance." Besides, I couldn't imagine dancing with anyone other than Chase. Or maybe Ben Taylor, but only because I thought Chatty might want me to describe the experience in detail so she could imagine attending the ball herself.

"Shhh!" hissed the dresses hanging across the room. In other words, Miriam. "They *will* find us if you guys keep chatting."

"One more question," Chase said. "Are we going or not?"

The dresses were silent long enough for us to know it wasn't an easy decision.

I imagined exactly what would happen if we didn't—house arrest in San Fran, explaining everything to my family, trying to convince my mom to let me go back to EAS. Knowing that I'd helped the Snow Queen escape, knowing that everything she did would be my fault.

Finally Miriam said, "Of course. He's my brother."

"Yeah," Kyle and Lena said, as if that explained everything.

And maybe it did. I could feel Chase nodding behind me.

I was the only one who didn't have a sibling. Yet.

Footsteps sounded in the hallway—the high-heeled kind and another quieter pair. We all went still.

"Well?" That was the Director, almost yelling. She must have been right outside the storeroom. "Can you tell me what this is?"

"It's my comb." Rapunzel was kind of quiet in general, but if we didn't breathe too loudly, I could make out what she was saying.

"Yes," said the Director impatiently. "I want you to tell me what it's doing here."

"I could not tell you. I took out all my combs for the ball, and I last saw it in the courtyard. I felt its absence when I visited the Table a half hour ago," Rapunzel said.

"You didn't search for it?" the Director demanded. "One of the four combs that finally captured Solange, the only bars powerful enough to subdue her?"

I choked a little on my own spit. As I fought to keep from coughing, Chase slapped a hand over my mouth. His fingers smelled like salsa.

"If it had fallen out of my hair, I knew that a search would be easiest in the morning, when the sun is up and the children are gone," Rapunzel said. "Who activated it?"

"If I knew, I wouldn't be questioning you," the Director said. "Deactivate the comb and let me get back to the library. I have every member of staff searching the corridors for these pranksters, but for God's sake, guard those combs *most carefully*. We'll surely need them in the war to come."

A few seconds later I heard a door open and then close. With relief, I batted Chase's hand away and let the last cough escape.

"Not yet!" Chase whispered. "Someone else could be in that corridor."

He was right. We heard slippered feet patter up the hall, and stop right in front of the storeroom door. I held my breath.

The door swung open. It was Rapunzel. I was a little too freaked out about what the Director had said about the combs to even feel relieved.

She whistled a low note. Then the room filled with light, coming from a slender glass vial on a silver chain. "Come out. Quickly."

But getting out of our hiding spots was a lot harder than getting in. We'd been squatting for so long that my feet had fallen asleep. My elbow knocked a huge jar of pickled ice-griffin eggs right off the shelf, and it would have met a loud and messy end if Chase hadn't caught it.

Miriam leaped out from behind the dresses with a lacy parasol held high. "I'm warning you, Rapunzel. I won't let you stop us even if I—"

"No!" I said, still trying to wiggle free of the shelves. "She's trying to help us."

Miriam snorted. "Help us? The Snow Queen's sister?"

Rapunzel ignored that, but I couldn't. "She *gave* me the comb," I said, and Miriam lowered the parasol slowly.

"Makes sense to me," Kyle said. "I would die for my brothers, but I sure as heck wouldn't do what they told me to. They're idiots."

"If the others are combing the halls, then the courtyard is clear. Most students are in the ballroom," Rapunzel said, but she wasn't really looking at us, not even Miriam, who stood right by her elbow. She just kept glancing over the walls. She frowned. "Forgive me. I am having difficulty looking directly at you."

"Oh, good! The wish worked," Lena said, triumphantly shaking the jar in her hand. The used-up wish sloshed around inside it. It just looked like turquoise water with a few gold flecks. "We'll get out without a problem."

"But what about telling people the Snow Queen escaped?" I said. "The others deserve to know."

"I can tell them," Kyle said automatically. Then what I'd said must have sunk in. "*What?* She's *out?*"

Oops. I'd completely forgotten he hadn't been in the library then.

"And you're still going to her palace?" Kyle added, glancing at Lena.

I have to hand it to him: He recovered quickly and sped off down the hall. "You guys should get out of here. I'll go to the ballroom and get the eighth graders together. After we spread the news, the grown-ups won't have time to search for you anymore."

After Kyle sped out of sight, Lena said, in her *I'm trying not to panic* voice, "I hope he tells them that he found out from us. Otherwise the Director will think *he* broke into the library."

Chase snorted. "The Director won't be in a position to punish *anyone* after word gets out."

"We're wasting time talking," Miriam said, charging down the hall.

I lingered behind Rapunzel. If she was going to say something to me, it would be now—right before we left.

"Here." Rapunzel took my hand and placed something metallic on my palm. The comb. No, three of them—all with the same tree design. "To return them to their original form, you touch the third bar from the right and whisper, 'Give way.' Do not let your enemies see, or they will be able to take down the combs as well. There is a fourth comb, in the possession of the sorceress Arica. You will find her home on your journey."

"You didn't tell me what the combs could do," I said, trying not to sound too accusing or needy. I'd kind of been counting on some ominous-sounding predictions. We needed all the help we could get.

Rapunzel knew what I was thinking. "Sometimes, it is better not to know too much. You will learn soon enough." I just stared at her blankly until she added, "Oh, Rory—to go or not to go is a decision. It rests on one person and one person only."

Wow. I'd been hoping for that kind of warning, but now that I had it, I couldn't see any possible way it could help us.

"And the dwarves are not your enemies," added Rapunzel, which sounded a lot more straightforward. "To earn their alliance, however, you will need to win."

"As in, win them over?" Lena had pulled out her pencil and notebook, taking notes just like she did with Rumpelstiltskin. Chase looked more skeptical.

"No, I mean that you will need to become champions," Rapunzel said.

"Are you three coming?" Miriam said, holding the door open for us. The courtyard was dark except for the lanterns over the Table of Never Ending Instant Refills. It was empty, except for that couple in the armchair, but they weren't interested in anything except—you know—kissing.

Lena and Chase hurried me down the hall, but I glanced back at Rapunzel.

I hadn't seen her look so stricken since we'd talked about the coming war last year, and suddenly I understood what she meant. Something bad was going to happen, something too awful for her to warn me about.

But it was too late to change our minds.

We sprinted across the courtyard to where Miriam waited, pack on. She passed a carryall to Lena, who was fastest, and she tossed the other two to me and Chase. I shrugged it on. The straps pinched my bare shoulders, and as we hurried through the door to Portland, I hoped we would get a chance to change.

Miriam banged through the outer door and waited for us under a huge tree, its bark covered in moss, its roots crumbling the sidewalk around it. When I followed her, my foot found a puddle of slick mud, and I would have slid straight into the tree if Chase hadn't grabbed my shoulder. Leaves dripped above us, and the whole street—houses to our left, shops to our right—gleamed wetly under the streetlamps.

Chase made a face. "Of *course* it's raining."

"Do we need to find a dry spot and recreate the map?" I asked Lena as she stepped out, pulling up her raincoat's hood. The emerald door swung shut behind her.

"No, not for this part. We don't have to go far. Only a couple blocks." Lena knelt beside the tree trunk, scooping up some dirt into a vial labeled HAWTHORNE (PORTLAND, OR). We would need that soil for the portal spell.

That step seemed really far away, though. We had a whole quest to survive first. Just getting out of EAS had been so much harder than I expected.

Miriam headed toward the shops. "Hawthorne's this way."

Most of the businesses were closed. Walking down the street, I spotted a bookstore with its lights on and a couple restaurants open, mostly empty except for a few shell-shocked couples, staring past their menus like their minds were thousand of miles away, as far away as their children in the Arctic Circle. The only people I spotted on the street were a policeman and the waitress he was interviewing. Right as we passed them, my phone decided to beep with a new text message.

My mind instantly flashed to the note I'd left.

Dear Mom,

*There was something I had to do—a matter of life and death.
I'll be gone for a few days, and I know—I'll have a lot of
explaining to do when I get back. I promise I'll answer all
your questions.*

I'm really really *sorry, Mom.*

*Love,
Rory*

She'd found it. She was texting to tell me that she was coming
to pick me up immediately, and I wouldn't be there. The Door Trek
door would be locked.

I groped around my carryall for my phone.

"You're really going to get that?" Miriam hissed.

But I had to. If Mom was already worrying, I needed to tell her
I was okay while I still could.

The text wasn't from Mom, though. It was from my stepmother:
IT'S A GIRL!!!! Any name ideas? XOXO. I snapped the phone shut,
furious, but not at her. Brie was having a girl. I knew it. Just like
Solange and Rapunzel.

Lena hung a left and stopped in the side street so fast I nearly
walked straight into her. I scooted those thoughts out of my head.
The quest was what mattered now.

"I *thought* this was it, but it's supposed to be abandoned," she
said. "Maybe I should have actually drawn the map after all—"

This little corner did have the most activity on the whole street:

about a dozen people around Amy's age lined up outside a door, all waiting to see a man in black. Inside a really fancy border, the sign on the door read MEMBERS ONLY.

"Crap." Chase stared at the line with the kind of horror he usually reserved for bones, tears, and troll armies. "Put in your gumdrops."

I scooped my translator out of my carryall and stuck it in my ear. I wouldn't mention what Brie's message said. Lena and Chase didn't need to know about one more parallel between my life and the Snow Queen's, and definitely not before we got back from the Arctic Circle.

Then Chase pointed at the sign. The border wasn't just fancy squiggles—it was Fey calligraphy: SEELIE COURT ONLY. EXCEPTIONS: NOBLE GUESTS, ENCHANTED HUMANS, INDENTURED ELVES, EMPLOYED GNOMES, AND ENSLAVED TROLLS.

"This is an entrance to Queen Titania's dancing pavilion," Chase explained. I gulped and scanned the line again. Only nine left. I wondered how many were as human as they looked and how many were wearing a glamour. "She has a Door Trek system set up all over the world for it. She likes to have a nice mix of humans to dance with her nobles, so she sends out Fey scouts to lure people in."

"Okay, but where's the *portal*?" Miriam said. "Philip's Tale didn't mention a pavilion, so it's not our problem."'

"Unless you want to buy a plane ticket to the Arctic Circle, it *is* our problem," Chase said. "This entrance to the pavilion is new. It's probably here to cover the Pied Piper's tracks and make it harder for us to reach the portal."

"The Seelie Court has allied with the Snow Queen?" I asked. That would be really terrible news.

"I doubt it," Chase said. "Solange insulted Titania and Oberon once, and the Fey don't forget that. But whoever suggested this place to her probably is."

I didn't like the idea of the Seelie Queen helping out Solange and not even knowing it. "Do you think we should tell her?"

"Do we have time?" Miriam asked, who clearly thought the answer was no.

"If she catches Characters sneaking around her pavilion unenchanted, she usually tries to imprison them for seven years," Lena said. "But on the upside, all the regular humans here can be enchanted for only one night. That was Queen Titania's deal with the Canon."

I bit my tongue to keep myself from throwing out any more stupid suggestions.

"Can you whip up another one of the illusion things?" Miriam asked Lena.

"Maybe," Lena said slowly. "It'll take me some time, and we might need to get a few more ingredients, and someone will need to chant with me . . ."

Chase took a deep breath, and then he thrust out a hand, showing us a stack of dragon scales. "I got it. An illusion trick my dad taught me." Suddenly, he looked about a foot too tall. Tiny raised dots lined his face, and scarlet wings rose from his shoulders.

A glamour *was* the best way to get us inside. The guard wouldn't be able to see through it, and with all the fairies around, he probably wouldn't even be suspicious Chase was wearing one. The Fey felt naked without a little magical covering.

But I couldn't believe he was using a glamour in front of the others. Maybe Miriam had bought Chase's story, but Lena's eyes were practically bugging out of her head. She was going to figure it out.

And as much as I wanted Lena to know, this wasn't the right

way to expose his secret. "What now?" I said, hoping that the other two would focus on the *quest*, not on Chase's transformation.

Pretending he didn't notice Miriam and Lena staring, Chase led us over to the line. "I think I can get us in," he whispered, "but I need you guys to try and act like the other enchanted humans." He jerked his head at the line.

In the group ahead of us, the girl looked pretty human in a long cotton dress, but her hair shone a little too gold, her eyes a little too purple. I wondered what color her wings were. Beside her, the human with a handlebar mustache couldn't focus his eyes, and his ponytailed buddy had a tiny puzzled frown on his face, like he couldn't remember how he got there.

When the guard opened the door, the glamoured Fey woman sauntered in, her two enchanted captives trailing behind her, their eyes half-lidded.

We were up next.

The guard had cropped silver hair and pretty burly arms for a Fey, but my eyes went straight to the dark stick in his hand, as skinny as a wand. It was Iron Hemlock, basically the Fey version of a Taser. One touch could make a fairy scream in pain. I didn't want to know what it could do to a human.

I concentrated hard on looking stupid, and not like I wished I could reach into my carryall and pull out my sword. Lena and Miriam weren't having any trouble seeming dazed.

Chase swept a bow. It went too low, and with him smirking like that, you could tell there was an insult hidden in it. "A guest, bring-ing his hosts a little entertainment."

"You doubt our scouts?" said the guard annoyed, but he actu-ally waved us *in*.

We didn't question it. We scurried through the doorway into a long corridor. One wall was prickly with branches, the real living kind growing through the blank white plaster. Leaves brushed my cheek, and twigs tried their best to get tangled in my hair.

The door clicked shut. With the glamour making him so tall, Chase towered over the rest of us.

I knew who he was supposed to be.

Cal. His nose was thinner, but besides that and the dots on his face, he looked exactly like Chase, just older. I never knew the family resemblance was so strong. I wondered if Brie's baby would look like me. Solange and Rapunzel looked alike, even though they had different mothers.

I shoved that thought out of my head. I couldn't afford to get distracted.

"Cool trick, Chase," Miriam whispered. "I can't believe they don't teach that to all the Characters."

I didn't want either of them asking Chase for a lesson. "Which way?"

"There!" Lena pointed to the far end of the corridor, where stairs curved out of sight. Miriam plunged down the hall, Lena on her heels. I fell into step beside Chase.

Part of me wanted to ask him if he should be wearing Cal's face. His brother was kind of famous. And no longer alive. But I was kind of glad I couldn't point that out while Miriam and Lena were in earshot. I was glad for the chance to see what Cal looked like.

"Are you guys coming?" Miriam asked when she reached the top of the stairs, glaring like she might strangle us if we didn't hurry up.

"Three floors," Lena said, right behind her.

Miriam trotted down first, and the rest of us followed. As far as I could tell, the steps were pretty normal concrete. Maybe that part of this place had been there before Titania messed with it, because the next floor down was much stranger.

First of all, the room was impossibly big, stretching on and on. I couldn't even see the back of it. *Trees* grew under ceilings so tall that no leaf brushed its surface. They were birches, so the silver trunks didn't throw me that much. But the silver *leaves* certainly did, rustling from every branch with light metallic rings, like wind chimes.

Between the trunks stood tiny sky-blue wardrobes. Fairies and humans clustered around each one. The Fey we'd seen in line had dropped her glamour. Her wings were blue-green and lighter at the edges, as if years of flying had rubbed away the color. She settled a top hat, embroidered with berries, on her ponytailed captive's head.

Lena whispered, "Do you think they would notice if I collected some samples? For some spells?"

Miriam didn't answer. She just grabbed Lena's wrist and dragged her down another flight of stairs.

Halfway down, the next floor came into view: another huge room with trees, but these were gold instead of silver. And it was apparently autumn in this room, because the fan-shaped leaves tumbled from branch to floor, glittering like giant confetti. This room also had *tons* more fairies, all holding goblets of Fey honey mead. Tables of food had been set up among the golden trunks.

Queen Titania sat near the back, elbow propped up on her golden throne, talking to a couple knights. Golden flowers had been woven through her dark blond hair, and her wings trailed golden glitter over her golden gown. It was easy to guess what her favorite color was.

Miriam didn't loosen her grip on Lena's wrist, as she led us along the banister.

We passed close enough to overhear one group's conversation—a grown-up Fey with bronze hair, a pale boy with silk clothes as black as his wings, and another Fey boy wearing a crown.

I recognized the first two. That meant Torlauth di Morgian and Prince Fael of the Unseelie Court could recognize us too. I grabbed Chase's arm to warn him. He followed my gaze and stiffened. His glamour lost three inches, his hair dulled to brown, and his chin grew an idiotic-looking goatee. I hoped he'd changed my face as well.

Torlauth's eyebrows lifted. "Your fathers haven't told you?"

Prince Fael had seen the older Fey's pitying look. "It's only for the heirs of the Seelie and Unseelie thrones?"

A huge hulking shape lurked behind them, like a boulder with cement-gray wings and chains around his wrists. Ori'an, Prince Fael's bodyguard.

I thought he was watching us for one scary second, but his gaze slid to Torlauth.

"A demonstration, you might say. Of the Courts' most ancient and powerful magics," Torlauth explained, and I could see the eagerness on Fael's face, even out of the corner of my eye. "But if the kings themselves haven't spoken of it, it isn't my place to enlighten you. Perhaps they think you're too young still—Princess Dyani didn't perform it until her two-hundredth year."

"You'll tell *me*," Fael said, who obviously didn't realize he was playing right into Torlauth's hands.

"Calm yourself," said the other boy Fey. His leafy crown looked a lot like Queen Titania's. Awkward to have a party in the same room as your mom. "Torlauth isn't one of your subjects, nor is he yet one of mine. But he's reasonable. . . ."

Before I could hear what else the Seelie prince had to say, Chase steered me down the steps behind Miriam and Lena.

"I guess we figured out which Fey is working with the Snow Queen," he whispered, once we were on the stairs.

He was probably right. A couple years ago, when Chase and I had ended up in the Snow Queen's hidden war room inside the Glass Mountain, we'd found a report Torlauth had sent her, describing all the skills of EAS's fighters. He'd organized a mini-tournament at the Fairie Market to spy on us. But I said, "Let's hope not, because it sounded like he was trying to trick Fael. And we all know he's not the sharpest sword in the armory."

"They didn't see us, right?" Miriam said. Chase and I shook our heads. "Then who cares?"

Lena spotted the next room first. "Trees of diamond! I don't care what you say—I'm taking some twigs." Breaking out of Miriam's hold, she flew down the rest of the steps and across the floor to the nearest tree.

I wasn't half as eager as she was. The forest in this room looked like it was carved of ice. It didn't have any leaves. It didn't even have any color, except for the rainbows that the see-through trunks threw off like prisms. This garden could belong in the Snow Queen's palace, and it gave me the creeps.

Miriam scowled, clearly not a fan either. "I don't see the portal."

"My guess is that it's in the pavilion." Chase pointed to a clearing ringed with extra-tall diamond trees, their crooked branches nearly touching the ceiling. Ribbons were strung from branch to branch, marking out the dance floor.

We crossed through the weird trees and lined up at the edge. The Fey nobles and their partners didn't glance our way as they twirled and glided, everyone perfectly in time.

This was definitely disturbing. There wasn't even any music.

No one needed to ask if the humans were enchanted. One girl in a lavender dress spun and stepped with her fairy partner, graceful and languid. You would have guessed that she'd been transformed into a perfect Fey lady, except for the way her eyes were wide with fear, the muscles in her neck as taut as bowstrings.

A dozen single dancers in red and orange flitted above the couples, pirouetting and leaping on half-extended wings. I didn't like the way a few of them watched us like a dragon that had spotted an EASer to snack on.

Lena thrust a handful of diamond sticks into her carryall and zipped it closed. "I *hate* the Snow Queen. I could be dancing with Kyle right now."

Miriam ignored her. "Does anyone see the portal?"

"Yeah, and the good news is that it's not far." Chase pointed straight ahead, right in the middle of the whirling dancers. An archway stood between two small, beribboned diamond trees, all by itself, like it went no place except for the other side of the pavilion. A hundred feet of dance floor stood between it and us.

"The bad news," Chase added, even though we'd all started to figure it out, "is that we have to dance to get there."

Miriam stared at Chase, one eyebrow raised, like she was wait-ing for him to tell us, *Just kidding! The portal's inside this tree*. But he didn't. "Okay, everybody," he said. "Let's see your shoes."

I gulped. If he was checking to see how durable they were, he probably thought that we'd be stuck dancing for a long time. I stuck out my foot, with its flat-soled sparkly slipper, and Lena and Miriam did the same. Lena's wedges had rhinestones at the toe, and Miriam's plain black heels were so high that I wondered why she hadn't changed out of them before we left.

"Rory, your shoes look the least dangerous." Chase grabbed my hand. His palms were hot. "You're with me."

"Oh. Okay," I said, taken aback.

Lena snorted very softly.

"I guess you're with me, then," Miriam told Lena.

"You can *try*," Chase said. "If the Fey let that happen, I'll eat my carryall. Rory and I will get to the portal, and then we'll grab you after."

I was ready to get *out* of this creepy room. "Let's go."

We stepped away from the hard dirt to the cool stone of the dance pavilion. A violin reel exploded in my ears. Suddenly Chase's glamour vanished, and my body wasn't my own.

I'd been under other enchantments that moved my limbs for me—usually from my sword's magic and once from the mother of the four winds. That just felt like I had forgotten that I'd told my sword arm to swing or my legs to run.

This felt like someone had tied puppet strings to every limb, every finger, every muscle, every eyelash. Painful tugs forced me to grab my skirts, sweep my arms open, and curtsy to Chase, as he bowed low to me. Out of the corner of my eye, I spotted Lena curtsying to a slender Fey with green wings, but I couldn't turn my head to see her face.

Then the enchantment straightened us up. Chase took one of my hands, positioned his other hand just below my shoulder blade, and we were off. The spell tugged our feet one step forward and one step back. Then Chase twirled me, and even though I felt invisible strings yanking me in a thousand directions, we moved so smoothly that the hairs on my arms stood up.

Miriam and her leafy-haired Fey partner did this complicated step-tap-hop-glide combination in perfect sync, and I knew we were doomed. This enchantment would never let us reach the portal. If we were lucky, Queen Titania would release us from the spell like the other humans. If we weren't, she'd figure out who we were and imprison us for seven years.

"You need to follow *me*—not the enchantment," Chase said right in my ear.

"What's the difference?" I said, too freaked out to be nice, but relief flooded me as soon as I said it—at least my mouth did what I asked. "You're under the enchantment too."

"Not the way *you* are." I couldn't see his face, but I could hear the grin in his voice. "The enchantment's set up for humans. I just feel a strong nudge the way it wants us to go."

That sounded too good to be true. He was probably just trying to make me feel better. "So you can dance like all these Fey?" I said skeptically.

"I told you I was good. Ballroom lessons are required in Unseelie preschools," Chase said. I must have made a *yeah right* face, because he added, "Iron Hemlock method."

He'd learned to fight that way too. The Fey instructor basically electrocuted his students if they made a mistake. I believed him now.

Chase squeezed my hand. "Listen, or we'll never get to the middle. I need you to look at me. The enchantment should let you do that much."

Well, the spell didn't *like* it exactly, but after another spin out and back in, I managed to lift my chin.

His face was very close, and his eyes were incredibly green.

Something warm fluttered in my middle. It almost freaked me out as much as losing control of my body.

"Good," he said. "Now concentrate on what I'm saying—I'm going to teach you how to resist a Fey enchantment. Okay?"

"Okay." My heartbeat galloped forward.

"Don't fight it directly, because it'll fight you back," he said. "The magic will just clamp around you tighter. You need to pick your moment, and when it pushes you in the right direction, you go a little farther. Got it?"

I got it, but I wasn't sure I could do it. "I'm dancing backward half the time. I can't see—"

"That's why you have me. Ready?" he said, and before I had a chance to respond, he added, "Here we go. Short step, short step, long step. Short hop, long twirl. Good. You just got us four feet closer in about twenty seconds. Now, again. Short, short, short, long, long, short."

I'd expected it to be weird, dancing so close, but it wasn't. It was kind of nice. It was just like Chase explaining a new drill while we trained. No, it was just like when Chase had talked me through the climb up the beanstalk. Except we hadn't even been friends then.

This was better.

This time Chase's gaze was locked tight on mine, not glancing away for a second, and stepping with him got easier and easier. The pavilion faded away, and the enchantment's invisible strings hurt a little less. "There you go. Try not to spin far," he said, raising his arm so I could twirl under it, in as tight a circle as I could manage. We came back together. "Good. Long, long, long, short. Long, short, short, long."

I grinned. This was almost a game. Beating the enchantment was way more fun than any EAS ball. Then he grinned back, his face inches from mine. The warm flutter in my stomach exploded into a hailstorm.

It wasn't the enchantment. *Chase* was what made me like this so much.

"Almost there," he said, as we tapped our feet out and in, out and in. I nodded, a little bit out of breath. "Short, long, long—brace yourself, I'm going to toss you through."

"What?" I said. Chase's "almost there" usually means "half-way."

But a doorknob clicked open, and then his arm slipped around my waist, scooping me forward and through the archway.

I tumbled onto my hands and knees, sprawled across a sheet of ice.

The chill crept through my thin dress and straight into my skin. Whoa. I'd never been so cold. My hands stiffened even before I unzipped my carryall and tugged out my coat.

"I still need to get Lena and Miriam." Chase stood in the doorway, steam rising off his back. "But don't come any closer. I can feel the enchantment trying to pull me back in. It'll be worse for you."

"Okay." My teeth started chattering as soon as I opened my mouth. Geez. At least the warm air from the dance floor was leaking over in the cave. Without it, we probably would get instant frostbite. "Just get Lena first. We need that warming spell."

"Already on it." Chase lunged back through the portal so fast that I was afraid that the pavilion had captured him again, but then he reappeared, dragging a stumbling Lena behind him.

When Chase let her go and turned back, she shuddered so hard I thought she might topple over. "Well, *that* was traumatizing. Next time I won't step into an enchantment without working out a counterenchantment first. I don't know how to do that, but I'm sure Melodie can—"

"Lena," I said, with as much patience as I could muster. "It's *cold.*"

"Yeah, your lips are almost blue," Lena said, not getting it.

Then with an *oh my gumdrops* expression, she swung her pack in front of her so she could dig through it. "I'm so sorry! I should have taught everyone the heating spell before we left!" She thrust a dragon scale in my palm—a heavy green disk, sharp at the edges. She held one too. "Repeat after me," she said, switching to Fey. *"No need for flames, no need for a blaze, just enough heat to survive these days."*

I repeated it, and delicious heat—like a blast of warm air from a car's vent—washed over my hands and down my arms, swallowing my shoulders, head, legs, and feet. I didn't even care that it stunk of rotten eggs. My fingertips felt like they'd been pricked by a thousand needles at once, and I didn't want to think about how easy it would be to freeze out here.

"The Fey dancing with Miriam saw me grab Lena," Chase told us from the portal. "They've moved to the outer edge of the pavilion. I can't reach them. Rory, get me the rope in there." He dropped his carryall in my lap.

When I unzipped it, all I saw was a puffy jacket. I tossed it at Chase, and it flopped over his head, like a fluffy fire-engine-colored curtain. "Put that on. You're no good to anyone if you freeze to death."

He stuffed his arm through the sleeves. I found the rope, all coiled up inside the back pocket. As I passed it over, I recognized the grappling hook on the end. His father had something just like it, but this one belonged to Chase, which meant Lena had added a bunch of improvements to it. Unfortunately, last time he had tried to use it in a fight, his aim hadn't been great.

"Thanks." Chase snatched it away and unscrewed the grappling hook, so the rope ended with a heavy metal cap instead. Then he started swinging it so fast the rope sang *Woop, woop, woop* as it cut through the air.

Forty feet. That was how far away Miriam's partner had taken her.

"Can you even make that?" Lena said.

I couldn't see how he could, not without accidentally hitting one of the dancers twirling between us and them. I groped inside my pack for my sword, just in case he brained a Fey and they decided to attack.

"I've been practicing." Chase let the heavy end of the rope fly. It sailed over the dancers. I winced, waiting to hear a clunk against someone's head—but the rope dropped just over Miriam's forearm, right above the hand she was resting on her partner's shoulder.

"That's the trick, knot real quick," Chase muttered in Fey. Then he yanked, like a fisherman hooking something at the end of the line.

Miriam jerked away from her partner, tripping between the other couples as Chase pulled the rope, hand over hand. The Fey were too astonished to stop her, and by the time Miriam passed through the portal, she was laughing.

It could have been the fairies' gaping jaws, but my bet was on plain, hysterical fear.

"Did you seriously just lasso me?" Miriam asked.

Chase bent over her wrist, fumbling with the knot in the enchanted rope. His fingers were red and clumsy. He was colder than he realized.

"Lena, I think we need some dragon scales," I said.

"Right here." She passed one to Chase and one to Miriam. "Here's the spell—"

"No need for flames, no need for a blaze, just enough heat to survive these days. Yeah, I heard you telling Rory," he said, looping the rope back up. Then Miriam repeated it too, but it took her two tries since she forgot to say it in Fey.

I slammed the portal shut as soon as the spells caught. My eyes started to adjust to the moon's glow flowing through the cave mouth.

"I think I'm going to change shoes." I didn't feel the *cold* anymore, but the spell apparently didn't extend to keeping stuff dry. Melted snow soaked through my slippers.

Chase nodded and kicked off his fancy shoes. I couldn't believe he hadn't started bragging about the awesome rope trick yet.

"Should I change out of my dress?" Lena said.

"Absolutely not. That'll take too much time. Just put on another layer," Miriam said shortly, pulling on a knitted blue and orange beanie, but her smile was huge.

Miriam's mood swings were even more intense than Chase's, and that was saying something.

"We're still about a day and a half's walk to the Snow Queen's palace." Lena had gotten her sketchpad out with her boots, scarf, and mittens. Her pencil flew over the paper, redrawing the map. Then she pointed to the bottom right-hand corner, to something labeled IVINHOOR'S BAY. "We're here."

The palace—marked with a ring of jagged spires—was in the upper left-hand corner. Basically, as far away from us as it could be and still stay on the same page. Not encouraging.

But I'd thought of a shortcut. "I have a couple boons left from the West Wind. He can carry us there."

"Bad idea," said Chase, lacing up his boots. "A giant flying personification is extremely easy to spot. The second he shows up here, the Snow Queen will know exactly where we are. I don't like our chances if we can't sneak up on her."

That hadn't even occurred to me. "So, we're actually *walking*?"

"Not to be rude or anything, but I don't care right this second." Miriam practically skipped over to the cave mouth, her carryall over her shoulder. "We're here, closer to Philip than I've been in days, and I'm finally getting to do something to get him back." She pointed outside. "Look! There are the footprints! Just like his Tale said!"

I finished tying my boots and joined Miriam. The moon was almost full, and the snow reflected the silvery light. Icebergs bobbed in the dark bay ahead. A snowy ridge rose up on our right.

It was so stark and still that fear crept inside me. We were traveling through this?

"Pretty, isn't it?" Miriam obviously didn't feel the same way. "See? There. Footprints."

A path—churned up by hundreds of feet—curved from the cave. It looked so fresh I counted toes on the closest tracks, but I was just relieved to see signs of life.

Miriam trotted down the path. She was a *lot* quicker without her heels on.

Chase groaned. "Any faster, and she would actually be running."

"Wait, let me lead!" Lena hurried too, but without looking up from the paper in her hands. I was amazed that she didn't take a nosedive. "Miriam, we need to follow the map! General Searcaster might have created fake tracks to throw us off!"

When she passed Miriam, Lena straightened up, squared her shoulders, and walked fast—her fearless leader mode. It was kind of hard for me and Chase to keep up. The ice on the bay's edge had broken to pieces recently, and the current had pushed them farther onto the shore. Every hundred yards or so, footprint-covered slabs clumped together like a pile of dishes in a full sink. Waves lapped in between them.

Miriam and Lena scurried over like it was nothing, but climbing them was *not* fun.

Chase had trouble too. I heard him cursing behind me at least ten times.

We traveled so long that my dragon scale shrank to the size of my palm. Lena had told me to expect the spell to eat away at it, but it was kind of weird to see it in action. She'd also said that we would need to switch out our scales every eight hours or so.

Hopefully Miriam would get tired and let us stop before then.

"Crap! Crap crap crap!" Chase said, with extra gusto.

I glanced back to make sure he was okay.

He'd caught himself, landing lightly on some flat ice, but his wings—the real, unglamoured ones—shone clearly in the moonlight.

Something was wrong. His wings weren't visible unless he used them for five whole seconds, and he was an expert at using them for just four and a half. He would never expose them on purpose, especially when he'd just used a glamour in front of Lena.

Luckily, she and Miriam were still plowing through the path ahead. I stopped, letting them get farther and farther away. "What's up?" I whispered.

"I'm fine," he said, panting. He was still sweating, despite the cold. "I just did too many spells in a row. My magic level is at, like, two percent right now." He reached me, his head bowed low.

"I didn't know that was possible." I fell into step beside him, ready to help him if he tripped again.

Being out of breath couldn't keep Chase from talking. "I don't have that much of it to begin with, compared to regular Fey. I try not to use it this much. Cal would be furious with me."

I could think of only one reason why Chase's brother would get upset about it. "So you're basically in the danger zone."

"I was in the danger zone even before we started dancing," Chase said. "I haven't felt like passing out so much since the beanstalk, when the portal in the giant's desk ran out of magic and stole all mine instead."

Oh. Well, that explained why he'd passed out first. I started watching Chase out of the corner of my eye, looking for signs he was going to faint.

He stumbled a little bit, and I slipped an arm around his waist, steadying him. He put an arm around my shoulders and leaned a little of his weight on me. We'd helped each other out this way many times, so I shouldn't have noticed how tightly we were pressed together. My arm around his waist definitely shouldn't have tingled, but maybe the magic in his wings had something to do with that. This was the closest I'd ever gotten to touching them.

"It's always eighth grade," Chase said, almost mumbling, he was so tired. "I thought we were immune, but everybody was just waiting for the dance."

I was officially concerned. He wasn't even making sense anymore. "What are you talking about?"

"Lena and Kyle. Dating and stuff," he said. "With Characters, it always starts before high school. It took our grade a little longer than the ones before us."

That didn't seem like something Chase would ever notice, let alone talk about. He must have been *really* exhausted if he wasn't even acting like himself.

"When we get back, Kyle will figure out a way to ask Lena out again," he said. "Paul and Vicky will probably be a thing."

Now he was *really* worrying me—imagining stuff about people. I'd never noticed anything between Paul and Vicky. "Chase, how can I help you?"

I was thinking along the lines of taking his pack before we got to the ice slab pile ten feet ahead, but he said, "Just let me sleep. I'll be okay after sleep. And food would be nice."

I sighed. This was why I wanted him to tell Lena about being half Fey. She would know exactly what excuse we could give Miriam to convince her to stop for the night. She would help us keep the secret.

We took the ice slab pile really slow. Chase slipped once, and he almost dragged me down with him. He really couldn't go much farther. At the top, when he stopped to catch his breath, his wings disappeared, and then I had an idea.

"Don't try to catch me," I warned him. "That'll defeat the purpose."

Then I stepped away from him and fell, shrieking a little to make sure Miriam and Lena noticed.

"Rory!" Chase said.

Sliding down the fifteen-foot slope, I made sure to include *lots* of arm flailing. The only part I didn't plan on was the gap between the ice slabs and the flat trail. Specifically the *puddle* inside the gap. My foot went straight into it.

"Ugh!" I said, splashing out. No need to fake frustration now.

"Are you okay?" Lena sprinted over the snow. Miriam came back more slowly, scowling hard, like every step in the wrong direction pained her. Chase slid down and stared hard at me, waiting to see what I was up to.

"Is it sprained? Can you still walk? Do you need some of the Water?" Lena asked me.

I stood up. My foot was fine, but my soaked boot squished unpleasantly. "I don't think we need to break out the Water just yet. But Miriam, this is ridiculous. It's dark. We should stop."

"I think we have a few more miles left in us," said Miriam evenly.

"I don't," I said, trying to sound less whiny and more authoritative. "My adrenaline wore off about a half mile ago. It's only a matter of time before someone breaks a leg."

Miriam glared down at me. "I know you three think you're the king and queens of all the other little eighth graders, but I have news for you: I'm in charge here."

That annoyed me. The three of us had been on quests before. *She* hadn't. "Or someone could break their neck. The Water can't fix that."

Lena was more sympathetic. "I know you really want to cover as much territory as possible tonight, Miriam, but I *am* pretty tired. And we really can't afford to make mistakes."

"You're just a bunch of bullies, aren't you?" Yikes. Miriam's good mood was gone, and it was my fault. "Fine, but we're getting an early start tomorrow. No more excuses."

"Great." Chase dropped where he was, dragged his pack in front of him, and pawed through it until he found his sleeping bag. "I call this nice flat spot with all the cushy snow."

"Wait! I adapted this spell." Lena moved behind me, unzipped my carryall, and pulled out that big tile, which she placed on the ground. Then she said, in loud clear Fey, *"Oh, snow servants, you're pretty swell, but we need a temporary place to dwell."*

Chase snorted. Using "swell" in a rhyme reached a new level of giggle-worthy, even for her.

Then a half dozen headless snowmen rose. They were shaped exactly like the dirt servants hiding in Mom's garden, except these had spades instead of fists. They immediately started cutting blocks out of the ice and arranging them into walls.

Miriam was too shocked to see walking snow to be mad anymore. "Are they, for serious, making an igloo?"

"Yes! Well, kind of." Lena beamed. "I downloaded snow structure building online yesterday and embedded the techniques in the tile with, you know, the usual—the clay figurines and powdered dragon scales. I wasn't sure whether or not I needed to burn it first—to get its essence—so I did *both*, and . . ."

She can chatter about new inventions for hours if no one

stops her. Miriam looked like she regretted asking.

Chase leaned in, so his voice wouldn't carry over the sound of the snow servants. "You're getting better at lying."

It was true. I'd had a ton of practice over the past few years. My mother had probably found my letter by now.

I wish I couldn't, but I could picture the horror on her face. She probably tried calling me first, then breaking through the San Fran Door Trek door, then calling people in the middle of the night. Mom was wondering where I was, just like the parents in Portland were worrying about their kids, because I was good at hiding the truth.

I hadn't even told Lena and Chase that Brie was having a girl. That might count as lying too.

But Chase had meant it as a compliment. So all I said was, "Be proud. I just channeled *you*."

He grinned sleepily. "Hey, your pack has the Lunch Box of Plenty, right?"

And so, while the snow servants cut and stacked their third layer of bricks, Chase ordered a cheeseburger from the Lunch Box. When the walls grew as tall as her shoulders, Miriam made us change out of our fancy clothes. She *said* it was only to save time the next morning, but I think it was punishment for forcing her to make camp. With the dragon scale clamped in my fist, I didn't feel the cold, but it was *super*awkward to change into my jeans out in the open. Even if Miriam had made Chase go on the opposite side of the snow hut.

Especially if. I mean, he *was* a boy.

Chase finished dressing first. When the tile servants placed the last block and collapsed into little snowballs, he dove through the rounded hole at the bottom of one wall.

"Okay. Right," said Lena, still trying to take out her contacts. "No need to test it out. The structure looks pretty sound."

"Thanks, Lena," came Chase's voice from inside.

Miriam kicked it once, hard. Lena yelped, but the blocks didn't shift. "Seems safe," said our Tale bearer, and she crawled inside.

"*Thanks,* Miriam. You got *snow* in my sleeping bag," Chase said.

"What if that Searcaster giant comes back?" Miriam said, as Lena and I scooted in after her. The roof was too close to stand up in, but it was kind of cozy. "Doesn't a little house made out of snow scream that people are here?"

"This is why we have watches." When Chase finished shaking the snow out of his sleeping bag, he flopped on top of it, eyes closed, and kicked off his shoes. "I call last watch."

"I'll do the first one since you guys are all tired," Miriam said, not in a supernice way. "What do I do? Just look for giants on the horizon?"

"Um. You could," I said politely, "or if you wanted to stay inside, you could just watch the mini magic mirror." I flipped open my M3 case and chanted the spell that turned the radar on: "*Show me our enemies, if you don't mind, please.*"

"Got it." Miriam snatched the M3 from my hand and stormed outside. She probably would have slammed the door if we had one. Not a great start to the quest.

I mean, it *was* her Tale. She should be in charge, and we *had* kind of bullied her into stopping.

Lena unrolled her sleeping bag. "I call third watch. Rory, I give you permission to poke me until I get out of bed."

Someone had to tell Miriam which one of us she needed to wake up for the next shift. I grabbed the Lunch Box and crawled out. At least I could bring her a peace offering.

Then I discovered another downside to not having a door: Miriam didn't hear me coming.

She hugged her knees, peering into the mirror she'd balanced on top of them. The M3's soft gray light lit up her chin, leaving the rest of her face in shadow, but a tiny tear glinted on the side of her nose.

I was a humungous jerk.

I would be a better Companion after tonight. I wouldn't get Chase and Lena to gang up on her ever again. I would let her make *all* the decisions. "Miriam?"

Her head jerked up. Two more tears dribbled from her eyes, and she didn't even *try* to hide them. "Philip never listens to me! I can't believe he decided to remember *that*. I wasn't even talking to him—Mom and Dad had both promised to come to my tournament in Eugene. College scouts were going to be there, and I *had* to make a good impression. But Philip's been sucking in geometry this year. My parents convinced his teacher to let him retake the last test he bombed, but it was on the same day as the tournament. Dad announced he was going to stay behind with him, and it seemed so important, and George and I had just broken up, so I just—I always say stuff I don't mean when I lose my temper, and it came spewing out of my mouth. I think that was the last thing he heard me say."

I'd made the right decision, not getting involved with Brie's baby. You didn't need to do anything as intense as locking a sister in a tower. Younger siblings were so easy to hurt.

"He *has* to know I didn't mean it," Miriam murmured, mostly to herself.

Well, I couldn't ask her if she wanted the Lunch Box *now*. So, instead, what popped out of my mouth was, "You and George broke up?"

They'd been together practically since my first day at EAS. Inseparable.

Miriam shrugged. "It didn't make any sense to stay together. I mean, he'll be a college student in, like, two months. We'll never see each other."

"Does Lena know?" I asked.

Miriam wiped her face. "I don't think George told his family yet."

Silence stretched out between us.

I remembered all the times the three of us had run into Miriam and George, and they'd been laughing, or holding hands, or studying together. When everybody got poisoned last spring, they'd picked beds side-by-side. I remembered Lena teasing George about it. I'd never imagined them breaking up. I'd always thought they were part of each other's *happily ever after*. That was what Sarah Thumb had said.

But once, when I was very young, I thought that about my parents, too.

"I'm sorry." Great. I sounded awkward, even to myself.

"It just sucks!" she burst out, almost crying again. "Now I'm alone in the *Arctic Circle* with a bunch of bossy kids, who just so happen to be Philip's best chance. I know you don't want to hear that right now, but it's *true*. And it *sucks*."

"I'm *really* sorry about earlier," I said, meaning it this time. I set the Lunch Box down next to her. "I thought you might want some coffee. To keep you up until it's time to wake me for the next watch."

Miriam snorted. "I barely slept last night—what makes tonight any different?"

"It's really cold," I offered.

She cracked a tiny smile, but it disappeared as soon as she remembered she was mad at me. "Thanks, Rory." When I hesitated, she waved me off. "We're *good*. You can go to sleep now."

I didn't feel very tired either, but I crawled back inside anyway.

By the time I'd pulled off my sword belt, boots, and jacket, Lena's soft purring snores filled the snow hut.

Chase was out too. His burger was still in his hand, only three bites taken out of it, I'd never seen him too exhausted to finish a meal.

He hadn't seemed tired at all when we'd danced. Fighting the enchantment hadn't shown on his face inside Queen Titania's pavilion. He'd just told me that we were going to be okay. He'd known that *I* was scared. He hadn't even bragged very much afterward.

I was lucky to have friends like these.

They weren't like Natalie and Shakayla. When I picked Lena and Chase for Companions, they would never let me leave without them. *Never*.

"You're awesome," I whispered to Chase, taking the burger from his hand.

I would have never admitted that if I thought he was awake, so I jumped when he mumbled, "I know."

Then he rolled away, closer to the wall, and fell asleep for real, and I wondered why I felt so embarrassed.

That night, I didn't dream of my ancient door.

I dreamed of Torlauth di Morgian, a sneer on his face and a sword in his hand. I had my sword out too, but I turned to the other people in the room. The Snow Queen smiled. Chase managed to look smug even with one of Solange's trolls holding his arms behind his back. Lena tried hard to nod encouragingly even though she was crying.

As my free hand slid into my pocket, I knew one thing: I had brought us here, and so *I* had killed us all.

So that sucked. But I can tell you something that sucked *more*: waking up to find the business end of a spear an inch from my face.

The others had woken too. Lena gasped, and Chase cursed.

"You have two choices," said the small white bear holding the spear. No, it was a bear *skin*, but the scowling face under it didn't look any less scary. "You can fight, and we slay you here for trespassing. Or you can surrender, and we take you to the king for questioning. I prefer the first. That's easier for us."

e'll surrender!" Miriam called from outside. "We'll go see your king!"

After less than a day in the Arctic Circle, we'd already been captured.

I immediately regretted deciding to let the Tale bearer make the decisions. Then again, I didn't see my sword anywhere. If they'd taken our weapons, then we didn't have much chance of fighting our way out right away.

"Miriam, did you fall *asleep* on guard duty?" said Chase, ticked off.

"Not now!" Lena and I snapped. I was pretty upset too, but we had other stuff to worry about. The not-bear didn't lower the spear a fraction, even when I lifted my hands from under the covers and sat up.

Still, these soldiers were being pretty civil, especially compared to the bad guys who had taken us captive before.

"All our stuff . . . ," Lena started, pushing her sleeping bag aside.

"We will see to it," said the not-bear. "Outside now, please."

Just so everyone knows, it's pretty awkward to lace up your boots when somebody is sticking a spear in your face. But it's twice as awkward to crawl outside with a spear pointed at your rear and two more spears bristling in the opening ahead.

When I got out, Miriam's wrists were tied together, her face pale. The soldier guarding her was a head shorter than she was and as wide as a hundred-year-old tree. Under his brown beard, his features were blunt and squarish, like a stone sculptor had started to carve his face but had gotten distracted before smoothing out the edges. A dwarf.

The dwarves are not your enemies, Rapunzel had said.

Well, if that was true, the dwarves didn't seem to know it yet. Neither did the other questers.

Miriam sounded like she was hyperventilating. "I'm so sorry! I'm so so *so* sorry! I really didn't think I could sleep—"

"It's okay," I said, trying to calm her down. Maybe it *was* okay. Maybe we needed to go with the dwarves. Rapunzel had also said we would have to earn their alliance. I'm sure that included not ticking them off. I raised my voice so Chase could hear me inside. "I think it's better if we cooperate!"

"Clasp your hands in front of you," said another soldier. He had a beard too, black and braided with red thread, and he barely looked at me as he tied a leather cord around my wrists.

An extremely wide dwarf led a herd of reindeer out from behind a giant ice pile. They snorted and tossed their velvety antlers.

Lena crawled out next. Standing up, she opened her hand and showed me what was in her palm: a small green coin. No, that was her dragon scale. "The heating spell won't last much longer. Should we tell them—"

The bear dwarf emerged from the snow hut and rose smoothly, a whole head taller than the others and the only one so far without a beard. This had to be the one in charge. "I heard, thank you. How much time is left?"

"About forty-five minutes," Lena said hesitantly.

I wondered how long we had been asleep. I couldn't tell what time it was. The moon was gone and the horizon glowed pale yellow. The icebergs on the water gleamed gold too.

The bear dwarf nodded. "Do not fear. We'll reach safety before then."

Safety sounded promising. If they really thought we were enemies, they would just leave us out here to freeze.

Chase wasn't very good at cooperating. He emerged with a scowl and took a good look around. "Reindeer? Seriously? You forgot Santa's sleigh."

Another dwarf slid out after him—probably second in command. He was the only other dwarf who didn't have a beard. "Permission to tie this one up behind Rebdo, captain?"

Chase glanced at me, horrified, but Rebdo just turned out to be the extra-wide dwarf in charge of the reindeer. Extra wide and extra messy. Gravy had dried in his beard, and he had stains all over his fur jacket.

The second-in-command lifted Chase up behind Rebdo as easily as tossing a bundle of laundry in a washing machine.

"It *smells*," Chase complained, thrashing around. "Geez. Is that the reindeer or you?"

"A bit of both," said Rebdo, not even a tiny bit embarrassed.

The second-in-command dusted off his hands, a faint smile around his mouth.

I thought the rest of us were in for the same treatment, but nope. The dwarves just lifted us onto the mounts. I barely had a second to get settled in the saddle before the second-in-command swung up in front of me. Then we were trotting across the stark white landscape, not superfast but plenty bumpy.

Lena leaned as far away from the dwarf sharing her saddle as she could, her eyes huge. I didn't blame her. The soldier with red thread in his beard wasn't exactly friendly.

"At least we're still going in the right direction." I pointed at the Pied Piper's trail under the reindeer's hooves, trying to cheer her up. Maybe the dwarves always arrested trespassers, no matter who they were. Maybe we could talk their king into letting us go.

"Rapunzel could be wrong, Rory," said Chase, his voice a little muffled.

"Wrong about what?" Miriam said, at the same time Lena asked, "Rapunzel told you something?" But I didn't want to repeat these predictions right in front of the dwarves. I wished I'd taken the time to fill the other questers in the night before.

The captain just frowned at us. I thought maybe he didn't like his prisoners talking so much, but he said, "Rory Landon, Chase Turnleaf, and Lena LaMarelle."

We were the Triumvirate. We had a reputation, because the last Triumvirate, which had existed centuries ago, had included the Snow Queen, the Director, and this guy named Sebastian. The Triumvirate before *them* had founded the Canon. I hadn't expected word to spread all the way up here.

"Wait, you know about them?" Miriam asked. At least that bit of news hadn't reached the eleventh-grade rumor mill yet.

"Her Majesty sent out a report," said the soldier riding with Lena.

I swallowed. Only the Snow Queen's allies called her "Her Majesty."

My dream came back to me with the force of a door slamming—Chase and Lena captured, Torlauth looming, Solange smiling.

It still might not come true, but if the dwarves delivered us to the Snow Queen's dungeons, it was very *likely*.

I didn't want Chase to be right. Rapunzel would never send us into danger on purpose, but maybe she didn't know these dwarves had allied with the Snow Queen. Maybe we *should* try to escape.

"You must be the Tale bearer, then," the captain told Miriam.

"Miriam Chen-Moore." She totally ignored my *shut up, shut up, shut up* glare. "And my Tale is 'The Snow Queen.' She and the stupid Pied Piper stole my brother, and if you think you can stop me from getting him back—"

She was gearing up for a TMI rant, but Lena interrupted. "Aren't we getting kind of close to that water?"

Dead ahead, the shoreline curved sharply out into the bay, where a massive iceberg floated. The dark water around it would probably kill us if we went for a swim, heating spell or no, but the mounts didn't stop.

When the bear dwarf's reindeer picked up speed, the others did too. They ran straight for the water, like they didn't notice the solid ice under their hooves was about to run out.

Toppling off a galloping reindeer didn't seem like a great improvement over my morning, but it was better than plunging in and freezing to death. I shifted to the edge of the saddle and hoped the others would follow my example. But before I could jump, the second-in-command reached back and clamped a hand around my tied wrists.

He turned over his shoulder, shouting so I could hear him over the wind. "Wait! Our captain knows what she is doing!"

"Whoa! The captain is—" I was going to say, *a girl,* but luckily, the second-in-command interrupted me.

"I wouldn't call her Princess Hadriane! She hates that when she's on duty!"

We'd been captured by the dwarf *princess*? Seriously?

When I squinted at her, I noticed the chestnut braid whipping around above her polar bear cloak. It looked wider than a human braid was, and a golden chain had been woven through it.

Her reindeer reached the edge—and kept going. A tiny ridge appeared under us, connecting the shore to the iceberg. I could see the city on it now, ringed with a wall of ice. Homes were carved into the hillside, like frozen boxes stacked on top of each other. From this far away, the ladders running up the slopes looked like stitches holding the houses together.

Princess Hadriane reined in her mount, and we trotted toward the city's wall, slowing so we could catch our breath.

"A cloaking illusion!" Lena said when she could talk again. "Like the one that hides Atlantis."

"Did we know this was here?" I asked Lena, a.k.a. the quester in charge of the map.

She knew exactly what I was thinking. "No, it wasn't on there."

"What are those?" Miriam asked, staring at the city gates. They looked like two huge icicles with giant brown carvings of dwarves frozen inside them.

"The Living Stone," the second-in-command replied. That sounded supercreepy, but maybe I'd just seen too many enchantments that turned people into statues. "You call it 'petrified wood.' We brought it from our homeland."

"Wait, you mean the Petrified Forest National Park? In Arizona?" said Miriam, as the gates opened ahead of us. The reindeer walked in. The wall was at least thirty feet high and too slippery to climb.

"We don't know what the humans call it," spat the dwarf riding with Lena. I was beginning to think of him as Cranky Beard. "We call it 'homeland,' which was lost to us when the Europeans invaded. First they stole the Living Stone from our cities, but they only passed through. Then they stole our land, and we were the ones who needed to pass on."

We could probably count Cranky Beard out as a possible ally.

The reindeer carried us down an avenue in the shopping district, with bricks of ice laid in the snow like cobblestones. The buildings on each side were made out of huge slabs that looked like they'd been harvested from a glacier. Cloth had been frozen in some of them to make certain sections less transparent. I craned my neck around the second-in-command so I could peek in the windows: a dress displayed on a snowman mannequin; frozen vegetables piled up in baskets; fine leather gloves and metal gauntlets stuck on upside-down icicles.

The only thing missing were the customers and the shopkeepers. None of the stores were open. On one of the doors, someone had written a message in dots and lines. The gumdrop in my ear managed to translate it: CLOSED FOR THE TOURNAMENT.

You will need to win, Rapunzel said.

Win another tournament? I hadn't had much luck at the EAS one, and I'd *trained* for it.

"It's warmer in here," Lena said uncertainly. "Right? I'm not imagining it?"

"An enchantment, under the dome that veils us," said the second-in-command. "It keeps the cold from stealing heat from the warm, and the warm from melting the frozen."

"A cloaking spell *and* an advanced stasis spell?" Lena said. I had no idea what she was talking about, but I recognized that excitement—she was a second away from asking if she could meet their magicians and do a little research.

"We owe the Snow Queen much," said Rebdo. "She gave us a

home of our own, the first since the Great Migration."

"Solange built this city?" I said. I couldn't imagine her doing anything that nice.

"*Dwarves* built this city!" roared Cranky Beard.

"Her Majesty chose this spot for our new home," explained Rebdo, "and Her Majesty's general set up the enchantment that keeps us safe."

"And how do you maintain it?" Lena asked eagerly.

"You EASers ask too many questions," said Cranky Beard.

So, of course, Chase made sure to ask one more. "Are we almost there?"

We were coming up on *something*. I could hear cheering up ahead.

"Oh, so you're still with us?" said the second-in-command. "You've been so quiet, I wondered if perhaps Rebdo slipped you into the ocean sometime back."

"I've been holding my breath," Chase said. "Rebdo's stink is beginning to *thaw*."

"I'm a well-seasoned dwarf," Rebdo said cheerfully.

Princess Hadriane turned her reindeer down a side street, and her squadron followed. Massive icicles held up a stage. Beside it stood a fancy brown tent, like the ones humans use for outdoor parties.

Beyond them was the square. Hundreds of fur-wrapped dwarves slowly made their way to the bleachers at the square's edge, and mounted soldiers lined up at the events.

The princess didn't even glance their way.

She just slipped off the reindeer, passed its lead rope to her second-in-command, and dashed through the tent's opening, her strange braid swinging. "I'm sorry I'm late, Father."

Her second-in-command jumped down too. "Off you get," he

told me. "Stand right there beside the tent—I want to be able to see you when I get your friend down."

I slid off the reindeer, and my feet jarred against stone. Wow. This part of the city had to be special. It was paved with discs of petrified wood. I made my way over to the tent, but the second I stopped, the second-in-command shouted, "Not there, Landon!"

I jumped and looked back.

The second-in-command was untying Chase and scowling at me. He jerked his chin to the left. "There. Between those two ropes."

I stepped to the side, wondering what *his* deal was. This spot wasn't any different from the one I'd just been standing on, except I couldn't see the square with the stage in the way, and the voices coming from the crack between the tent's panels were so loud I—

Voices.

". . . event is so important," said a voice inside, much deeper and gruffer than Hadriane's. That had to be the king.

"This tournament is a farce," said the princess. "It doesn't address the real problem. Ima and Iggy—"

"That's precisely its merit," said the king. "The twins' disappearance has alarmed our people. They worry for the throne's future, and this event will give them peace of mind."

Okay, just because I could hear didn't mean I could *understand*.

"But Ima and Iggy didn't disappear," said the princess. "I told you what happened to them. The Pied Piper marched the human children past our gates. The twins heard him playing, and they followed."

Oh. I didn't realize the dwarves had lost children too.

"A misunderstanding—" started the king, but he sounded miserable.

"You know it's not," said the princess. "The tune changed before the twins got up and joined them. The giant smiled when they came out. It was their intent."

They were both quiet for a moment—so long that I wondered if they'd left, but then the king spoke again, sounding a lot more grief-stricken. "My hands are tied, Haddy. What would you have me do?"

"The EASers have sent a Tale bearer and the Triumvirate to retrieve the children," said the princess. "We could *help* them, Father. We could go *with* them and get Ima and Iggy back."

I blinked. Somehow the whole spears-and-imprisonment routine hadn't given me the impression that Hadriane wanted to join the quest, but I wasn't complaining.

"No. We trade them." The dwarf king obviously hadn't considered the rescue idea at all. "If you have Rory Landon, the Snow Queen will surely return the twins."

The relief in his voice made me swallow hard. If he did give us to the Snow Queen, my dream would *definitely* come true.

"*No*. Remember: Solange is too greedy. She never gives her prisoners back, unless she kills them first," said Hadriane. "But if anyone has a chance at freeing the children, the humans' *and* ours, it is these Characters, aided by the magic of a Tale."

The king was silent.

"Father?" said Hadriane eagerly. I hoped, too.

He sighed. "Get ready for the tournament, Haddy. We're to open it in a few minutes."

"Will you at least *think* about it?" said the princess. "Before you report them to the Snow Queen?"

"Yes, I'll wait until after the tournament," he replied. "But in exchange, you must play your part. None of that polar bear glare. Show us your smile. You have your mother's smile."

"Yes, Father." And then there was an *oomph*, and a patting sound. I'm pretty sure those were the sounds of the princess tackling her father in a hug.

Rapunzel was right. The dwarves could be our allies. I had no idea how winning could earn their trust, but we only had until the end of the tournament.

"You heard that, right?" I asked Miriam and Lena, who had lined up beside me.

"Heard what?" Miriam asked, mystified. The perfect eavesdropping spot beside the tent obviously didn't extend to her. "Hey, could you do something about Chase? He's not exactly making us any friends."

The second-in-command had untied Chase from the back of Rebdo's reindeer, all right. Chase had apparently returned the favor by dumping Rebdo out of the saddle. The poor big dwarf was still recovering, sitting in the alley and rubbing his head. Chase yanked the reins, trying to turn the reindeer into the square, but it wasn't moving. The second-in-command had hunkered down like an anchor, holding the reindeer's lead rope in his hands. Cranky Beard was trying to pull Chase off the mount, but every time he got in range, Chase aimed kicks at the dwarf's head.

Well, that was a stalemate if I ever saw one. Chase was great at fighting his way out of scrapes, but if that didn't work, he wasn't so awesome at figuring out Plan B.

"Chase, cut it out and get over here," I said.

"Give me one good reason," Chase said, not ready to back down.

He had me there. I couldn't exactly shout, *Because I have a plan and I want to tell you about it.*

Luckily, Lena came to the rescue. "Your scale is all used up. If you try to leave the city, you'll freeze to death."

"Very good reason." Then Chase hopped off the reindeer and walked over. He pretended not to notice when an enraged Cranky Beard raised his spear and the annoyed second-in-command stopped him from nailing Chase in the back.

"*Do* you remember what Rapunzel said?" I asked Chase.

"Yeah. She said we needed to win," he said. "I was trying to win that fight over the reindeer."

We were definitely interpreting that differently. "She said we would need to become *champions*," I reminded him, jerking my head toward the tournament.

Chase was unconvinced. "You can't win all tied up. We need to free ourselves first."

"Okay . . . ." Confused, Miriam glanced at Lena for an explanation.

Lena just sighed. "Half the time, I don't know what they're talking about either."

"Sorry—" I started, but I didn't get a chance to explain what I'd found out. Booming drumbeats filled the air, and the whole square grew quiet. All the contestants turned their reindeer toward the stage.

The tent's door was knocked back, and out strode a dwarf even more square-shaped than the others. His hands were like cutting boards, his beard like one big reddish rectangle. Even the gold crown on his head had four flat edges.

When he jogged up the steps to the stage, the crowd clapped and roared. He raised his massive hands for silence and said, "My good dwarves, I welcome you to the first tournament ever staged in our fair city of Kiivinsh. My family and I have been looking forward to this for months. It's true that Princess Imelda and Prince Ignatius can't make it today—"

I gasped so loud, several dwarves glared at me.

"I know," Chase said. "Those names *suck*."

Ima and Iggy. The Snow Queen had stolen Princess Hadriane's little brother and sister.

"—but my eldest daughter is here," the king said, turning back to the tent. Hadriane emerged, looking a lot more like a princess. Her brown velvet dress was struck through with gold, and she'd brushed out her chestnut hair until it hung in waves down her back. Her polar bear skin was draped across her shoulders like a cloak.

Maybe her features were a little bit too squarish to be super-beautiful, but when she flashed a smile as dazzling and empty as a Fey's, she was definitely striking. She was also several inches taller than her father.

"It's time that Hadriane takes part in this tournament, so we've set up a new event. Go on, my dear," the king told the princess. Still smiling, she swept down the steps in front of her father. The crowd drew back, bowing and curtsying as she made her way to a giant hill, positioned about fifty feet from the stage.

It was made out of ice and about three stories tall, way too steep to make a good sledding hill. She climbed up a ladder and took a seat on the flat top, smoothing her skirt. Her father continued, "The challenge is to ride up to the princess. She will toss an apple carved of Living Stone to those who come the closest." Hadriane pulled something round, heavy, and brown from her dress's deep pockets and held it up.

So far, this seemed like the stupidest event ever, even stupider than the ring event, but I knew where this was headed. Kyle had told us about this tournament just a couple days ago.

"She has three to give away," the king went on. "And from those three winners, I'll choose the recipient of my daughter's hand in marriage."

"Wait, *what*?" Miriam said. "That's, like, archaic."

Yeah. After meeting her, I kind of thought Hadriane should have been a competitor, not one of its prizes.

She must have thought that too. She was only doing it to convince her dad to save her little brother and sister.

"For the other two who earn apples, I've prepared these chests," said the king, and soldiers behind him whipped big furs off a corner of the stage. The chests had the usual—strings of pearls, gold cups, loose emeralds and opals, plus big chunks of petrified wood. They were kind of obsessed with Living Stone here. "The prizes for the other events are either a golden spear or a favor from your sovereign. If it's in my power, I will grant it."

My whole body went tingly, like electricity had snuck through the ice and made my hair stand on end. Now I knew what winning would get us.

I searched the courtyard for an event I recognized. The closest lane ended in a slender metal tree that reminded me of the witch forests in Atlantis. But metal hoops dangled from the branches on leather cords. The ring joust.

That tree's trunk looked bendable.

"And now, " added the king, as the drumroll sounded again, "let the tournament commence!"

I tried to raise my hand, but I'd forgotten that my wrists were tied together. So I just ended up flapping my arms up and down like an idiot. "Wait! I have a question."

The entire square looked our way. Even Hadriane turned to listen. My face burned. If the dwarves had been too excited about the tournament to notice the humans beside the stage, they definitely noticed us now. Miriam's eyebrows were sky-high, her mouth stern, like she was two seconds from telling me off.

The king's face was unreadable. "Well?"

"Can, um . . ." It didn't seem polite to call us prisoners. "Can guests compete? Even if they're not dwarves?"

"You wish to enter the tournament?" said the king, astonished.

"I think so." I pointed to the ring joust. Dwarf warriors armed with lances were lined up at the end of the lane, their mounts pawing the ice restlessly. "What are the rules for that one?"

"Whoever can capture the most rings and drop them in the snow wins," explained the second-in-command.

"That's the only rule? Get the rings in the snow?" I asked, and the king nodded. "Can I, then?"

The king scratched his beard. "I suppose so, but the bonds stay on."

The dwarves began snickering, but none of the events started. They were waiting for me. Nothing started a tournament off better than watching a human make a fool of herself.

Hadriane wasn't amused, though. She just watched me, eyes narrowed. Lena's lips were pressed together, and Miriam said, "Are you *sure* this is a good idea?"

Chase just shrugged, hands in the air, which was his way of saying, *Okay. We'll try it your way*.

I stepped up behind the line, but one of the dwarves already waiting pointed at the metal tree with his lance, smirking. "Oh no. You go first. We want to see this."

"Would you like to borrow a reindeer?" asked another, and his friends laughed.

"No, thank you." I walked straight down the lane to the metal tree, where the rings dangled at least five feet above my head.

I grabbed the trunk in my left hand, and with the strength of the West Wind, I began to bend it. The metal protested with a squeal, but when the branches lowered to the ground, the leather cords and the rings attached to them dropped too. With one more good push, I bent the tree almost in half, and the rings hit the powdery snow.

Every single one. So no one had a chance at beating me.

The snickers across the courtyard stopped, leaving an eerie silence.

When I looked at the stage, the king's eyebrows were a big, scary V that basically said, *Forget about the Snow Queen. You'll rot in* my *dungeon for the rest of your days.*

I'd miscalculated. The Fey would have been cool with it, but dwarves did *not* appreciate sneakiness.

But Princess Hadriane started laughing. "She has you there, Father. She asked for the rules, and we told her. You're a dwarf of your word—deliver her prize."

I really wanted to ask him for help saving Ima, Iggy, and the kids from Hawthorne, but since he hadn't told Kiivinsh what *really* happened with the twins, I didn't think he'd be too excited about an alliance if I blabbed his secrets.

So I said, "Let us go?" Maybe later we could sit down and discuss rescue strategies.

The king smiled so happily at Hadriane that I thought she'd convinced him, that he was going to go with her plan. But he said, "I'm afraid that request is too grand for a mere favor. The best I can do is let your party roam free at our tournament, on the condition you bend that tree trunk to its original position. Would that satisfy you, or would you rather have a golden spear?"

It was weird to be relieved and disappointed at the same time. "That's good. Thank you." It took me a minute to bend the metal tree back up. The trunk was a little warped where it had been folded, but the rings dangled from their leather cords high above my head, like they had before.

The king turned back to the square. "I said, let the tournament commence!"

Arrows thunked into targets in the archery lanes, and the first reindeer tried to gallop up Hadriane's ice hill. It took maybe two strides before its hooves slipped, and it fell, tossing its rider. That didn't bother Hadriane—she was still laughing.

"Remove their bonds," the king told the second-in-command.

The soldier immediately moved down the line, sawing through the leather cords around our wrists. When he was done, the king continued, "Forrel, you and your squadron are officially off duty. Enjoy the tournament."

He didn't have to tell Rebdo and Cranky Beard twice. They leaped on the backs of their mounts and galloped toward their favorite events. Forrel lingered a little, watching us.

"So," I told the others, rubbing my wrists to get feeling back into them. "We should have a questers' meeting."

Miriam plunged into the crowd and hurried behind the stadium seating. Chase, Lena, and I had to run to keep up. She didn't stop until we reached an event that looked like a logging contest with ice picks—the dwarves were hacking so furiously that I knew we couldn't be overheard.

Good thing too. A bunch of dwarf ladies in the bleachers, all with the funny extra-wide braids, were definitely trying to eavesdrop. They kept glancing over at us, like they couldn't decide if they wanted to say hi or start pelting us with their frozen popcorn.

"Rory, I see the brilliant plan now," Chase said. "We steal our supplies back while they're distracted by the tournament—"

"—and we hightail it out of here before they realize we're gone," added Miriam.

"No, we're going to convince them to let us go. We need them to help us," I said. I repeated everything I'd overheard, as quickly as I could.

To their credit, they all listened, but Chase started to look more and more concerned. "Interesting," he said when I finished. "Miriam, you're the Tale bearer. Use your power of veto."

"Your plan has problems *too*, Chase," Lena pointed out. "The king said we could walk around the tournament. If we step one foot outside the square, the dwarves are going to stop us."

"Wait, I can't hear you all that well with the pickax action," Miriam said. "Lena, you're with Rory? You think we should bring the princess on the quest with us?" She jerked her thumb to the ice hill, one event over.

Hadriane looked bored, and no wonder—none of the contestants were having any luck. Most dwarves who took a turn toppled off their mount when it slipped, and I'd seen a couple warriors spit out teeth. The reindeer that had just reached the front of the line was refusing to sprint straight at the ice wall.

"I don't know," Lena said. I was hurt. I was *sure* she would side with me. "I think the king might not have a choice, Rory. The spell over this city needs some upkeep, and the dwarves don't have the magic to do it themselves. It's not just the prince and princess that the Snow Queen's holding hostage. She could freeze every single person under the dome, just by turning off the enchantment."

Oh. That sounded a lot like the Snow Queen I knew. She'd sent them a nice invitation for a hostage situation, and the dwarves walked into it willingly. They even thanked her for it.

"On the other hand," Lena said, "Rory's plans always sound kind of crazy, but they definitely work."

"Yeah," Miriam said thoughtfully. "I thought you were nuts when you entered the tournament, but without you, we'd still be all tied up."

Chase knew he was losing ground. "Rory, Rapunzel said we needed to become champions, and you did that at the ring joust. Now we have a golden opportunity to get out of here. We can't let it pass. The dwarves haven't exactly been buddy-buddy since we got here. Those soldiers were ready to kiss Solange's feet."

Well, when he put it like that . . .

But Miriam had decided. "Okay, so we try to win the dwarves over. How will we do it?"

I hesitated. That was the part of the plan I needed help with.

"Definitely don't try to escape," said a voice directly behind Chase. "We'd hate that."

It was Forrel, watching us with that tiny smile. "My captain ordered me to keep an eye on you. I could see you were plotting some mischief, but I couldn't hear you from my hiding spot."

"You're not very subtle, are you?" Miriam said. "Isn't the point of spying not to let us know you're doing it?"

The dwarf ignored her nasty tone. "I can keep a very good eye on you from right here. Now what were you children whispering about?"

"The tournament," said Lena, too quickly. "We were trying to figure out which event to enter next."

"And you pointed at the hill?" said Forrel, with a look that clearly said, *Do you think I'm as dumb as a troll?* "They won't let you anywhere near it after the trick Landon pulled. The winner of that event could be our future king, you know."

It did sound pretty far-fetched, but Miriam had clearly decided that the best defense is a good offense. "We think it's stupid. She doesn't need a king to rule for her."

"She would make a wonderful queen. I won't deny that," Forrel said, so calm and polite that he was getting on my nerves. "But her people won't allow it—she's only half dwarf."

That explained why she was so much taller than everyone else.

"Oh," said Miriam and Chase together.

Both Miriam and Lena turned to look at Chase, kind of shocked to hear him sound so sympathetic, but he didn't notice. He just added, "What's the other half? Fey?"

"Human," Forrel said. "Her mother was a Character. She went easy on you this morning. You should have seen the trolls we caught trespassing last week."

"Remind me again why we should trust you?" Chase asked, taking a step closer to Forrel, but I hoped they wouldn't actually start fighting. Even though Chase was taller, I didn't think he could beat the soldier easily. I hadn't seen someone so unmovable since Iron Hans. The only difference was that Forrel always seemed slightly amused by everything.

"He helped me eavesdrop. He told me exactly where to stand," I told the others. That didn't mean I totally trusted Forrel, but we could probably use him for information. I pointed out the mounted dwarves standing back from the hill, just watching other participants try and fail. "Why aren't they taking their turns?"

"Strategy," said Forrel. "No reindeer could conquer that slope as it is now, but some of these hooves are leaving divots in the ice. Soon the divots will make a trail."

I pointed to familiar faces at the end of the line—Rebdo and Cranky Beard. "And they're allowed to compete?"

The corners of Forrel's mouth twitched a little more. "If one were to win," he said, as if he seriously doubted their chances, "they would replace me as lieutenant, so I would not outrank the third heir to the throne."

"Why aren't you out there?" Miriam asked.

"The captain ordered me here," Forrel said.

"So, would you help us?" Miriam said. "Like, do you have any supercharged reindeer at home? Could we borrow it when the trail gets a little higher?"

"A Dapplegrim could make it without any dumb trail," Chase said. I rolled my eyes—he'd been obsessed with Dapplegrim ever since Atlantis. Then he added, "I can get one."

"You have a boon from a Dapplegrim *and* the means to transport it here?" Forrel said, disbelieving.

No, Chase had a boon from Iron Hans, who did have them. Chase had *also* sworn to keep Iron Hans's hideout in Atlantis a secret, so he couldn't tell anyone but me and Lena about that boon. So he did—over and over and over. He loved that boon so much that I'd been sure he would keep it forever.

In other words, I was too shocked to speak.

Not Lena. "He doesn't joke around about Dapplegrim," she told Forrel.

"One Dapplegrim won't be much help," said the dwarf. "Its hooves will blaze a trail any half-decent reindeer could follow."

"Three Dapplegrim, then," Chase said. "Three of us can ride up at the same time. We'll do it disguised, so nobody will stop us."

"Not a glamour, though," said Lena. "The king needs to recognize the riders."

My eyebrows flew up, and Chase said, with lots of hostility, "Who said anything about a glamour?"

"I mean, illusions," Lena said, a little too fast.

She had definitely noticed what Chase had done at Queen Titania's pavilion. She *was* figuring it out.

I think Chase knew it too. He strategically changed the subject. "So, where can I go to contact my source without anyone yelling, 'jailbreak'?"

Forrel escorted Chase through a restaurant on the square, into its back lot, but he kept shaking his head with a tiny smile, like this was a huge waste of time.

About a minute later the dwarf reappeared in the doorway, his dark eyes so wide they were rimmed with white like a spooked horse. He waved Lena, Miriam, and me inside and through to the back.

Yep. Chase definitely got them here.

The Dapplegrim were way too fiery for this ice-filled city. They'd melted a puddle in the middle of the alley they pranced on, and when they tossed their heads, flames flickered along their manes. Beside them, three empty suits of armor stood at attention.

"Oh my gumdrops," Lena whispered.

"Wow! They're gorgeous!" Miriam cried, and I just sneezed.

I'm *really* allergic to horses, even if they happen to be from a magical talking herd that lives in southern Atlantis.

The black one lifted his head and stared straight at me. "Not *you*. I have been insulted by Rory Landon's sneezes for the last time."

They were magical, not superfriendly.

"You know him?" Lena hung back, clearly too freaked to go any closer. Not Miriam. She started stroking the palomino's nose. Looking a little jealous, the chestnut one nudged her shoulder.

"He's the one who raced me to the Unseelie Court," I explained to Lena.

The dark one preened a little until Chase said, "Dude, how many boons do you owe? You must get trapped a lot."

The other two let out great whinnying laughs. "All the time!" said the chestnut. "He's the fastest of us, but he's also the clumsiest."

"Because he never looks where he's going," said the palomino, who was a mare, judging by her voice. "But if you're going to owe someone a boon, it might as well be—"

She couldn't reveal Iron Hans in front of the Snow Queen's allies. Solange would hunt him down and force him to rejoin her side.

Luckily, the grumpy Dapplegrim thundered, "We do not speak his name!"

"Yes, Brother," said the palomino meekly. Oh wow—these two were the dark Dapplegrim's younger siblings. I liked him a lot better after meeting them. Come to think of it, I liked Philip a lot better when Miriam was around too. I wondered if Brie's baby—

No. I wouldn't let myself think about that.

In a tiny voice, the palomino added, "Well, our mutual acquaintance always sends us to the best places."

"We're the first Dapplegrims to ever set foot in Kiivinsh," said the chestnut excitedly.

"Yeah, and you're about to become a legend." Chase stepped toward the suit of copper armor and touched its shoulder with one finger.

It rippled and flew, like a hundred giant metal butterflies taking off at once. It clanked so loud I had to step back, wincing. When I looked again, a giant copper knight swung up onto the dark Dapplegrim's back. Chase looked a lot smaller on top of that huge horse.

"Hey, I didn't get a saddle!" I said, noticing the Dapplegrim's saddle and reins.

"You didn't have armor," said Chase's Dapplegrim. "Armor pinches."

The silver armor rippled onto Miriam, and she climbed on the palomino.

"Who's our third rider?" said Chase.

Lena and I glanced at each other.

"You have experience," Lena pointed out hopefully.

"I also have allergies," I replied.

We'd hurt the chestnut's feelings. "Fine," he said. "I'll take a tour of the city if you don't need me. I'm just here to visit the Arctic Circle anyway."

But Forrel touched the golden armor. As it rippled over his skin, he bowed low to the chestnut. "I would be honored if you would consent to be the first Dapplegrim to carry a dwarf in three centuries."

For a shocked second, no one said anything. Not even Chase.

"The honor is mine, dwarf," said the chestnut.

Forrel took a running start and leaped in the chestnut's saddle, landing surprisingly lightly for a guy wearing gold armor. "Well?" he asked, waiting for one of us to challenge him.

Chase just turned to me and Lena. "Meet us out front."

Then all three Dapplegrim leaped up on the restaurant's roof. Wow. They'd obviously decided to make an entrance.

Lena and I ducked inside, weaving through the tables in the dining area. She hesitated before she opened the front door. "Do you think Forrel will sabotage the plan?"

"I really hope not." If he rode straight to the king's stage and turned us in, it would be our fault for not volunteering.

Outside, the Dapplegrim had definitely gotten everyone's attention on the roof. The archers and loggers had stopped competing to stare at them. Then the Dapplegrim and their riders leaped down. Dwarves stumbled back, clearing a path to the ice hill. Sparks flew up from the three horses' hooves, spooking the other mounts. Cranky Beard's reindeer actually threw him as it skittered out of the way.

But no one tried to stop the Dapplegrim. Only Hadriane looked like she might protest. She stood up, clutching her skin-cloak to her like a polar bear defending her territory, but the Dapplegrim were too quick.

In a few lazy strides, each Dapplegrim conquered the hill. They paraded around the flat top, circling the dwarf princess until she tossed each of them an apple of Living Stone. Chase and Miriam caught theirs and guided the horses down immediately. Forrel must have said something when the apple hit his golden glove, because suddenly, Hadriane looked a lot less sullen and a lot more freaked out.

The king waved them over. "Let me congratulate our winners."

My insides started churning, like a thousand mini Dapplegrim were galloping around my stomach. "Why do I have a really bad feeling?" Lena whispered to me, and I couldn't answer her.

Forrel offered a golden arm to the princess, and after giving him a dirty look, she swung up into the saddle. Then the chestnut Dapplegrim leaped down and joined the other two in front of the king's stage.

Hadriane dismounted and marched up the steps to her father, without breaking the withering glare she was aiming at poor Forrel. Maybe she didn't think this counted as keeping an eye on us prisoners.

"Please remove your helmets," said the king, oblivious.

The three disguised knights all glanced at each other—we hadn't planned this far ahead—but when Forrel flipped up his visor, Chase and Miriam did too.

"We give her hand in marriage *back* to the princess!" Miriam tossed her apple.

Hadriane's eyes widened as she caught it, and then the apples Chase and Forrel threw her way. She peeked around her polar bear hood to see what her father thought.

If he'd looked ticked after I won the ring event, that was nothing compared to the fury on the king's face now. But this time, he pointed straight at the dwarf who'd helped us. "Forrel, son of Freidel, you were given a direct order not to compete in the tournament."

Forrel had definitely not mentioned that.

"I had good reason, Your Majesty." Forrel's tiny irritating smile was back. "I saw no one in this city more suited to lead the dwarves than your daughter."

I didn't realize it was an insult until Princess Hadriane buried her face in her hands and groaned. Apparently, the "no one in the city" included the king himself.

So they threw us in the dungeon. I wasn't shocked.

Only Chase resisted arrest. He tried to make a break for the city gates. Knowing him, that had probably been his backup plan all along. But his mount stood still and announced, "*No.* You used your boon for three Dapplegrim to win the tournament. Freezing to death was never agreed upon, and that will happen if we step outside Kiivinsh."

The Dapplegrim didn't seem to mind getting arrested at all. They were pretty docile when the dwarf soldiers marched us all— questers, Dapplegrim, and Forrel—out of the square, down a long boulevard, and into a building with metal sheets frozen into its walls. Then the dwarves locked us behind iron bars glistening with ice.

Two stayed behind to guard us—Rebdo and Cranky Beard.

"Now we're the first Dapplegrim who've ever been in Kiivinsh's prison!" said the chestnut gleefully in the cell next to ours.

"Be silent," whinnied the grumpy Dapplegrim.

"And hope the transportation spell of our mutual acquaintance brings us home swiftly," added the palomino. "All this ice makes my hooves ache."

Everyone else took a seat, even the three in armor, but I couldn't sit still. I paced up and down the length of the cell.

I'd made such a huge mistake.

The dwarf king must have reported our capture to the Snow Queen. She was probably sending someone right now to fetch us. The dwarves may not have been our enemies, but they were definitely not helping us.

Mom would be terrified if she knew where I was. If I never came back . . .

No. I refused to believe that it was that bad already. We would just have to wait for our moment.

I squeezed in between Lena and Chase. She scooted over to make room, but Chase just kept scowling down at his copper armor. He probably couldn't believe he'd used his awesome boon just to land us in prison. That was my fault too—Chase had just wanted to escape. I wouldn't have blamed him if he'd said, *I told you so*.

"It was really cool of you. To use your boon," I told Chase. What I really meant to say was that I understood why he wanted to help out another half human, but I couldn't say that in front of others.

He brightened. "Don't worry. I'd do it for you too."

"I *know* you would do it for me and Lena," I said. He deflated a little, but I hadn't meant to insult him or anything. "I'm saying it was cool of you to do it for Princess Hadriane and Miriam."

"I didn't do it for Miriam," Chase said, mock-horrified. "George would kill me if I tried to win Miriam's hand in marriage."

Instant awkward. Miriam stiffened, but she didn't say anything. Neither did I.

Then Cranky Beard spoke up. He had become a lot crankier after losing his chance to become the next king. "The beardless should never enter the tournament. You're a fool, Forrel."

Rebdo didn't turn around. "We're not supposed to talk to them."

Forrel flipped up his golden visor and stared hard at Cranky Beard. "Perhaps less of a fool than you. At least my mistress looks after her own, unlike your Snow Queen."

"You won't disrespect Her Majesty with that traitor's mouth!" Rebdo launched himself at Forrel, reaching through the iron bars.

But then the three suits of armor vanished, leaving our riders with severe cases of helmet hair. Apparently, the Dapplegrim vanished too.

"The hooved prisoners have escaped!" Cranky Beard ran out

for backup. I don't know why. No one could do anything about Iron Hans's three-horse return ticket to Atlantis.

Lena sighed. "When I finally get to meet our mutual acquaintance in person, I've *got* to convince him to share that transportation spell."

"You would need fifty boons for that," Chase warned her.

Then Forrel grabbed the arm Rebdo had stretched into the cell and yanked. The guard's head hit the iron bars so hard that the ice cracked off, and Rebdo slumped to the frozen floor, unconscious.

Poor guy. He was going to hurt when he got up, but at least we were getting out of here. "Can you unlock the door, Chase?" I asked.

"No need." Forrel jangled some skeleton keys. "Present from Rebdo."

"We need our packs back," Lena said anxiously. "We can't leave the city without casting more heating spells."

Chase took the keys from Forrel and set to work on the door. "We have a better chance of finding them outside of this cell."

"Yeah. It would help if someone told us where they took our stuff." Miriam turned to the dwarf. The skin around her eyes was red and puffy—she'd obviously been crying under her helmet. "Any ideas?"

The dwarf was silent.

I couldn't believe he was refusing to help us *now*. "You owe us a little information, Forrel. You should have told us you weren't supposed to enter the tournament. The king wouldn't have been as mad if it had just been us."

The cell's lock clicked. Chase pushed open the door. "Save it. We can interrogate him after we escape."

Miriam stepped over Rebdo's unconscious body and out of the cell.

"I'm not going with you," Forrel said.

"You are," said a steely voice in the doorway. Princess Hadriane had changed back into her riding clothes, and the straps of our carryalls hung over her arms. "And that's a direct order from your captain."

Maybe we were never meant to win over the king. Maybe we were just supposed to convince Hadriane to disobey her father.

or anyone planning to escape from a dwarf city, I totally recommend recruiting their princess.

She led us farther into the building. A very large hole had been cut out of one hallway, revealing a dark sky and a moon blasting the city with silver light. A ladder leaned against it, and waiting at the bottom were six saddled reindeer.

It took me forever to climb down the ladder and mount up, but we didn't see anyone. No one even came out when the reindeers carried us to the city wall. In fact, the only problem we had was the princess and her second-in-command arguing the whole way out of town.

"You shouldn't risk this, Haddy." No more smiles from Forrel. He hated this plan, and he made sure everybody knew it.

"That's not your choice to make," Hadriane whispered back.

"You could lose your father's trust, your *people's* trust."

"I could lose Ima and Iggy. I *will* lose them unless you help me rescue them."

"I'll always help you, but this is not the way. You are the Princess of Living Stone—you shouldn't be sneaking prisoners out of your own kingdom, especially not me."

"This isn't about you, Forrel. And I tried reasoning with Father—you know I did."

We reached the wall, but there wasn't a gate at the end of the lane, just an ice sculptor's studio. A cluster of ice blocks—some as low as a coffee table and some as tall as a train car—were pushed up against the wall, in order of size. Hadriane urged her mount forward. It was apparently used to this routine. It leaped from the shortest block and up to the next tallest one with ease.

Oh no. A reindeer-friendly staircase.

I was still recovering from the ladder. My stomach couldn't handle more heights, and my mount didn't exactly come equipped with barf bags.

I guess my face was looking pretty green, even in the moonlight, because Lena said, "It's okay, Rory. Just close your eyes. Chase and I will watch out for you."

"You're afraid of heights?" asked Forrel. "I thought you jumped off a beanstalk."

"We did. Which means I've had enough of heights for *life*," I snapped, but then my reindeer decided to follow Hadriane's. I had to shut my mouth, afraid I really would hurl. I squeezed my eyes shut and clutched the reins.

"If you don't like heights, you might not want to watch this part either," I heard Hadriane say gently. Then my reindeer and I were rushing down. We landed on something, so hard I bit my tongue, and we rushed down again. "It's safe to look now."

I did and immediately turned away from the wall. I definitely didn't need to see *everyone* jump.

Dismounting, the princess pointed at a red line in the ice, half hidden under a dusting of snow. "This is the boundary of the city's protective enchantment. Take care not to cross it before you have cast the necessary spells."

As the others landed behind me, I pulled out a dragon scale, but

Lena was distracted as soon as her reindeer touched down. "Oh my gumdrops," she breathed, sliding off her mount and staring at the enormous bell attached to the wall. "Is that what I think it is?"

"The origin of the stasis spell, yes," said the princess. "You will examine it and remove any device that allows General Searcaster to control it from a distance."

Chase glanced up from his scale. "You want us to wait outside the city we just escaped from? So we can get captured again?"

I shot him a look. "We don't question the nice princess who just masterminded our escape."

Hadriane apparently thought so too. "This is a condition of Forrel's and my involvement. I've arranged for its guard to be absent for this purpose."

Lena paused, suddenly looking a lot less excited. "Okay. Let me see what I can do." She took a deep breath and ducked under the bell's lip.

"You could have just asked," Miriam said, watching Hadriane's stony face. "Lena has a thing for this stuff—she wanted to look at it anyway."

"Plus, we're not big fans of General Searcaster either," I agreed.

"We thought she might eat us this one time," Chase added.

Hadriane looked a little less haughty.

Lena stuck her head out, in full-on magic mechanic mode. "I think I figured it out. But I need someone to come in here and hold the light for me while I dismantle it. Probably one of you guys," she added, pointing at the dwarves, "so I can explain how you refuel the enchantment. Searcaster has left you enough juice for about a month, but after that runs out, you'll need about twenty dragon scales, phoenix feathers, or cockatrice teeth a week to keep it going."

"I'll go," Hadriane said, and she slipped inside the bell with Lena.

Either Forrel was determined not to trust us, or he was upset that his princess had somehow gotten demoted to Lena's flash-light-holding assistant. "If that girl harms one hair on my captain's head—" he started.

"Dude, *chill*," Chase said. "Lena is not the type. Go back inside and recruit a couple of your buddies if you're so worried." Wow, the EASer-dwarf alliance was off to a great start. I was busy trying to think of a way to smooth things over when Chase nudged his reindeer closer to mine. "You never told me what do you think of Lena and Kyle."

"What?" I said, startled.

"The way Characters start pairing off in eighth grade," he said. "Any thoughts?"

I couldn't believe he'd bring this up again, especially now. A few minutes ago he'd told Hadriane off just for stopping. "I think we have a lot of other stuff to deal with right now. None of the other eighth graders have to worry about a bunch of kidnapped kids."

After a pause, Chase said, very quietly, "Okay."

It wasn't like him to keep asking me weird questions. He wasn't telling me something. *"Why?"*

He shrugged. "No reason."

But he was lying. He only sounded that casual and matter-of-fact when he was trying to hide the truth. Then he flashed a grin. "Well, Lena could start gushing about Kyle any second. Now I know what to say to make her stop."

He was just joking, I was pretty sure.

Before I could tell him that he better not try, Hadriane and Lena crawled out from under the bell. Lena gave Hadriane a hazel stick wrapped with thick strands of Searcaster's ugly gray hair—the icky-looking long-distance device. The princess dropped it into the snow and cheerfully chopped it into tiny pieces with her axe.

After we returned to the trail, the dwarves grinned for a whole mile. The princess even promised to let Lena examine her bear cloak, which apparently had been prepared with an enchantment to keep her warm. Hadriane explained it was standard procedure in Kiivinsh. Forrel's fur jacket had it too. Of course, when Chase asked Forrel whether or not our mounts were *war* reindeer, and if they were trained to charge at enemies with their antlers lowered, the dwarf just gave him a tiny smile that said, *Do you really expect me to give away all our secrets?*

We skirted around the bay until the footprints headed away from the water, down an empty field of white. Huge craterlike tracks stretched out beside them. Those *had* to belong to General Searcaster.

After another mile, our quest grew kind of quiet, but a companionable kind of quiet. And I have to say—it was really *awesome* to have reindeer. We covered a lot more ground than we would have on foot, and it was nice to let our mounts do all the work for a change. All we had to do was relax and enjoy the ride.

And apparently stay awake.

I totally blame Lena's heating spell. It kept me extra toasty, just as warm as I would have been tucked in bed.

One minute I was riding along, staring at the moon and trying to gauge how long until it set. The next thing I knew, I was flat on my back in the snow, my side stinging, my reindeer snorting at me.

Lena turned her mount back toward me. "Rory!"

"I'm okay," I wheezed, rolling to my feet. And I was, except the breath had been knocked out of me. "What happened?"

"You started snoring, and then you fell off your reindeer," said

Chase, laughing, "and you're still dreaming if you think I'm ever gonna let you forget it."

"I wasn't snoring," I said automatically. I wouldn't have been embarrassed if it was just me, Chase, and Lena, but Miriam and the dwarves were smirking. The princess was at least polite enough to try and hide it.

"We should stop and make camp," Hadriane said, and I resisted the urge to cheer. I had the feeling that Miriam would listen to the dwarf princess. "If she's that tired, then she'll be useless in a fight."

That was true—I was having enough trouble grabbing my reindeer's bridle.

"Not here, though. At least a quarter mile from the trail," added Forrel.

"*More* riding?" I said, hating how whiny I sounded.

"It is necessary to camp out of sight of the footprints." The princess raised an eyebrow. "This morning it was easy to find you beside them."

Oops.

So the princess led us away from the trail. Forrel tied a bunch of rags and leather skins to the top of his spear and used it to cover our tracks, and when we were far enough away, Lena set up the tile of the snow-hut-building servants, which fascinated both dwarves.

Forrel taught the rest of us how to groom the reindeer—removing their saddles, attaching their lead ropes to a stake in the ground, brushing down their thick coats, and finding out if Lena's Lunch Box of Plenty could supply reindeer food.

It did. *Big* buckets of thin, dry grass.

Then the snow hut was finished. When we could *finally* crawl inside, I wasted no time unrolling my sleeping bag.

Forrel slipped inside after me. "I may decide to drag my captain home to her father before dawn."

"Try, and I will show no mercy," promised Hadriane, who clearly wasn't too pleased with him either.

Geez, these dwarves were intense. At least the Fey sounded like they were joking half the time. But my last thought before drifting off was that I was glad they had come. At least I wouldn't have that dream again. With the dwarves as our allies, we couldn't get dragged off to the Snow Queen in chains.

I was wrong.

Again the Snow Queen smirked, triumphant, as a troll held Chase's arms behind his back, and Lena tried to smile. I hated the way they watched me, hopeful, like I could do something to save us.

Just me and my sword against the grinning Torlauth.

"Isn't this what you've always wanted?" said the Snow Queen.

I couldn't stop thinking about it during my breakfast the next morning. I was so freaked out that I could barely swallow my bagel.

I jumped when Forrel popped his head into the snow hut's entrance. "Captain," he said.

The dwarf princess grabbed her spear, pulled up her bear hood, and slid out the door before I had a chance to ask what was up.

Miriam, Lena, and I exchanged glances. Chase, as usual, was too busy devoting his full attention to his egg-and-cheese burrito.

"I guess we should go see," Miriam said with a sigh, crawling out. Lena and I followed her.

Still tied up, the reindeer stamped their hooves and snorted out big steamy breaths. Well, all but two of them. Hadriane and Forrel's mounts galloped hard back to the trail. The dwarves raised their spears above their heads.

"Maybe Forrel convinced her to go back?" I said.

Miriam gasped and pointed. "Wolves!"

Half a dozen black and gray figures pounded across the snow-packed plain, headed straight for the dwarves. Forrel cocked his arm back.

"They're totally outnumbered!" I sprinted for the reindeer, grabbing a saddle.

"I think they've got it under control, Rory," Lena said.

I stopped fumbling with the buckles and looked up. One wolf was already still, pinned by Forrel's spear, and the soldier beheaded another one with his axe as he thundered past. Hadriane charged the line to cover Forrel's back and speared a black-furred wolf in the heart.

We were too far away to hear much of the battle, but as soon as Forrel chopped down a fourth pack mate, a white wolf gave a long howl that sounded like, "Retreeeeeeaat!" It and another gray one turned tail and ran.

Chase wiggled outside. "Wait, the dwarves went to fight, and nobody *told* me?"

"It all happened kind of fast," I said.

Hadriane launched her spear, and the white wolf dropped. The only member of the pack left was the small gray one, with white paws. He had to be the same wolf I'd knocked into Stow Lake, the one younger than all the others. His pack mate had called him Mark.

Forrel retrieved his spear and threw. It flew for so long I bet he could have won the Spear event at Kiivinsh's Tournament. I held my breath, but it fell short, sliding to a stop on the ice.

I was weirdly, stupidly glad that the little wolf was okay. To hide it, I said lightly, "Well, five out of six isn't bad."

"Who's glad they're on *our* side now?" Miriam said. We all raised our hands, half grinning.

The dwarves weren't nearly as pleased with the battle as we were. After they rode back, Forrel called, "We should get moving. One got away, and it's only a matter of time before the beast reports our whereabouts."

"My father must have informed the Snow Queen," said Hadriane apologetically. Hopefully, the king had made his report *before* he'd found out the princess had joined our quest. "We should expect trouble ahead."

"We're used to trouble." Chase shoved the rest of his burrito in his mouth, and he busied himself with saddling, talking through his mouthful. "Here's what I really want to know: Can we get another war reindeer demonstration? And can you teach *me*?"

After we returned to the trail, the terrain changed. From far away, it still looked pretty flat, but up close, you saw the jagged cracks in between big blocks of ice. Some of them were barely as wide as my finger. Some were so huge a troll could fall into the puddles of water below—I had to close my eyes when my mount leaped over those.

And wince when we landed. These reindeer saddles weren't all that comfortable after you'd been sitting for a few hours.

That wasn't what was bothering me, though.

I just didn't want to believe that the Director was right. I didn't want to believe our mission was doomed. Besides, the dream didn't make any sense. Maybe getting captured was likely, but the Snow Queen would never ask me if it was what I always wanted.

"You okay?" Lena said. "You're being really quiet."

"She's trying not to fall asleep," Chase said before I could answer, and I *really* wished I had something to throw at him.

Instead, I fought back the only way I could think of. "Lena, I really loved that dress you wore on Saturday."

She grinned. "Thanks! I loved yours too. That green looked really amazing on you."

Chase shot us a look of pure disgust. "Fine. Be that way. I'm going to make Forrel teach me about dwarf fighting." He urged his reindeer farther ahead, where the soldier was leading us right down the middle of the Piper's trail. As soon as he caught up, Chase unclipped his scabbard from his sword belt and started poking the dwarf with it.

Forrel didn't even turn his head, but Chase was unstoppable.

"Wow. I'm going to laugh if Forrel smacks Chase upside the head," I said.

But Lena was looking behind us, where Miriam and Hadriane were bringing up the rear. "Do you think they can hear us?"

Their voices drifted across the ice.

"The twins can annoy me as well," said Hadriane. "If I tell them that I don't have time to help them practice their spear work, they threaten to tell Father when I sneak out with my squadron for extra patrols."

"Philip does that too," Miriam said. "Except it's when I won't let him borrow my DVDs."

"What are DVDs? Are they like M3s?" asked Hadriane.

"I think they're pretty involved in their own conversation, Lena." But I leaned in a little closer just in case. Maybe she'd noticed something in the stasis spell she didn't want to share with the dwarves.

"Kyle asked me to dance!" Lena whispered. "I can't stop thinking about it. *Kyle* asked me to dance, and now I have to wait, like, three years before EAS has another ball. I *hate* the Snow Queen."

After Queen Titania's pavilion and the dwarf city, *this* was what she couldn't stop thinking about? I was glad Chase wasn't around to hear.

"What do you think it means?" Lena whispered. "Do you think he likes me?"

I laughed. "Come on, Lena. Kyle ran all the way to the library to warn us that the Director was coming. Do you really think he did that for me and Chase? Or for Miriam, Philip, and the kids in Portland?"

Lena let out a happy little squeal. I smiled too, ignoring the uneasy feeling that wormed into my chest. I was pretty sure, but I didn't want to be responsible for getting her hopes up if I was wrong.

Up ahead, Forrel had finally had enough of Chase's poking. Quick as a winter hare, he knocked the scabbard out of Chase's hand and struck him hard in the stomach with the blunt end of the spear.

Laughing, Chase swung his reindeer around and leaned far out of the saddle, scooping up his sword without even dismounting. "Come on, Forrel! Teach me how you did that!" he called. "Or I can keep poking you! That's fun too."

"Anything from Saturday *you* want to talk about?" Lena asked with a sly look.

I didn't get a chance to ask her what she meant.

Chase's mount tripped. The reindeer recovered, but Chase toppled out of the saddle.

Lena and I reached him in two seconds. He was fine, just dusting the snow off and cursing.

I grinned. "Chase, if you think I'm forgetting *this,* you have another thing coming."

Forrel trotted over, leading Chase's mount by its bridle. "Take a look at what he tripped over before you get carried away."

Half sticking out of the ice was a thumb as big as my leg and the same pale blue as the sky. Rust-colored stains were embedded under its cracked nail. I was almost sure it was blood.

I could see the hand partially hidden by the cloudy ice beneath our feet. The faint shape of an arm lay up ahead. "Um, did someone lose their giant?" I said.

"Likon, the cold one," replied Hadriane gravely. I looked at Lena for a better explanation.

"You know, one of the four pillars," Lena prompted, like this was something I should definitely understand. Then she added in her tinny, reciting voice, *"'On the day the Snow Queen was defeated, it took the magic of both Fey kings to bring Likon down, and even then, Solange's protection spells wouldn't let them kill him. So the exhausted monarchs dragged him off into the frozen wasteland and buried him beneath the ice, never to be seen again.'"*

"Except by us." Chase jabbed Likon's thumb with his scabbard.

The explanation had definitely freaked me out. "Don't wake him up!"

"That's not gonna happen. King Oberon and Fael's father used both Seelie and Unseelie magics to bind him here," Chase explained. "Two Royal Fey would have to work together to get Likon out. Do you know how often that happens?"

"When Atlantis first became a hidden continent," Lena said. "That's the only other time I can remember."

I had a really terrifying thought. "But what if you were a young and stupid prince and Torlauth kept telling you and the Seelie heir about this 'demonstration of ancient and powerful magics'?"

The color drained from Chase's face. "Oh, crap. Torlauth's going to bring them here. He's going to tell them the test is raising Likon, and then he won't let them put the giant back."

"Are two princes enough?" asked Hadriane. "The enchantment was cast by two kings."

"Two *heirs*, though. They can probably do it," Lena said nervously. "Maybe the Snow Queen doesn't know Likon's here."

"With years to search the wasteland?" Forrel said. "I am sure she does."

"The trail goes right over him, Lena," Chase pointed out.

"We can't let them wake him up," I said. "Whoever these pillars are."

Every single face turned from Lena to me in disbelief, and I hated it. I hated the blush creeping up my cheeks even more.

"The pillars are the Snow Queen's giant bodyguards," said Lena. "She said, 'These are the pillars on which I'll build our new era.'"

"Come on, Rory," Chase said. "You've met all of them now: Ripper, Ori'an, and Likon here."

That left one out. "Who's the fourth? Searcaster?"

Lena shuddered. "No, the sorcerer giant is in a class all her own."

"Dad killed the fourth one," Chase said. "After that, the Snow Queen cast some protection spells. Nothing can kill them now except another pillar."

Every day I found out the Snow Queen had bigger and scarier allies on her side. I was starting to get tired of it. "Maybe we could keep her from getting this one back."

"And what do you propose to do?" Hadriane asked. "Wait here and guard? Split our forces? Which is more important to you—the possible return of one giant or the possible return of those children?"

The kids, obviously. But I couldn't imagine not even *trying* to stop Torlauth. "Lena, could you set up an illusion? Or something to confuse the Fey into thinking that Likon isn't here?"

"Well, there's a disorientation spell I've been meaning to try." She dug through her carryall. "It'll only slow them down a little, though. I *think* we have enough spare dragon scales."

"Worth it," Miriam said, "especially if we can rescue Philip and everyone before they defrost Likon."

We waited while Lena ran around the giant, burying dragon scales under loose snow and murmuring the enchantment over each one. Forrel followed along behind her, erasing her tracks, and then we were on our way again.

The mood was a lot less festive after that.

It was Monday. Chase, Lena, and I were missing school. Mom had probably called into work and asked her understudy to take over. She was probably in our kitchen right now, her hand on the phone, waiting for it to ring.

I might have called, if I could, just let her know I was all right, but I had no way to contact her.

The Pied Piper's trail cut through miles of frozen plains. Once a snowy hare bounded up and watched us pass, but otherwise all we saw was white and white and more white, the icy patches glittering in the sunlight. My eyes began to ache. I should have brought sunglasses.

Finally Lena said, "Hey, are those mountains?"

She pointed at a part of the horizon that looked a little more jagged than the rest. She unfolded the map. "That's probably the Avaker mountains. That's the halfway point."

"The halfway point?" Miriam sounded way less excited. "Shouldn't we already *be* there? The kids reached the palace in a night and a morning. We're mounted. We should be faster than them."

"They didn't take a pit stop in the dwarf prisons," Chase reminded us.

"Or take time to sleep and eat, either," added Forrel.

"So, after we get to those mountains, how long till we reach the Snow Queen's palace?" I said.

Lena squinted at the map. "Maybe a day."

That cheered everyone up. Getting back by Tuesday night sounded good—Mom wouldn't have to worry too much longer. I could explain everything to her. I could even tell Dad and Brie.

Hadriane started chatting with Miriam again. "You are better traveling Companions than the twins would be. They have no patience for journeys."

Miriam grinned. "On car trips, Philip used to kick the back of my seat and whine, 'Are we there yet?' He still does that when I drive him to school sometimes."

"When they were younger, Ima and Iggy used to steal my cloak," said Hadriane, patting the polar skin. "They liked to play bear and knight. They tore three big holes in it once," the dwarf princess added ruefully, showing us the black stitches mending it.

Miriam laughed. "God, little brothers and sisters are so much trouble."

Solange had probably said that about Rapunzel, too.

I wondered if I would ever say that about Brie's baby. Or maybe I would end up like Jenny, who was so bossy that she drove Lena crazy. Then I remembered I wouldn't get the chance—I was hardly ever going to see Dad's new family after the birth.

"Yes, it's a wonder why we're going to so much trouble to get ours back," said Hadriane. I didn't realize she was joking until she and Miriam burst out laughing again.

Forrel drew his reindeer alongside us. "Have you Characters heard the story of the day my captain earned her bear skin?"

"Uh," I said, with extreme amounts of eloquence. "No."

"It was just after Her Majesty the second queen passed away, and before the dwarves began the construction of Kiivinsh," Forrel said. "The king took a small party here to the North—only his family and my captain's squadron. We were distracted with the city plans. We did not notice the twins wander off, and when we realized they were gone, we could not find them. Their white mourning clothes hid them from our eyes."

He glanced at Hadriane to see if she was going to help tell the tale, but she just raised her eyebrows, waiting for him to get to the point.

"We split up to search. We called their names but heard no answer. We began to fear that they had disappeared into the frigid water. Finally the king and the squadron heard our captain cry, *'Here! They're here!'*

"And then we heard a roar so terrible it froze our blood in our veins."

The bear.

"A great polar bear had come to shore, lured by the smell of the children, hungry for dwarf blood," Forrel continued. "Ima and Iggy had hidden themselves under snow, afraid to run lest the bear see them. When our captain raised the cry, the polar bear attacked, knowing it was about to lose its meal. And our captain—alone, without armor, armed with only a spear and an axe—faced it." He smiled. "And won."

Wow. I wanted to be like the dwarf princess when I grew up.

"Ima and Iggy helped," Hadriane said. "I told them to make snowballs and aim for the bear's eyes—to blind it."

"There is nothing our captain wouldn't do to save the twins," said Forrel, and I knew this was the point of the story. "She has buried her mother and her stepmother, but Ima and Iggy, she will not."

I couldn't imagine losing both Mom and Brie, but I *could* imagine facing down a dragon or some trolls for the baby. I wouldn't even need to be in her life to save her.

Miriam turned to Hadriane. "And now you've graduated to taking on the Snow Queen."

"Yes. Why do you think I've recruited such talented allies?" replied Hadriane, smiling like she was joking, but she wasn't looking at Miriam.

She was looking at Chase, Lena, and me.

No pressure.

Our wolf problem came back just as we began to climb the mountains. Chase pointed out a couple white ones sniffing around the frozen fields below, west of our trail. From this far away, it was impossible to tell if they were the regular kind or the kind that called the Snow Queen "Her Majesty," but since we hadn't seen a ton of wildlife, I was guessing they were the second.

"What do we smell like right now?" Forrel asked Chase. Lena and Miriam both gave the dwarf weird looks.

Not Hadriane though. And not me.

Chase's glamours were strong enough to include a phony scent, perfect for fooling wolves, but I hadn't expected the dwarves to know.

"A family of polar bears." Chase didn't meet anyone's eyes.

I wondered how long he'd been keeping the glamour up. Actually, I worried about how much magic he had left. Chase had already exhausted himself once on this quest.

"Not sulfur?" Miriam checked the smelly dragon scale in her hand.

"If we smelled like *Draconus melodius*, the wolves would report that some of Solange's pets had escaped," said Forrel.

Someone was going to have to tell the dwarves that being half

Fey was Chase's secret. Lena didn't need to become any more suspicious. Behind Miriam and Lena's backs, I met Hadriane's eyes, pantomimed wings, and shook my head, eyes wide. She got the picture. I guess if anyone would understand Chase trying to pass for human, it would be a half-human daughter of a dwarf king.

"Better to—" continued Forrel, but Hadriane interrupted, "Enough. One thing is certain: they'll catch us if we stay in one place."

Then she charged up the slope before anyone could argue with her.

I looked back once. Someone else had joined his two white packmates—a gray wolf with white paws, like socks. Mark sniffed around the other two and then skittered away to pounce on an especially big mound of snow.

Hopefully Chase wouldn't spot him. Otherwise he'd tell me that this is what happens when I insisted on not killing bad guys.

We stopped at the summit. A huge bay was spread out below us, the water nearly black in the dusk. The floating icebergs reflected the orange and gold sunset.

Lena unrolled her map, biting her lip. She didn't have good news. "It's still supposed to be frozen. I'm betting that a few nights ago, it *was* frozen, and"—she pointed right to the middle of the bay—"the Pied Piper led them straight to the Snow Queen's palace."

"So spring struck early?" Miriam asked.

"Spring . . . or maybe General Searcaster's cane. She probably cracked the ice to keep a rescue party from following," Lena said.

"Oh," Chase, Miriam, and I said heavily.

"But we can still skirt the bay's edges," Hadriane said.

Lena nodded glumly. "Yeah. Going around will just take us a little longer."

Yay. More time in this cold. More time for Mom to worry.

So we made camp. Before we finished grooming and feeding the mounts, Hadriane and Forrel were arguing again. I wondered if this is how other people felt when Chase and I bickered all the time.

But we weren't *this* bad. We fought over how to do stuff all the time, but never for days in a row. Me killing enemies and him telling Lena were the only things we *kept* arguing about, and usually we did that when no one else was around.

"Let it go, Forrel," said Hadriane.

"They'll say it was my influence," Forrel said. "You'll lose all the popularity you've had since you earned your polar bear skin."

"What people say won't matter as long as we return the twins. Who knows?" she added in a sly voice. She reminded me of Lena right before she tried to bribe Chase with one of her new inventions. "The people may be so grateful to get their heirs back that they'll restore your right to a beard."

"I don't care about that," said Forrel, who obviously did care. A lot.

When Lena's snow servants finished up, I slid inside the hut, hoping it would be quieter there, but the dwarves just followed us. The Lunch Box made the rounds.

"You actually need permission to grow a beard?" Miriam asked Forrel.

Lena flipped the snowmen tile upside down, and as she made tiny adjustments to the writing there, she explained in her tinny reciting voice, *"In most dwarf cities, a beard is not merely an object of pride. It is a mark of full-fledged citizenship, and every adult male dwarf proudly remembers the day he won the right to grow his beard and became a true warrior. By extension, one of the harshest punishments in the dwarf cities is to force a criminal to shave his beard—for a month, or a year, or—"* She stopped, realizing what she'd kind of just accused Forrel of being.

Hadriane only looked amused. "She does this often, doesn't she? Speak like a history book?"

"Oh, all the time." Miriam grinned fondly at Lena. "Drives her family nuts."

Forrel, despite all his earlier grumpiness, didn't look offended. "Well, your speaking history book should know this too: The very *worst* punishments extend well past a dwarf's lifetime. Those are inflicted on his son and his son's sons. I inherited mine from my father."

"Forrel has requested a repeal three times," Hadriane whispered.

Even though I'm pretty sure we questers were *all* thinking the same question, not one of us said it out loud.

Hadriane grinned. "Forrel, it seems you've scared them. They won't even ask what your father did to deserve such a punishment."

That actually cheered him up. "He entered the last war and fought alongside a great friend of his, the Frog Prince in your Canon."

"Henry?" I said. The Frog Prince was super-old. He walked with a cane. He'd never struck me as the fighting type.

"My father died in battle, and his punishment fell on his children," said Forrel. He didn't sound upset about it.

"That's not fair," Miriam said.

"It isn't about fair. It was an example. My father's transgression was very serious," said Forrel. "The neutrality of our people was our only defense. We were in no position to enter a war, and as long as no dwarf of Living Stone joined a side, we would not be attacked."

"But you're obviously allies of the Snow Queen *now*," I said. Hadriane grimaced, like that thought made her dinner taste bad. "What changed?"

"Solange has planned her return for a long time," Forrel told us. "She has courted many once-neutral parties, and that is why what we are doing now is so dangerous."

"Forrel—" Hadriane said, in a warning kind of way.

"No, captain. They need to know what they've asked of you." Forrel leaned in. "Our city is the closest free settlement to the Snow Queen's base. We will be the first to see war when it comes here. If a single dwarf joining an EASer could be considered suspicious, a princess joining a Character's quest will be deemed an act of war."

I hadn't thought of that. I kind of wished I *still* didn't know.

"Stealing both our heirs—*that* was an act of war," said Hadriane.

"And Solange's response will be to strike," Forrel said. "If Searcaster can't reach our spell, troops will come, like those wolves this morning."

"Well, you beat those wolves in, like, three minutes," Lena said uncertainly. Maybe she had the same sinking feeling in her stomach that I did. Maybe she regretted getting the dwarves involved too. "If Kiivinsh has more warriors like you guys . . ."

Forrel shook his head. "*Skirmishes* are won with warriors. Battles are about tactics, but *wars*, they're won with numbers and weapons. Our numbers are small, and the numbers of the Characters are even smaller. If the Fey decide not to ally with you this time, it will be a grim war indeed."

Okay. It was official. This conversation had stolen my appetite.

Hadriane broke the silence. "Conviction is a sort of weapon."

"Even then, you are outmatched, captain," Forrel replied. "Our people don't know the Snow Queen stole the twins. They know only that she offers us our homeland if we promise to go to the human world and fight for it."

"Can she do that?" Miriam asked, alarmed.

"She makes a lot of promises like that," Lena said. "That's how she gets her allies."

"Too bad we can't just tell her allies the truth about her," I said, but when everybody's head turned to me, I wished I hadn't. I didn't know what I meant. I fumbled around, thinking out loud. "I mean, she *makes* all these promises, but has she ever delivered? Even once?"

"She will only say that she must win the war before she can dispense what she owes," Forrel said. Hadriane looked kind of interested, though.

"But she doesn't treat her allies much better than her enemies," I said. "So she made your people promises. So she gave you guys a city. She also basically held the whole city hostage *and* she kidnapped the heirs to the crown. How many allies has she treated the same way? How many of them haven't spoken out because Solange is such a huge bully?"

"You are forgetting how many of our people are already devoted to the Snow Queen," said Forrel, not unkindly. "They may believe her if she says that she is only giving the twins a place of honor in her court. It's difficult to overshadow the lure of our homeland."

"There has to be *some* other way to get your homeland back," I said, frustrated. "A way without fighting."

Forrel smiled. "Now you sound like someone else I know."

"Quiet, Forrel," Hadriane said, smiling too. Definitely an inside joke.

"She's scared of Rory," Chase said. "Maybe we can use that."

I squirmed. I hated how discussions of the Snow Queen *always* shifted back to me somehow. I hated the reminder that maybe I was meant to stop her. "She is *not*."

"Yeah, why would the Snow Queen be scared of *Rory*?" said Miriam.

"Well, maybe not you *exactly*, Rory," said Lena slowly, thinking. "But however you're *like* her, that scares the Snow Queen."

"You mean you don't know? Rory's—" Then Hadriane's face twisted sharply, like she'd almost swallowed her own tongue.

I sighed. I knew what that meant. "The Director put that secret in the Pounce Pot. You won't be able to tell me, Lena, or Chase."

"*What* secret?" Miriam asked impatiently.

"That's the problem with the Pounce Pot," Chase said. "We don't know, and the dwarves physically *can't* tell us."

"It doesn't matter," said Forrel. "What you three have done to oppose Solange is admirable, and it has been on the lips of many. But the Snow Queen's resources are old and the stuff of legends. It is impossible to compete."

Well, that was *super*depressing. The only thing worse than believing that I was the one who was meant to stop the Snow Queen was believing no one could defeat her, no matter *what* I did.

"You won't convince any of us to turn back," Miriam said edgily.

Hadriane raised her eyebrows. "The secret to truly understanding Forrel is to ignore what he says and examine instead what he *does*. He's here, isn't he? He didn't turn back."

Yeah, but he *would* probably turn around if he convinced his captain to go with him. He was loyal that way.

"Of course I am here," the dwarf said impatiently, "but the humans should know the consequences of taking action."

He was right. I hadn't really thought this through.

"And what about the consequences of *not* taking action?" said Miriam. "If we didn't come, I would lose Philip forever, and I would know that I didn't even try to save him. I couldn't live with that."

"Nor I," said the princess. Forrel raised both hands in surrender under Miriam and Hadriane's glares. But even though I agreed with them, I couldn't help worrying now—over the king and Rebdo and the city we'd put in danger.

Hours later, the dwarves shook me and Lena awake for guard duty. I don't know how we got stuck with the second shift. It was hard to get up in the middle of the night, and it was harder to get back to sleep after you've been watching for bad guys.

Lena went straight out. I couldn't face the cold without ordering a steaming hot chocolate from the Lunch Box.

Hadriane shuffled over to the fleeces the dwarves had brought instead of sleeping bags. She dropped onto it so fast that Forrel reached up to steady her, his tiny smile making a brief reappearance. The dwarf princess caught his hand and squeezed it before she bent down to unlace her boots. Trying not to feel jealous about the dwarves wriggling under the covers, I crawled out the door after Lena, careful not to spill my cocoa.

The moon hovered just above the horizon, and a chilly silver glow hung over the big ice chunks scattered below our ridge. From here, the plain we'd crossed today looked so smooth, so *easy*.

"Hadriane and Forrel made up, I think," I whispered. "They have such a weird relationship."

"Of course they do," Lena said, examining her dragon scale in the moonlight. It was about the size of a quarter. "They're in love."

For a second I thought my sleepy ears had misheard her. "Really?"

"Yeah." Lena looked up, surprised. "I overheard Hadriane telling Miriam last night. Everybody in Kiivinsh knew it. That was the *real* reason he couldn't enter the tournament. Hadriane would just toss an apple as soon as Forrel got close." She giggled. "Geez. You didn't figure that out? Even Chase knew before you."

Wow. If Chase knew, I must have been *really* clueless.

Seeing how tired I was, Lena took pity on me and stopped teasing. "Let me see your dragon scale."

Groggily I tried to remember which pocket I'd left it in. After patting down half of my jacket, I pulled it out of my jeans, careful not to drop it.

She squinted at it. "I thought so. They're shrinking faster now. It must be colder here. The spell has to burn up the scale quicker to keep up."

I'd never noticed Lena could be so perky in the middle of the night. After an embarrassingly long pause, I figured out a good reply. "Is that a problem?"

"I don't think so," Lena said. "I brought extras, but we should start rationing them just in case. No more unnecessary spells. But that means I brought all those baseball bats with me for no good reason."

I slurped from my mug, trying to remember. "You mean, like the Bats of Destruction?"

Lena nodded with a proud grin. Oh gumdrops—I knew that look. She was going to talk my ear off. "I tested a few more the day before we left, but they all moved exactly the same, tried to hit the exact same spot. It wouldn't help us if they all concentrated on just one wolf, so I asked Melodie, and Melodie said maybe I should try cross-enchanting them with the same spell that powers the practice dummies, but I didn't have time to do it before we left. I brought them anyway, thinking I could change the spell up here, but if I can't use the dragon scales . . . I guess I'll just have to sit out the battles like always."

I didn't follow all that, but she sounded so unhappy about it. "You don't have to. You still have your spear."

"So I can take out *one* wolf while you and Chase take out tons of them?" Lena said. "That's not much help."

"Depends on the wolf you take out," I said. She'd forgotten to defend herself in *several* battles before I convinced her to start training with the spear again. "I don't want you to get hurt."

But Lena was still focused on her inventions. "Maybe *this* is what Rapunzel meant. Before I left, she said . . ." She pulled her notepad out of her jacket and flipped through it. "'Not every invention needs to be brought forth. A sword has two edges.' We must need the dragon scales for something else."

"That sounds right to me," I said softly, and her face fell. She must have really wanted to invent something to help the quest, but I didn't understand why. I was happy she was here, whether she brought her inventions or not.

I pulled my M3 out of my pocket and flipped open the cover. My sleep-deprived brain was trying to remember the spell for bad-guy radar, so I was completely unprepared for what Lena said next.

"Rory, I think Chase has Fey blood," she said in a rush. That startled me awake. "Like, a lot of it."

Yep. She'd figured it out.

"The trick Chase's dad taught him, the one he used at the pavilion, I'm almost sure it was a glamour," she continued. "I researched all the ways to cast an illusion for the one at the ball, and it's impossible for a normal person to cast with just dragon scales. If there was, Melodie and I would have done it. I think he can even do a glamour with scent. The dwarves think so. What they asked him this afternoon . . ."

I didn't say anything. I *couldn't*. The Binding Oath he'd made me swear would break the magic in my sword if I even hinted Chase's mother was Fey.

"And what Forrel said about the whole beard situation, it reminded me of something," she said. "Do you know what 'Turnleaf' means to fairies?"

Lena looked at me. I felt my face smooth out. The Binding Oath even made sure my expression didn't give anything away.

"You do, don't you?" she said. "He told you already."

"Um . . ." Either it was a really eloquent "um," or Lena knows me *really* well.

"And he made you swear not to tell," she said.

I braced myself. I wouldn't blame her if she got mad. And possibly grilled me until I dished, Binding Oath or no.

But she just looked really thoughtful. "Well, if he was going to tell anyone, he was going to tell you. When I found out what a Turnleaf was, I asked Rumpelstiltskin if Chase was related to a Fey who'd joined the mortal world. And Rumpel just pointed to the part in my book that said 'Turnleaf' becomes the last name of the first Turnleaf's descendants. So I always figured there was a fairy way back in Jack's family tree, and that was why he hated them so much. The Fey aren't kind to Turnleafs, no matter *how* many generations away they are from the original one."

Oh. Lena thought she'd been keeping secrets too. I was definitely telling *Chase* that, the next chance I got. "You never told me."

"Well, it was way before you came," Lena said quickly, like she was worried that *I* might be mad. "Besides, a lot of Characters have a touch of nonhuman blood. But it changes things if Chase can do glamours. That means he might be the great-grandson or even the grandson of the last Turnleaf, who left the Seelie Court in 1899. Ienna di Morgian, Torlauth's sister."

Chase leaving the Unseelie Court must have not entered the history books yet. That was the only reason Lena hadn't read about it. He would be relieved, and as much as I wished Lena knew, I was a little relieved for him too. Maybe because I was glad he was *not* a close relative of Torlauth, who was—let's face it—kind of evil and twisted, even for a Fey.

"Am I close?" Lena asked. "Can you tell me?"

The answer was no, but something flickered across the white horizon, a dark shape with four legs. "Lena, look. Is that what I think it is?"

"You're *always* changing the subject," Lena complained. "You're as bad as Chase now."

The dark shape was joined by a dozen others, then dozens more. "Lena, as one guard to another—*Look, wolves!*"

With a gasp, she grabbed my M3 and whispered the spell for bad-guy radar, just to double check. Lots of gray specks appeared on it. I didn't waste any time. Fumbling for my sword hilt, I ducked my head back into the snow hut. "Battle stations, everyone! We have company!"

Everyone crawled out, but sleepiness had taken its toll. Chase wiped drool from his chin, and before Forrel pulled his hood up, I saw a patch of his dark hair sticking straight out. The dwarf princess glared down the mountain like a scowl could turn back the bad guys and give her more time to sleep. The wolves were still a couple miles away, which gave us a chance to discuss strategy, and as an added bonus, being so high up let us count them—around fifty, plus an extra big one. Ripper.

The dwarves looked to Chase first, who shook his head. "It's no use. They're downwind. They've already smelled us." So another glamour was out. I guess not even a talented half Fey could keep one up when he was asleep.

"No chance then. Not against so many." Forrel turned to Hadriane. "Saddle the reindeer. I'll hold them off."

That sounded like the dumbest idea ever.

Hadriane apparently thought so too. "Please try to limit yourself to *helpful* suggestions."

Chase zipped up his jacket. "Yeah. Don't forget: You haven't seen me and Rory fight yet. We'll stay in front—take the offensive."

"Lena, I think you'd better get your spear," I said, and she nodded, grabbing her carryall to find it.

"I propose that the rest of us defend the reindeer," said Hadriane.

"If a wolf gets even one of them, we'll need to double up," said Forrel. "That will slow us down. Increase our chances of getting caught again."

The dwarf was clearly still on his pessimistic streak, but this time, Hadriane nodded. "We should fight on foot. A reindeer's throat is an easy mark for a wolf. A dwarf with a spear and axe is harder to defeat."

"Rory," Chase said sternly. That was his teacher voice—the one that said, *argue with me and I'll make you do a thousand sword raises in practice*. I braced myself. "Today would be a good day to *kill* a few wolves. So we don't have to keep fighting the *same* bad guys."

So he *had* recognized Mark.

I tried really hard not to lose my temper. He needed to stop nagging me. I never pressured him this much about telling Lena his secret, and definitely not right before a battle. "It doesn't matter if I do. The Snow Queen will just make more. Maybe stronger ones. At least this way, we know what we're dealing with."

"It's not just that. It slows you down," Chase said. "You can't afford to waste any time when we're this outnumbered. You would take out more of them if you didn't turn your sword and use your hilt. That's why you lost the duel with Hansel."

Bringing up the duel was a low blow. "That's not true. I take out just as many as you do. Maybe more."

"Wanna bet?" Chase said quickly. "If you win, I'll never bug you about this again, but if *I* win, you try my way."

I had just walked into one of Chase's hands-on lessons, the sneaky kind where he got me to try something I didn't want to do. "And exactly how long have you been *planning* this bet?" I asked suspiciously.

"Since January. How many times do you think we get a five-minute warning before we fight?" Chase replied, not even the slightest bit sorry.

I glanced at the wolf pack. They were so close now that we could see the moonlight gleaming on their teeth. Their breaths rose in steaming clouds.

Well, I *would* really love it if Chase got off my back. "One condition: If you win, I start *training* for your way now, and I try it after the school year ends."

I stuck out my hand to shake on it, but Chase hesitated.

"Come *on*, Chase. That's, like, eight weeks from now," I said.

"It's *this* quest I'm worried about." He shook my hand anyway. "I don't trust you to count, though."

"Same here. Mirrors? Magic camcorder mode?"

"Deal."

"God, Lena, are they always like this?" Miriam asked, as Chase and I clambered out onto the ridge, trying to find a rock with a nice view to set up our M3's on. "How do they get anything done?"

"I'm still trying to figure that out," Lena admitted, obviously distracted. She had half her body inside her carryall. She hadn't found her spear yet.

Forrel pointed down the slope, right beside the bay. A tennis court–size piece of solid ice still clung to the shore. "We need to get down there."

"You want to leave this ridge and lose the upper ground?" Chase said disbelievingly. "That's our only advantage!"

"No, it isn't," said the dwarf with a huge un-Forrel-like grin, and he began to explain his plan.

We waited for the wolves down beside the bay. We waited for so long I began to worry that maybe they had their own strategy meeting. Then Miriam screamed, spooking our mounts, war rein-deer or no.

A huge black wolf's head peeked over the ridge. I guess Ripper was disappointed that he didn't get a chance to eat us in Golden Gate Park. He must have figured he'd be the first to take a bite out of us this time.

I suddenly remembered the weapon we'd forgotten.

"Not good," Chase said, as I swung my pack in front of me and unzipped the pocket. "They were all supposed to go around. We need them to come at us from the water."

The rest of Ripper's body came into view, his massive legs bent in another crouch. He was preparing to jump, even from a few hundred feet up.

Forrel saw it too. "Get ready to dodge."

My hand scrambled around even faster.

"That fall will kill him," said Hadriane.

"Not if you're *the* Big Bad Wolf," Chase said.

They were both right: Ripper bounded down the slope, three huge leaps that stirred up a cloud of snow and caused half a dozen mini-avalanches. Then he jumped. Miriam screamed again. My fingers closed on Rapunzel's comb, and I threw it, as hard as I could, at the base of the ridge.

Iron bars as thick as tree trunks shot up beside the slope, and they clanged when Ripper's body struck them. The giant wolf whimpered a tiny bit as he slid down the new fence, stunned, and I let out the breath I'd been holding.

"I'm sure that's *not* how it looked when it blocked our path from the library," Lena said wonderingly. "What craftsmanship."

"You can examine it *later*, Lena," I said.

Ripper was beginning to stir and *growl*. He wore a cuff made from white leather around his left leg, and above his paw dangled a silver charm, an *S* with a snowflake hanging in the bottom curve, its spikes as sharp as a throwing star.

It was the Snow Queen's symbol.

"Awesome. Toss us the other two," Chase said. When I did, he caught one and dropped the comb. Another wall sprang up fifteen feet opposite the first. Lena caught the third. She threw it behind us, and bars sprouted up, linking the two sides and climbing up until they wove together into a roof.

Ripper laughed. "You've just made the cage you'll die in," he said, in such a creepy growl that I wished we had an archer who could nail him in the eye. Then he howled so loud the bars hummed.

Now the wolves *had* to attack us from the water. A dozen of them streamed down the ridge, right between the M3's Chase and I had set up. Mark stopped to sniff at one, but when his pack mate nipped at his white paws, he turned away. A larger group rounded the ridge and followed the water's edge to join their leader.

If the reindeer didn't like Miriam screaming, the wolves *really* freaked them out. One yanked its lead rope loose and tried to make a break for it. Hadriane caught it almost instantly, but I was glad we had the comb cage to keep them corralled.

"Ranks!" barked Ripper. The wolves formed lines on the ice hugging the shore: a row of big white wolves and a row of nimble grays and blacks, and another row with white wolves.

Around every left leg was a white cuff with that snowflake charm. They didn't just look like a pack. They looked like an *army*.

Wars are about numbers, Forrel had said.

Then creepy to end all creepies, they all barked back, "Yes, sir!" And they grinned, tongues hanging from every pair of jaws, as if they *knew* how much hearing them talk made me shudder.

I'd been an idiot to leave Mom and Amy guarded by just the tile servants. If the Snow Queen really decided to go after them, the dirtballs wouldn't stand a chance, and neither would my family.

"You're going to die," called a wolf in the back, and his pack mates howled in triumph.

But we had them *right* where we wanted them.

"Now!" Forrel called.

I darted forward and smashed my left fist into the ice. The ground beneath the wolf pack shattered, and the pieces shot apart. Some chunks were big enough so that the wolves could keep their footing, but half the pack slid into the water.

Ignoring their yelps and whines, I leaped back onto the solid rock shore.

Chase jogged out to me. "None of those count, Rory. You didn't use your sword at all."

"You can't just make up rules," I said, shaking out my stinging hand. "That's not fair."

"Not fair? Who's the one of us with a magic ring *and* a magic sword?" Chase replied, and I rolled my eyes. He'd known about them before we made the bet. "Ripper counts for five."

Not a good idea. Bet or no, Chase had *no* business fighting Ripper. The giant wolf couldn't be killed except by Likon and Ori'an. Besides, the Big Bad Wolf was safely out of the way. Ripper leaped from ice chunk to ice chunk, trying to make his way back to land, but he was having trouble finding ones big enough to float under his weight. He kept sinking up to his huge furry ankles.

"Will you two give it a rest?" Miriam said, still in the cage thirty feet behind us. "They're regrouping!"

"We can see that, Miriam!" Chase stared down a trio of white wolves who had managed to stay afloat on a nice-size raft of ice.

Either the Snow Queen had turned these guys so long ago that they'd forgotten how to speak, or they were just stupider than the others. They didn't talk at all. They didn't even show any strategy. They just waited to float closer to shore and growled, watching Chase.

But Forrel threw his spear and nabbed the one on the right. It splashed into the water.

"What will we get if we dwarves kill more wolves than you and Rory put together?" asked Forrel.

"Nothing!" Chase said, annoyed. "Stop killing my targets."

He took a running start and leaped on to the white wolves' ice raft. Forget my sword and ring. He'd just used his invisible wings. He beheaded one wolf and stabbed the other, and then he jumped to the next big chunk of ice to deal with the black wolves stranded on it.

I waited for the wolves to come to me.

Some grays managed to make it to shore. They ran up along the ridge, intent on revenge and—you guessed it—growling. These wolves were big on growling.

Behind them, the littlest gray hadn't been so lucky. He doggie-paddled over to the nearest chunk, so soaked that his fur lay flat on his skin, making him look more like a seal than a wolf. His white paws scrabbled against the ice, trying to get a grip so he could pull himself up. "I *hate* you EASers! Why do I always end up *swimming*?"

"We'll get her for you, Mark!" yelped the gray who ran in front.

I took a deep breath, concentrating on protecting the fighters holding the line at the comb cage behind me. My sword's magic flowed into me, and when the first gray wolf leaped, it jolted my body into action.

I ducked and struck up with my left fist, smashing the wolf's ribs. It crashed into the rocks beside us, whimpering. But not knocked out—out of the corner of my eye, I could see it trying to get up.

The next wolf skulked in low and tried to bite my sword arm. A snap kick sent him straight into the water.

Recovering, the first one tried to jump on my back, but the sword's magic sent me down to a crouch. Instead, he landed on his buddy's shoulder, teeth ripping, a bite probably meant for my neck. The third wolf howled, just for an instant, before I smashed my sword hilt at the top of his head and the first wolf's.

So, three down. I wasn't about to ask Chase what his score was, but judging from the trail of bodies he'd left behind on the ice islands, I had some catching up to do.

"I will get you, Rory Landon! They won't go unavenged!" cried the little wolf, but since he still hadn't managed to get out of the water, I wasn't too worried.

Hot breath blasted my neck, and I threw myself to the side, waiting for wolf teeth to sink into my flesh.

Instead, something thwacked behind me—Lena's spear on the wolf's head. And just in time. It landed, unconscious, just a few inches from me. "I guess it does depend on the one I take out," she said.

If we'd had more time, I would have hugged her. "Thanks, Lena."

"I want to try something! Can you come fight a little closer?" she said. Twelve white wolves had closed in on the cage. The reindeer were safe for now, pressed back against the bars, but the dwarves' spears were barely holding off the pack. Miriam's sword was bloody, her face ashen—she'd killed one who'd gotten too close.

They definitely needed help.

We sprinted back to them.

"No! Keep them separated!" Ripper said. "If Rory helps the magician cast another spell, I will personally rip out all your throats."

"Dude, don't worry about them. Worry about *me*," said Chase from a couple ice floats over. I really hoped he didn't get any closer to the Big Bad Wolf, and not just because of the bet.

Then the line of Arctic wolves attacking the others turned and faced me. I threw myself at them, carving a path for Lena.

My world dissolved to a storm of white fur, yellow teeth, black gums, and my next move: left punch, snap kick, duck, hilt smash, duck, roll, jumping snap kick, strike with the flat part of the sword, duck again . . . I barely had time to register what my body was doing, but it was hard to ignore the big ragged breaths that started when I got tired.

I couldn't see what Lena was up to, so I was kind of shocked when she called, "That's good, Rory! I'm ready now!"

I let go of one wolf's tail—I'd yanked him back when he'd tried to jump at Miriam—and looked up. Beyond a clump of unconscious wolf bodies—*had I done that?*—Lena had laid out dozens of bats inside the comb cage. Metal ones, wooden ones, ones so old all the lettering had been rubbed off, ones so new they were still in their plastic wrappers, and one particularly scary one with nails driven into it.

"Whoa." I hilt-smashed the wolf who tried to take me down while I was talking. Lena had told me she'd brought some bats, but not how *many*. "When did you leave the quest and raid a sports consignment store?"

She beamed. "Up, bats!"

They stood on their handles. Lena had her own very *skinny* army.

"Beat some furry backsides!" Lena cried. "And you five, break Ripper's nose!"

Just like the one in the Shakespeare Garden, the bats rose up into the air, sailed around me, and headed straight for the wolves. Some of the pack tried to run away, but most of them just stared as the baseball bats found their targets.

A big batch found some wolves staggering out of the water—their wet fur was tipped with icicles—and the bats shoveled the dripping soldiers back in, winging into their ribs. The canines flew back in a long arc that ended with a huge splash. Mark howled as he went in again.

I lowered my sword, impressed. With the Bats of Destruction, there weren't any wolves left for me to fight.

My favorite bats were the five Lena sent after Ripper. One minute, the huge wolf was staring at Chase with a huge toothy grin, probably imagining the best way to eat him. The next, he was ducking and yelping as big metal sticks took turns dive-bombing at his face.

"Retreat!" Ripper howled, until another bat struck him in the nose. Then he bit down on the silver chain hanging from his left leg and yanked it off.

He disappeared, and so did every single wolf in his army.

"They're gone," Lena said. Her bats hung in midair, spinning slowly, giving me the creepy impression that they were *looking* for something.

"So, that means . . . we won?" Miriam said, disbelieving. It *did* kind of seem like a miracle.

"Indeed." Walking back to the mounts, Hadriane stroked their noses, trying to calm them down. Then, with a pretty good impression of Forrel's deep voice, she said, "No chance, then. Saddle the reindeer. I'll hold them off."

Forrel just kept glancing at Lena, the comb cage, and then the bats with a stunned frown. He hadn't totally figured out what had happened.

"Crap. I was so close to getting Ripper." Chase pulled that funny rope thing from his pack. After whirling it a couple times, he hooked the shoreline and started towing himself back to the rest of us. I guess he didn't want to risk exposing his invisible wings outside the battle.

Lena gasped. "The cuff things! They were rings of return! I mean, not *rings,* obviously. It's hard to use rings when you don't have hands, but it's the exact same spell—it *must* be—but Ripper's must have been rigged to activate everyone else's if he used his." She only talked this fast when she got excited about an invention, so I knew what she'd say next. "I can't believe I didn't get a sample."

Yep, that earned her a weird look from Miriam, Forrel, and Hadriane. I smiled. Obviously they weren't used to my favorite inventor yet. "Next time we fight the wolves, I'll try to get one for you."

Still disappointed, Lena lifted her carryall and held the biggest pocket open. "Up, bats! Back to the sack!" The bats swung around and swooped toward Lena, sailing straight into her backpack, one by one.

I laughed, shaky and giddy with relief. Not even the fang-shaped rip I found on the hem of my jacket could freak me out. "You fixed all of those just now? While we were fighting?"

"Yep!" Lena said happily. "It wasn't *hard*, but . . ." The last Bat of Destruction dropped in, and she zipped up her carryall, looking a little worried. "I did have to use ten dragon scales."

Then we probably didn't have any spares left. "I'm not sure we could have won without them."

"Speak for yourself," Chase said, still reeling his ice raft in. "We had things under control."

"But she totally kicked the wolf army's butt in what—less than forty-five seconds?" I pointed out. "Chase, I think she just won our bet."

"No way. And if you think our bet is off just because Lena—" Ten feet from shore, Chase paused to shoot me a glare, and then his face changed. "Watch out!"

A blur of gray fur bounded out from behind a boulder and sprinted straight for *Lena*. Unfortunately for him, I was in his way. One punch was all it took to knock him back on the ice, and he lay still for a second, stunned.

It was Mark. He'd managed to get out of the water again. I lowered the point of my sword to his throat.

He scrambled up on all four white paws, shivering so hard I felt sorry for him.

Lena crept up behind me, pointing to his cuff. "His charm's gone! Look! That's why he didn't go back with the others. He must have broken it when he was trying to climb back to shore."

So now we had a prisoner. One who was whining in the back of his throat and dripping water so cold that the puddle underneath him was already turning to ice.

"What do we do with him?" Miriam said, her lip curling.

"It's your Tale. It's up to you," Lena replied.

"We could use him, couldn't we?" I said. Last year Chase and I had defeated Iron Hans, and just look at how helpful *he'd* been since. Even Forrel and Hadriane had seemed like enemies at first. Maybe Mark could lead us the rest of the way. Maybe he knew a back entrance to the Snow Queen's palace. Maybe he knew where the kidnapped kids were being held. "Binding Oath, maybe?"

"Wait," Chase said, sounding worried. He jumped the last five feet to land, dumped his rope, and ran toward us. "I'll take care of him. Just wait for me."

I shouldn't have looked away.

"I'll *never* help you." Then Mark leaped.

Lena screamed and fell, pinned under his huge paws. She threw an arm out to keep his teeth from her throat. His jaws closed over her wrist instead. He whipped his head from side to side. Her skin ripped. I saw red.

It happened so fast, too quickly for the sword's magic to flow into me and take over.

One slice, and his head was shorn from his shoulders.

One slice, and he was dead.

I'd killed him.

I t's okay, Rory," Lena said, but she was sobbing, her chest all scratched from the wolf's claws, her arm torn up from his teeth.

I tried to dig the Water of Life out of Lena's carryall, but Miriam gently pushed me away, looking pointedly at my hands. They were trembling. When Forrel placed the combs in my palms, all three dropped to the ground before I could close my fingers. Right beside them, a pool of blood stained the snow.

I couldn't look at the body.

Chase put my sword back into my hand. The blade shone silver in the moonlight—he must have cleaned it for me. It took me three tries to sheathe it, my hands shook so much.

"I'll get your M3." Then Chase fled. He probably thought I was going to cry.

I didn't feel like crying. I felt hollow and raw and leaden, like a witch had scraped my insides out and left metal replacements instead.

When Miriam squeezed out a few drops of water, Lena didn't wait to check on her wounds. She just launched herself at me, murmuring, "It's okay, it's okay, it's okay."

And I stood there, letting her hug me.

But it wasn't okay. I wasn't the same Rory I'd been when I woke up that morning, and I liked the earlier version better.

We mounted soon after that. We couldn't exactly go back to sleep.

Every time a thought nudged its way in my mind, I shoved it back out again. Instead, I noticed things on the ride.

I noticed how pretty the ice islands were. I noticed how massive the bay was, the way it stretched on and on, out of sight, even after the sun climbed above the horizon. I noticed Hadriane, Forrel, and Lena debating about how much time going around the bay had added to our journey. Miriam took the lead, forcing the mounts faster and faster until Hadriane called her back, saying that pace would kill the reindeer. Chase stared intently at the M3's as he rode, counting on his fingers. He was still trying to figure out who won the bet, even though it didn't matter anymore.

I'd killed someone. Finally. It probably made him happy.

He glanced my way every few miles, but I looked back only once. He didn't seem triumphant like I expected, just worried.

Around midday the wind picked up, and Lena passed out another round of dragon scales so we could refresh our heating enchantment. Except I didn't say it right the first time: *"No need for flames, no need for a blaze, just enough to kill—"*

That was what I was now. A killer. Thirteen years old, and I'd killed someone who wasn't much older than me. My hands started shaking again. I clutched my dragon scale, so hard that I felt its edges bite my palm.

Lena noticed. "Are you okay?" I just nodded, but the numbness was beginning to wear off.

Hours later, as the sunset dyed the bobbing icebergs pink, the bay ended. Ahead of us was the trail of footprints, leading straight into a gorge.

"Yes!" Miriam cried, spurring her reindeer forward.

I didn't really look.

Chase drew up. "Here." He held my M3 out to me, and when I just stared at it stupidly, he reached out, unzipped my carryall's pocket, and shoved it inside. "Hey, Forrel—me and Rory's mounts are starting to wheeze. That means we should stop, right?"

"Yes. Miriam, I'm sorry, but the reindeer will suffer if we go any farther," Hadriane said, before our Tale bearer could protest. "We've ridden more than a full day already."

So out came Lena's tile and the snow servants. Up went to snow hut, and in we went. Out came the sleeping bags and the Lunch Box of Plenty.

The food smells turned sharp and metallic, like wolf blood, and suddenly I remembered how easily my sword had sliced through Mark's neck, easier and messier than hacking down a beanstalk.

Nausea flooded me.

"I'll take first watch," I heard myself say, and I stumbled outside. I managed at least ten paces before I started retching up bile. It steamed on the ice and started to freeze, edges first. Being upset didn't stop me from thinking that was gross.

I dragged myself over to a hunk of ice to sit. All the thoughts that I'd managed not to think earlier crashed through my head. Mark's little socks. The way he'd kept looking for permission from the older brown wolf in Golden Gate Park. The way he'd snarled, "I'll never help you," right before he attacked Lena, right before I murdered him. Those were the last words he'd said, and now he'd never say anything again. Now he'd never get turned back into a human.

So, yeah, I was crying pretty hard by the time Chase came outside.

"You don't want to be out here." I wiped my face, but my

sniffly voice made it pretty obvious what I'd been doing.

Chase didn't even pause, but he looked down into the steaming bowl of soup in his hands. "You can cry. I don't have to watch."

Considering how much he hates seeing people cry, this was actually really generous. Suddenly I was glad I wasn't alone.

The soup was for me. He put it in my hands as soon as he reached my ice chair.

"I'm not hungry," I said automatically.

Chase pulled a spoon out of his pocket and passed it to me. "You don't have a choice. Lena says that even with the heating spells, we're using up more energy being out in the cold. It's dangerous not to eat *anything*."

He sat down next to me. "You never forget the first one. You never forget their *face*."

Sometimes I felt like there were two Chases—the one who liked to show off and pester us, and then this one, who said things that actually mattered.

"The first person I killed was a goblin. He had a scar on his right cheek, a hole in his right ear, and eyes as green as a parrot," Chase said softly. The details shocked me more than the story. "The Snow Queen's war had begun. The Fey weren't part of it yet. But Cal had his suspicions, and he shared them with Dyani's father, who doubled the patrols. The kids in my sword class were assigned guard duty at an old portal. The others, especially Fael, kept complaining that everyone had forgotten it. They thought nobody would come through."

Chase had been *five* when he lived with the Fey. Just five.

"But three goblins did. The Snow Queen's messengers," Chase said. "I didn't even mean to kill him. He tried to jump me from behind, and I turned. My dagger just slid into his stomach. He looked right at me, and then. . . . His eyes were still open, but he wasn't seeing anything."

I pushed away the memory of how sharp my sword really was, how smoothly it sliced.

"Since we just captured the other two, I was the only one who killed anyone," Chase continued. "Everybody congratulated me, but for the next three days, I kept throwing up. Amya thought I had food poisoning.

"But Cal knew. He took me on a long flight, far from the others, and he told me, 'You'll never forget your first. You'll carry his face with you always.' And since I'd spent the whole day throwing up every time I remembered the goblin, that wasn't what I wanted to hear. I think I kicked him."

"Not shocked," I said.

Chase shoved me, not hard, just enough to let me know I wasn't getting away with that. "And then he told me that if I hadn't killed that goblin, the goblin would have killed me instead. 'Amya and I would be devastated if anything happened to you,' he said. 'We would never be the same.'"

I knew where this was going, and it ticked me off. It wasn't that simple. "You're trying to remind me that I saved Lena, aren't you? I *know* that. I'm glad she's okay. It's just—" When I went home, I would have to tell Mom about this too, and the look on her face when she learned I was a killer on top of everything else. . . .

"'You've decided who should live and who should die, and you cannot take it back.'" It took me a second to figure out that Chase was still repeating what his brother had said. "'You don't know whether or not it was the right decision, choosing your life over the goblin's, and I can't tell you that. But I can tell you that you will make peace with the decision you made. The horror you feel will pale in comparison to the horror of what might have happened instead.'"

He meant losing Lena. That was so awful I couldn't even imagine it.

"'And it will be easier when the choice comes next time,'" he continued. "'And easier the next time still.'"

That was probably true. But I didn't think it would ever be as easy for me as it was for Chase. I didn't think I could kill someone during every single battle, even when I was older.

"That was one of the last things Cal said to me," Chase added softly. "He and Dyani were dead a few days later."

I knew how much Chase cared about his brother, but Cal must have loved him too. War had been destroying their whole world, and he'd still taken time to make sure his little brother was okay.

I let myself imagine it, just for a moment—suggesting names like Brie had asked, flying down to L.A. for the birth, waiting with Dad through Brie's labor, meeting the baby for the first time. She would be so tiny, so helpless. She would be family, for me to protect like Mom and Dad and Amy and Brie, and maybe someday, I would be the one telling her advice, like Cal had for Chase.

Pointless to think that way. It made me feel even worse.

"You miss him." It wasn't a question.

"Every day." Chase shrugged. "But recently, every hour."

Because we were getting closer and closer to the place where Cal died.

"What was he like?" I'd never asked him this. Chase was too touchy about the Fey and his life with them.

"It's impossible to tell you about Cal without talking about Dyani. They were always together," Chase explained. "She was the Unseelie heir, and she liked the attention. She drew people to her. She was fair though, because Cal was fair. And he was just about the only person she listened to. And Cal—"

He paused. *Here's when he changes the subject,* I thought, but I was wrong. "Dyani told me once that Cal was like a light. He just made everything better and brighter. He wasn't the first person you noticed in a crowd, but if you got to talking to him, he was the one you remembered afterward. He was the one you wanted to see again. It was hard to feel alone when he was around."

But then he was gone, and Chase *had* felt alone.

"Brie's having a girl." It just popped out. I hadn't planned on telling him.

Lena would have immediately started telling me that this still didn't mean I was like the Snow Queen, that I wasn't turning into Solange, but Chase just stared at me, searching my face so intently that I had trouble looking back at him.

Then he said, "You'll make a good sister, Rory."

He meant it, and I was grateful, even though I still had to decide what being a good sister meant. Afraid I was going to cry again, I told him. "Chase, Lena noticed that you do glamours. Last night she told me that she thinks you're the grandson or great-grandson of a Turnleaf."

"That stupid pavilion—" Chase sucked in a huge breath, think-ing it over. "I can live with that," he said finally.

"Even if she thinks Torlauth is your great-uncle?" I said. "She wouldn't tell. She spent the last few years believing you're descended from a Turnleaf, and she never said. You might as well—"

He raised his eyebrows, and I knew I was pushing it. Oh well. It *was* his secret.

"Get up. You're helping me train." Standing, he unsheathed his sword and pulled out his M3. *"Please, please don't be botched. Come on mirror, it's time to watch."*

"I don't want to train." I didn't feel like *touching* my sword.

Chase knew that, I think. "You don't get a choice. *I'm* the one training this time, and you owe me about a thousand training sessions. I watched the mirrorcordings from this morning, and I figured out why you're so good at fighting in big groups. You move around so fast that you get your opponents to accidentally fight each other. You know, like human kung fu. We're going to go through every single move, very slowly, till I get the hang of it. Then we'll do it faster. You're playing all the bad guys. I'll be you."

I could think of only one reason why Chase would show a sudden interest in my magic sword's techniques. "Does that mean I actually won the bet?"

Chase didn't answer that directly. "Tackling the islands was a strategic mistake, but if I'd gotten the five points from Ripper, I would have won."

"It doesn't matter anyway," I said, trying not to think about Mark. "You got what you wanted."

"I didn't *want* this," Chase snapped. I looked up, surprised he was so angry. "I never wanted you this upset. I was afraid you would get backed in a corner and have to choose between you and the bad guy. You would hesitate and then there would be no more Rory. I knew this would suck for you, no matter what. I pushed you anyway. Be mad at me if you want. If I have a choice between you being mad at me and being dead, you can just be mad."

"I'm not mad." I really wasn't, not anymore. "But you should have told me *that*. You just kept complaining about fighting the same bad guys over and over." I would have listened better if I had known he was worried about me.

Chase shook his head, turning back to the M3. "You would just have said there's nothing to worry about."

He was probably right, so instead of arguing, I peeked at the M3 over his shoulder. I couldn't really follow it. I just saw white fur, and then my brown jacket. But Chase did. He stared at the mirror, totally engrossed, like it was an instructional manual for awesome.

Cal would be proud of him. I hoped Chase knew that.

"Chase?" I said.

"Yeah?"

"I wish I could have met your brother."

"You would have gotten along." Chase tapped the M3 twice to rewind the last section. "You two are a lot alike, actually. Okay, looks like you need to be over on the right and aim a slice at my throat. I wish this mirror had slow mo. You think Lena could add it while we're out here?"

I don't think he even noticed what a nice thing he'd said. But I did.

And I would have trained all night if he'd asked.

I hadn't really expected to sleep after we woke up Lena and Miriam at the end of our watch. Every time I closed my eyes, I kept seeing Mark's white paws, but eventually, the paws grew boots, Mark started walking on his hind legs, and he sprouted cobalt wings threaded with red.

Then Torlauth towered over me, a sword in his hand, a sneer on his face.

"Isn't this what you always wanted?" said the Snow Queen.

The scared questers were lined up beside me, Forrel's pale face, Lena's weak smile. Then Chase gaze's hit mine like a magnet, and I couldn't look away, even as my hand crept toward my pocket.

I was terrified that they were going to be hurt, and I was even *more* terrified that I would kill Torlauth.

I'd had the dream three times. I really needed to report to our Tale bearer, and it didn't help that Miriam was in a good mood when Lena woke me up.

"It isn't very different," the princess explained as she braided Miriam's hair the dwarf way. "We merely braid with four pieces instead of three, but it is an honor among the women of our people, much like the beards are for our men. The four strands remind us what qualities we dwarves seek to embody: endurance, strength, courage, and loyalty."

Her voice faltered on the last one. She was thinking of her father.

Miriam heard it too. "Well, that's a lot to live up to first thing in the morning, but I'll try," she said. Hadriane smiled as she tied the braid off with a leather cord. "Thanks. My hair was grossing me out. The worst thing about these quests is that you can't take any showers."

I grimaced. I was about to tell her something much worse than getting smelly. "I dreamed that we all got captured by the Snow Queen and Torlauth and some minions."

That got everyone's attention. Chase even stopped stuffing his face.

Forrel said, in a supercondescending way, "Nightmares are to be expected—"

"No, it's not that," Miriam said. "Characters sometimes have dreams that come true. How many times, Rory?"

"Three," I admitted.

Miriam nodded grimly.

"That is how many times you will dream it if it'll come true?" asked Hadriane.

"Usually, yeah," I replied, and when a funny expression crossed her face, I remembered that her mother had been a Character. "Why? Did *you* dream something three times?"

She just shot me a tiny, unreadable smile. She'd definitely spent too much time around Forrel.

"Okay." Miriam attacked her packing with enthusiasm. "Let's get going. The sooner we get there, the sooner we can get captured and break out and get home."

We rode off. The sun squatted on the horizon. The icy footprints reflected it like gold mirrors, making me squint. Keeping my eyes mostly closed was *not* helping me wake up. Even the bruises I felt from yesterday's ride weren't doing enough to keep me awake, and I knew Chase would never, ever stop teasing me if I dozed and fell off my reindeer *twice*.

I moaned. "Lena, I know what your next invention should be. Something that can keep you in the saddle and let you sleep at the same time."

"Um . . ." Lena said, thinking about it.

"They've invented it already," Forrel said. "We dwarves call it rope."

Chase grinned. "I have some, if you need it."

Obviously the *Rory's had a bad day so let's be nice to her* period was over. But that was okay. I would have a lot of time to be upset after we got home and Mom locked me in my room for the next few months.

"Forrel," Hadriane called from where she was riding in front with Miriam. The sharp note in her voice made us all look up.

I didn't realize what I was seeing until Forrel dismounted and walked over to it. Or rather, what I *wasn't* seeing.

The golden trail of footprints ended just twenty feet away, and the white landscape stretched ahead of us, empty as far as the eye could see.

14

For a second, we all stared at the spot where the tracks ended. One of Searcaster's footprints was only a half, like someone had cut off part of her foot midstep.

My heart stopped. "A non-Fey glamour spell? Like the one over Kiivinsh?"

If that was true, then we had probably reached the Snow Queen's stronghold, and I wasn't sure if I was ready for that yet.

Forrel shook his head. "I would see the palace from here."

"Maybe it's a disorientation spell! Like the one I cast around Likon!" Lena said. "We can find the dragon scales they buried. . . ."

"No." Forrel patted the snow beside the end of the trail. "The tracks have just vanished."

"Even farther on?" Miriam whispered. She was so tense, her reindeer started to prance nervously.

Forrel took a few steps forward and searched the ground, frowning. Then he did it again. "Nothing."

"Searcaster erased them," Hadriane said dully.

"Yes. Probably after we defeated the wolves," Forrel replied, and Miriam looked like she was wrestling back tears.

"Is that even possible?" I asked Lena.

"General Searcaster is the only sorceress-giant history has ever seen," Lena said. "There's really no telling what she can or can't do. But in Philip's Tale, it seemed like she'd completely used up her magic keeping the kids warm during the run. This isn't a small spell. Sending the wolves gave her enough time to recover."

Chase didn't look very freaked out, but maybe it was hard to look nervous when you're forking hash browns from the Lunch Box of Plenty straight into your mouth. "What's the big deal? We have a map."

"Yeah, but . . ." Lena unrolled it, turning it around so we could see. She pointed at one spot, a little bit past something labeled the Bay of Vinyais. "This is about where we are, and this is where we're headed," she said, moving her finger to the castle icon.

There were no landmarks between us and our destination. None at all. Just a whole bunch of white space.

"Compass?" Miriam said, kind of desperate.

Hadriane shook her head. "They don't work very well this far North."

"It will probably be too cloudy tonight to navigate by the stars," Forrel said, looking up at the sky. That hadn't even occurred to me, which shows how good my sense of direction is.

"So, basically," Chase said, *finally* starting to look worried, "we're screwed."

No one responded, which I guess was answer enough.

"I know what my next invention will be," Lena said after a moment. "Magical GPS."

Miriam nodded mournfully. "Turn-by-turn guidance even in the Arctic," she said, and we were still optimistic enough to find that kind of funny.

Our Tale bearer decided to keep going in the same general direction as the trail where the footprints ended. We all knew it was a long shot. But lots of quests were long shots.

It was Miriam's *Tale*, after all—the help the Tale bearer needed the most usually showed up right when everything looked bleak. Maybe Searcaster had only erased a piece of the trail; maybe it would show up again. Or maybe Iron Hans would appear ahead, worried about us after those Dapplegrim got back to Atlantis.

Then a sudden gust blasted us, hard enough to blow our reindeers off course. The chill invaded our clothes and our heating spells. It was hard to imagine a happy ending when the wind pelted you with tiny bits of ice and your teeth chattered too hard for you to think.

My reindeer stumbled once, and when I looked down to see what had tripped it, I glanced down at the ice, blown bare of snow.

Something dark swam underneath it, as long as a fireman's hose.

"What was that?" I yelped, my voice shaking from the cold. "The tentacles of an evil Arctic squid?"

Forrel looked back, annoyingly calm. "Probably the sea serpent."

"But it's the Snow Queen's pet, right?" Chase said. "That means we're probably in her backyard."

"Except her backyard is about the same size as Denmark." Lena sighed deeply—I couldn't hear it with the wind whipping around us, but I could see her jacket heave up and down. Then she nodded shortly, like she'd come to a decision.

"Okay, everybody—we need a stronger heating spell." She pulled out a couple fresh dragon scales. In Fey, she pronounced, *"We need more heat, please make us warm, don't make us wish we'd never been born."*

She trotted down the line, passing out two scales to every quester, even the dwarves. When the princess refused to take them,

Lena said, "I can *see* you shivering in that big polar bear skin."

"You can't save the twins if you lose your hand to frostbite, captain," Forrel added, and even Hadriane couldn't argue with that.

I was last. She stuck close, biting her lip as I repeated the spell. She was worried about something. "What is it?" I asked after she refused to meet my eyes for a whole mile.

"You know those fifty dragon scales I packed? To make a portal to get the kids back home?" Lena whispered. "Well, I just dipped into them. I didn't know what else to do."

"It's okay," I said. Maybe it wouldn't be if she told the others that she'd made such a big decision on her own, but she couldn't let us freeze. "I mean, there's bound to be some dragons at the Snow Queen's palace, right? We can get more there."

"That's what I thought too." She didn't sound that relieved though. "But we're running out of dragon scales. Those fifty won't last between the six of us."

"How long?" I said. She'd packed enough for weeks.

"Maybe two days," Lena whispered.

It felt like the cold had seeped into my chest and frozen it, refusing to let my lungs pump air. Maybe three days was enough to search the Snow Queen's backyard, but not two.

"Do you think I should tell Miriam?" Lena added.

"Yeah, I think you'd better," I said, but I knew why she hadn't. Miriam was at the front of the line, her face still eager. She didn't believe the quest could fail. I didn't want to burst her bubble either. "But maybe wait until we stop for food or sleep or something."

A few hours later, Mirriam pointed over to our right. "There! Look there!"

My heart gave a great big thump, warm with sudden hope. I

looked for Solange's palace and saw . . . an icy plain. Also, snow blowing in the wind.

In other words, nothing. "Um…" I said.

Hadriane pushed her polar bear hood back and squinted, trying to see what Miriam saw. So at least I wasn't the only one confused.

Miriam slipped down from her reindeer. She pulled off her glove and picked something small and square from the ice. She must have been watching for footprints. I'd forgotten to keep searching the ground.

"One of the kids must have dropped it," Miriam said excitedly. "Leaving a trail, like Hansel and Gretel in the woods. Philip would do that."

It could be. Some more dark squares were scattered on the ice. But I couldn't figure out why the kids would start dropping them *here*. I nudged my reindeer a little closer.

"Is it Philip's?" Lena asked. "Do you recognize it?"

"No. But that doesn't mean anything," Miriam said. "He's always picking stuff up."

I jumped off my mount and crouched over the nearest little cardboard square. It was a book of matches, inside a silver and black case, easy to see against the white snow. I didn't see any lettering.

Light flared up. Miriam had struck a match. "Well, at least it's warm." She stared at the flame.

My mitten closed over the matches in front of me, and suddenly I shivered, like someone had stuffed icicles down my jacket. The matches were making me *colder*.

The Snow Queen's magic could do that. The letter in the giant's desk, the one she sent villains through, it had chilled me when I touched it too.

"Miriam, I wouldn't—" I started.

She turned my way and gasped. "The trail! There it is!!!"

I glanced over my shoulder, searching the flat white space. "I don't see it."

"Does anyone else see it?" Chase said, but no one answered.

"But it's— Oww!" The match had burned too low, all the way down to Miriam's fingers. She dropped it, and it sputtered out on the snow. She scowled. "Great. Now *I* can't see the trail."

"Miriam, I think the Snow Queen made these—" I started, wanting to explain.

"That must be it! It might cancel out whatever spell Searcaster used on the trail," Miriam said. "To help her minions get back! Let's see." She struck another match and looked around wildly.

"Lena, have you ever heard of such a thing?" asked Forrel.

"I don't think so. . . . ," Lena said.

"There's the trail again!" Miriam cried. "Oh my God, is that—? That bump on the horizon, it's the Snow Queen's palace, isn't it?"

We all turned again to check it out. Hadriane stood in her stirrups, like the extra height would help her see farther.

I looked too. Sometimes your Tale *did* bring you to the only thing that could possibly save you. But sometimes an enchantment discovered your deepest desires and used them against you.

"Hold on, Miriam. Let Lena take a look at it really quick," I said. "Maybe she can figure out what the spell is—"

"OWW!" The second match had burned too close to Miriam's hand, and she dropped it too. "Stupid matches. They're too short."

"Miriam, wait!" Lena said.

Without even glancing at us, Miriam struck another one, and I was furious at her for blowing us off, Tale bearer or no.

"Put it out!" I shouted, running at her.

"I see some people. Some kids! They've escaped!" Miriam said, and it was so far-fetched that we didn't even bother looking now. My hand shot out. I was ready to rip the box of matches away, even if I had to wrestle her to the ground to do it. "Look, it's Phil—"

Then flames whooshed across Miriam's whole body. She screamed. I flinched away from the fire and tripped. Before I hit the ground, she was gone.

All that was left was a small pile of ashes, dotted with scorched shreds of her jacket. The wind began to scatter them across the ice.

We'd lost our Tale bearer. We'd lost Miriam.

It was Hadriane's idea to scoop up the ashes, so we could take them back to Miriam and Philip's parents. Lena held one of the little vials she used to collect samples, and the dwarf princess packed them in until her fingertips turned blue.

I was sure I would cry, or at least throw up. But I didn't. The tears and the vomit just hung out close to the surface, making sure I felt good and rotten.

And I was pretty sure I deserved it. "It's my fault," I whispered to Chase.

"You told Miriam to stop," he reminded me, as Forrel rode up with the two reindeer that had bolted away from the fire. "We all heard you."

But that's not what I meant.

Miriam was a Failed Tale now. She would have still been a Failed Tale if she'd stayed at EAS, but she would have been alive, too. She wouldn't have died if I hadn't had the brilliant idea to come out here.

We pitched camp to discuss our options. They weren't good, and everybody knew it after Lena explained about the dragon scale supply.

"I wish we'd found those rings of return," Lena said.

"Can't you make a temporary-transport spell back to Portland?" Chase asked.

The dwarves would look pretty weird there, but we could probably get them through the pavilion and back to Kiivinsh. And then Lena, Chase, and I could take the Door Trek door back to EAS.

And explain what happened to Miriam.

Sometimes, it is better not to know too much. You will learn soon enough, Rapunzel had said. She *must* have seen this. She hadn't wanted to tell us. We wouldn't have gone if she had.

"I can try," Lena said slowly. "The ingredients for a temporary-transport spell are a little different than the one I was planning. I may be able to do a substitution, but there's no guarantee that it'll work."

"We should avoid that then, until the worst happens," said Forrel.

"It's true that Characters' quests have a much greater chance of completion if they have a Tale bearer among them, isn't it?" Hadriane asked.

Chase, Lena, and I all nodded glumly. Without the magic swirling around the Tale bearer, putting the helpful things in her way, our impossible task became even *more* impossible.

Mom would want us to try the spell that could bring me home.

But Rapunzel wouldn't have let us go on the quest just so Miriam could die. She had to see more than that. She had to have seen us do *something* right. Otherwise she would have stopped us. Plus, she'd told us that we would find the fourth comb with that sorceress. This quest couldn't be over yet.

"We have to keep going," I whispered. "We have to rescue Philip and the others."

Lena half smiled. "I knew you'd say that."

Forrel stared at me, so Chase explained, "Rory has this annoying habit of looking on the bright side. *All* the time."

I didn't feel like I was looking on the bright side, but I didn't want Miriam's death to be for nothing. At least I could save her brother for her. "We can't be *that* far away."

"That is true." Hadriane probably still wanted to save the twins, more than anything.

"*If* we have traveled in the right direction," Forrel pointed out. "We could already be going the wrong way."

"They are the new Triumvirate, Forrel," the princess said. "If anyone could find their destination through sheer luck, it's them."

And the second the decision had been made, I started worrying again about what we'd gotten ourselves into.

Hadriane and I took the first watch. We huddled in our bedding and sipped hot chocolate from the Lunch Box to keep warm. I tried not to think about how Miriam would be sharing the shift with the princess, if she were around.

I wished I hadn't felt *so* sure that we needed to come, and I also *really* wished that feeling would come back.

"Guilt is a useless emotion," the dwarf princess said suddenly. "The loss of Miriam is no more your fault than the loss of the twins is mine. The Snow Queen is behind it all."

I goggled at her. "You want me to just stop thinking about it?" I wasn't sure that was possible.

"My advice is to turn your thoughts to the future, to things you might actually be able to change, rather than imagining different outcomes of your past choices," said Hadriane. "Such tiresome thoughts have taken many of my nights. I remember when my father first allied with the Snow Queen. Back then, my people lived in a small town on Atlantis, crowded because the Unseelie refused to let us build a bigger one. I knew the alliance was a mistake. I used to fantasize about convincing my father not to move to the Arctic; I used to imagine picking *just* the right words—what Mother would have said—to make him see.

"But the lure of our homeland, the hope of returning to the land of Petrified Stone . . ." Hadriane sighed. "It would take much more than words to fight it. When we first left the place you call Arizona, the only home our grandfather's grandfathers could remember, the dwarves of Living Stone walked softly on the earth, heads down, always apologizing for their presence."

Honestly, I couldn't see Cranky Beard apologizing for anything.

"So," the princess continued, "it was easy to listen when the Snow Queen told us that we had been pushed to the forgotten corners of the earth, that we should take back what was rightfully ours."

I resisted the urge to shudder. I'd heard the exact same words come out of Searcaster's mouth.

"In Kiivinsh, my people were proud to be dwarves once more. Even if I cringed every time they spoke of murdering humans and taking the land back again, the Snow Queen's task gave my people hope again. It made them come alive. Sometimes people don't mind being wrong as long as they feel alive, too. I do not blame them," she added softly, "but I don't want our homeland back the way they want it."

"How *do* you want it?" I asked.

Hadriane didn't quite smile, but her face softened. "Before the Snow Queen reached out to my father, I had a different daydream. I imagined the humans learned what they had done and invited us back to Arizona. They helped us rebuild our City of Living Stone, and my mother's human family came to visit me as much as I wanted."

I didn't see why they couldn't go back. National parks had a bunch of rules to keep people out—the dwarves would probably have to hide during the day, but . . .

"But these were the daydreams of a lonely child," Hadriane

said swiftly, like she was kind of embarrassed. "For now, I'll just settle for the twins' safety."

Miriam had been a good sister too.

"It would take something truly tragic for my father's people to change their minds," Hadriane said softly. "I'll warn the twins of that when we reach the Snow Queen's palace."

When, she'd said. Not *if*.

I wished I could believe it wasn't an *if*.

In my dreams that night, I trudged across a frozen lake, hip-deep in snow, head bent against the wind. I was searching for Miriam, except Miriam didn't look like Miriam. In the dream, I knew she had my father's chin dimple and Brie's bright red hair.

Then the frozen lake folded up into a white hallway.

I turned a corner, and I wasn't searching for Miriam anymore. There was the black door, with its ancient cracked wood and the scrolling *S* underneath the doorknob. I was exhausted right down to my bones, the kind of tired I'd never been before traveling to a place as cold as the Arctic Circle. I knew I had to go through the door, and I fought the fear that kept me from opening it.

The fate of the world depended on what was on the other side, but I wasn't thinking about that. I was thinking about the others, who had sacrificed so much to get me this far. I was thinking of how I owed it to *them*.

So my morning obviously didn't get off to a great start.

I wasn't the only one. After we saddled up the reindeer, recharged our heating spells, and moved out, Lena recounted the dragon scales we had left, shuffling them in her hands as smoothly as a stack of cards. I knew something was bothering Chase, because he only ate a tiny bowl of oatmeal for breakfast. Even Forrel was jumpy—once, across a river of melt water, we spotted a white-furred, four-footed figure with pointy ears and a great fluffy tail. The dwarf cocked his spear back, taking careful aim, but the princess threw out an arm.

"Only a fox," she said as it pounced away. "Much too small for a wolf."

Hadriane apparently had taken it upon herself to keep Miriam's spirit alive. She started off the morning ride with a chipper "Let us go!" She kept saying stuff like, "Just beyond that cove, we'll see it." Then, when that cove was behind us, "Just beyond that rise."

Hours later I was sure that if she pointed at some other unspecial feature of this bleak landscape, I would scream.

This quest *was* different from the others—Rapunzel had been right. Up the beanstalk and on Atlantis, we'd been in a lot of danger, but we'd *chosen* this journey. *We'd* decided to rescue the kids.

No. *To go or not to go is a decision. It rests on one person, and one person only,* Rapunzel had said.

That person was me. I'd talked everyone into coming, even the dwarf princess.

I hadn't saved the kidnapped kids. I'd only thrown our lives in with theirs.

Mom was waiting with my note, waiting for me to come home. But I would never come back, and she would *never* know what happened to me.

That afternoon Lena passed out a pair of dragon scales to each of us and said, "That's it. This is the last of them. If we use any more, we won't have enough for a temporary-transport spell."

"Can you do a scrying spell instead?" Chase had apparently been brainstorming during the ride. "To see how far away we are from the palace?"

Lena shook her head. "I didn't bring any of the ingredients."

"Could we take a sample from *here*?" Chase asked. "Sneak back into EAS, grab more supplies, and come right back?"

"No," said Lena. "Ice won't work as a sample. Just dirt."

So we could stay here and freeze, or use a temporary-transport spell that may leave half of us behind, or plop us down somewhere in between here and EAS.

Forrel held up his dragon scales. "How long will these last?"

"Three hours, I think," Lena said.

"And how long do you need to set up this spell?" Forrel said.

"Fifteen minutes," replied Lena. "Ten for the tile's servants to build a snow hut, and five for me to set up the spell in its doorway."

"Then we still have two hours or so." Hadriane pointed to a plateau of ice standing above the rest. "There! That's where we'll find it."

I didn't scream, but I did snort a little. When the reindeer reached the ridge, a lot of white stretched out ahead, with a big dark bay scooped out of it.

"Nothing?" Lena said, drooping. I guess Hadriane's attitude was getting to her too.

"No," said Forrel, his voice suddenly heavy with relief.

"Yeah. Right there." Grinning, Chase pointed to the shore.

Hadriane whooped and urged her mount down the slope. Then I spotted it—a blue-gray square about as big as my thumbnail, so close in color to the water beside it that it had completely blended in.

Relief flooded me, but I didn't want to trust it. "That's way too small to be the Snow Queen's palace."

"It doesn't matter," Lena said happily, her map flapping as the reindeer galloped forward. "They'll at least be able to tell us where we are."

"If someone actually lives there," Forrel pointed out.

But he didn't need to worry. Riding closer, we could see the round stones in the house's walls, the gray door and shutters, the smoke puffing from the chimney, the white picket fence, and the woman kneeling in the yard, wearing a red cloak.

She stood when she saw us. Her face was unlined, with smooth round cheeks and black eyes, but her hair had gone completely white. It hung loose and straight all the way to her ankles.

Tucked under her arm was a wicker basket with a small shovel in it, dusted with snow. I kind of couldn't believe she was actually gardening, but when I looked around her yard, I noticed a leafless tree, its forking branches gilded with ice. Frost-covered vines snuck up the pillars on each side of the front door, and short-stemmed lilies grew beside the fence.

They'd been bleached of all color, except for the one at the woman's feet. She'd probably just finished planting that one. It was turquoise blue near the center, framed with paler petals.

If I didn't know any better, I'd say that flower was looking at us. Actually, all the lilies seemed to be bobbing their petal-framed heads in our direction. Which made sense. A garden this close to the North Pole definitely had to be magical.

"Hi! We're a little lost," said Lena, like this woman wasn't our very best chance of surviving our quest. "Would you mind pointing out where we are?"

The woman waved a hand. I thought it was some sort of strange sign language until Lena glanced down at her map. "Oh! That's perfect! Thank you so much!"

A new landmark had appeared in the upper right-hand corner, a cottage exactly like the one in front of us. It was labeled ARICA'S HOUSE.

"We passed it," Lena explained, showing the others. "We went too far west."

It was all going to be okay. Lena and I grinned at each other.

Then I remembered where I'd heard of Arica before. "Oh! You're the sorceress with the fourth comb! Rapunzel's friend!" I had no idea how they knew each other, unless they'd met in a club for people with young faces and old-lady hair.

"Yes. You are Rory Landon. I've been waiting for you." Arica pointed at the front door. Her whole arm was black, metal, and bare up to the shoulder. Pretty easy to guess what body part had been replaced to make her a sorceress. "Come inside."

I slipped off my reindeer and stepped through the front gate. Strange whispers hung over the garden. I didn't realize that it was coming from the flowers until I got close to the new one with the blue center.

It turned to me. "Won."

Okay, so the weird flowers talked too.

"Weave." It flapped its side petals, like it was annoyed at me for not responding. "Wisten!"

They talked nonsense apparently, but hey, they still talked.

"Come," said the sorceress again.

Chase shook his head at me, and Lena said, "Um . . ." They obviously couldn't believe I was holding up the quest for this.

"You have three combs. You really need a fourth as well?" Now Hadriane *really* reminded me of Miriam. Forrel just grabbed my mount's reins before it could run off.

"Ten minutes," I said, trotting up the steps as the sorceress opened the door. As soon as I was inside, Arica slammed it. Her smile was so wide that I could see half her teeth were metal too.

rica was obviously a *lot* creepier than Rapunzel, and I tried really hard to keep her from seeing how much she freaked me out.

Unfortunately, her house didn't exactly inspire warm fuzzy feelings either.

The gray floorboards were warped with age. Long strips of ancient wallpaper rippled along the walls, reminding me of used bandages. The doors hung loose and crooked in their hinges. Some of the steps in the stairwell had rotted away, leaving gaping dark holes.

"Nice high ceilings!" Then I glanced up and noticed the cobwebs attached to the dusty chandelier. Eww. I didn't even think spiders could *live* in this cold.

I'm pretty sure Arica could tell I was just trying to be nice. "Come with me."

She walked down a dim hall. Her feet fell heavily with weird clicks. They must have been metal too. I tried not to imagine what had happened during her Tale to make her lose so many limbs.

Something stepped out of the shadowy place under the stairs and followed us. I jumped back, but it was just a woman exactly Arica's height, with straight white hair the exact same length.

"Oh, hello," I said, but she didn't respond. When we stepped into the light, I could see why—her face was wooden, her carved eyes fixed, the hinges around her mouth a little bit rusty. A puppet without strings, moved with magic. I'd seen only one before, and considering that it had tried to kill everyone at EAS last year, I wasn't a huge fan. "Um, the Snow Queen had one of those. . . ."

"Yes, Solange stole the design from me." Arica sounded kind of bitter.

Little warning bells went off in my head, but then a bigger dummy crawled out of the next room. It had a long serpentlike tail, four clawed feet, and lots of sharp teeth, but what really got my attention was its shiny, green-gold hide.

"Whoa, are those real dragon scales?" I asked, walking backward to get a better look.

"Yes," said Arica.

Jackpot. Well, kind of—I just had to figure out how to convince the sorceress to let us borrow some of the scales. That would get the others off my back. We could even replace them after we returned to EAS. I tried to figure out how many we needed.

The next room wasn't as empty or colorless as the rest of the house. Wicker birdcages hung from the ceiling on bright ribbons. Something rustled inside the nearest one.

Bright fuchsia lily petals formed a body, a head, and two wings over stem legs with tiny green claws. It cocked its head at me. Its eye looked all polleny, like the inside of the flower.

"Wow," I said. The two puppets shuffled over to me, standing on each side. "Did you make these yourself?"

Before the sorceress could answer, the fuchsia flower-bird chirped, "Run!"

Automatically I reached for my sword, but the woman-shaped

puppet snatched my right wrist. A click came from the dragon's head as its fangs disappeared into its wooden gums, and then its jaws nabbed my left arm, latching on so hard I knew it could snap my wrist in a second.

Before I even thought, *Hey, struggling might be a good plan,* Arica raised her hand, and a thread of magic unfurled from her fingers. When it struck me, my muscles went all . . . floppy. Something sent me rushing down, twisting my insides together. The pain lasted only a second, and then I was sitting on the floor.

I was also only a few inches tall. With emerald and yellow petals lying beside me instead of arms.

"Oh, crap," I said, my voice much higher than usual.

The flower-birds in the cages didn't realize the damage was done. The whole flock started shrieking. "Run! Run! Run!"

"Hush, little ones." Arica tipped up a mask—it must have had an illusion embedded in it to make it look real. Underneath, her skin looked like crumpled paper. "Unless you would like to join your fellows in the garden."

The bird room was instantly and eerily silent.

Oh no. The blue flower, who had spoken to me, had been planted outside for rebelling. Freezing had turned its edges white and garbled its words.

Not "won." *Run. Leave. Listen!*

I was an idiot. And now I was a flower-bird.

If Chase started calling me birdbrain after this, I would totally deserve it.

I sprinted toward the door, my petal wings spread for balance, because my awkward little body was *definitely* not built for running.

Arica scooped me up off the floor and held me to her chest. "You're so much more trusting than the other one."

I was too freaked out to reply. My green legs dangled over empty air as she carried me across the room. I didn't want to know what would happen if I fell. I could barely *walk* in this body. Flying must have been a lot more complicated.

The sorceress thrust me inside an empty birdcage and latched the door. The woman puppet tied my cage to a ribbon, and horror of horrors, the cage started *rising*. My claws clutched the bottom of the cage as tightly as I could. That was a weird feeling, like making a fist with my feet.

Arica folded her arms, the metal one and the real one, with a stern look that reminded me a lot of Gretel. "Solange would never have been caught in such an obvious way, and yet they say that you'll—" She stopped suddenly, looking like she had swallowed her own tongue.

The sorceress was trying to tell me how I was like Solange.

"Ah, Mildred has kept the Pounce Pot. She has *used* it." Arica's eyes blazed so much that the flower-birds chirped with alarm. "It was *mine* before it was stolen, but that little Triumvirate paid the price for taking it from me."

Then I knew how this sorceress fit in. Way before she turned into the Snow Queen, Solange and her friends went on a quest for the Pounce Pot. I'd never thought about who it had belonged to *before*.

"You won't ask me what kind of price?" Arica asked. "You *are* a strange one."

She didn't get a lot of visitors out here, in the middle of a frozen nowhere. I guessed I could play along until someone rescued me. "What kind of price?"

"They left behind one of their own," said the sorceress, sounding like Jack bragging about the giants he'd slain. "I caught Solange

229

taking the Pounce Pot from its pedestal. I flicked a finger—in those days, that was all I needed to turn someone to stone—but the boy stepped between us. The spell hit him instead."

My petal-feathers ruffled—another very weird sensation. "You're the one who turned Sebastian into a statue." I'd seen him at EAS, in the same room I'd seen the Pounce Pot.

"Yes," said Arica, "and despite all her sorcery, Solange could not turn him back."

"She was a sorceress when she was a Character?" I said. "How did *that* happen?"

Arica shot me a dark look, like I should know what a stupid question that was. "No one knows, and no one knows how she became so strong. She did not have such power as a child."

Another mystery about the Snow Queen. Just what I needed.

Arica was obviously way more interested in her story. "Solange and Mildred couldn't carry Sebastian, so they had to leave him behind. Three months later, Solange lost Mildred to the Sleeping Beauty curse, and she was alone." She sounded so proud of herself, but Solange had been a kid then—a Character just like me, facing a destiny she wasn't sure she could handle.

"I sang the day I heard of it. I sang the news straight into Sebastian's ear," said the sorceress. "One day, after her curse was broken, Mildred and her husband came to collect Sebastian. She paid me with a comb that could keep the Snow Queen from crossing my threshold, and I was happy to receive it—I knew it was only a matter of time before Solange came for her revenge."

Yeah, well, I couldn't fault Solange for that. Look what I'd done when Mark bit Lena. "What did the Director want with Sebastian?" It obviously wasn't to break the spell.

"Poor naive Mildred, she rolled the boy into battle," said Arica gleefully. "Fresh from her curse, she did not know her friend was beyond saving. She asked Solange what Sebastian would think if he could see them. And in answer, the Snow Queen thrust an icicle through the heart of Mildred's beloved."

I'd known Solange had killed the Director's husband right in front of her, but not why. Geez. "And the Director swore a Binding Oath to stop the Snow Queen." No wonder the Canon had refused to explain all this to me, Lena, and Chase. The last Triumvirate was so messed up.

That couldn't be our future. It didn't matter what had transformed Solange from a Character mourning her friends to the villain hurting them. I wouldn't become her. Never.

"She wasn't the Director of you Ever Afters then," said Arica, "but yes. The best friends make for the best enemies. With Mildred's help, they defeated her."

And they hid Sebastian away, deep inside EAS.

"But even Mildred could not stop her for long," said Arica.

I knew she meant that was my job, but the Pounce Pot wouldn't let her say so.

"Are you so blind?" Arica said, annoyed with me. I fought the urge to remind her which one of us had turned the other one into a flower-bird. "Solange will come after your loved ones before she comes after you, because that's what happened to *her*."

The thought sliced through my little petal body, straight into my tiny heart.

Down the hall, the front door squeaked open. "Hello? Rory?!"

Chase.

I panicked.

"R—" That was as far as I got in my *Run! Save yourself!* speech. Arica flapped both hands at me, and it was like she'd hit the mute button on my squeaky-toy voice. No matter how much I squawked, no noise came out.

"Don't worry, my little one—you will both leave this place. I want what you want. I want Solange dead," she said. That was definitely *not* what I wanted, but I couldn't exactly argue. "However, you must allow me my little games. I cannot leave this house, but I *can* keep my reputation intact."

"Where are you?" Chase called again, his voice closer now. "The others are coming in after us if we don't leave in ten minutes."

"In here!" Arica called, and she used *my voice*.

Oh no.

She stepped away from the cages, and when she flicked her mask down, she was wearing my *body* too, plus my new sword belt, my carryall, and my jeans, complete with the pizza sauce stain on the knee. She smiled at me, but it wasn't *my* smile—it showed way too many teeth.

Chase *had* to know that wasn't me.

He walked in, his sword swinging at his side. "Hey. Where's the sorceress?" he asked Arica.

If Arica had been impersonating *him*, I would have guessed right away. I tried to yell again, indignantly, but no sound came.

"Getting the comb. She'll be back in a minute," Arica-Rory said. "Then we can get out of here."

Chase nodded, glancing around the room. I threw my little body against the cage bars, waving my wings frantically, but it didn't do any good. All the other flower-birds were doing exactly the same thing. "Yeah. Can't say much for her decorator."

"I think they're pretty. But thanks for the rescue," said Arica-Rory, smiling at him with a syrupy Adelaide-like smile. Then she made a huge mistake: She slipped her hand through Chase's.

He would know *now*. Maybe Sebastian and Solange had had been like that, but never in my life had I ever grabbed Chase's hand. Not unless I was dragging him away from a dragon or trying to break an enchantment.

But he just stared at her and then their hands. He didn't even drop it.

Arica-Rory's eyes shone. "We could be there by tonight."

"Yeah," he said in a tiny, un-Chase-like voice, the corners of his mouth tilting up, and I started to wonder if *he'd* been replaced too.

"We could kill her before the—"

Chase's sword pricked Arica-Rory's throat.

Okay. So he'd been playing along to get her to lower her guard.

"What are you doing?" said Arica-Rory, all pouty. Now she *really* reminded me of Adelaide.

"Where *is* she?" Chase hissed.

"Getting the comb—" started the sorceress.

"No, Arica—where's the real Rory?" Chase pushed the blade closer to her skin. "And get out of her body before I cut it to pieces."

Now she smiled with the smile that wasn't mine, and she flicked her mask up again, revealing her true ancient face. "You wouldn't want that. My death would bring yours. Only my magic is holding this house together, and it will vanish if you kill me. The roof will collapse and crush you all. Better to simply ask me to break the spell."

"*What* spell?" Chase's gaze strayed to the flower-birds. "You turned her into one of those?"

"Very good. You're quicker than she is," said Arica. I resented that like whoa. "If you can tell me which one she is, the comb is yours."

"I could torture you until you turned her back," Chase said, and for a second, I thought he really might do it. He looked mad enough.

I really hoped he didn't. This whole day was already guaranteed to give me nightmares.

"Finding her in the crowd would be faster," said Arica calmly.

Chase didn't lower his weapon, but he skimmed the cages.

"Me! It's me!" the flower-birds chirped, throwing themselves at the cage bars. I stopped feeling sorry for them. Now that I was enchanted, it was every flower-bird for herself.

I figured waving just one wing would look pretty human, but trying threw my cage off balance. It swung crazily, and for a second, all I could do was squeeze my eyes shut and trust my stupid stem legs to hold on.

"There," Chase said, and when my eyes snapped open, he was pointing straight at me. "She's the only one who looks like she's afraid of falling."

He didn't *need* to keep telling people I was afraid of heights.

"Are you sure?" asked Arica.

"Positive. Only Rory gives me that look when I rescue her."

I was busy wondering what *that* was supposed to mean when Arica flapped both hands at me again. My body grew—I yelped when that sharp twist hit me, and yelped again when the twiggy cage busted to pieces around me—and then I was *falling*. Thirty feet to the floor.

Luckily I crashed into someone first. Chase. I'd knocked him flat.

He looked me over, his peach-orange wings fluttering into view behind him. He must have flown to get over to me so fast. "You okay?"

"Yeah, you threw me a little bit when you let her grab your hand.

You *know* I'd never do that." I stood, reaching out to help him.

Chase's jaw clenched. He knocked my hand away and got to his feet.

Arica laughed, a soft sound that made all the flower-birds go a little crazy, screeching and flapping their wings. "Oh, Rory. You *are* blind."

That did *not* help my mood.

I drew my sword. The sorceress took a nervous step back, but I turned to the puppets sitting quietly in the corner, hacked off the dragon's tail, and tucked it and all its nice scales under my arm. "I was going to ask nicely if I could have this, but then you turned me into a *bird*. Maybe I should just keep chopping to make sure you can't catch anyone else."

Chase caught on fast. He pointed his sword at the woman puppet. "Give us the comb, or the puppets get it."

"Such impatience." From her pocket, the sorceress drew out a comb, decorated with the same emerald-and-silver tree as the others. She held it out and said, "I will even pass on a warning: that comb may not help you. I threw it across my threshold when Solange came for her revenge. Magic cannot pass through its bars, and the walls here were fortified with similar protective enchantments. And so, instead, the Snow Queen cast her spell over the house itself, locking me inside this crumbling prison."

Oh. Well, I guessed that explained why she wanted to kill Solange.

"Sucks for you," Chase said. Then he stomped down the hallway. I hurried after him.

"Protect them, Rory. Doubtless, you'll need their help," the sorceress called, but I slammed the door behind me.

The enchantment had left me kind of confused, but I didn't

know what Chase's excuse was. By the time I'd caught up to him, he had his hand on the front door's handle.

"Chase, *wait*!" I said, throwing myself against the door before he could walk out.

"I don't want to talk about it, Rory," he said at the same time I started, "Your wings—"

They vibrated with agitation until Chase took a deep breath, concentrating until they stilled. Now we just had to kill time until they disappeared. "Talk about what?" I said.

"Nothing." He refused to look at me.

"Are you mad?" I asked, trying to figure out what I'd done.

He shook his head, but he was lying. He still wouldn't meet my eyes.

"I'm sorry I gave you that weird look when you rescued me," I said softly.

Chase's fists clenched and unclenched. "Rory, that's not it. It wasn't a big deal."

I was starting to babble. "It just surprised me, that's all. She took your hand, and you didn't react, and we've—"

Chase doubled over, his hands tearing at his hair, and said something like, *"Uuuuugggggghhhhhhh."*

I jumped. Either this had been the wrong thing to say, or Arica had just cast a long-range spell over him.

Then he thrust his face close to mine, eyes blazing. "Listen, Rory—I will tell you if you really want to know, but I don't think you do. I think all you want is get to the palace, rescue those kids, and deal with everything else afterward."

"Everything else . . . ?" I repeated, barely breathing. Our faces were inches apart, and I wanted to lean forward and shrink back at the same time.

But when Chase's glare softened, I remembered the way he'd

glanced at his hand linked with Arica-Rory's, the way he'd started to smile . . .

Oh my God. *No*. He couldn't.

He'd told me, two nights ago, that I reminded him of his *brother*.

He jerked away. "Forget it."

But I couldn't forget it, even when he stared down at the floor and swallowed hard.

I wanted to tell him that that I couldn't think past finishing Miriam's quest for her.

But that wasn't true. Thinking about Miriam made me think of George too—how they'd been inseparable and how they'd still broken up. It didn't matter if Characters started pairing off in eighth grade. It couldn't possibly be worth it. I couldn't risk losing Chase. I couldn't imagine my life without him.

So I just froze, like a complete idiot.

Finally his wings winked out. "They're gone," I said. Without even glancing at me, he slammed through the door, marched down the stairs, leaped on his mount, and urged it back to the trail, like he couldn't wait to leave me behind.

The others were happy to see the scales I brought. Hadriane and Forrel beamed at each other. Lena actually *squealed* and started prying the scales off the tail stump with the dagger she used to chop up spell ingredients. But when I told her about Arica and being a flower-bird, she looked seriously freaked out. She even started watching me as we rode. When the symptoms started about a mile later, I found out why.

One minute, I was staring at Chase's back, wishing he wasn't ignoring me and wondering how to get us back to normal. The next, my arms and legs felt like they weighed a thousand pounds. My eyelids felt even heavier. I couldn't keep them open.

Apparently getting enchanted and unenchanted is really hard on your body, especially when it involves shrinking that small. Lena said I just needed to sleep, but since we had to keep moving, they had to tie me to my reindeer with Chase's rope to keep me from falling off.

I drifted in and out of consciousness for the rest of the day. Chase didn't even tease me about it. I wished he would. I kind of missed it.

When Lena woke me a couple hours later to refresh the heating spell, I could barely stay awake long enough to say the rhyme. When I opened my eyes again, it was dark, and Lena was leading her reindeer down from a ridge, whispering, "Oh my gumdrops, it's *there*! The Snow Queen's palace! Maybe a mile out!"

"We can't go now," Chase said, behind me. "Rory's still asleep."

"No, I'm not." I wanted to see. It was torture to be this close and not be able to go any farther. "We can go."

"We can't." Forrel had crawled up on his stomach to spy over the ridge. "The Snow Queen has wolf and troll patrols guarding the perimeter. We'll be easy targets crossing in the moonlight."

Hadriane protested, and Chase offered to disguise us. I guess now that Lena knew he was part Fey, he didn't bother to hide his glamours. I wanted to argue too, but my stupid overenchanted body drifted off again.

I came to when Hadriane began untying the ropes around me and my saddle. Forrel tethered the rest of the mounts in front of a dark cave.

I wished I could have stayed awake for the planning. "What happened?"

"We're stopping for the night." The dwarf princess was clearly unhappy about it. "Forrel thinks we should move in after the moon sets."

Yeah right. *I* was holding up the quest. I could tell by Lena's worried face. I couldn't let them lift me out of the saddle and tuck me into bed like a baby, so when Hadriane got the ropes off, I said, "I got it."

Unfortunately, when I slid off the reindeer, my legs had other ideas. My feet struck the ground at a weird angle. I would have taken a nose dive if someone hadn't grabbed me.

"Easy," said Chase. He looked at me this time, but as distantly as a stranger.

"Let's get you inside," Lena said. She tried to lead me into the cave.

Chase's hand dropped from my arm, but I didn't go yet. I couldn't leave it like this. This was bigger than fighting over me killing or him keeping secrets. This could push us apart. I might lose him anyway. "Chase . . ." My voice cracked.

He waited, face hard.

"Thank you for coming after me." That was all I could think to say.

He looked me straight in the eye. "Rory, if you're in trouble, I'll *always* come for you."

I could hear how much he meant it, and I felt better. Some things didn't change.

"I'll always come for you too." According to Arica, I would probably *have* to. "And Lena."

"Lena too." Then he smiled, in such a familiar, exasperated way that I knew we'd be okay in the morning. "Get some sleep. You can't rescue anyone like this."

The dream came again, despite the enchantment.

Torlauth smirked, his bronze hair reflecting more light than his sword, his wings flapping in anticipation.

The Snow Queen smiled too, her eyes alight with triumph under her towering icicle crown. "Isn't this what you always wanted?" she said.

My left hand drifted toward my pocket, and I looked down the row of prisoners—at Lena's shaky smile, at Chase's smug grin, at Forrel's white face, at Miriam's desperate tears—

Miriam. Alive, I thought, and hope bloomed in my chest.

Hadriane shook me awake. "Lena said you should be all right by now. Are you?"

I sat up and rubbed my face. I was a little achy, but otherwise, I felt fine. I nodded.

"Then join us. We've had a messenger." She sounded eager, so obviously it was the *good* kind of messenger.

The others sat in a circle around a white, fluffy creature with a pointed face, dark eyes, and a long snout. The fox turned her little nose up at me, deciding I was less than awesome.

Lena passed me a note. It was written on paper torn from a

small notebook, the writing cramped and tiny. "It's from *Evan*."

"His Tale's 'The White Snake.' He can talk to animals," Chase explained to the dwarf princess as I started to read.

To the rescue party (if you're out there):

The Snow Queen has us. If you're heading toward her palace, I guess you already know this, but here's what you don't know: She's planning to give us to some allies she's invited out here. If you get this after dawn on Friday, April 8, don't bother coming—she's already given us away. If you get it before *Friday, wait and come then—your best chance is to sneak in with the guests.*

Then follow the fox. She knows how to get to where they're keeping us.

—E.

P.S. Feed her if you can. I've promised all these foxes an unguarded henhouse of their very own if they help us.

Lena tackled that last part and ordered a bowl of raw chicken from the Lunch Box.

I started counting days. "It *is* Friday, right?" I couldn't believe we'd been out here for that long. Poor Mom.

Lena nodded, fighting a smile. The note had gotten her hopes up too. That's the thing about bad luck. It makes you really appreciate *good* luck, and also not to trust it. "What are the chances?"

"I don't think chance had much to do with it," said Hadriane. "Do you remember the fox Forrel wanted to shoot yesterday? How many foxes did Evan send to find us?"

But I knew what Lena meant. "It's like Miriam's Tale is still helping us."

She could still be alive. But I didn't tell anyone about my dream. If I'd misunderstood it . . . "What time is it now?"

"An hour before dawn," said Forrel. "The Snow Queen's guests have lined up at the entrance. Most of them are on foot. We should leave the mounts behind."

"Untethered," said Hadriane. "So they can start the journey back."

She didn't need to say we would find our own way home. Since we were heading into the Snow Queen's palace, filled with her minions *and* her allies, we would definitely need to.

It took us only two minutes to pack everything and get out the door, but the fox still managed to finish her breakfast before then. She stared at us impatiently from the cave mouth until we left and climbed up the ridge.

The Snow Queen's palace spread out ahead of us like a crown. A long line snaked out in front of it, flanked by ice griffins and dragons. The fox padded up ahead, leading us down the slope and across the ice.

My heartbeat thudded in my throat.

The giants were easy to recognize—a brown-haired one shivered in a gray coat and red apron, but the green-skinned one next to her didn't seem to mind the cold at all. Matilda and Jimmy Searcaster. We'd stolen Melodie from them during Lena's Tale, so I definitely hoped they wouldn't recognize us.

But Chase had it covered.

When I glanced at the others to see if they'd noticed the Searcasters, all I saw were trolls. Not the kind that wore hockey masks and worked for the Snow Queen, or the huge kind that hid under bridges. These were like the ones I'd fought in the Hidden

Troll Court—short and squat and wearing just one piece of armor.

The one in shin guards looked me up and down and said, with Lena's voice, "Oh, that's *creepy*."

Up ahead, Forrel's laugh came from the troll in the helmet, and the troll wearing a skirt of chain mail smacked his arm. At least the dwarves were enjoying this.

The scratched-up breastplate in my glamour even had a little blood on the bottom. Gross. "Great detail, Chase," I said, making a face.

"I know," said the troll wearing a shoulder guard to my right, but he stumbled over an uneven patch of ice. I wondered how low his magic was running.

"You okay?" I asked him.

"Yeah." Chase was practically grunting, very troll-like.

Right. *Totally* okay. I could tell by the grumpy sidelong look he was shooting me.

Then I remembered, kicking myself for *not* remembering. Suddenly my heartbeat thudded *everywhere*, booming in my ears so loud I couldn't hear the snow crunching under our feet.

Chase grinned. It weirded me out that I could recognize that expression even when it was hidden under a glamour, complete with troll tusks. "I reserve the right to be cranky. I also have epic plans to sleep for roughly a hundred years after this."

He didn't actually say anything. I must have imagined it, I thought, smiling back, but the thumping in my ears didn't calm down. It might have even gotten worse. I felt kind of light-headed.

"Are *you* okay?" Lena-the-troll asked me, way too observant for a moment like this, and I really, *really* wished Chase had given me the glamour with the helmet.

The fox stopped for a second and shot us a look like, *Are you going to talk the whole way there?* We probably did need to keep our voices down. We were getting close, but we definitely weren't the only ones talking. Hundreds of voices hummed from the line, speaking dozens of languages.

Chase nudged me, looking hard at a spot in the line, right after a bunch of goblins and bulky bridge trolls. A man with a pointy face and a goatee slurped some coffee. A handful of his teeth were gold.

"Ferdinand the Unfaithful," I whispered. We'd fought him in the giant's desk. "Didn't we see him turn to stone?"

"Well, somebody turned him *back*," Chase said grimly as we stepped into line.

Now Hadriane turned around, her troll eyebrows raised, demanding quiet.

We shut up. A clan of witches stepped into line behind us. They had green skin, warts on their hands, and giant black hoods over bushy clouds of gray hair. The Wolfsbane clan—I'd kind of stolen their Dapplegrim in Atlantis. Chase's glamour must have been good, because none of them spared us a second glance.

So many people were in line. Ten times as many Characters as we had at EAS, and she probably had more inside.

Wars are about numbers, Forrel had said.

If that was true, we were screwed.

From here, the palace looked like an arc of skyscrapers. Its ice walls gleamed as brightly as mirrored glass, and its doors—at least five stories tall—were silver, the Snow Queen's black symbol etched over them. When they cracked open, the waiting line grew so quiet that you could hear the hinges groan.

Then the line moved forward, and cloaked in our troll glamour, we went with them. The fox darted around, trying not to get stepped on, until Lena picked her up.

A Wolfsbane witch gave us a weird look. Apparently trolls didn't keep foxes as pets.

"Pretty," I grunted, trying to sound like I wanted to fight for it.

Lena caught on. "Mine," she grunted back, hunching over the fox protectively.

Satisfied, the witch looked away and followed her sisters.

Thanks, Lena mouthed as we moved inside.

Nothing could have built the Snow Queen's palace except for magic. The building shouldn't have been possible. High ceilings are a challenge when giants are regular guests, but I couldn't even see the top of the receiving room. The space overhead just disappeared into shadow.

It was *way* darker inside. The Wolfsbane witches blinked at each other, rubbing their eyes and scowling.

We had just enough light to see that those lumpy things on the walls weren't icicles. Half were gargoyles, carved to look like ice griffins but with sneering human faces, and the other half were people—real ones, clawing at the ice they'd been frozen inside.

I didn't mind at all when the crowd pushed us away from them, farther into the room.

Lena pointed out an enormous balcony, about three stories from the ground, easily twice as wide as the house Mom was renting. A dozen figures stood up there, but I only recognized the Pied Piper. His red tracksuit definitely stood out. "I think the fox wants us to go that way. Maybe there's a door underneath," she whispered.

We shuffled forward, trying hard not to touch people since the feel of our hands wouldn't match our glamour. We got a lot of glares, but no one stopped us. Maybe trolls usually tried to get front row seats.

Lena stopped so abruptly that Hadriane crashed into her. A black door was closed in the milky white wall under the balcony, barely visible. I stopped breathing until I realized it couldn't be the door in my dream. It was made out of metal, not old wood.

Then I noticed what had halted Lena in her tracks—the row of gray wolves guarding it. The leather cuffs with the Snow Queen's symbol hung around their left forelegs.

The fox tried to squirm free. Lena-the-troll held her even tighter. *Now what?* she mouthed.

I looked at Hadriane, but the dwarf princess's head was craned back. Even the troll glamour couldn't hide the horror on her face.

At the balcony's edge was the Snow Queen, smiling at all the guests who had answered her invitation. Freedom agreed with her.

She looked like she had been carved from the freshest, smoothest snow. When she turned her head, her face glittered like snowflakes in the moonlight, and her hair fell around her like smooth spun gold. The white cloak hanging from her shoulders had those funny black specks in it, like you see in portraits of famous kings, and a crown of towering icicles sat on her brow. It was at least a foot high, impossibly heavy-looking for her slender neck, but she wore it like it was as natural a part of her body as her hands.

Lena clutched my arm—she'd never seen the Snow Queen in person before. Even Chase's shoulders had gone rigid, like they do when he's scared.

I think I'd been hoping, just a tiny bit, that the Glass Mountain had messed her up for good—that she would never recover all her magic, so I would have a better shot at stopping her.

But she was really back.

"Welcome to my palace." Even her voice had changed. It was more musical and more cutting at once, twisting straight into your brain like a song you hated but got stuck in your head anyway. "I thank you for coming. I know it was a long journey, and I would not invite you here unless I had a matter of import to share with you."

She gazed out right over our heads.

We were in the Snow Queen's palace. We were literally under her nose, and she had no idea we were here. It was a terrifying thought, but kind of awesome.

It would be way *more* awesome if we got past these wolves without getting captured.

I tapped the dwarves' shoulders and mouthed, *Wait for a diversion.* They nodded.

"A meeting to discuss the state of our world is long overdue," continued the Snow Queen, "and I fear the fault is mine. I was detained."

Detained? That was what she called it? No, she was downplaying it on purpose.

At least one person in the audience refused to swallow that. "You were defeated, Your Majesty." The people near the speaker shrank away until he was standing by himself—an old goblin, with his arms crossed and a circlet of rusted metal above his batlike ears. "Forgive me for being so blunt, my queen. I mean no disrespect, but these years without you have been long."

The wolves guarding the underside of the balcony didn't like that. They growled.

Solange spread her hands with a wistful *what can an evil queen do?* kind of smile. "I admit, my imprisonment was a great setback, but defeated? I don't believe so. Can a mere jail cell—even one as mighty as the Glass Mountain—smother a true and just cause such as ours? The years in prison stoked a fire within me, a fire to see our cause realized. For too long, our peoples have been squeezed into the forgotten corners of the world, squeezing out our might, our dignity, our very lifeblood. We have subsisted on the land left over from the humans, and that is no way to live."

The goblins around the one with the rusty circlet stood taller. She was winning them over.

"If we band together once again, we can end our exile," the Snow Queen said. "Together, we will make those who have stolen our homes tremble at our strength, and together, we will destroy them. We will take back the lands that the humans stole from us, and we can live as we were *meant* to live—as the proud masters of this earth."

The wolves guarding the balcony howled, and near the walls, some trolls in hockey masks beat their spears against their shields. But what really freaked me out was how much of the audience joined in.

Conviction is a kind of weapon, Hadriane had said. These people thought they were fighting for their very existence.

And worst of all, after meeting the Dwarves of Living Stone, I didn't really blame them.

"Forgive me again, my queen, for expressing such doubts," said the rusty-circlet goblin, "but I have grown old listening to your speeches. I do not want to spend the rest of my life making war if we won't live to see the results. Today I see an army still scattered—there, I see Ripper. . . ." My head whipped around to the back corner he pointed at, where the teeth of a huge furry shape gleamed in the shadows. "But one of your pillars is lost to us forever. And where are Likon and Ori'an? Where is General Searcaster? Where are the witches, who were your earliest supporters?"

With outraged howls, the wolves abandoned their posts and bounded into the audience.

"Stop!" the Snow Queen cried, and the pack halted in a tight circle around the rusty-circlet goblin. His face shone with sweat. "Wolves, your loyalty is commendable, but King Licivvil is not to be harmed. As I expressed on the invitation, this is a free forum, a chance to discuss our future openly and honestly."

Of course, the Snow Queen didn't call the wolves back, either. She just let them bare their fangs in a circle around the goblin.

Good. That left the door unguarded. All we needed was a diversion, and we could sneak over to it.

"I did not sit idly in my prison," admitted the Snow Queen. "My plans have already been set into motion. The Pied Piper's work last week is only one part. Searcaster and my other pillars have undertaken a task vital to our cause, but I have received word of their success—they will return momentarily. As for the witches, I confess I do not know." Here, her smile glimmered again, soothing and inviting at once. "However, a few of them are in the audience. Perhaps they can speak for themselves."

"I will speak for the witches." That cold angry voice sounded familiar, but I didn't recognize it until the crowd cleared around the new speaker.

Kezelda, the gingerbread witch. She pointed a crooked finger at the Snow Queen. "You poisoned me and twelve of my sisters when you poisoned Mildred Grubb's Ever After School, and you framed us to take the blame. You left us to die. I have brought proof."

She thrust something silver and square in the air: one of Lena's M3's. Then an illusion unfolded above her: the Snow Queen, as she looked in the Glass Mountain, with strawlike hair and slush-colored skin, saying, *"Rapunzel is the only suspect. Well, besides the witches, and all the witches are disposable."*

Chase grinned. *He* was the one who recorded that, back when Solange had us trapped in the Glass Mountain. We had no idea that the Director had shared it with the witches. I elbowed him—all the other trolls in the audience just looked confused.

Triumphant, Kezelda slapped the M3 shut, and the recording of the Snow Queen disappeared. "Since we witches are so disposable, I'm sure you can fight without us." Then she turned and strode toward the open doors and the glittering landscape beyond them.

A few wolves abandoned King Licivvil to go after Kezelda, but the Snow Queen raised a hand. "No, let her go. It's regrettable, of course, that Kezelda and her sisters have succumbed to the Ever Afters' trickery, but one clever illusion spell should not be enough to break our alliance. Our armies would be stronger without those with such weak allegiances."

I barely kept the fury off my troll-glamoured face—she was just going to pretend that the Director had made it up?

The Snow Queen turned to the green-skinned witches. "I trust you agree, witches of the Wolfsbane clan?"

One of the older-looking ones, bald under her hood, spoke up. "We have seen this already, as have all the witch clans, but its truth or falsehood doesn't concern us. We only ask that you allow us the opportunity to kill the Character named Aurora Landon."

I felt Lena peeking at me, and I froze, afraid to gulp or do anything else to give myself away.

"Granted, gladly," said the Snow Queen indifferently. "The girl is not significant."

"Aurora Landon has made an enemy of the Wolfsbane clan for life," replied the old green-skinned witch, "and we will see her dead."

Death seemed a little harsh.

"You're not the only one," said Ferdinand the Unfaithful, rubbing his jaw, and in the back, I saw Jimmy Searcaster's SUV-size head nodding.

I'd made a lot of enemies without realizing it. If the Snow Queen sent them after my family at the same time, I'd never be able to fight them all off.

The Snow Queen frowned just a little, the first time that morning that her gracious hostess act had slipped. She opened her mouth to say something else, but then a shadow crossed the doorway.

"We have arrived, Your Majesty," said Genevieve Searcaster, leaning on her basilisk-wrapped cane. A boulder with cement-gray wings sat on Searcaster's shoulder—Ori'an. Behind her ankles, a cloaked figure snuck in. He was human-size, but his wings tented the material above his shoulders. Like *that* fooled anybody. It had to be Torlauth.

Another colossal, blue-skinned figure stepped up behind Searcaster. Likon.

My heart sank. They'd found him. Searcaster had probably broken Lena's disorientation spell.

The whole audience scrambled out of the giants' way.

"Now," Hadriane-the-troll whispered in my ear.

Right. No one was looking at the balcony. Even the Snow Queen's gaze was fixed on her giants.

The black door under the balcony was locked, but Chase had it open an instant after he touched it. Hadriane slipped through after him, then Forrel, then Lena, and I brought up the rear. I looked back once.

Following Searcaster inside, Likon grinned, showing off teeth the exact same color as a fresh bruise. In each fist he carried a struggling winged figure.

Fael and the Seelie prince, the first Fey hostages in the Snow Queen's second war.

None of us wanted to talk about it.

So Lena just let the fluffy fox down in the long, dim tunnel behind the door. She bounded off, and we ran after her, clamping our hands on our weapons and packs to keep them from jingling. The floor was even but kind of slippery.

That wasn't a forum in there. It was a war council.

If only we'd known Solange was out, we could have stopped her from regathering her armies. If only we hadn't given her exactly what she needed to break out of prison. . . . No, I couldn't think like that. Hadriane was right—it didn't help anyone if I kept worrying about something I couldn't change. The quest was the only thing that mattered now.

The tunnel hit a dead-end. One sputtering torch lit up three more black doors, the Snow Queen's symbol carved under their doorknobs. All metal, not wood.

The fox pawed at the one on the left.

"Ready?" Forrel-the-troll asked, his spear slightly raised. Chase unsheathed his sword and nodded, his tusked face grim. Hadriane turned the handle, and I made sure to step in front of Lena, who just looked stunned.

The door swung open to a bright room full of small, round

tables. On each of them was a white card propped against a small chest of gold coins.

Not so scary, I thought, relaxing just slightly, but then a furry gray head popped up in the back. "You're not supposed to be here!" the wolf barked. "All trolls are to stand beside the doors and wait for Her Majesty's orders. Go back where you came from."

At least we knew Chase's glamour was still working.

"Pretty," Hadriane grunted, moving toward the closest coins as if entranced. Behind her, Forrel raised his spear.

"Dumb trolls! This is the third time this week!" The gray wolf trotted forward, weaving through the little tables. "Do something!"

A second voice piped up, much closer to us. A small red-brown wolf sat just inside the door. "Calm down. We know what to do. This way, trolls. Back in the entrance hall are the prettiest pretties of them all."

I stared at them, dumbfounded. Promising trolls "the prettiest pretties" never actually worked, did it? Even trolls weren't *that* stupid.

"Just two?" Forrel asked Chase in a low voice.

"Looks like," Chase replied.

The red-brown wolf's ears pricked up. "What?"

Then Chase's sword slid through his neck. Forrel's spear sailed through the air and nailed the gray wolf through the heart. That one gave a sort of strangled yelp, but then it was still.

The room filled with the metallic smell of blood. My stomach churned.

Hadriane squatted down and peered through the tables' legs, checking for hiding wolves. "Do you see any more?" I still couldn't look at the wolves' bodies. Instead, I moved to the closest table and picked up the little card leaning against the coin chest. KING LICIVVIL, it read.

The little fox sniffed at the first wolf, mildly interested, until Forrel pulled his spear free of its heart. "It seems we have found the treasury," the dwarf said.

"You mean the bribe room," said Chase, holding another name card. "I bet the Snow Queen only brings them back here after they've sworn Binding Oaths of allegiance."

"But only two wolves to guard them?" Hadriane said. "There must be some trick."

"Her wolves and trolls are spread kind of thin," Lena said. "Didn't it seem weird that she started the meeting without General Searcaster?"

This was as close as any of us had gotten to talking about the meeting.

"These coins—" I picked one up. Just touching it made me shiver. It had Solange's face on it, complete with her favorite icicle crown. "I mean, if you're trying to bribe people, shouldn't the chests be bigger?"

"Maybe she's hard-pressed for money too," Chase said hopefully.

"I found her accounts ledger!" Lena was probably the only Character in the world who bypassed all the coins in a treasury and went straight for a book instead. The ledger was bound in silver leather, small but thick. She started to read. "'General Genevieve Searcaster: 35 coins—paid. 50 children—handpicked, to be exchanged after meeting.'"

My hands balled into fists without me realizing it, and I crumpled the name card in my hand. "There's something wrong with the world if a kid is worth less than a gold coin."

"Maybe there's Fey fudge inside. I mean, which is tastier?" Chase said. The joke was so inappropriate that I just stared at him.

Hadriane didn't need to hear Searcaster might eat the twins.

The princess crossed to the corner of the room where the fox waited. "We can't stay and examine the treasury. The children are more important."

"You know, Chase," I said, as we streamed around the tables, "sometimes I wish someone would stop you from saying stuff like that. Your big mouth is going to get you in trouble someday."

Chase grinned, but before he could say anything else, Forrel slapped a hand over Chase's mouth, silencing him.

It was so unexpected and un-Forrel-like that I started to giggle. Lena and Hadriane too.

Chase shoved Forrel's hand away and glared at the dwarf. "Dude, not funny!"

"I didn't—" the dwarf sputtered, mortified. "I—my hand—it had a mind of its own."

"You just watch your back, dwarf," Chase said, "because sometime soon, when you least expect it, I'll—"

Lena gasped. "Rory, you're holding a coin, right? Look at the coin!"

This was such a bizarre request that I didn't question it. I just opened my palm and checked. "Oh, weird—it changed colors." Now it was a tarnished sort of pewter—the metal around Solange's carved face had gone black.

Lena stared at the coins on the table beside her. "It's a portable wish."

"Like the one that you used at the ball?" Chase asked.

Lena nodded. "Mia kept sneaking around the workshop, going through my papers. She must have found the recipe for a wish. But you saw it. That recipe makes a liquefied wish in a tiny jar. The Snow Queen has bound it to the metal. . . ." She scowled down

255

at them for a second, thinking. "Quick. Take as many as you can carry."

"Yeah, I guess the Director will want to see them." I scooped up a handful of coins and shoved them in my pocket.

"We are wasting *time*," Hadriane snapped. A frayed rope hung in the corner behind her. The fox jumped up, gripped it firmly between her teeth, and yanked. With the squeak of ice rubbing against ice, the walls rumbled apart, revealing a hidden stairwell twisting down into the darkness.

Oh yeah—like *that* was inviting.

The fox bounded down the steps, her fluffy tail waving at us as she moved out of sight.

"No, we need *all* the coins," Lena said. "What if one of the Snow Queen's allies makes a wish like I did—that no one can see them even if they're in front of you? What if you face someone a month from now who has wished that his blade would kill one hundred warriors before the battle ends?"

"Okay, okay, we get it." Chase picked up the heaviest chest he could find and poured it into the front pocket of his carryall.

But Hadriane was right too. There were dozens of chests here. We couldn't really spare the time to get them all.

The princess stomped over to the nearest table and picked up a coin. "I wish that no one—whether it be the Snow Queen, her allies, or enemies—be able to remove a coin from these tables."

"Oh. Good idea," I said, but Chase lifted a coin out of the nearest chest and raised one skeptical eyebrow.

"That wish is too big," Lena said encouragingly. "You need to add a limitation. Like, unless you sing the ABC's backward fourteen times in a row, or some sort of time limit."

"Until a hundred years have passed," Hadriane added.

When Chase tried to collect another coin, it stayed there no matter how hard he yanked, like the whole pile had been super-glued down. "Yep. That did it."

"We go *now*," Hadriane said. "As soon as they reach this room, they will know that someone has interfered."

Forrel nodded. "And if the Snow Queen can't give them the coins, she will go straight for the children instead."

The dwarf princess disappeared down the secret stairway. I went next, trying hard not to think about how far down we were going, trying not to imagine what would happen if my foot missed a step. . . .

Finally the stairway stopped twisting and opened into a cramped chamber. Thick icicles hung from the ceiling, heavy-looking and tipped with sharp, gleaming points. Under them, two doors stood opposite each other.

The one made out of rusting iron was massive—wider and taller than a bridge troll. The bars over the window were crooked, like someone had bent them out of shape and then bent them back.

But the smaller one made my heart stop. It was the first wooden one I'd seen. It wasn't the cracked, ancient wood from my dream, but except for its pale color, it was almost identical. Etched into the metal under the small silver handle was that scrolling *S*, with a snowflake hanging out in the bottom curve.

More wooden doors probably waited on the other side. My Tale was *that* way. I was almost sure.

It wasn't fair, having to choose between it and Miriam's quest.

The lock on the big metal door clicked under Chase's hand, and, gripping my sword hilt, I turned my back on the wooden door. I knew what I needed to do.

I'd gotten everyone out here, and Miriam had given *everything* for this quest. I had to make sure Philip got home safely. I owed her that.

My Tale would have to come later.

When Hadriane swung the metal door open with the screech of rusty hinges, I sprinted through first.

Two trolls in hockey masks sat across from each other, their spears leaning against the wall. They both had their hands outstretched for a game of knuckle-thumping—I guess trolls are too stupid to play cards—and when they saw me, they jumped to their feet. The closer one was still reaching for his weapon when I ducked inside his guard and smashed my sword hilt into his temple. He dropped like a stone. When the second one tried to jab his spear in my face, I blocked it easily, trapping it against the floor. Before I could deliver a knock-out punch, a Bat of Destruction walloped the troll, so hard that his hockey mask broke. *That* troll didn't get up either.

"I wish that they would sleep until we leave this palace," Lena said, and then she dropped a pewter coin beside them.

The troll glamour over us disappeared.

I turned to Chase, wondering if he would say I should be over this killing thing by now, but he wasn't looking at me. His gaze was locked on the hall ahead.

"The Snow Queen's prison," Hadriane whispered.

It was so big. The cells stretched down and down, and even though the corridor was wide, I felt locked in. It was too white. Even the metal doors were bleached pale with frost. It didn't remind me of a dungeon at first. It was as bare and stark as a hospital room.

"That witch, Kezelda, was very brave," said Hadriane, staring too. "By the end of the day, she will be imprisoned here. Or dead."

Forrel nodded. "She couldn't have made it very far before they took her."

The fox walked briskly down the corridor.

"Well, if they're taking her *here*," Lena said, her voice kind of squeaky but her face determined, "then we'd better not hang around and wait to be caught." She followed the fox.

I peeked inside one of the cells. It was just a hollow block of ice, empty except for the frozen manacles hanging from the wall and the stains below it, a patchwork of sickly browns and ugly yellows and reds so dark, they were almost black. They had frozen solid a long time ago. They were part of the floor now. No one could ever wipe them away.

The dwarves didn't seem to notice—they walked carefully, their weapons raised like they were expecting more guards—but then I glanced at Chase.

He was whiter than the walls around us. He put one foot in front of the other as mechanically as the sorceress's doll. Even though it was so cold that our breath fogged in front of us, sweat dripped from his curls.

Cal and Dyani had died here.

I'd done this too. I'd forced Chase to visit this prison. I was responsible for that look on his face—like he was going to throw up. Or worse, stop and search the cells for something his brother might have left behind.

I wanted to tell him that I was sorry or to give him a hug, but the others would notice. They would wonder what was wrong.

I just took his hand, so he would know that he wasn't alone.

We didn't stop walking, but Chase looked at me.

He lifted his other hand—in his palm was a gold wishing coin. Then, so softly I barely heard him, he whispered, "I wish I knew what happened to my brother here."

If I'd known this was what he was planning, I would have snatched it away.

His gaze unfocused, and he turned *gray*. That wasn't even the worst part. Chase was years older than the rest of us, and suddenly, he *looked* it. As the coin dulled to pewter he looked older than his parents ever had, more ancient than even Rapunzel. More devastated too.

And I couldn't do anything except walk beside him, my hand squeezing his, and watch Lena, Hadriane, and Forrel's backs, willing them not to turn around. If they did, I would step in front of Chase—I wouldn't let them see his face, not when he looked so vulnerable.

I wondered when this had happened. Not long ago, I'd tried to convince him to share his secrets. Now I was just grateful he had someone watching out for him.

When his grip around my hand grew stronger, I knew his mind had come back from wherever the wish had taken him. His gaze was on that awful floor.

"You couldn't wait?" I could think of a thousand better times to make that wish, but I wasn't mad. Not when the color was coming back into his cheeks.

"It was worse not knowing." His voice was ragged but quiet.

The others were way ahead of us, too far away to hear, but pretty soon, they would reach the door at the end of the corridor. They would wonder where we were. They would look back.

"He died first," Chase said. "They made her watch. She almost broke free, the second the last blade fell, but when he was gone, she was gone too."

I couldn't see what he'd seen. I couldn't even imagine it, but I could see *Chase*. I could see the new shadows haunting his eyes. I could hear his deep shaky breaths and the way his voice had been stripped raw.

I hated the Snow Queen. I hated how I could never make this

better, no matter how many wolves I killed and how many coins I wished on.

"It's all right," Chase said. "I thought it was the other way around. I thought he lost Dyani, and he decided not to even try to come home. I didn't want to think that, but I did."

I stared at him. There was no way watching your own brother die could actually be comforting, but I didn't have time to say so.

"You guys?" Lena whispered. She'd reached the door at the end. It must have been two stories tall. "Did you see something?"

"Sword out," Chase told me. Then he let go and unsheathed his own weapon. He strode down the hall, head held high. "Just a pile of rags in one of the cells. Nothing to worry about," he said, so confidently that the lie rang true.

Someday I wanted to learn that trick. I wanted to be able to feel that much and then just push it aside. I didn't always want to be the one trailing behind, my feelings written all over my face.

"You okay?" Lena asked me.

I nodded, not looking at Chase, because I couldn't trust myself to speak.

Hadriane patted my shoulder. "I feel it too. This place has seen much death."

"All the more reason for us not to linger here," Forrel said, lifting Chase up to the lock.

It took him less than ten seconds to open it. Then the door squealed open, and Chase leaped through, sword raised high, his gaze sweeping back and forth. "No guards?" he said, lowering his weapon.

I'd kind of expected another long white hall, but it was just one enormous holding cell, about twice the size of a basketball court, probably built to hold a giant.

But not that day. Right then, the only prisoners were kids in their pajamas, lying on the stained floor, so very still.

The fox darted over them, and I had no idea if she was just leaving after a job well done or if we had a little farther to go. None of us made any move to follow her, and none of the Portland kids flinched as she ran past, not even when she stepped on them.

It was too dark in here to tell if they were breathing.

The ledger in the treasury hadn't said anything about the children being *alive* when they were given away.

Hadriane gave a panicked almost-sob. That freaked me out even more. I couldn't imagine her crying.

Forrel knelt next to the nearest body—a lanky middle-schooler in green flannel pants with yellow O's all over them—and pressed fingers to the boy's neck. "Just asleep, Haddy."

"Whoa. Are those Tables of Plenty?" Chase said.

Tables had been pushed against the wall. They looked like silver patio furniture for the Unseelie Court, all twisting vines and elaborate metal flowers. But I sincerely doubted the Fey would eat any of the food: mac and cheese with bits of bacon; fancy thin-crust pizza; grilled cheese with sundried tomato; falafel; fajitas; and a *bunch* of yummy-looking sandwiches. There was a table of steaming soups and another with fancy breads, biscuits, and pastries. There was even a table of chocolaty-smelling coffee drinks.

Chase walked closer, obviously hungry. "Wow. This spread blows the Table of Never Ending Instant Refills out of the water."

"No, it doesn't," said a clear, *distinctly* nonsleepy voice behind us. "All that food is laced with some drug. Eat anything on there, and you'll be knocked out in five minutes."

"Oh. I'll pass then," said Chase, abandoning free food for maybe the first time ever.

"Evan!" Lena cried, and there he was. He picked his way carefully over all the sleeping bodies, carrying the fox guide in his arms and grinning. Lena darted through the drugged kids. "Are you guys okay?"

"Fine. Hungry, but fine," said Evan. "I haven't eaten in a couple days."

We'd actually *found* them. We'd made it in time.

"Better set up that portal," I told Lena. "It'll take a while to evacuate if most of the kids are unconscious."

"They're not all unconscious," said Evan. "We could either starve and keep watch, or eat and pass out. Some of us have been taking turns. Philip and Mary have just woken up. They'll be glad to see you."

Philip.

He was almost safe. When this was all over, I would repeat what Miriam had told me our first night of the quest. I'd tell him how much she'd regretted what she'd said.

I concentrated on not stepping on anybody, which was harder than it sounded on a slippery floor crowded with sleeping kids. They didn't need to wake up with bruised fingers on top of everything else.

Evan led us to a few dozen kids stumbling around like sleepwalkers, their steps kind of jerky, their eyes red and half-lidded. "These guys are kind of on patrol. They've been eating just a few bites, which might explain the zombie impressions."

"You don't even have guards," Chase said, clearly delighted about it.

"We *do*." They must have caused some problems if Evan sounded so bitter. "It took us a couple days to spot them. We think they're dolls, like that Mia kid last year, but they look like people we know. At first they mixed in with the sleepwalkers. But then Jamal, Philip, Mary, and I tried the door, and they rushed us, blowing these silver whistles. The wolves were here in five minutes. They said they would let us off with a warning, but they had permission to eat the next kid who tried to escape."

"So you sent the foxes out instead," said Lena.

Evan nodded. "On the march here, I saved a den of kits from getting trampled. The mom fox convinced some of her friends to help us out."

"But where are the dolls *now*?" I asked.

Forrel stared at the cell's shadows. "You've chased them to the walls."

"Mostly to the back. They haven't blown their whistles, so they haven't seen you yet," Evan said. "We threw food at them, to mark which of us were spy dolls. Since then, they've just been pacing."

I was impressed. They hadn't just waited around to get rescued. They'd gotten ready—they'd *helped*.

These weren't just a bunch of scared little kids. They were *Characters*.

We got past the circle of sleepwalking patrollers, where a few people sat on the floor. I recognized some of them. Mary's jaw actually fell open, and a split second later, she burst into tears. Beside her, Philip blinked at us blearily, unhurt, even *smiling*. Jamal had obviously eaten recently—he'd passed out behind them.

Hadriane pushed her way to Evan's side. "Have you seen two children? They were dressed in white and brown. Sleeping clothes made out of rabbit skin."

"Oh, yeah," Evan told Hadriane. "And they're the bossiest little kids I've ever—"

"Haddy?" said one young voice. It came from a stocky little girl. Her messy pigtails were the exact same shade as Hadriane's chestnut hair.

Then Hadriane was running, and Ima too. Out sprinted another figure in ripped brown furs—Iggy. They collided halfway, and the twins' hug knocked Hadriane down. The princess was laughing and trying to get her arms around them both and kissing their faces all at once.

I felt a tiny bit sad, which was stupid. The happy reunion should have proved the long quest had all been worth it.

Maybe because it wasn't over yet. We still needed to get them out of here. "Lena," I said.

"On it." Lena knelt down, and out of her carryall, she pulled dragon scales, the snow servant tile, and a Tupperware labeled INGREDIENTS FOR A PORTAL.

From the floor Mary grinned weakly at us. "How long?"

Lena was already counting out dragon scales. "Fifteen minutes."

Philip's eyes weren't blinking so much. He focused on me. "So you finally got your Tale?"

"No, it was Miriam's Tale." My heart sank, especially when he glanced around, hopeful.

Then he asked the question I'd been dreading. "Where is she?"

I couldn't tell him. Lena's hands paused on her Tupperware. It was Chase who put a hand on Philip's shoulder. "I'm really sorry, but she's gone."

He just nodded, completely gutted, like Chase had been in the prison a few moments ago, and I felt even guiltier than I did when we first lost her. "I knew it. A new guard showed up the day after we tried to unlock the door, and the doll looked exactly like Miriam. I hoped the Snow Queen was just punishing me for trying to escape, but . . ."

Lena's hands started mixing. "She came even though the

Director cancelled the quest. She was so brave, Philip. She—"

A Miriam doll?

The Miriam in my dream had been in tears, but the Snow Queen wouldn't make one of her spies cry.

"Where exactly *is* the Miriam doll?" I had to see it, before I said anything to get Philip's hopes up.

Chase and Lena both shot me a look that clearly said, *Don't bother him with questions*. But Philip only pointed over my left shoulder, kind of numbly.

I stood on my tiptoes, trying to see over the patrol. "Chase, lift me up."

"What?" Chase stared at me.

"Or you could jump up for me—" I started, already having second thoughts, but then Chase's arms were around my waist, and my feet left the ground. Wow, he was a *lot* stronger than he used to be. Steadying myself on his shoulders, I scanned the room.

There she was. Miriam, her straight black hair falling out of the braid Hadriane had done for her, her eyes on me, her expression flat.

Lifting a slender silver whistle to her mouth, about to call the wolves.

But *alive*.

The whistle screeched. I winced and planted hands over my ears as Chase set me back down, but the sound just multiplied. The other spies must have blown theirs too.

"Are you insane?" Evan demanded. I could barely hear him. "What do you think the sleepwalking patrol was for? We didn't want them to know you were here!"

Oops. "Miriam, she's—her braid—" I started, but with that noise stabbing my eardrums, forming whole sentences was impossible.

Lena held up a gold coin. "I wish the whistles were silent!"

It was like she'd hit a mute button, but my ears still rang. The patrol crouched down, cringing. Even some of the drugged kids were starting to stir.

"It's no use now." Evan started to pace. "You don't understand how many wolves will come down here. Way too many to fight!"

I pointed at Miriam. "That's not a doll! That's *her*! Look at the braid! It has four strands, and a leather tie thing. Hadriane did that."

Beyond the sleepwalking patrol, six spies crept out of the shadows. I bet all of them were real kids, just like Miriam.

We'd heard about this in Philip's Tale. Searcaster had told the Pied Piper that the Snow Queen had a plan.

The matches must have been a trap. Freezing out on the ice, the escapees must have struck matches until a transport spell kicked in and whisked the kids here, where the Snow Queen had enchanted them. Miriam would never spend a few days right in front of her brother without trying to break him out, unless she was under a spell.

"The Snow Queen's matches could have copied what she looked like. . . ." Lena said doubtfully.

Explaining was taking too long. I pulled a gold coin out of my pocket and told it, "I wish you would show us the living Miriam Chen-Moore. The original, not a copy."

The coin flew away, over the patrol, and sailed straight into Miriam's forehead. She didn't even flinch. The coin—now a dull pewter—tumbled to her feet, and she stepped over it.

"You're right," Lena whispered.

"I don't get it," Philip snapped. "How can a dumb coin tell me whether or not that spy is Miriam?"

But we didn't have time to answer his questions.

"We can't change her back if the wolves get in here," Chase pointed out. "Evan, how much time do we have?"

"Five minutes, at most," replied Evan, taking the axe Forrel handed him. "Small entrances will open up along the walls."

"The dreams . . ." Hadriane hugged the twins so close that they tried to squirm free. "The ones in which we are captured."

I went cold. This couldn't be how that happened. After standing unnoticed under the Snow Queen's balcony, after snooping through her treasury and sneaking through her prison, I couldn't have just called the soldiers that captured us into this room.

But I couldn't just leave Miriam to that brainwashing spell either.

"The combs," I said suddenly. "We can set them along the walls so nothing can get in."

Chase was tempted. "No," he said reluctantly. "They're too valuable—we won't be able to retrieve them, and we can't risk losing them."

"We can't risk losing *period*," I reminded him.

He still shook his head. "Save them in case we need a second line of defense."

So I dug them out of my carryall and stuck them in my pocket, where I could reach them.

Already distracted with the portal, Lena passed her pack to Chase. "The Bats."

I breathed a sigh of relief. Maybe we didn't have to be captured after all. If *anything* could hold the wolves off long enough for us to get these kids out, it was the Bats of Destruction.

"You saw bats?" Evan said, confused.

Chase took the pack. "Evan, Forrel, come help me put these along the wall."

The line of spies reached the sleepwalking patrol, and then they stopped, waiting for backup. When the boys jogged past them, the closest spy—a tall, skinny boy in sweatpants and a faded hockey jersey—tried to grab them, but Chase, Forrel, and Evan were way faster.

"Focus on Miriam," Chase called back to us. "We've got this."

Hadriane lifted a coin. "I wish that the enchantment over the spying children was broken." But the wish must have been too big. The coin stayed gold.

Lena was obviously stressing about creating the portal under these conditions, but she told Hadriane, "The enchantment is too strong for the coin's magic to reverse. Try another wish."

Iggy snatched the coin out of his big sister's palm. "Show us how to break the enchantment."

Nothing happened.

"No, you have to phrase it right," Ima said, grabbing it from him. "I wish you would show us how to break the enchantment over those spy kids."

The coin flew up out of her hand and zoomed straight to the floor, carving out a message so fast that Hadriane and the twins scurried out of its way: *Save one, and you'll save the others*.

"I hoped for more detailed *instructions*," Ima told it indignantly, but the coin clattered to the ice, pewter-colored and useless.

Now we had three minutes left before the wolves arrived.

Miriam's stare was so blank. I wondered if we could just capture all the spies and haul them back to EAS. The grown-ups probably knew how to fix them.

"That's really my sister?" Philip said, his voice cracking. "She's alive?"

"Yes," said Hadriane.

Then Philip sprinted for his sister. I should have guessed that he was just as impatient to save Miriam as she had been to save him.

Every single one of the spies' heads snapped straight in Philip's direction, perfectly synchronized.

"No, wait!" I stumbled after him. "Don't go alone!"

"We'll help!" cried Ima, and the footsteps of two small dwarfs pounded behind me.

I thought Hadriane would protest, but when I glanced back, she was passing some cords to the twins. "I know you're angry that they've been working for the Snow Queen, but be gentle with these humans. They didn't know what they were doing, and the tallest is a friend of mine."

Philip wove through the sleepwalkers like he'd borrowed

Chase's wings, and then he was right in front of his sister, grabbing her shoulders. "Miriam!"

She tried to punch him. The rest of the spies swarmed.

I threw myself between Philip and a little girl with cartoon unicorns and a chocolate stain on her nightgown. She kicked me in the shins with her bony bare feet. Then I had the really embarrassing job of wrestling with an elementary-schooler.

The royal dwarves were way more efficient. When a burly teenage girl reached for Philip with both arms, Ima stuck out a leg and tripped her. Hadriane pinned her flat, arms behind her back, and Iggy tied the teenager up.

Miriam slapped her brother's face hard, but Philip didn't let her go. "You are Miriam Yu Chen-Moore. You're *obsessed* with tennis. When Dad told us he got a new position at the University of Portland, you cried, because you thought moving meant quitting tennis."

It was hard to tell with Unicorn Nightgown kicking me, but I thought Miriam flinched. Obviously this was an embarrassing story even if an enchantment made her forget who she was.

"Nobody messes with you on your team," Philip continued. "They know you can smack a tennis ball in their face. No one messes with you period. Or me, when you're around. The last time someone tried was kindergarten. A fifth grader hit me on the bus, so you knocked him down and kicked him. You said . . ." Miriam punched half-heartedly at his chest, but a frown creased her face, the first expression we'd seen on any of the enchanted spies. Even Unicorn Nightgown had gone still. "You said, 'We come as a package. You touch him, and *I* come out swinging.' You are *my* big sister, and if you don't stop trying to hit me, I'm telling Mom when we get home."

Then Miriam looked at her brother. "Philip?"

"Hey," he said weakly.

"Oh my God, *Philip*!" Then she hugged him so hard that they both fell down, and they were doing the same laugh-cry thing that Hadriane and the twins had done.

I wanted that. I wanted someone in my family to know me that well. I wanted someone who could understand exactly where I was coming from—from Mom's insane worry, Brie's constant talking, and Dad's general cluelessness to the awesome strange truth of EAS. Not as someone who could ground me, but someone who could live it with me. I'd *always* wanted that. I'd *always* wanted to be a sister.

I should have been happy that Brie was having a baby, *just* happy and excited to suggest names and come to the birth and help my sister grow up. But the Snow Queen had ruined it.

I hated her for that, too.

The unicorn nightgown girl head-butted me. "Who are you?"

Wow, she was back to normal, and after getting kidnapped by a magic piper, she had definitely learned the stranger-danger lesson.

"Uh. Why am I all tied up?" said the kid the dwarves had just taken down.

"'Save one, and you'll save all the others,'" repeated Hadriane. "Ima, Iggy, release them. Quickly."

Not that Miriam or Philip noticed any of this.

"I bet you're glad you're not the only child *now*," Philip said, laughing.

"Of course." Miriam wiped her face on her sleeve, but her smile was humongous. "I mean, whatever. Shut up. I come all this way to rescue you, and—"

"I just rescued *you*." Philip grinned as they got to their feet. "You realize that, right?"

"Maybe." Then Miriam threw an arm around his shoulders, hugging him hard.

Getting jealous was stupid. So was getting mad that I might never have that with my own sister, but that didn't stop me.

At least one disaster had been averted. "Lena, how's it coming?"

"Five minutes more," she called back, and *that* was the moment dark narrow doors slid open along the walls, close to the floor. In the vast chamber, they looked like tiny coin slots.

The wolves were coming.

I pointed to Lena and told Unicorn Nightgown, "Go over there. That's where the portal will be." Then I unsheathed my sword. Shadowy shapes moved in the openings. "Chase!"

He grinned. "Up, bats! Hole them up in those tunnels. Don't let them in here."

All across the chamber, the Bats of Destruction sailed into the slots. All across the chamber, yelps and whines rang out, but not one wolf managed to make it inside.

"Whoa," said Evan, impressed.

It was just like Golden Gate Park. We *could* escape—we just had to hold the pack off.

Then the wolves tried squeezing inside two at a time, so that the bats had to beat back both of them. Some bats managed, but a few of our enemies wiggled through. The first one had an X-shaped scar on his snout. Lieutenant Cross. His black lips curled away from his fangs, his gaze fixed on the sleeping kids on the floor, spread out like a wolf's feast.

The magic of my sword flared, and I sprinted. Cross's hind legs bent, but by the time he left the ground, I was there, smashing my sword hilt between his ears. He dropped, his four legs sprawled. A white wolf bounded in three slots to my right, and it took a snap kick and a two-handed smack with the flat of my blade to bring it down.

"We have incoming!" cried Miriam, standing beside Philip. Trolls marched through the huge front door, seven hockey masks across and five deep. Their spear butts struck the floor in unison.

"We will take care of it!" called Hadriane.

Then the dwarf siblings charged, and with a flurry of Ima's throws, Iggy's kicks, and Hadriane's axe, four trolls went down.

A red-brown wolf and a black ran at me together, and while I was ducking away from one and punching the other, I heard Chase shout, "Lena?"

"Two minutes!" she called back.

"Oh, crap." And he sounded so upset that I looked over to see if he needed backup. Seven wolves lay in a bloody circle around him, but he wasn't looking at them. His eyes were on the door.

"What do we have here?" said General Searcaster, blocking the whole entrance.

She surveyed the prison cell—the trolls and the dwarves pausing their battle, Miriam and Philip standing side-by-side, Lena kneeling inside the ring of sleeping children, the sleepwalking patrol and ex-spies guarding her, the fallen wolves around me and Chase, and the Bats of Destruction still whaling away at the slots.

None of us could fight a woman as big as a building, who had almost as much magic as the Snow Queen herself.

I *knew* we should have set up the combs.

I ran, a hand in my pocket. If I could just get between her and the rest of the kids . . .

"Ah," the giant said, like she'd finally understood what was taking so long, and she pointed her basilisk-wrapped walking stick at the walls. "Up, bats! Quash this insurrection!"

No, I thought. It wasn't possible. They were *Lena's*.

The Bats of Destruction swiveled away from the slots. Then one of them flew at my face.

I twisted away. It glanced off my cheek, hard enough for dark spots to open up across my vision.

Another bat struck Forrel across the shoulders so hard he fell.

Miriam screamed, then Lena.

Not every invention needs to be brought forth. A sword has two edges. Rapunzel should have just *told* Lena that Searcaster would hijack our weapons.

Chase ran for me. "Rory, get down!"

Too late. A bat smashed into the back of my head, knocking me to the ground. One more burst of pain, and everything went black.

Something cold pressed up against my aching cheek.

I thought, for a second, that we'd managed to get back and Gretel was holding an ice pack to my face in the EAS infirmary. But if we were safe, who had trapped my arms behind my back? I looked.

The Snow Queen's face was only a foot from mine, her glacier-pale eyes inspecting me like a troll inspects a pretty war trophy, with glee and triumph and *appreciation*. Her hand was touching my *face*. With a gasp, I jerked away from her.

Bad idea. Moving made my head throb and the room spin. I would have probably fallen if two troll guards weren't holding me up. Geez, was this what bad guys felt like after I knocked them out? Dying probably hurt less.

"Wonderful of you to join us, Rory Landon," whispered the Snow Queen.

"You're okay," came Lena's relieved, trembly voice beside me.

Her glasses were bent, her eyes swelling, and she was very still, trying to lean away from the troll pinning her arms.

Three trolls held Chase down on Lena's other side—rust-colored blood had dried beneath his nose, but he stopped struggling when he saw that I was up. Miriam wept with fury, trying to squirm out of her guard's grip, but Philip just stood there, stoic, not acknowledging anyone. Behind them, a troll held all four of our carryalls in his arms, like they needed guarding too.

I looked on my other side. Forrel, Ima, and Iggy must have fought the hardest—they had all been forced to their knees. Ropes covered their entire torsos, spears inches from their throats. Hadriane was the only dwarf standing, but she wouldn't fight, not when the twins and Forrel were down.

We couldn't die here. I couldn't do that to Mom.

Then the Snow Queen walked to the very edge of the balcony, and once I saw the audience, stretching out and out to the colossal open doors, I realized we were back in the entrance hall.

"How did we get *here*?" I asked.

"Stairs in the walls. They had to carry you," Lena whispered. "It's my fault—the bats—"

"No talking," grunted one of my troll guards. The Snow Queen had decided to speak.

"We have already discussed the Pied Piper's most recent catch." Solange gestured below her.

Oh no. The kidnapped kids were here too, right in the front, under the balcony—all of them, even the ones who'd been in a drugged sleep. The Pied Piper guarded them, his wooden flute raised to his lips. He would enchant them the second they tried to resist.

"But we have had a new development." The Snow Queen's

arm swept back to us, and my face flamed. "Behold the rescuers that the Canon has sent. These are their best, their strongest—one Tale bearer and the so-called Triumvirate. It took my forces only a moment to subdue them."

All of her forces gloated about it too. Searcaster stood to the right of her mistress's balcony, and in front of Ripper's wolf army, four pillars guarded the other side. I guess the sorceress-giant had convinced the Snow Queen to promote her son, even though Jimmy Searcaster definitely wasn't the scariest villain ever. Likon still held the Fey princes, but they had stopped struggling. The Seelie kid looked like he had passed out. Prince Fael just stared at us, terrified.

"We have expected the EASers for some time, but it hurt to see these dwarves with them," said the Snow Queen. "Their people are my sworn allies. I am willing to listen to an explanation for this betrayal. One of them has volunteered to speak on their behalf."

When her guard let her go, Hadriane stepped forward, her jaw set.

I started shaking my head. She *wouldn't*.

Lena whispered, "They're *making* her, Rory. Searcaster threatened the twins if—" Then a troll shook her to shut her up.

"Haddy, *no*," Forrel said.

The princess bent down and whispered, "You'll keep them safe? You'll see them home?"

"Of course—" Forrel said.

"Don't watch," Hadriane told the twins. Iggy's face was white, and tears glinted on Ima's cheeks. When they closed their eyes, she added, "I love you."

"Come here, child." The Snow Queen sounded kind, but her impatience was written all over her face. "Tell them."

The princess stepped to the balcony's edge. She was so *calm*. "I am Hadriane of the Living Stone Dwarves. My father allied with Solange more than ten years ago. You may have heard of Kiivinsh, the city of ice her sorceress-giant built for us, and my father has often said we can never pay back what she has given us. It is true that her gifts are great."

The Snow Queen smiled graciously, pretending she hadn't fed Hadriane all her lines.

"But it is also true that she *takes* what she wants," said Hadriane, and a scowl darkened Solange's face. This wasn't part of the script. "Seven nights ago, when the Pied Piper led the children past our gates, he called out my brother and sister, heirs to the throne. She kept them prisoner alongside the human children."

"Don't—" Forrel whispered. His troll guards looked to the Snow Queen, waiting for her to give the order to start slaying the hostages.

Hadriane didn't look back. She didn't see the twins' eyes pop open with sudden delight. "She calls us her allies, and yet she is as ruthless with us as she is with her enemies. She speaks of making her allies masters of the earth, but in truth, I believe she sees only one master in her vision of the future. And she crowned herself queen long ago."

Solange raised a hand in Hadriane's direction. I thought that she was just doing a spell, like the one Arica used to take away my voice when I was a flower-bird, but when the Snow Queen flicked her fingers, shards of ice flew. All four thudded into Hadriane's chest, straight into her heart.

The three dwarves cried out, and I did too.

Then Hadriane collapsed, her head turned toward me. I saw the resolve in her eyes.

And then I saw the light go out of them.

It would take something truly tragic for my father's people to change their minds.

It had been on purpose. She had *meant* to die. She'd wanted to show everyone who the Snow Queen really was.

"That was necessary, I'm afraid." The Snow Queen mixed regret and apology in her voice. She even bent down to close Hadriane's eyes, and I hated her for touching my friend. "In private, the princess confessed that her father had ordered these questers imprisoned as I'd requested, and she had defied him and me. Alone among the Dwarves of Living Stone, she was a traitor."

A few members of the audience were *nodding*. No, the Snow Queen couldn't actually *recover* from this. Hadriane's death couldn't be a waste.

"And traitors cannot be tolerated. They must be executed as swiftly as possible. For without trust among us, we're at the mercy of one another, and the humans have won," said the Snow Queen. "Is that what you want?"

"No!" screamed voices from the crowd.

But only a few. The rest were silent. Either watching Solange murder the dwarf princess had shaken them up, or they were still deciding.

I could practically see the wheels inside the Snow Queen's head turning as she calculated. "But never let it be said that I am without mercy. My first impulse is to execute these questers as well, but I suppose I could content myself with seeing them in my dungeons. I will give them the opportunity to save their lives. A duel, I think. I will nominate my champion, and they may nominate their own. Is that not fair?"

None of us were stupid enough to think that the Snow Queen

actually meant it. We would only live as long as her guests were here.

Then Forrel said, "Yes."

Of course. He'd promised Hadriane he'd keep the twins safe. He would play by the Snow Queen's rules from now on.

"Very good. As for my champion . . ." The Snow Queen peered into the audience, making a big show of looking over her allies. A bunch of trolls actually raised their hands, but she ignored them. "Torlauth di Morgian," she said finally.

He'd been in the very back, trying to creep toward the door, still hiding behind that stupid cloak. When he threw it off, I could see the fury on his face. Word was going to get back to the Seelie Court that Torlauth had allied with Solange and sold out their heir. The days when he could play both sides were over.

He flew, his bronze hair waving like a banner behind him, and after less than a minute, he landed at the Snow Queen's side, his hands curled into fists, his cobalt wings buzzing behind him. He glanced over us eagerly.

He couldn't wait to take out his frustration on one of us, and that made him twice as dangerous.

The Snow Queen looked our way too. "Well? Who will you nominate as your champion? Who is the bravest among you?"

I thought Forrel would volunteer, but Chase was faster. His voice was so smug you would have thought he'd won already. "That would be . . ." He paused for effect, and I was *furious* at him for making the choice for us, for putting himself in so much danger.

His gaze slid straight to me. "Rory."

veryone stared, like they couldn't believe what he'd said.

Even me. Especially me.

Then the Snow Queen said exactly what I was thinking. "*What did you say?*"

"You heard me." Chase grinned. I wished he wouldn't. I wished, just once, he wouldn't act so confident. "You didn't ask for the strongest fighter, or the smartest, or the one of us who wanted to fight ugly Fey traitors the most. You asked for the bravest, and from day one, that has always been Rory."

It would have hurt less if someone had pried open my ribs and punched me in the heart.

What he said wasn't true. If it was, I would have listened in Arica's house. I would have asked Chase to tell me what he'd said I didn't want to know.

"This loyalty is touching." The Snow Queen gestured to the trolls clutching my arms. They let go.

"It's not loyalty. Rory's going to win." Chase sounded so sure.

A troll returned my sword to me, hilt first, and I took it, trying to think.

"Only a naive child believes without question that his side will win," said the Snow Queen. "You probably also believe that good triumphs over evil, and all those simplistic ideals."

"I'm not talking about good versus evil," Chase said. "I'm talking about Rory against you. *You* just put a sword in her hand and said you'll kill us unless she does something. Let's look at the track record for how that worked out the last couple times. Rory: two. Snow Queen: zilch."

He was picking up where Hadriane had left off. He was going to get himself killed. "Chase, *shut up*."

"She is just a scared little girl," snapped the Snow Queen. I stared at her hands, terrified that they would flick ice darts at Chase. "Look at her—paler than me. You've chosen a poor champion."

"She is your equal," Chase said, and I hated how brave he was. "And in a few minutes, everybody in the audience will know it. Then maybe they'll think twice about allying themselves with some washed-up villain who's met her match in a thirteen-year-old."

He'd gone too far. One of his guards backhanded him across the mouth. He started bleeding, and I completely lost it. "No! Don't hurt him!"

Two trolls tried to hold me back, but the runner's high had taken hold. I stabbed the first in the shoulder and punched the second so hard he flew into Torlauth. More trolls rushed me, and I snap-kicked and sliced through their ranks. The guard hit Chase again and raised his hand to hit him a third time. I would cut it off. I would *kill* him for touching Chase, and this time, I wouldn't even be sorry.

But someone else caught the guard's arm. The Snow Queen.

"You aren't to hurt him, do you understand me?" she said. "The moment her friends are threatened with physical danger, her sword's magic takes over, and then she *does* become a real threat. Magical danger, however . . ." The Snow Queen dropped a hand on Chase's head. Frost crawled from the tips of her fingers, over his hair, down his face to his split lip. He shuddered, so I knew it hurt. "This has no effect on her sword. So Rory will still need to behave."

She was right. The sword's magic flowed out of me, and I backed off. "Okay."

The Snow Queen patted Chase's head and let him go.

"Rory's still going to beat you." Chase's voice was shaking now, but at least his skin was losing that icy sheen.

Torlauth was tired of being ignored. "Don't forget, Turnleaf. It's me she has to fight."

Chase snickered. "Some fight. Rory, you have an advantage over Torlauth. He hasn't seen you fight, but you've watched him."

That was true. At the Fairie Market, two years ago, I'd watched his duel with George. George had disarmed Torlauth, and the second his blade flew through the air, Torlauth had planted a kick on George's chest, knocking Lena's brother thirty feet back.

"I didn't even beat Hansel," I said weakly.

"You almost beat him." One of the trolls approached with a grimy looking gag, but Chase just talked faster. "And it didn't take much for him to beat me."

Then I understood what he was telling me to do.

"Go, Rory!" Lena burst out, two octaves squeakier than normal. Since the troll was tying the gag on Chase, she must have figured I needed the encouragement.

"You can do this," said Miriam, like she actually meant it.

Philip stared at them like they were crazy. The twins were fierce in their grief, Forrel pale and broken. Gag or no, Chase didn't look away from my face.

Torlauth stepped closer, facing me, and I froze. I even forgot to breathe.

"Well, Rory Landon?" said the Snow Queen, eyes narrowed. "Isn't this what you always wanted? A chance to save your friends? Isn't that your greatest wish?"

Here it was. My dream. The one I'd feared since the first night of the quest.

Lena even smiled at me encouragingly, like she'd done then.

"No." Even though I couldn't see the point, my hand drifted to my pocket. "I wish I had a plan to get all of us out of here," I said, just as my fingers brushed metal. *The wishing coins.* A plan bloomed in my mind, sudden and *complete*, down to every last wish I needed to make. "And while I'm at it, I wish all of us knew the plan."

Without giving it away, I added silently.

Hope flared in Lena's eyes, and Miriam stopped crying. Chase started to grin through his gag. Out of the corner of my eye, I spotted the kids from Portland pressing closer to the balcony, like they were trying to get a better look. But those were the only signs that the plan had sprouted in their brains too.

"A foolish wish from a foolish girl," said the Snow Queen. She obviously had no idea. She took a snowflake-shaped throwing star from one of her trolls. "When this hits the ground, the duel begins. Don't fail me, Torlauth."

The Fey bent his knees slightly and drew his sword. "I'll kill her with pleasure, Your Majesty, as long as I can kill Chase Turnleaf next."

That wasn't going to happen. We were going to make it out of here.

The Snow Queen tossed the throwing star high. Then she

retreated to safety, behind the trolls guarding the back of the balcony.

I turned to Torlauth.

The silver snowflake clattered to the ground, and the Fey lunged at me, sword held out. He was practically inviting me to hook my hilt guard with his and twist his sword out of his fingers. So I did.

When his sword flew up, well above our heads, I swear he smirked at me.

Then he leaped into the air and aimed a kick at my chest, but my left hand—the one with the strength of the West Wind's ring—was ready. I caught his foot. His face barely had time to register his surprise before I hammered the pommel of my sword straight into his knee. Something cracked, nauseatingly loud, and Torlauth screamed.

Then I snap-kicked his face, and his wings stopping flapping. He dropped onto the balcony.

I'd won.

The trolls just stared, stunned, at Torlauth's crumpled figure, his bronze hair fanned out around him.

Before anyone could speak, I pulled a comb from my back pocket and tossed it between us and the Snow Queen. It struck the balcony floor with a clang. Bars as thick as beanstalks sprouted up, but not fast enough, the ceilings were too high. The Snow Queen raised her hand, readying her ice darts . . .

I scooped the wishing coins out of my pocket. "I wish the first spell that the Snow Queen cast backfired on her!"

That made her pause. I sprinted along the edge of the balcony and tossed another comb over the side between us and the four pillars. Fresh metal columns raced up to the ceiling, just as Ori'an and Ripper moved closer.

Chase threw his head back into the nose of the closest guard, freeing his left arm, and he elbowed the other two in the face. He didn't bother to find his sword or even take off the gag. He just held out a hand, and I tossed him a comb.

I ran to the front of the balcony, past Hadriane's body. There was a gap between the Portland kids and the rest of the audience, at least forty feet away. "I wish, just once, that I could throw that far with perfect accuracy," I said.

The comb sailed beyond the kids and dropped right beside the baffled Pied Piper. When metal columns sprang out of the ice floor, he got squeezed between two of them. He hollered and dropped his wooden flute. One of the Portland kids happily crushed it under her bunny slippers.

"They've gotten to the treasury," the Snow Queen told General Searcaster, furious.

The bars from the first comb clanged against the ceiling. Then the second.

The sorceress-giant raised her cane. "I wish the first spell that Searcaster tried backfired on her!" I said quickly. Then Chase reached the edge.

"Don't let him throw—" the Snow Queen started, and he dropped the comb between us and the sorceress-giant. Those bars grew so fast that they snagged Searcaster's fingers as she snatched her hand back. Her *blood* was green too.

"Kill them!" the Snow Queen ordered. "Execute them immediately!"

The bars from the third comb crunched into the ceiling too, and the fourth set raced up, out of sight.

"Rory!" Lena cried.

I turned. Her troll guard had recovered. He'd forced her to her knees and raised his spear to stab her.

My plan was great, except for the fact I'd locked us in a huge metal cage with a dozen and a half enemies.

It took me three steps to reach Lena and one punch to send him to the floor.

Chase had found his sword, and he went after the nine guards in charge of the dwarves. Once the dwarves were free, they helped him—except for Ima, who charged the trolls holding Miriam and Philip, a stolen spear held high.

"Thanks." Lena pried my left hand open. I only had three golden coins left—the rest had faded to pewter—but she took one. "I wish that the ingredients I brought made a portal right below this balcony, one that would send every single one of us back home, but would collapse on itself the moment the last of us went through."

There was a pause, and then Evan yelled. "It worked! I'll start evacuating!"

"Good wish," I said, flicking the used-up coins out of my palm. "We should have thought of that one when we were still in the prisons."

"I *know*," Lena said, obviously upset. "I've been kicking myself since I thought of it."

General Searcaster grabbed the comb's bars and shook them. "No!" she boomed when they held, but something snapped, way above us. A great white chunk of the ceiling, as big as an iceberg, came loose.

"Haddy!" screamed Ima. The chunk was headed straight for the front of the balcony, where the dwarf princess had fallen. Lena and I grabbed Hadriane's feet, dragging her out of the way.

The falling iceberg smashed down a couple inches from the dwarf princess's head. Ima ran our way, sobbing, "Thank you, thank you." Like we'd really saved *Hadriane*, not just her body.

"The bats! Bring me the bats!" boomed Searcaster. On the other side of the cage, a dozen wolves streamed into a slot in the wall.

"Feel free to help any time!" said Philip. He had two trolls trying to spear him in the stomach.

"We were a little busy not getting squished!" Lena shouted back, but the sword's magic sent me running.

One troll had backed Miriam into the bars. That sucked, especially since she didn't have a weapon, but from the other side of the comb cage, Jimmy Searcaster was trying to work his hand in and grab Miriam, which would definitely complicate our escape plans. I gave myself a running start and then slid on my knees, holding my blade level. My sword rammed straight into Jimmy's green fingers.

He yowled and stumbled away. Trying not to get grossed out by the weird-colored blood on my blade, I spun around to deal with the troll. I stepped in front of Miriam, caught the spear handle just below the point and shoved back hard. The troll tripped, fell, and smacked his head on the ice floor. He didn't get up, so I passed the weapon to Miriam.

"I could have done that," said Philip, coming over to join his sister. He'd picked up a spear too. "But *I* don't have a magic sword and magic ring."

Miriam smacked the back of her brother's head. "Don't ask for help unless you can handle it if she saves you. These eighth graders are in a different class."

Chase, Forrel, and Iggy had taken on the rest of the trolls. I ducked in, cut three spears in half, and snap-kicked four others.

Then I spun around one last time, weapon raised to smash my hilt on the next troll's head, but Chase was standing there, his sword arm cocked back too. He grinned so wide the gag cut into his cheeks, and I noticed the trolls' unmoving bodies lay in a circle around us. We'd taken them all out.

He's safe, I thought. Relief made my knees all wobbly.

Hands shaking, I reached for his gag—it was gritty; obviously, it had been used before—and I cut it away with the very tip of my sword. His smile softened as the gag fell away, and when his fingers curled around mine, all I wanted to do was throw my arms around him.

"Yes!" growled Searcaster.

But I guess it wasn't time for that yet.

Outside the bars, the wolves had returned, their jaws clamped around Lena's Bats of Destruction, like this was the evil-giant version of fetch.

"Up, bats! Destroy the Characters and the dwarves!" cried the sorceress-giant, and a dozen Bats escaped the wolves' teeth and sailed up toward the balcony. They were *definitely* skinny enough to fit through the bars.

"We can dodge them," Chase said, "but Rory, you'll need to use your ring to smash them. That's the only way to take them out—"

But when the first bat tried to fly into the comb cage, it burst apart. Fragments of pale wood flew everywhere.

I ducked and felt Chase's arms shield my head. Then another explosion sounded across from us, this one tinkling like someone had thrown a box of tacks against the bars. Then another hit, and another, and another, until they all went off together with the crackling *boom-boom-boom* of a fireworks finale.

Then the room was silent.

Chase looked first. "We're okay," he said, helping me up.

Not even a splinter had made it inside, but the Bats had done plenty of damage on the *other* side of the comb cage. Jimmy Searcaster, Ori'an, and Ripper were closest. Jimmy bled from hundreds of wounds, the splinters stuck fast in his skin like a dozen archers had emptied their quivers into his forearms. Ori'an was on his back, orange blood pumping out from a jagged metal shard in his neck. It didn't matter that we couldn't kill him. He wasn't going to be in shape to fight anytime soon. Ripper was howling and pawing at his face. I was pretty sure he had lost an eye. Dozens of his wolves whined at his feet. Another dozen lay still, not even whimpering, probably dead.

They didn't have anything else to send after us.

So Chase decided to gloat. "What did I tell you? We're going to walk out of here, and there's nothing they could do about it. What side are you going to bet on now?"

"Of course. No magic or weapons can pass through these combs. I should have remembered." At the back of the balcony, the Snow Queen stepped out of the shadows. Even she hadn't escaped the shrapnel. A metal shard, as long and slender as a sword, pierced her chest in exactly the same spot her ice darts had stabbed Hadriane.

Following my gaze, the Snow Queen looked down. Surprise flickered across her face—she hadn't even *noticed* it—and she plucked it out. It was clean. There wasn't even any blood.

She tilted her chin up, not exactly smiling, but I knew how much she appreciated my horror.

The Glass Mountain wasn't the Fey and the Canon's first choice for punishing the Snow Queen. They had *tried* to kill her. *They executed her no less than eighteen times,* Chase had told me once, but nothing had worked.

I was supposed to stop her, and she couldn't be killed.

"There's *nothing* me, Rory, and Lena can't do!" Chase bragged, oblivious.

I should have used a wishing coin to stop him, because as soon as he said it, determination slid into the Snow Queen's glacier-blue eyes.

"Run today, little Rory. Run fast, and run home," whispered the Snow Queen. "Perhaps it is true—perhaps you can defeat me every time we meet, but know this: I will come for them, and you cannot be everywhere at once. Who will you bid fare-well to first? Your friends, who are so helpful? Your parents, who gave you life? Your stepmother's child, who has not yet seen the world?"

Oh no.

It didn't matter whether or not the baby was born yet, or whether or not I was in her life. The Snow Queen could still use her to get to me. Maybe that had been the problem all along. Maybe I just didn't want to love one more person I could lose.

"You won't touch my sister!" I said, slamming against the bars between us. The Snow Queen just *laughed*.

"Rory! Most of the kids have gone through!" Lena called to me, our carryalls in her arms. "We're going to need a way down!"

I held up my second-to-last golden coin. "I wish that there was a very safe, very solid staircase leading from the balcony straight into the portal."

"Perfect! Now hurry up!" Lena said.

Turning my back on the Snow Queen was the hardest thing I'd done all day. Leaving her here alive meant putting everyone I loved in the worst kind of danger, the kind that hangs over you like an axe ready to fall.

So I ran.

When I reached the others, Chase was inspecting the two flights of white steps leading down to the floor, with chest-high banisters of milky ice. "Total waste of a wish. Where's my pack? We could have used my rope . . ."

He drifted off when the dwarves picked up Hadriane's body—Forrel at the princess's head, each twin holding a foot, their faces like stone. They went down first, and Miriam walked beside them, holding Hadriane's wrists in place. Philip followed, carrying the princess's polar bear cloak, all bundled up in his arms.

"We will meet again, Rory," the Snow Queen said as I stepped down onto the first stair.

I froze so quickly that Lena grabbed my arm, peering into my face worriedly.

"Count on it!" Chase called back. "And you'll be dead!"

When we reached the ground, the kids were gone, all of them, and only the portal was left. It was the first one I'd ever seen that wasn't attached to a doorway, and it was just wide enough to let the dwarves and Miriam pass through together. The sunshine on the EAS side of the portal was already lighting up Forrel's face, and beyond them, I could see the Tree of Hope.

One last thought occurred to me. "The combs."

Chase took my very last wishing coin. "I wish to tweak the enchantment over these four combs, to add a condition that they'll return to their owner when she says, *'We're leaving this land, come to my hand.'"*

The giant bars around us didn't change, but the gold drained away from the coin.

Then we stepped toward the portal. Lena and Chase stood at the edge with me as I turned back and shouted the new retrieval spell. The four combs clinked into my palm. With the bars gone,

I could see the huge doors at the end of the entrance hall, taller even than the Searcasters. Half the audience had marched through them, out into the white landscape. The Snow Queen's allies were abandoning her.

Then Chase and Lena dragged me through, and the portal collapsed.

tumbling, I crashed into a very solid chest covered in golden chain mail.

"Easy." Hansel dropped hands on my shoulders and steadied me. "You're safe now."

We were, but my family wasn't. Mom and Dad and Brie and the baby and Amy—they were all in danger. That wouldn't change until I stopped the Snow Queen for good.

I needed to go home.

"Miss us?" Chase wiped the orange troll blood off his blade and onto the grass. Lena just looked wrung out, head bent over the carryalls.

Line after line of metal dummies stood at attention behind Hansel. We must have set off EAS's intruder alert. I waited for the yelling to start, like it did *last* time we dropped an unapproved portal in the courtyard.

"Are you hurt at all?" he asked us.

I shook my head. I was pretty sure I should thank the sword instructor. Without him, I would never have known how to beat Torlauth. I probably wouldn't have remembered the other weapons in my pockets either. But I was too freaked out by the way he wasn't telling us off.

"Um. Did you guys see a thousand and one kids come through here?" Lena said.

"There." Hansel nodded across the courtyard. The kids had formed a line in front of the door to Portland. In the daylight, their pajamas and sleeping sweats looked dirty and rumpled, but every face gleamed with impatience. "We're trying to send them all home before the Characters got here. They'll start arriving any minute."

Gretel and Ellie stood to the right of the Portland door, holding a mirror shard in their hands and making each kid look at it before they passed through. The Mirror Test. Unicorn Nightgown must have seen something in it, because Gretel pulled the girl aside and put her in line with a couple other kids.

Hansel stepped out of the way, letting us pass. "The Director will want to talk to you before long, but go and say your good-byes."

The dwarves waited on the grass. Miriam and Philip were with them, and the three of us headed over too.

The elves from the Shoemaker's workshop arrived with a stretcher, the kind they use to carry wounded Characters to the infirmary. The dwarves lowered Hadriane onto it and took the handles. Miriam and Philip spread the polar bear cloak over her, covering her face.

Something hard lodged itself in my throat, and I swallowed and swallowed around it, trying not to feel so awful. With her head raised and her eyes clear, Ima looked so much like a princess that I knew her big sister would be proud, but I remembered her crying back at the balcony.

"We cannot stay," Prince Iggy told Gretel. "We will visit briefly with Queen Titania at her pavilion and tell her of what transpired this afternoon. She may not yet know that the Snow Queen has kidnapped her son. Then we will return home. We have been too long from our city, and I know my father will be anxious. But we thank the Characters of Ever After School." He turned to me, Lena, and Chase, and he bowed, as low as he could with the stretcher in his hands. "We will be indebted to you forever."

Thank you, thank you, Ima had said, and suddenly I knew why it bothered me.

Hadriane was gone. She wouldn't show up enchanted, like Miriam; a swallow of the Water wouldn't heal her, like Lena. She wasn't coming back, and these kids would miss her every day of their lives, like Chase missed Cal.

And I'd convinced her to come with us.

I didn't deserve to be thanked.

"Our father will know what the Snow Queen did to our sister," Ima added fiercely. "The Dwarves of the Living Stone will never ally with that sorceress again."

"I'm so sorry about Hadriane." My voice wobbled all over the place, and my nose prickled like it does right before I cried.

Forrel must have guessed what I was thinking, because he said, "Listen, and listen well, Rory Landon. Haddy has had *one* dream, and one dream only since she was born, and that was of facing the Snow Queen's allies and speaking the truth. Do you understand?"

I nodded, blinking hard. She had told me about it, that night we shared a watch.

But Miriam said, "You mean like the *Character* dreams, right? The ones that show the future?"

Forrel nodded. "Why do you think I fought so hard against her coming? She never expected to return home."

I should have noticed.

"And for that, Forrel, you have earned your beard," said Iggy. "Whether it will be under my rule, or my father's."

Forrel's tiny smile reappeared. "Prince, it's not a beard that I want."

Then my heart fractured a little more.

"We know," Ima said gently. At least Forrel had the twins to look out for him. "Now, let us return home. Before nightfall, I want to convince our father that we should *move*."

The kids from Portland moved aside to let the dwarves through first. Maybe they didn't understand everything that had gone down in the Arctic Circle, but they definitely knew that Hadriane had died for them. The twins didn't look back, but Forrel nodded a good-bye to us as he stepped out of sight.

"Should we be worried about three dwarves carrying a stretcher covered in a polar bear skin down the middle of Hawthorne?" Philip said.

"It's Portland," his sister said. "They've seen weirder things."

Then I remembered how *very* close we'd come to bringing *Chase*'s body home, and my whole body started shaking.

"Whoa, *Rory* . . ." Lena said.

I'd come close to losing Lena, too, but dealing with Mark hadn't made me lose it like that. I just handled it with one clear-headed slice.

When I thought I was going to lose Chase, it was like the whole world was crashing down. I couldn't even think straight. It wasn't that I cared about Chase more, but the feelings weren't the same. They'd changed, and I hadn't noticed until now.

But I didn't say that. I turned to him and shouted, "You *idiot*! She was *this close* to killing you."

He reeled back. "No, she *wasn't*. I figured it out the second she went after Hadriane instead of the twins. She wanted them alive, so she could blackmail their dad. I'd knew she would want me alive for the same—"

But I didn't care about his excuses. I cared that he was *alive*, and I threw my arms around his neck. "Don't *ever* do that again," I whispered, trying so hard not to start sobbing right there, because I knew how much he would hate it.

A hand patted my back, kind of awkwardly, just like Chase patted his mom's shoulder when she was upset. But that was Lena struggling to hold onto all the carryalls and comfort me at the same time.

Chase's warm arms slipped around my shoulders, and he rested his head on top of mine. "It's okay, Rory. It's over."

And then it was even harder not to cry.

It wasn't over. Hadriane was dead, and today just marked the beginning of her being dead. Nothing was ever going to be the same. Not for Ima and Iggy. Not for us—not when the Snow Queen wouldn't stop until she had murdered everyone I cared about.

Then the hand on my back went still. "Gran!"

Lena dumped all the carryalls and took off running.

Her whole family was on the lawn. Her grandmother and Jenny squished Lena between them. But George sprinted straight for the Portland door—for Miriam.

She saw him coming and sent him an awkward half-wave that clearly said, *I have no idea what to say*. George wasn't having it. When he reached her, he scooped her up, lifting her a couple feet off the ground. "You should have called me. I would have come back—but instead you took *my sister* on a quest?" George said angrily, but he didn't set her down until he'd kissed her.

For a *really* long time.

Chase and I glanced at each other, and I was about to roll my eyes until I realized we were still hugging. We let go and hastily backed away.

One thing at a time, I thought. Then I couldn't believe I'd thought that. My blush even kicked in.

But I peeked at Chase. He was blushing too, wasn't he? Maybe I *could* think that.

Doors slammed across the courtyard. School must have gotten out on the east coast. Characters were arriving.

"Oh, yeah," Philip said when George finally set Miriam down. "You guys have *really* broken up."

"We had a *fight*—we didn't break up." George turned to Miriam. "Have you been telling people we broke up?"

"I didn't mean it," Miriam said, wiping a tear from her cheek. "Not really."

Some eighth graders were gathering in front of the training courts, but then Adelaide cried out, pointing at us. It took them maybe ten seconds to mob me and Chase, sparing us from having to watch Miriam and George make up some more.

"Where's Lena?" Kyle demanded, before anyone else got a chance to speak.

"She's okay," I said, making a mental note to tell Lena exactly how worried he'd sounded. I pointed to her and her family. It looked a lot less like a happy reunion now. Jenny and Gran were both chewing Lena out.

Kevin pushed his brother out of the way. "Tell us everything."

"In her last update, the Director made it sound like you were dead for sure," said Tina.

"So we planned some extra training," said Vicky.

"We were going to avenge you," said Paul, who was standing

299

right next to her. No, they were *holding hands*. Chase had been *right* about them being a couple.

"Updates?" Chase said, confused.

"Well, she was keeping some *huge* secrets," Kyle reminded us.

"We swore we would rebel if she didn't update us every afternoon," Tina said.

Yikes. The Director definitely wouldn't go easy on us now.

Adelaide elbowed her way to the front, her eyes rimmed with red. I *almost* felt bad for her, but then she smiled in that syrupy way I couldn't stand. She sauntered right up to Chase, her long blonde hair swinging. "Who cares about that? Did you bring me anything?"

She stepped so far into Chase's personal bubble that he scooted away, shooting me a look that clearly said, *Help!*

"It wasn't exactly the kind of trip where you can buy souvenirs," I said icily, and Adelaide backed off a little.

"But we did get a few things." Chase went through the packs Lena dropped, unzipped one, and groped around inside until he pulled out a handful of gold coins. "Wishing coins, people. It'll turn silver if it works."

Then he *threw* it like confetti. He was enjoying this a little too much. The stepsisters didn't go for it, but Kevin, Connor, and Paul tried to catch them. Adelaide actually *did* catch one, and then she clutched it to her chest with both hands in a *very* irritating way.

Chase scooped out another handful and shoved them *all* in Kyle's hand. "You deserve these the most. We would have never made it out of here without you."

I guess Chase did have some cool moments left in him.

"Chase! Rory! Lena!" Ellie called, her frizzy brown hair huge. She was definitely stressed. "Head to the Director's office, please. She wants to talk to you immediately."

All the eighth graders drew back, like getting in trouble was contagious. Chase and I glanced at each other. We'd known that this was coming. "Let's go get it over with," I said.

I'd been in the Director's office only once before, during my orientation in sixth grade, but it looked exactly like I remembered it: the fountains in the corners, filling the room with the sound of trickling water; the marble floor, inlaid with pink roses; the overstuffed, rose-covered chairs, and the large wooden desk, carved all over with roses.

But the Director was a mess. Her silk dress was rumpled, and the curl had fallen out of her blonde hair. She and Rumpelstiltskin were bent over the current volume. "Take a seat," she said without looking up.

That was all. No *how was your trip to the Arctic Circle?* No *I hear my ex–best friend tried to kill you.* No *you three are in so much trouble that you'll be doing chores around EAS until you graduate high school.*

The Director was definitely a fan of the guilt trip. She wanted us to squirm.

I thought watching Hadriane die had squeezed out all my fear of getting in trouble, but the Director still knew how to get to me. "Your mother has been calling, Rory," she said. "I've heard from her almost hourly, and so has Lena's grandmother."

"Did she come here?" I asked, scooting to the edge of my chair. If she was around, I would go straight to her. I would let her see I was okay.

"She *tried*," the Director said, "as did other members of your family. The Door Trek system wouldn't let them through."

That meant she was still worrying. "Then what do you need from me before I go home? A report?"

"I do *not* need a report," said the Director. "I have learned everything I require from this book. The current Tales are very thorough. But you will need to surrender all the wishing coins."

"We gave them away already," said Chase, sounding pleased about it.

"Then retrieve them from the eighth graders who received them," the Director said, her voice like iron. "It is a matter of *safety*, Chase Turnleaf. I'm certain that spying spells are embedded in the metal. Lena, you will examine them and tell us for sure."

That shut Chase up, and Lena nodded miserably.

The Director pushed one of her papers across the desk. "I would like you to explain this."

It was a letter, written all in spiky caps:

DEAR KEZELDA, WITCH OF THE GINGERBREAD CLAN,

WE KNOW THAT YOU HAVE RECEIVED SUMMONS FROM THE SNOW QUEEN TO JOIN HER ON THE EIGHTH OF APRIL. WE WRITE TO TELL YOU THAT YOU SHOULD GO WITH THIS IN MIND:

DO NOT UNDERESTIMATE AURORA LANDON. WE BELIEVE THAT THE CHILD AND THE OTHERS OF THE NEWEST TRIUMVIRATE HAVE THE RESOURCES TO STOP THE SNOW QUEEN ONCE AND FOR ALL.

SIGNED,

MUIRE, UNIZI, VIONNIA, AND CIONA,

PRIESTESSES OF THE GOBLINS

I stared at it, confused. I knew who the goblin priestesses were. We'd never actually met in person, but I'd gotten stuck in a vault they'd made once. Even their statues made an impression—they were so dignified, so certain of their power.

Chase ripped it out of my hand, scanned it, and passed it to Lena.

"Well?" the Director asked.

"I don't know. I've never seen it before," I said.

"I have been informed that every group that received the Snow Queen's invitation also received this," said the Director.

That was definitely weird. "I didn't ask them to send any letters, if that's what you're asking."

The Director sighed heavily, like she was the reasonable grownup and I was the little kid making her day difficult. "Aurora, I know that you are angry with me for keeping news of your Tale from you, but I can't help you if—"

"Wait, *what*?" I said. "Did my Tale start?"

Chase sat forward. "It started while we were *gone*?"

"Don't insult our intelligence," said Rumpelstiltskin. "We know that you have seen the book."

"You must have seen your Tale," the Director told me.

"You are telling them now," said a voice from the door. Rapunzel. Her dark eyes were fixed on me. "And none too gently."

"This doesn't concern you," Rumpelstiltskin said, glaring at her. "Go back to your tower."

"I know my sister better than anyone else living. Of *course* it concerns me," said Rapunzel sharply. "Besides, I came to confess: *I* contacted the goblin priestesses. *I* gave them the list of potential allies Solange would invite. I am responsible for those letters, and I alone."

The Director groaned. "How many boons does the mother of the four winds owe you?"

"Many," replied Rapunzel. "But the goblins would have done it without a boon, I think. For I told them that the new Triumvirate would go to the Arctic Circle, and they would rescue the stolen children in front of an audience. Rory, Lena, and Chase demonstrated their own strength just as my sister demonstrated hers. Between this letter and young Chase's words, many of Solange's old allies have been convinced to leave her."

I stared at Rapunzel. *Sometimes, it is better not to know too much. You will learn soon enough,* she had said. I'd thought that she was just being skimpy on her quest advice, but she hadn't wanted us to know how high the stakes were. She'd known I would freak out.

She'd *used* us. I didn't want to be angry with her, but I kind of was.

"I made everything up as I went along," Chase protested.

"I foresaw it," Rapunzel said. "My sister will have to work hard to earn her allies back, but she *will* do it. This has only bought precious time. We must prepare ourselves."

I channeled all my anger into turning the conversation back where I wanted. "Tell me about my Tale."

"Rory's Tale was the secret you put in the Pounce Pot, wasn't it?" Lena said. I'd assumed she'd been quiet because she hated getting in trouble, but she had just been thinking. "We should have discovered it when we snuck into the library and read the current volume, but we didn't see it because we only looked at the very last pages."

"*When* did it start?" Chase said, ticked.

Rapunzel put her hand on the back of my chair, and then I understood why she had really come—she was moral support. I wondered what was so bad about my Tale that I was going to *need* moral support.

The anger left me, and now I only felt afraid.

"Tell her, Mildred," said Rapunzel. "It is time."

I was sure the Director would refuse. She *never* took orders from Rapunzel.

But the Director slid the book away from Rumpelstiltskin's fingers, opened it where the bookmark was, and set it down in front of me. Lena and Chase leaned in on both sides, reading with me:

THE TALE OF RORY LANDON

And underneath was an illustration of a girl and boy on top of some gold coins, and the green-and-gold dragon getting ready to eat them. My first day at EAS.

That was how long they'd been keeping the truth from me.

My hands trembling, I reached for the book and turned pages, not bothering to read when it had so many pictures. There we were, the three of us, camped out in Matilda Searcaster's desk, reading the Snow Queen's letter. There was the Snow Queen talking to Jack in the Glass Mountain. Chase and me falling from the beanstalk. The snowflake throwing stars hanging from the ceiling in EAS's kitchen. The West Wind, trapped in that glass vial. The goblin vault in the Hidden Troll Court. The staircase of talking stones. The Mia doll chasing me, Chase, and Ben to the throne room.

I stopped there. I didn't want to see any illustrations from *this* quest. I didn't need to see myself slay Mark or the Snow Queen execute Hadriane.

"The Canon meeting at the Fairie Market," Chase said, practically spitting he was so mad. "You were voting not to tell us."

"Yes." The Director obviously didn't regret making that decision. "And the day you left on Lena's Tale, I put the secret in the Pounce Pot."

I still didn't understand. "Why does it just say my name? What Tale *is* it?"

"It's an Unwritten Tale," said the Director. "A Tale without precedent. It follows no guidelines, because no Tales that occurred previously compare to it. Lena was the last in a long line of Jacks, but you are the first and only bearer of this Tale."

"In the history of the Ever Afters, only one other Character has gotten an Unwritten Tale," Rumpelstiltskin explained.

"The Snow Queen," Lena breathed.

All that time I'd wondered, but what we shared was so simple: We both had Tales no one had seen before.

"My sister's Tale was called 'The Tale of Solange de Chateies,'" said Rapunzel gently, "so we knew right away that your Tale was Unwritten as well."

Solange de Chateies—I hadn't realized that the Snow Queen even *had* a last name.

"The magic clinging to the Tale bearer of an Unwritten Tale is much stronger than the magic around an ordinary Tale," the librarian continued. "Thus, like Solange's Tale, Rory's Tale has made changes in all the Tales around her. Time frames expand or shrink. Endings change. Two Tales overlap, or even combine."

Like "The Snow Queen" and "The Pied Piper."

"So that's why *my* Tale took five days, not four? And we managed to steal all three—" Lena gasped. "That's why I got my Tale so soon after Rory came to EAS! Her Tale sparked mine, right?"

The Director nodded wearily. "Yours and your brother's. The first of *many* Rory's Tale has ignited."

"Then why didn't Chase's start?" Lena asked, like she was hoping to shoot a hole in their theory, to prove it wasn't me. "I mean, between all those sword practices, I'm pretty sure he hangs out with Rory even more than I do. Her Tale should have sparked his too."

Oh no. For the first time, I glanced at Chase, and he looked so *lost*.

This was pretty strong proof that he wasn't ever going to get a Tale. And from the resigned looks on the grown-ups' faces, I was pretty sure they thought the same.

It wasn't fair for me to wish that my Tale had never started when Chase wanted one so badly.

He shrugged it off. "It doesn't matter. But *when* were you planning on telling us? You could have at least given us some tips on the Snow Queen or the last Triumvirate, but we had to learn *everything* the hard way."

"I had hoped to wait and tell you when you were older," the Director said, and now *she* sounded upset. Not in a *you're so disrespectful* way, but in a *I have really bad news* sort of way. "But the time frame has shortened in the past week. When the Tale first appeared, its beginning cited 'four years' as the time frame, but . . ."

Her voice drifted off. I flipped back through the pages.

Once upon a time, the first lines read, *there was a girl named Rory Landon. Though she did not know it, the fate of magic would fall into her hands during the month she turned fourteen. With it, she would meet winter, death, and despair.*

My mouth went dry.

Well, I didn't have to worry about messing up Brie's baby the way Solange messed up Rapunzel. My sister wouldn't even miss me, like Chase missed Cal. I would barely get to meet her.

"Last spring, the Snow Queen's spy snuck into the library and saw those lines. So, Solange hastened her plans to return,"

Rumpelstiltskin said, even more dry and distant than he'd been when he'd explained Lena's Tale years before. "We believe that is why the text at the beginning revised itself to 'during the month she turns fourteen.'"

I couldn't believe he was rattling on about the time frame. That wasn't the part that stuck out the most.

"It says I meet death," I told them, and Lena burst into tears. "In less than four months. My birthday is in July."

"Not necessarily *your* death," Rumpelstiltskin pointed out, but that wasn't good news. I just started worrying about Lena and Chase—about my family. "It says you meet winter followed by death followed by despair. It is hard to despair if you're not also alive."

I shuddered.

"Not helping," Chase told the librarian.

"But it's a possibility, isn't it?" I asked. No one answered me, not even Rapunzel, although she moved her hand to my shoulder.

"You're not going to die." Chase sounded just as confident as he had when he'd said I would beat Torlauth. I stared at the book, wishing I could believe him. "You're *not*," he said louder.

But when I went home and explained the truth about Ever After School, when I told my parents where I'd *really* gone, when I explained who the Snow Queen was and why she was after us, I had to tell them this too. I had to tell them about my Tale, and how it might kill me.

Tears streamed down Lena's face. She took off her glasses to wipe them, but Chase handled the situation the same way he handled most conversations he didn't like. He changed the subject. "So, what's our punishment?"

Wow, I thought numbly. *Things have gotten really bad if that's the less intense topic.*

"Punishment?" repeated the Director, startled.

"Yeah," Chase said slowly, the voice he uses when he really wants to tell someone they're as dumb as a troll. "You called us in here to tell us off for going on a quest you'd forbidden, right? This is the part where you say we have to scrub all the practice dummies with a toothbrush or something."

"It's my fault," I reminded them, my voice sounding very far away. "It was *my* idea to go. Punish me if you're going to punish anyone."

"What would be the point? You are filled now with the burden of Hadriane's death, the terror of your Tale's first lines, and the dread of explaining to your parents," the Director said. "No punishment I could inflict could ever compare."

I stared at her, wondering for one awful second if she had a mind-reading enchantment she'd never told us about. But then my gaze fell on the huge book between us.

She didn't have to read my mind. My Tale could tell her everything. And Rumpelstiltskin. And probably the whole Canon.

They'd kept all these secrets from me, and since they had that book, I couldn't even have one.

I sprinted for the door—not the one back to the courtyard, where more people would stare, but the one that led deeper into EAS.

"You couldn't have made it even a tiny bit easier?" snapped Rapunzel.

"How could I make it easier?" replied the Director, as I ran out into the hall. "The children are thinking the same."

Then the door shut behind me.

I ran down a hall with spinning wheels inlaid in the floor, a corridor lined with doors numbered one through seven in scarlet paint, and a long wall carved with three little pigs. I dashed across an indoor courtyard, past its gazebo and its tulips, and I sprinted down a corridor covered in murals of trees and another with dragon-scale wallpaper and another with portraits of the first Canon, and another and another.

I thought I didn't want anyone to find me, but maybe I did. When I finally stopped running, I found myself at a spiraling stone staircase, the one that led to Rapunzel's tower.

I collapsed on the bottom step and buried my face in my arms, but I didn't want to cry—I wanted to hide. I wanted to sit still and figure out what was happening to me before I faced the world again.

Rapunzel's footsteps were so quiet. I didn't notice her arrival until she spoke. "Mildred didn't mean it the way it sounded. She understands what it is to punish yourself. She has blamed herself for the death of her husband all these years, and being deeply unhappy, she spreads her unhappiness to others."

I didn't say anything. I didn't even lift my head. I felt safer down there.

Rapunzel just settled on the step, waiting for me to get around to talking. It took a while, because the guilt had caught up with me too. It lodged itself, huge and tangled, in my lungs, squeezing out the air. I didn't know how to begin to unravel it.

Thank you, thank you, Ima had said.

"You knew she was going to die. You knew I was going to lead her straight to her death," I whispered.

"You? No, Rory," said Rapunzel. "That is not what happened."

"But you said, 'to go or not to go is a decision. It rests in one person, and one person only,'" I reminded her. "That person was me. It *was* my idea."

"You misunderstood. It was your idea, yes, but Hadriane's *decision*. You did not force anyone to come with you," Rapunzel said softly. "To believe that the responsibility lies with you would belittle her sacrifice. Knowing that the quest meant her own death and choosing to rescue the twins anyway—that was truly an act of great love and great strength."

She was trying to make me feel better. It worked, kind of, but another guilty thought rose up to take its place. Maybe Hadriane had broken us out of prison, but she had always been honest with her dad, even when she was telling him something he really didn't want to hear.

Not me. Maybe the Director had been lying to me since I first arrived at EAS, but I was even worse. I'd been lying to my parents. That wasn't anybody's fault but mine.

"I'm pretty sure that Hadriane was a better daughter than I am," I whispered.

"You could not keep your mother from worrying about Solange *and* tell her the truth of your life here. You could not give Hadriane the opportunity to save the twins *and* ensure her safety," Rapunzel said. "Doing both is impossible. So you made a choice and sacrificed one for the other. Your guilt merely tortures you for not being able to do it all."

Yeah, I was glad we'd saved the kidnapped Portlanders, but I also wondered . . . if I'd followed that wooden door in the prison, if I'd found out what was behind the ancient black door in my dreams, maybe I could have defeated the Snow Queen for good. Maybe I could have prevented the war that was coming, and all the deaths it would cause.

It was too horrible to say out loud—even to tell Rapunzel. Besides, she was right. I couldn't have followed the door *and* rescued the kids, not at the same time.

"Guilt is a useless emotion," I murmured. "That's what Hadriane said."

Rapunzel hesitated. Then she said, "That may have been true for Hadriane, who pushed guilt away, but it was also true for my sister, who never felt guilt at all. I have always taken a great deal of comfort in my own guilt. It means that I can learn from my past. Next time, I can take action to avoid doing what will make me feel that way again."

I didn't want to think about a next time. I didn't know if I could make myself go back in July, knowing what I would face, and I was sure that selfishness made me just like Solange. "I don't want to turn into her."

"You are making the same mistake the Canon has," Rapunzel said. "Having an Unwritten Tale, as Solange did, does not mean you'll follow in her footsteps. You can choose not to. *I* did not. You are more like Hadriane than Solange, I think, and that is why I worry for you."

I glanced up. Her dark eyes were full of kindness. She looked like she always looked—young and ancient at the same time, but not like the Fey did. She looked like she had seen more of the world and weathered more of its sadnesses than anyone ever should.

She did know things. She knew more than that stupid book did.

So I asked. "Am I really going to die?"

I would believe it, I might even accept it, but only if Rapunzel told me so.

"I do not know," she said, and all my hopes of having the answers to all my questions—all of *Mom's* questions—went completely out the window. "I see great danger but not the final outcome. Perhaps that is best. I fought the Director when she hid the truth of your Tale, but she may have been right. It is hard to be happy after being warned of 'winter, death, and despair,' and you *have* been happy. Sometimes, it *is* better not to know too much."

I would know soon enough. I would know in July.

"I kind of don't agree right now," I said quietly, but mostly I was thinking about telling Mom. "That's the worst part of having an Unwritten Tale. At least Lena, Ben, and Miriam had some clue what was coming, even if it changed a lot."

"Is an Unwritten Tale very different from the way your parents live their lives?" Rapunzel asked. "So much of a Character's life is unknown. One's Tale only sheds light on one small part. Our lives are shaped instead by the stories we tell ourselves. Perhaps you cannot change your destiny, Rory, but *you* are writing your own story. You have some say in how it turns out."

I sighed. "You're telling me not to count high school out just yet."

She nodded. "It is sometimes the hardest thing of all—to know so little and to refuse to lose hope."

I didn't *want* to hope I would live past July. I wanted to take it for granted like every other eighth grader, but I guess that would never happen again, not after watching Hadriane die.

A couple voices drifted down the corridor.

"Lena, you've got to stop crying. We're going to be there in a second, and you're going to upset Rory."

"She's not *you*, Chase! Give it a rest."

I smiled. Lena couldn't be crying *that* hard if she could tell Chase off.

"I told them where they might find us. I knew you wouldn't mind," Rapunzel whispered.

Then Lena and Chase rounded the corner. They were exactly who I wanted to see. "Hey!"

Lena waved, looking relieved. I guess I looked more like myself.

"I've decided that I'm going to follow you around," Chase said. "Eventually, it'll jump-start my Tale."

"I told you, that's not the issue today," Lena said.

But I knew that this was Chase's way of telling me he wasn't dwelling on his Tale. "Do I have any say in this?" I asked.

"Not really," said Chase, but he smiled at me, kind of shy, as if he'd been kind of planning to follow me around anyway.

Wow. Not even learning about my Tale could keep my cheeks from turning red.

Lena didn't seem to notice. "The Director told us to find you and come to the courtyard."

Somewhere, a bell started ringing. Like it does when a Tale starts.

Rapunzel waved us off. "Go. I will see you soon, but you will not wish to miss this."

The Director had already reached her podium when we stepped outside. The elves had set it up in its usual place, under the Tree of Hope, but they'd also added a little stage so that we could all see her. She'd brushed her hair.

The Snow Queen may be loose, but the Director had an appearance to maintain.

"As I'm sure you've heard, the questers have returned successful." The Director nodded to her right, where Miriam and Philip stood side-by-side. "The Tales of these two siblings as well as those of Evan, Mary, and Jamal combined within the current volume, and I'm happy to announce 'The Pied Piper and the Snow Queen' has reached its final page."

Some kids clapped. Miriam ruffled Philip's hair.

"Another long-standing Tale has reached its conclusion today—Evan Garrison's 'The White Snake,'" the Director continued. It took me a second to find Evan, but he was grinning as he stroked the white fox tucked inside his shirt. I guess he wanted to make sure she got her henhouse reward. "He recruited foxes to carry messages to the questers, without which they would have most certainly been caught, and the children of Hawthorne lost."

People clapped again. Some ninth graders whooped. I was happy for him too. He'd lost two fingers to his Tale a couple years ago, but at least it ended okay.

"I need to announce another new Tale, one that I believe has sparked all the others," said the Director. "'The Tale of Rory Landon.'"

No clapping for me. Just staring. I wish she'd given me a heads-up about what she was announcing. I might have stayed in Rapunzel's tower.

"It is an Unwritten Tale, which means that it is the only one of its kind," said the Director. "So no one knows what will happen to Rory. Her Tale is still ongoing, as it has been since she joined us. Do not blame her for not telling you this. She didn't learn of it until today."

Wow. The Director had gone from keeping secrets to oversharing.

If she tried to read *everybody* the first few lines of my Tale, if she even *hinted* at us being the new Triumvirate, I was going to charge the podium. That was *private*.

But she didn't. She didn't even ask me who I wanted as my Companions, but maybe it was too obvious that I'd picked Chase and Lena.

"This week, we've spoken a great deal about the Snow Queen," said the Director. "However, we haven't mentioned how we will protect you and your families."

Suddenly she had everyone's attention again.

"We have received intelligence that the Snow Queen will strike in July," the Director said. "In the past, her pattern has been to hunt down Characters one by one before such a battle. She may try to attack you in your homes." I swallowed. I knew who she would go after first. "The Canon and I are prepared to offer asylum to any Character who asks for it." She looked my way, so I knew that the next line was meant for me. "We strongly encourage you to convince your families to relocate here as soon as possible. For those of you who are interested, Ellie and Gretel have leaflets containing more detailed information. The building will expand as needed, so there is definitely room for all."

I forgave the Director for everything right then. She was inviting me to move to EAS. She was offering me a chance to keep my family *safe*.

"I need to go home," I told Chase and Lena.

I had some explaining to do.

n the workshop, Lena fixed up a temporary-transport spell to go straight to my house. She used some dirt from a jar labeled RORY'S BACKYARD—I'd collected it as soon as we moved in, just in case of emergencies, but we'd never risked using it till now.

Appearing out of nowhere wouldn't matter anymore. Also, I was way too exhausted to figure out which bus could take me home.

"Are you *sure* you'll be okay?" Lena asked for the fiftieth time as I painted the ruby doorway. Chase had scurried off in an annoyingly good mood, and every time I looked, he was talking to a different eighth grader. This was a dream come true for him. He was probably trying to convince the whole eighth grade to move before the end of the month.

I tried not to let it bother me. I would see him at school, after all.

"I'm fine," I told Lena again. The sooner I started explaining, the sooner I could convince my family we needed to move too.

Finally she chanted the spell and hugged me, hard enough that her bony elbows dug into my ribs. "Good luck," she whispered.

I nodded and stepped through. I arrived in the backyard, just between the wooden fence and some hydrangea. It was misting here in San Francisco, and moisture settled over my eyelashes as I stared at the back of the house.

A light brightened the kitchen. Mom was in there.

I walked across the lawn and up the steps, concentrating on finding the right words.

Then footsteps thudded inside, and I knew I'd been spotted. I froze when someone threw the door open.

Dad's eyes squeezed shut *hard*, and then he opened them again, like he was checking to make sure I was still there. Then he turned back into the house. "She's here, Maggie!"

"Dad? What are you doing here?" Not the greatest opening in the world.

He gave me a stern look, one I almost *never* saw on his face. "I've been helping your mother search. I've flown from here to North Carolina to L.A. twice, looking for you."

Then Mom appeared in the doorway—her eyes red, a tissue crumpled in her hand. She grabbed me to her as tightly as she could, and I hugged her back, filling with guilt as she took long, shaky, trying-not-to-sob breaths.

"Who's my favorite mother?" I whispered.

She jerked back and scowled at me, her hands tight on my shoulders. "Don't be cute. I'm not even remotely in the mood."

Amy ran out on the porch, looking scarier than General Searcaster.

I wished Brie was here, and the baby too. I wanted my whole family right in front of me, where I could see they were okay, where I could protect them.

Then the questions came at me.

"We tried tracking your phone, but it was malfunctioning,"

Mom said. "It said you were in Portland, Oregon. Then nothing for days. Did you not even charge it? Didn't you know how worried we were?"

"We went to EAS's door every day, but we couldn't get in," Amy said. "Why is the door always locked? And why didn't any other kids go in there?"

"Mrs. LaMarelle said Lena ran off too," Mom added, "and the Director said you went on an unauthorized 'quest.' What on earth is a 'quest'?"

"I flew to the LaMarelles to see if you went there," Dad said. "Did you know they don't even live in North Carolina? Jacqueline LaMarelle and her grandchildren are listed at an empty lot in Milwaukee."

Whoa. At least that gave me an idea of how much they knew.

"And *what* happened to your *face*?" Mom asked.

I lifted a hand to check. My cheek flared with pain. I'd completely forgotten about getting hit by the bats.

That last one was easy to answer. "I was in a fight. A couple of them, actually."

"You better come inside," Amy said. "There's no point in catching a cold on top of what Rory has put us through."

Guilt ate me up from the top of my throbbing head to the soles of my muddy sneakers, but I knew what I had to do.

The Snow Queen would come whether my family believed she was real or not.

Dad locked the door behind us, and I was glad, even though I knew it was to lock me *in*. Mom didn't let go of my shoulders as they steered me into the living room and onto the couch. The coffee table was cluttered with old mugs of tea, tissues, and lots of cell phones. It must have been really bad here while I was away. Mom took the love seat, Dad took the armchair, and Amy leaned against the back wall, arms folded.

They waited. Their stares pinned me to the cushions.

"I'm really *really* sorry for lying to you." I couldn't stop my voice from trembling, but their faces didn't change.

"You've run off *twice*, Rory," Dad said. "You never even contacted us to let us know you were okay. You were just gone. For a week."

"I don't know how we're ever going to trust you again," Mom said, and it clawed at me, hearing how sad I'd made her.

"Ever After School is a program for Characters—fairy-tale characters—to train and get ready for their Tales," I started.

That went over like Iron Hans trying to swim.

"Fairy-tale Characters," Mom repeated dully.

"Magic is real. You've seen it." I showed them the band of plain silver on my left hand. "This is a ring forged by the West Wind, and when I use it, it makes me really strong."

"Uh-huh," Amy said, obviously not believing me.

"I can prove it." I looked around for something to demonstrate on, but I didn't see anything they wouldn't mind me smashing. They were mad enough without me destroying furniture.

"*Rory,*" Dad said, like a warning.

I'd known that they wouldn't believe me—I'd let that be my excuse for putting off telling them, but I couldn't do that anymore. We were in too much danger.

I tried a different tactic. "It runs in families. Dad, the Director told me it mostly comes from your side. *Your* father had a Tale too. I think it was 'The Boy Who Went Forth to Learn What Fear Was.' Did he ever mention it to you?"

He was about to blow his stack. "My father died when I was

eight, Rory, and he worked too much to tell me bedtime stories."

"I'm telling the truth this time," I promised. They just kept scowling.

I should have told them on a day they weren't *furious* with me. That was the real problem.

Then the doorbell rang.

We all sat there, ignoring it, but then it rang again. And again, but this time, it didn't *stop* ringing. Someone was leaning on the buzzer.

Amy pushed away from the wall and opened the door, and I could hear someone scolding, "Don't make them mad before we even get inside."

My head popped up.

"Lena?" Amy asked.

"And Chase and Kyle. We're all friends of Rory's," said another familiar voice.

Mom and Dad's glares got even *less* friendly.

"Did you invite them here?" Mom asked, and I shook my head quickly.

"Well, right now is a really bad time," Amy said. "Rory probably won't be allowed out much again ever, so— Hey!"

"We know Rory's in trouble. That's why we came." Lena barreled into the living room in full-on fearless leader mode, and I knew right away that this was her idea. She swerved around the couch and sat right next to me, pulling a bag off her shoulder.

I wondered if I could kick them out of the house before they made things worse. Dad looked like he might explode, but Mom said, pretty calmly, "I know Rory appreciates you trying to help, but this is really a family matter."

Then *Kyle* strolled into the room and zeroed in on the TV. "I completely agree, ma'am. We'll clear out of here after we set a few things straight. I'm Kyle, by the way."

"Chase Turnleaf." Chase was actually trying to be charming right now. He even tried to shake Dad's hand. They'd never met before, and Dad kept glancing from Chase's split lip to Lena's puffy eye. Great first impression. "Nice to meet you."

"What are you doing here?" I whispered.

"We're backup," Lena told me, like this should be obvious. "How far have you gotten?"

"EAS is a school for young fairy-tale Characters," I said. "The West Wind's ring makes me strong. Dad's dad was a Character."

"Wow. It's going over *that* well, huh?" Chase said, sitting down so close to me, the butterflies started up again. I shot him a look to let him know he was being unhelpful.

"Put the remote down," Amy snapped.

"Yes, ma'am." Kyle clicked the TV on, put it on mute, and flipped through channels. "Just as soon as I find the right station."

Well, that explained why Kyle was here—he was awesome at handling parents. He managed to be extremely polite, even when he was doing exactly what they didn't want.

Lena took over for me. "It's true what Rory said. Ever After School is full of Characters waiting for their Tales. My Tale was 'Jack and the Beanstalk.' When Rory told you we went to . . . Rory, where was it they thought we went?"

"Raleigh," I said.

Dad's mouth was open—I guess I knew where I'd gotten that from.

"When you thought we were in Raleigh, that's where we really were—up in the beanstalk. You know, with giants," Lena said, but horror grew on my parents' faces. They didn't think I was lying anymore. Now they thought EAS had deluded us as much as the matches had brainwashed Miriam.

"Time to bring out the big guns," Kyle said without looking away from the TV.

Lena dug into her pack and pulled out the golden harp, who was *not* happy to be here. Melodie was trying to stay as still as a real statue and to cling to the bag at the same time. "I have evidence! This is the harp we got on my Tale."

She set Melodie on the coffee table. The harp wasn't even breathing.

"Is it supposed to *do* something?" Mom asked uncertainly.

"Melodie, that's your *cue*," Lena said sharply, letting the harp know exactly who was mistress.

The harp moaned and covered her eyes. "But it's so *humiliating*."

"Oh my God," Amy said, stumbling back, and now Mom's mouth was open as well as Dad's.

"Ventriloquism," Dad said, glancing at me. "Robotics."

"I beg your pardon. Have you ever seen a robot with hands like mine?" The harp wiggled her fingers at him.

"That's your mind trying to figure out a logical explanation," I told Dad, encouraged. "It's like a defense mechanism."

Mom gave a shaky little laugh. "Then we're dreaming."

"That's the *other* defense mechanism," Lena explained. "You'll probably think that you're crazy or that you're dreaming for a while—just until you get used to the idea that magic is real."

"Bingo." Kyle set the remote on top of the TV. "*That's* where Rory has been this week."

Everyone turned. Kyle had found the news, where kids in grubby pajamas were embracing their parents. Two moms were covering their son's face with kisses, and the banner at the bottom read, BREAKING NEWS: RETURNED!—KIDNAPPED CHILDREN OF PORTLAND.

"You *were* in Portland?" Dad said, confused.

"We passed through there," I said.

"There has been a lot of rejoicing here this afternoon, but not a lot of answers," said the newscaster. *"So far, none of the kids have been able to tell authorities exactly where they've been. The police have a few leads—the kids were held somewhere surrounded by snow, where music was used for some sort of hypnotic effect, and several have mentioned that they were kidnapped by a man wearing red. But many other children are so traumatized that they've made up stories about evil giants and big bad wolves. It may be a long time before we find out exactly what—"*

Amy turned the TV off, but Kyle explained, "The man in red was the Pied Piper. The Snow Queen sent him to take the kids and bring them to her palace in the Arctic."

"From the fairy tale?" Mom was clearly having just as much trouble as Dad with this conversation.

"The grown-up Characters at EAS gave up on them," Kyle said. "But Rory didn't. They went on a quest to rescue those kids—the three of them on the couch, and this girl named Miriam. From what I've heard, it was Rory who managed to save everyone in the end."

"To you, Rory's just your daughter, and you're really mad at her," Lena said softly. "But to us, she's a hero. That's what we came here to tell you."

"And if you come to EAS, a bunch of people will say the same thing," Chase added.

I loved my friends. I really *really* loved my friends.

Mom glanced at them and back to me, her eyes narrowed. Lena

pressed her shoulder against mine, like she was ready to prop me up if I keeled over under the pressure.

"Okay," Dad said, but it wasn't like the "okay" you say when you're trying to get someone to shut up. It was the kind of "okay" you say when you're pretty sure you've put all the pieces together. "Lena, right? I take it you never had appendicitis?"

I'd forgotten that was the story Lena's grandmother had told them last spring.

Lena shook her head, looking a little hopeful. "Cockatrice poisoning."

"A cockatrice is like a lizard with a rooster head, but with teeth. It can turn people to stone with its eyes," added Melodie. "Lena ate a Fey fudge pie laced with its poison."

"Okay," Dad said, and he sounded even steadier now.

"You can't be serious," Amy said, but I always knew she was going to be the hardest to convince.

Mom said nothing. Her face didn't say a lot either.

Kyle pointed at the door. "Everybody out."

"But . . ." Lena didn't want to leave, not when we were finally making progress.

"No, this nice lady was right. This is a family matter. We've said what we came here to say, and now it's up to Rory." Kyle waved as he opened the front door. "Pleasure to meet you," he said, and then he was gone.

"Nice to see you again, Ms. Wright and Amy. Nice to meet you, Mr. Landon." Lena hugged me hard so she could whisper in my ear. "Call me on the M3 if you need more backup." Then she was on her feet too, gathering up her bag and reaching for Melodie.

"Can you leave the harp?" Dad said. He wanted to examine her.

Years of working with props made him want to see exactly how she worked.

"I don't know. Could you maybe ask the *harp*?" said Melodie, who clearly hadn't gotten over being called evidence.

Chase leaned in close, right in front of my parents, and I could *feel* my dad noticing. "We'll be right outside."

"Outside?" I peeked out the window. All the eighth-grade archers stood in a line along the sidewalk. They tried to act like they were just chatting, but that was hard to do when they had quivers and bows slung over their shoulders. When Kyle appeared behind them, they all spun around, obviously waiting for news.

Lena gave Chase a look like, *You better follow me,* and then she headed for the open door, taking Melodie with her. "Bye!"

Dad stood up to see better. "Are those *real* bows?"

"Longbows." Chase walked out *really* slowly, like my parents were even more dangerous than a bunch of trolls, but eventually, he did go. I didn't feel even a tiny bit sad.

My friends had come, and they weren't leaving.

"He just drew a sword," Dad said, still watching through the window. It was a good sign Dad noticed the weapon. Logic sometimes made your eyes skip over a sword, so maybe he was starting to really believe us.

But I wished Mom would say something. Her eyes were locked on mine, her face smooth, and it freaked me out that I couldn't read her expression at all.

"Why do you need bows and swords here, Rory?" Dad asked.

This was it. This was when I made them understand the danger.

"They're guarding us," I whispered. "The Snow Queen. It may not be tonight or even this week, but she's definitely coming."

Maybe Mom could hear how scared I was. Maybe she'd just

decided to hear me out before grounding me until my twentieth birthday, but concern filled her face.

She moved to the coffee table, not even noticing when she sat on a pile of tissues. She took both my hands. "I want you to start at Saturday night, right after I dropped you off. Don't leave anything out no matter how dangerous it was, or how complicated it is to explain. Tell us *everything*."

So I took a deep breath as Dad drifted back to the armchair, and Amy took over the love seat.

Then I began.

ACKNOWLEDGMENTS

This book was written and revised on a shorter schedule than the other two, which means lots of people had to put up with behavior weirder-than-usual from me for months straight:

To my awesome agent, Jo, thank you for being totally understanding about my inability to form complete sentences after turning in a new draft. To my patient, savvy editor, Julia, thank you for reining me in and making sure I didn't clutter up the plot with too many Tales, and thank you for giving me those last couple weeks when I really needed them. To everyone at S&S BFYR, thank you for believing in and supporting (and acquiring) The Ever Afters. To Chloë Foglia and Cory Loftis, thank you for being an amazing cover-creating team.

To my parents, thank you for enduring all my complaining about how tired I was. To my friends, thank you for understanding when I disappeared this spring. To my roommates, especially Megan, thank you for taking on more than your share of housework and for not saying anything about the crazed, off-in-another-world gleam in my eyes when I emerged from my writing cave (at the time, anyway). To Lancer and Shakayla, thank you for suggesting I borrow your names.

And most of all, thank you to my readers. This was the first time I've ever written a book when you guys were impatient to find out what happened to Rory, Chase, and Lena. I couldn't have done it without your enthusiasm, so thank you for writing to tell me. ☺

Don't miss the thrilling conclusion to

THE EVER AFTERS!

The morning before my fourteenth birthday, the witches ambushed us before Mom had a chance to finish her coffee. We were arguing about the usual things.

"The triplets will be here any minute," I said, shoving my cellphone and my M3 into my carryall's front pocket. Those guys were always a couple minutes late for guard duty. Sometimes they slept through their alarm. It *was* summer. That happened. "Then we can get out of here." I slung on my raincoat. Big heavy drops pattered on the window.

Mom set down her mug and folded her hands carefully. I knew what that meant: I wasn't going to like what she said next. "I've been meaning to talk to you about that, Rory."

Amy didn't even try to break it to me nicely. "No. They're not coming with us today. We're meeting with the play's producers."

"You *need* protection." I reached for my magic combs and reminded myself that it wouldn't do any good to get irritated. They just didn't really understand—not yet.

"They're teenagers." Amy crossed her arms. "It *looks* like we're babysitting them, not the other way around."

"It is beginning to look strange, Rory," Mom said. "Normally, I'm fine with them tagging along with us. I know that it makes you feel better, but today's meeting is important—"

"Makes me *feel* better?" I wrestled with my temper and lost. "The Snow Queen attacks a new Character almost *every day*."

Mom took a very deep breath, like she usually does when she thinks I'm exaggerating but doesn't want to call me on it. "We've taken all these precautions, but we haven't been in any danger since that wolf attacked us in the grocery store."

She *always* brought that up in arguments, and it was getting old. "You didn't want to move to Ever After School, even though it's the safest place for us," I reminded her, "and I said okay, but only if you accepted bodyguards. That was the deal. You promised me."

Mom winced. She'd obviously hoped I'd forgotten about that. "They're just kids, Rory. Just like you."

"You could come with us," Amy said. "That wouldn't look as weird."

"I have responsibilities too." I had class in Hansel's training courts in an hour, and I was on call for rescue duty until dinnertime. I'd explained this to them at least a hundred times.

"Besides, your mother made that promise more than three and a half months ago," Amy said. "Maybe the Snow Queen forgot about you."

"She hasn't." I was about to turn fourteen. According to my Tale, I would hold the fate of magic in my hands some time this month. The Snow Queen had to move now, but I'd been saying that since before Independence Day. They still weren't convinced.

I wished the triplets would hurry up and get here. Company always cut our arguments short.

Something pounded against the roof. No matter what they said about the Snow Queen losing interest, Mom and Amy both jumped just as high as I did. Outside the window, white spheres bounced across the back porch. "Just hail," I said. We didn't usually see it in San Francisco.

"Great." Amy dug through her purse for her keys. "I better check on the car."

Movement flickered in the yard. It had to be one of the dirt servants. Lena had rigged them to patrol the yard's perimeter—our own magical security system. And this one was shuffling toward us, as fast as its stubby dirt legs could carry him. It was hard to tell in the crummy weather, but it looked like it was missing a foot.

My heart stuttered. I reached for one of my combs.

It could be another false alarm.

The dirt servant jolted to a stop in the middle of the backyard, its mangled limbs bleached to gray. It toppled over. Turned to stone.

"Found them!" Amy stepped toward the exit, her keys jangling from her hand.

"No!" I tossed the comb in front of the back door. It fell with a clunk, and bars as wide as my wrist sprang up from the floor.

"Not again!" Amy said. Bars crunched against the ceiling. "Rory, you damage the house every time you overreact. We'll never get our security deposit back."

Mom tried to be more soothing, but she was obviously a tiny bit peeved too. "It's probably just the neighbor's dog again. The dirt things always think he's a wolf."

I picked up the other combs. The Snow Queen's allies were coming, just like I knew they would.

The front door banged open. Someone—*several* someones—stampeded into the living room. We couldn't see them, but we could definitely hear them squawking and cawing through the drumming hail.

I threw the second comb across the entryway to the living room. In two breaths, it knitted up the door frame with a chain-link fence. I tossed a third comb between the island and the kitchen table, and metal bars sprouted from the wooden floor.

Amy shrank back. "Oh my God."

Four green-skinned, black-haired witches trampled in from the dining room, the only entrance to the kitchen the combs hadn't sealed off yet. They wore toothy grins under their warty noses and raised long wands in their gnarled hands.

So, the Snow Queen had kept her word after all: the Wolfsbane clan would get their chance to kill me. They had even gotten first dibs.

One witch fired off a spell. I grabbed Mom's elbow and yanked her aside. The enchantment landed on the fridge, turning it to stone. Mom would have to pay for that too when we left this rental.

"Get behind the island," I said, snagging my carryall and dodging another shot. The top was marble. It would protect us from most spells. "Where are those rings I gave you?"

The week after I'd gotten back from the Arctic Circle, I'd made them *swear* to keep the rings on them at all times. When school was still in session, I refused to get in the car unless they both showed me the rings, but I hadn't done a check in a while. I definitely should have.

"My nightstand," Amy confessed.

Mom's mouth thinned and twisted, the face she always made when she realized she'd messed up. "It's over there." She pointed to where her red purse sat on a side table—on the other side of the chain-link fence.

I pulled my own ring out of my jeans' pocket and stared at it. One ring for three people.

"Well, you know what you have to do," Mom said. Calm as anything, she placed a hand on my arm. "You go to EAS. Get help. Come back and rescue us. The bars will keep us safe."

There were a million things wrong with that plan. I hadn't heard the third comb's bars hit the ceiling yet. Mom and Amy knew nothing about fighting, even less about magic. But I didn't bother arguing.

I squeezed her fingers reassuringly. With my other hand, I gripped the ring.

"I love you, sweetie," Mom said. The only way she could have been more obvious was if she actually said she never thought she would see me again.

"I love you too." Then I slid the ring on her finger.

She didn't have time to look surprised. She was just gone.

"She's not going to like that," Amy said quietly. "She wanted you safe first."

"If they captured her, they would use her against me." I'd explained this a hundred times too. I didn't mention that the witches would do the same with Amy.

"I never said I didn't understand your *reasons*." Amy scooted up just enough to peek over the counter at the witches. "Is that supposed to happen?"

I poked my head around the island, just for a sec. A spell whistled past my hair and blasted the dishes drying beside the sink. A mug—the one I'd painted and given to Mom for her birthday a couple years ago—exploded, and its clay shards cascaded to the floor.

I ducked back to safety, but I'd seen what I needed to see.

Three of the four witches had leveled their wands at the third comb. The bars were still growing toward the ceiling, but slowly. Maybe just an inch a second. I'd never seen this spell.

"No, it's never happened before." The Snow Queen's forces were adapting. They had trained just to stop these combs—just to fight *me*.

"I thought so." Amy crawled over to the last cabinet, where we kept most of our canned goods. She opened the door, plucked out some green beans and some cream of mushroom soup, and launched them over the island.

The first one struck a witch's elbow. She shrieked and dropped her wand. The soup can caught the second witch in the face. She crumpled, her nose gushing blood.

"Wow," I said, impressed. Only two witches were still performing the spell that countered the enchantment. The bars rose faster—two inches a second.

"I was the pitcher on my college softball team, remember?" Amy reached for another can. The witches outside must have sensed trouble. Their footsteps thudded across the patio, louder than the hail. "You do your thing. I got this."

I reached into my carryall and pulled out my sword. I felt calmer, having it in my hand. Then I grabbed my M3. "Chase?" I shouldn't have tried him first. I *knew* he wouldn't answer. "Lena?"

The mirror stayed blank. I frowned. Lena never left her M3 lying around.

Two more witches stamped in. Their spells hit the marble island with wet sizzles. Amy launched a counterassault of diced tomatoes, but these witches were ready for her. They raised their wands. The cans exploded, and red chunks rained down on our heads.

The bars grew, inch by inch.

Only one witch was left on comb-enchantment duty. She had gray hair and a huge gap between her crooked teeth. I didn't understand why the other three witches had stopped helping her. "Now!" she shouted to someone behind her. "It must be now!"

"You don't need to tell me," said another voice.

A witch stepped out from behind the rack where we hung our raincoats and umbrellas. The edge of her long cloak was stitched with silver, and a string of moonstones was braided into her dull black hair. Her lashes were long, and her eyes tilted up at the corners like a cat. If witches hadn't been cursed with ugliness, this one might have been beautiful.

The three witches turned their wands on the newcomer. An invisible current crackled through the air. The moonstone witch rose, her cape flickering around her ankles. She bent her legs and hugged her knees, and the three witches floated her toward the comb cage. More specifically to the three-foot gap between the bars and the ceiling.

I could guess where they were going with this.

I grabbed a can of chicken soup in front of Amy, and I launched it at the witch in charge of slowing down the comb. It went wide and clattered on the table. That was why I usually stuck with weapons you didn't have to throw.

"Please don't waste my ammo." Amy threw three cans in rapid succession. One hit a witch on the shoulder, another in the arm, and the last in her huge warty chin, and all three casters levitating their sister witch stumbled back.

But it was too late.

The moonstone witch had floated past the bars, and when the spell dropped her, she landed hard on the kitchen floor. Plates and glasses clinked inside the cabinets.

"She's inside with us, isn't she?" Amy asked me.

I swallowed. "Yep."

The gray-haired witch lowered her wand. The bars zoomed up and buried themselves in the ceiling, cracking the plaster. "It is all up to you now, Istalina," she said.

The moonstone witch drew herself up taller. So she was Istalina. "Come out, Aurora Landon, or I shall flush you out."

"Stay where you are," Amy hissed, grabbing another can. "I'm sure I can get her."

But Amy had no idea what we were dealing with. The last time I'd had to fight some witches, I jumped off a moving train to get away from them. I couldn't throw the fourth comb. I couldn't risk her using that slowing spell again. I couldn't risk her *capturing* it.

I wished that Chase and Lena were here instead of Amy. They would know what to do.

It doesn't matter if you've never fought a witch before, Chase would probably say. *Magic users usually stick to spells. Most of them have no close combat skills.*

I poked my head out. Istalina was waiting for me. She raised her arm and fired, only ten feet away. I jerked back just in time—the spell took a big chunk out of the island's cabinets and blasted the pot Mom had used to make macaroni the night before.

I knew what Lena would say too. *Wait! You need something to intercept her magic*. I forced myself to stop, to look at the materials around me the way she would look at it.

We had the fourth comb. We had all this kitchen stuff. I opened the cabinet next to me. Pans and their lids. I started shifting through them, careful not to touch the one Istalina's spell had hit. It burned a glowing orange.

"What are you doing?" Amy asked.

I ignored her.

"I doesn't matter what you try, Aurora Landon," said the witch. "It won't work. We have you trapped."

I ignored her too.

I found the lid I wanted. It was bigger than most and pretty heavy, but it had an extra strip of metal, almost two inches wide, that ran all the way around the rim. I dropped the comb inside it.

Please let this work, I thought. *Please please please please*.

It did. Slender metal rods sprouted from the pot's lid. Tentatively, they wove themselves together, like the comb wasn't totally sure about my plan either.

"Stay here, Amy." I concentrated on protecting her and stood up, my lid-shield in one hand, my sword in the other.

Istalina threw off her cloak. It puddled around her feet. Her cheeks were even greener than the rest of her face, like she was flushed or something.

Beyond the cage, seven green-skinned witches lined up, their beady eyes watching us, like crows circling a picnic. A fight with an audience, just like dueling with Torlauth at the Snow Queen's palace.

Before I could shudder, Istalina launched a spell. My sword's magic flowed into me, and my left hand shifted slightly. I caught the spell on the pot lid right in front of my belly. Good. My sword had adapted to the new shield, just like it had with my ring.

The moonstone witch's eyes widened above her warty nose. She launched a few more. I couldn't see the little zings, but I heard them sizzling toward me. The runner's high seeped through my body. I danced to one side and then the other, dodging three more blasts. I caught a fourth, right in front of my face.

Okay, defense was solid. Time for some offense.

I sprinted forward. Istalina tried to fire off another shot, but I was already in range. I bashed my shield down on her wrist, knocking the wand off course. I flipped my sword over and swung the hilt toward her temple.

A dagger blocked the blow. Istalina's weapon was black, its blade made of shiny stone instead of metal. The witch twisted her dagger around my hilt. I was so surprised that she almost managed to wrench my sword out of my hand.

The Wolfsbane clan had sent the witch who could actually fight.

The witch's heel shot out, trying to smack me in the chest. I caught it with my left hand.

But it was a feint. She squeezed off another shot from her wand. I ducked, crouching low to the ground so that it sailed over my head.

"Rory!" Amy cried. I whirled around, checking to see if she was all right, but it turned out to be just one of those *be careful* kind of yells.

Mistake. I shouldn't have looked away.

Did you LOVE reading this book?

Visit the Whyville...

IN THE MIDDLE BOOK HIVE

Where you can:

- Discover great books!
- Meet new friends!
- Read exclusive sneak peeks and more!

Log on to visit now!
bookhive.whyville.net

is just the beginning....

Mystery, murder, mayhem.
That's no excuse to be rude.

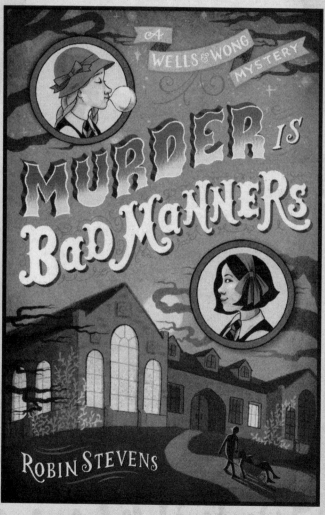

TOM SAWYER *and* HUCK FINN
have their stories. Now it's time you heard the truth!